_Regards
To Dave L._

BREAKUP!

Glen (Maloney) Alderton

Glen Ellen Alderton

Note: This is a work of fiction. Names, characters, places and incidents either are the product of the author's imagination or are used fictitiously, and any resemblance to actual persons, living or dead, business establishments, events or locales is entirely coincidental.

Published by Zailsky Associates
ISBN-10: 0615799426
ISBN-13: 978-0615799421 (Custom)

In loving memory,
John Edward Zailsky, M.D.
(1908 – 2004)
the stepfather Arnie wished to be.

L ooking into the mirror, the woman saw her reflection, the stark tear-streaked face and haunted eyes. It was the face of the person she had become. It wasn't the face she had wanted. It wasn't the person she had hoped to be or deceived herself into thinking she was. It was the face of someone in utter despair.

She began sobbing again, shaking even, and white-knuckled she tightly grasped the sink, trying to maintain her precarious balance. Taking several deep breaths, she forced herself to let go. At last determined, she leaned over the tub and started a warm bath. Returning to the sink, she began to search the medicine cabinet. There was a small disposable razor. She regarded it a minute, having a flashback of a little girl watching her father inserting a blade into a safety razor. Then another of the same child as her grandfather carefully sharpened a straight edge. Before beginning his shave, the old man dabbed some soapy lather on the little girl's checks so she could pretend to mimic his gestures while she laughed in delight. Now that grown-up child despondently dropped the bit of cheap pink plastic into the sink and renewed her search, becoming more and more frenzied in her frustrated hunt. After knocking bottles and tubes askew, she finally located a pair of nail scissors, half concealed behind an economy-sized bottle of aspirin.

Taking a last look at her ravaged likeness, she turned. Scissors tightly clutched in one hand, she stepped into the tub. The warm water was soothing as water always was. Opening and shutting the tiny blades, she stared vacantly ahead, occasionally making hesitant, feeble pinpricks to her wrist. Suddenly, she slashed the sharp points across one wrist. For a second nothing seemed to happen. She didn't even feel the pain but then the blood started to gush. Her interest was almost academic. Bright red drops bubbling across the gash like some perverted ruby chain. Ruby chains…she half remembered, and water, always water.

Switching hands, the woman took the scissors and stabbed at her other wrist but her left hand was awkward.

Pain was radiating so it took several jabs to get a decent cut. She bit her lips from the smarting wounds, but at last blood was flowing. Then, only then, did she drop the scissors outside the tub and lean back, surveying her throbbing, living, blood-ruby bracelets and feel the attendant ache. With one foot, she opened the drain part way and then adjusted the hot water knob with agile toes so the water would continue to trickle in. Closing her eyes, she lay back, waiting, trying not to think, trying not to hurt—all that hurt—mental, physical, past, present. Just waiting to drift off, to forget, to end it.

PART I: THE YEARS 1980 - 2000
CHAPTER 1

Arnie was standing by the crowded bar, a beer in hand, waiting for his business associate. A headline on the TV about an upcoming show on survivors of the Jonestown massacre made him shake his head. Murder by Kool-Aid? What next? Maybe the 1980s would be a more peaceful decade, although he had a feeling that the upcoming election would be heated. Carter, who had great ideas on energy and some other important issues, probably didn't have much of a chance, especially after the Iran debacle. And to think one of his main opponents was an ex spook and the other an over-the-hill movie actor.

Turning away from the television, he glanced into the mirrored reflection behind the busy counter and suddenly noticed a strikingly beautiful blonde sitting on a stool one seat over. She was talking to her escort, a tall, dark and very distinguished looking man about ten to fifteen years older. He made an attractive contrast to his young companion, who was undoubtedly one of the most stunning women Arnie had ever seen—shapely in a form-fitting sheath, the color of rich plum wine like his grandmother used to make. Fascinated, Arnie was unable to look away. Then, embarrassed, he averted his eyes, hoping the couple hadn't noticed his interest. But somehow, he kept returning to the reflection and found himself inadvertently eavesdropping on their conversation, words filtering through the prevalent din. It was apparent the young woman was uncomfortable. Particularly, after the man leaned over and placed his hand firmly on her wrist.

"Time to go, little darling."

"Go? We've only been here fifteen minutes. What do you mean?" the young woman replied. Arnie could tell she was feeling pressured. Although barely noticeable, she was also trying to pull her captive hand free, but the man's fingers had tightened.

"You know what I mean, little girl. We're going back to my place to have a couple drinks."

"I'm sorry. I told you already. When you asked me for a drink, I thought you meant here. I never said I was going any place with you."

The man's face changed, the smile fading, his features becoming harsher, less engaging. In low and somewhat intimidating tones, he persisted, "Don't play with me, Becki. You knew what I meant when I asked you for a drink."

"Let me go and no, I obviously didn't know what you meant. You asked Jenny and me for drinks. Since she seemed to know you and had to leave, I said fine. I took the offer at face value, but going to your place wasn't part of the deal." The young woman's voice, soft with a gentle southern accent, was becoming agitated and her lovely, aristocratic face was beginning to lose its calm composure.

"You're an adult," the man said in a sneering tone. "Of course you knew what I meant." His hand tightened further and the woman winced.

"A moment ago you were calling me a little girl, not an adult, and now you're hurting me." The young woman's speech was still hushed, but becoming more breathy and determined. "Let go or I'll make a scene."

"You think anyone would pay attention to you here with this crowd? We came in together. You stayed when your friend left. I'll just tell them you've had too much to drink. No one's going to pay any attention—especially in a singles bar. So come on. You know I'm not going to hurt you. We're just going to have a little fun."

She opened her mouth to reply when suddenly a short, stocky man had his arm around her and was saying hurriedly, "Becki, I've been looking all over for you. Jenny told me you were coming here. Listen, Aunt Mary called. There's been an accident. I've got to get you right home." He turned to her escort, shoulders shrugging in apology. "Sorry. I'm a family friend and this is an emergency!" Then without another word, the little man took her arm and pulled her off the stool, rushing her out of the bar.

Astounded, the young woman found herself going with him. "Who are you?" she asked as soon as they reached the street, eyes widened in surprise. Arm now free, she was rubbing and shaking the previously constrained wrist.

"Sorry," he said again, smiling and stepping back, giving her space. It was a nice smile that made his otherwise undistinguished looking face suddenly very winning. "I couldn't help overhearing that fool. Since he was about a foot taller than me, this was the only thing I could think of. I mean, I'm not very good at bar brawls. Also, I'm harmless. I just wanted to get you out of there since you seemed upset. Can I get you a cab or something?"

She looked at him, uncomprehending at first, and then suddenly burst into soft, tinkling laughter. "My knight in shining armor!"

Arnie looked down. "Actually a tweed jacket."

She laughed again. "Well, I should thank you, kind sir. No, I didn't want to get into a brawl either but I was afraid I'd have to start screaming or kick him just to make him let go. And no, I don't need a cab. I've just got to get to the Metro. It's only a couple blocks."

"Should you be walking around here at night?"

"It's not that late. I'll be fine."

"Well, let me walk you that far, just in case that idiot comes out and tries to follow you."

She looked at him. He was at least two inches shorter than her, not counting her low pumps. Luscious Larry inside had turned into a real disaster, but this little man? Of course mad rapists seemed to come in all sizes, but he really did seem nice and he, at least, had released her the second he'd spirited her out the bar. "Well, all right. But just to the subway."

"My pleasure. Just show me which direction."

"You're an out-of-towner?"

"What gave you the clue?" her surprise escort asked with a disarming grin. "Actually, it's my first time in our nation's capital. My name is Arnie, Arnie Miller." Reaching into his pocket, he pulled out and presented a business card, which indicated he was James Arnold Miller. "I use my middle name," he explained.

"How do you do," she responded politely. "I'm..." she hesitated for a moment, but then after all, he had come to her rescue, "I'm Becki Thatcher."

"You've got to be kidding. Where're Tom and Huck?" She looked at him, startled. "Sorry," he apologized, "you must hear that all the time." She remained quiet at first and he feared she might not have understood the reference.

At last she remarked slowly, "Actually, I don't and I spell Becki with an *i* not a *y*. Most people nowadays have never read Mark Twain's books, and I don't whitewash fences nor do I find caves fascinating."

He smiled, relieved she was a reader. She was so spectacular looking that that might have been low on her list of priorities. "You may not have whitewashed fences, but I bet you did memorize all those Bible verses."

Becki returned his engaging smile, finding it hard not to respond to the cheery little man. "No, and my father wasn't a judge. He ran a seafood place."

"Well, Miss Becki Thatcher with an *i*, I'm delighted to meet you. I heard there were pretty women in D.C., but now I know that's true."

Becki scrutinized him for a moment, a severe appraisal. No one could be coming on with such a line, but he was still just smiling innocently so she refrained from comment. The two started walking at a brisk pace towards the subway. "Are you here for long?" she finally asked, making conversation.

"Two weeks. I'm here on business, and I'm staying at the Key Bridge Marriott. I'm supposed to meet some guy at that bar in a half hour about a project. I came early to kill a little time. I don't know anyone in town, and I hate sitting around at the hotel almost as much as I hate business meetings at night, but sometimes that's what one has to do," he responded a bit winded. This Becki's long legs were really making time. "Are you from this area?"

"No, not really. I'm from the Northern Neck, but I'm living with my sister and her husband in northern Virginia now." And why did I tell him that, she wondered, as she hurried along. But he did seem pleasant and harmless. Besides, he was the first man she'd ever met who had caught the literary significance of her name—a family in-joke especially appreciated by her mother, who had preferred keeping her nose in a book to any other activity.

"I'm from Boston," Arnie volunteered, "and came down here to talk to the World Bank and some people at Treasury."

"Oh." Becki couldn't think of anything else to say. He looked quite ordinary, not at all the type who would be going to the World Bank. She had met a few through work and they always seemed so cosmopolitan. This man was young, probably not even thirty, and very low key with no hint of sophistication. He couldn't be more than five foot seven, with a sturdy built and a round nondescript face when he wasn't smiling. Yet he had a pair of the most alert brown eyes she'd ever seen and matching straight brown hair.

"Yes, I'm into computers and software, as you can see from my card."

Actually, she hadn't taken a good look at his card, just glanced at the name to see if it corresponded, before stuffing it into her jacket pocket. "Well, I guess we're here," she announced, stopping at the Metro entrance, relieved she'd escaped a humiliating situation. "Thank you again. That was an embarrassment back at the bar. I really didn't want a scene."

"It was my pleasure. You're sure you're going to be all right taking the train at this time of night? I mean the Metro's pretty nice, but…"

"It's only 8:00," she answered amused. "That's fine. Are you sure you'll find your way back?"

"Of course. I left a trail of bread crumbs."

Becki burst out laughing, and held out her hand to shake his.

"Becki…Miss Thatcher," he started to say and she

thought, oh dear, here it comes, but he continued, "I'd appreciate it if you'd phone the hotel when you get home. I really hate to leave you here. I'd feel a lot better if I knew you got there ok."

Becki was so surprised at this request and the good will it implied, that she found herself saying she would. Thanking him, she made her way into the subway. Just as she was halfway down the escalator, she looked back and saw that he was still standing there, obviously waiting until she was safely inside. What a nice person, she thought; maybe she would phone to let him know. But, when she got back to her sister's, she was so busy telling her about the evening that by the time she remembered, it seemed too late to make the call.

The next night when Becki returned from work and her evening class, reached into her jacket pocket and found the card. It was a day late, but then she was always a dollar short too. The little man had been truly kind and had seemed sincere so she picked up the phone book, found the hotel number, and dialed. If he didn't answer, she could at least leave a message and thank him, but the operator connected her to his room and he picked up almost immediately. "Mr. Miller?" she asked hesitantly.

"Yes." His voice was more resonant than she had remembered and actually very attractive. He should have been on radio. People would have thought he was really handsome.

"Hi, this is Tom's girl friend."

"Tom...oh, Miss Thatcher. I didn't expect to hear from you."

"I'm sorry I didn't call when I got home last night. I got into a conversation with my sister and then it seemed too late. But I wanted to thank you again. That was very kind of you to step in like that."

"As you said, knight-errant at your service. I was a little worried, but since I didn't see any lurid details about a missing blonde in the morning paper, I just assumed you weren't going to call."

"Well, I am sorry, especially since I had said I would." Becki wondered why she was apologizing so much.

"Miss Thatcher?"

"Yes."

"Would you care to have dinner one night with me while I'm here? No strings, no grabbing your wrist, just a plain and simple dinner at some place you choose. I'll meet you there and get you back to your subway after."

Becki considered the invitation. There was nothing exceptional about the little man, but he had been concerned about her, which was not what she usually encountered. And, it had been so long since she had had an evening out, Jenny's friend, Larry the Loathsome Lounge Lizard, excepted. "Well, yes, I guess so."

"Great! When? You pick the night, the place, the time. If you can't decide yet, you can just call back, leave a message, and I'll be there."

"You haven't said what your schedule is."

"Nothing I couldn't change at this point."

"Today's Tuesday. Why don't we say Friday, but what kind of food do you like?"

"Anything lower on the food chain."

Becki burst into laughter. "In that case, how about Adams Morgan? I can meet you around 6:00 in front of the McDonald's and we could just pick a place. There're all sorts of small restaurants there including a couple of good Ethiopian ones if you like that kind of food." And none too expensive she considered, not knowing his circumstances, although probably he had some travel per diem. Still, all would have seemed costly to her budget.

"That sounds fine to me. Should I call and make a reservation?" he asked.

"There're so many places, I don't think that will be a problem even if there is a crowd."

"Swell, I'll look forward to it and thanks. Oh, how do I find Adams Morgan?"

Becki laughed again. "Ask the hotel. It's becoming a fairly popular area and I'm the one who should be thanking you."

"Naw, just part of the service—dragon disposal, evil knights eliminated, whatever, but I guess I'm really thanking you for calling."

Smiling to herself, she replied simply, "Good night."

When she hung up, her sister Marty looked at her in amazement. "You really mean you're going to have dinner with this man?"

"Well you've been telling me to get a life. Besides, he's only in town a couple of weeks and he was nice about last night. He seems to have a sense of humor and not be the sort of self-impressed egoist I usually attract. Lothario Larry being a prime example. I told Jenny what happened, but she seemed to think I was crazy not to go off with him. He apparently is Mr. Lover Boy himself. She actually thought she was doing me a favor," Becki added in astonishment.

"You don't need favors like that," commented Marty acidly.

"No, I certainly don't. Why is it that the big, tall, good looking guys I meet are such jerks?"

"You meet them because you're a big, tall, good looking woman, but why they have to turn out that way, I don't know. You're going to find someone again, Becki. You're too nice not to and Drea needs a dad."

"She has one, Marty."

"Yes, but he's a jerk too. Leaving you in the lurch, never sending any money, and what's the most she's ever gotten from him? A doll when she was three and then another one a couple years later." Marty could have said more but she hated to distress her tenderhearted sister, and this unfortunately was an old topic.

"Maybe that's better than having him around," responded Becki sadly. "Next time I'm falling for brains the way you did. Jerry's so great. You both are. I don't know what I would have done if you two hadn't let me and Andrea come here to live."

"You're my baby sister," said Marty soothingly. "You and I are all the real family that's left, and I love you and

Drea. I couldn't let you end up on the streets. Besides, you help us by contributing part of the rent. I've told you that dozens of times. You just have to believe me. With Jerry still in law school and me having to leave work after the baby comes, it will especially help. You know that."

And life would be so much easier for you, if you'd only gone after Billy and gotten the support you're due, Marty thought; but, such conversations always led to grief for Becki and frustration for her. It was as though they were opposite sides of a coin, even though they loved each other dearly. Marty had learned to remain relatively quiet about Becki's ex, hoping someday Becki would come to her senses, even though Jerry would hear her continued aggravation later and counsel her to accept. Marty wished she could, but being unable to forgive sometimes came with her side of the coin.

"Oh, Marty," Becki sighed, "I don't know if I would have made it without you."

"Sure you would, honey. You just made some wrong decisions when you were too young. Billy was too cute for words but he had no substance."

"But he sure was sexy," remarked Becki reflectively, remembering the beautiful boy of a decade before.

"Yes, and look where that got you—pregnant with Drea and dropping out of high school. Then as soon as he comes up here to be in the Army, he moves out on you. No sense of responsibility. That whole damn family was no good."

"Well, I guess I wasn't either to get into a fix like that," Becki commented wryly.

"Honey, how can you say that! You weren't even fifteen. If you'd told me, maybe we could have done something. You were so good in school. You're the one who should have had the William and Mary Scholarship, not me," Marty asserted, not for the first time. Becki's ego needed to be primed at regular intervals, even if she did have the kind of looks that turned heads. If her sister weren't so sweet, Marty sometimes thought she'd gladly strangle her for the unfair distribution of beauty in the family—and also for signing the unfair divorce agreement without her and Jerry's input.

"I thought I loved him, Marty. I wanted the baby. Maybe now that I'm older I would have made a different decision but I have Drea and I love her."

"We all do. She's a wonderful little girl, but you've just turned twenty-four with an eight-year old daughter."

"Hey, I'm getting by. I've got a decent job, and I've been able to take some classes. I should have the associate's degree by next Christmas, provided I double up on those summer courses. Maybe I'll even try to go for a bachelor's."

"You should. You're so smart."

"So are you…and so nice. I couldn't have done it without you, Marty." She leaned down to give her older sister a kiss. "Good night, little big sister."

"Good night, big little one," Marty replied with a grin, completing the ritual begun some ten years before when Becki, to everyone's shock, had grown almost ten inches and towered over her sister and mother. Then drawing herself up to her full five feet, Marty admonished sternly, "And Giantess, watch out for bean stalkers." She might be small, but she still was the elder in their relationship and worried about her beautiful sister. Being picked up by strange men qualified. Becki had been hurt often enough.

"Hey, he's just from Bean Town. That doesn't mean he knocks giants off. He's a little guy. I've never dated anyone shorter, but it's only for dinner. We'll be sitting down, and at least for once I won't have to wear high heels."

CHAPTER 2

Friday night, Becki rushed as fast as she could up Connecticut Avenue, refraining from even a single glance at the stylish shops. Then at Columbia Road, she continued to the trendy Adams Morgan area. Sure enough, Arnie Miller was pacing in front of the centrally located McDonald's waiting for her. The second he saw her, his face lit up. "I was worried you weren't going to make it."

"Sorry, I got out of work late," she said, out of breath from the hurried walk. "I don't know why people have to have something done immediately when it's the last hour of the work week. They're not going to look at it until Monday anyhow. Then to make it worse, my boss left right after he assigned it."

"You're here; that's what matters. Hungry?"

"Enough, that it's dangerous for me to be out on the streets. You aren't the only one who understands food chains. Are you sure that Ethiopian food is all right with you? There're lots of other places around here too. All sorts of immigrants have been moving into this area, particularly Latinos."

"And chains like this?" Arnie asked slyly, glancing at the McDonald's.

Becki looked at him as if trying to decide whether he was joking. After all, she knew nothing about him. Maybe he meant it, or maybe he was broke. "Well," she hesitated, "I like Big Macs."

"Me too," he smiled, "but Ethiopian food sounds fine to me. I don't think I've ever had any."

"It's spicy...very hot."

"Mexican food is too and I like that, so let's try it." They walked back down the block to the nearest Ethiopian place, where taking her arm, he steered her into the dimly lit restaurant. Within minutes they were seated on large leather cushions covered with bright geometric designs, a small, low round table in front of them.

"I should have asked if you minded sitting on the floor," Becki said, suddenly concerned.

"I usually do in Tokyo," he answered casually, as he looked with interest at the walls. These were decorated with hand-woven baskets and paintings of handsome dark people in exotic, colorful costumes. More interesting, though, was the girl in front of him, soft and feminine. He'd wondered over the last few days if he'd imagined her spectacular beauty, but she was even prettier than he remembered. She also looked younger, and he wondered about her age. Definitely not the late twenties as he had originally thought.

"Tokyo as in Japan?" she asked surprised, her blue eyes lighting with interest.

"Yes, I go there sometimes on business."

"My! I've never been out of the States. Where else have you been?" Her voice lilted, excited.

"Oh here and there," he remarked casually, "but what about the important issue, the food."

"Well, they do all sorts of vegetables and then some chicken and lamb. We can get an assortment if you like. And beer, they have good beer, and it helps with the fire."

"Fire?"

"From the peppers and seasonings," Becki explained.

"Sure, beer's fine. You order. I'll be the official taster."

"If you can after you've tried a bite," she joked.

A slim youth, as exotic looking as any of the pictures, appeared to take their order. Somewhat to Becki's surprise, Arnie smilingly refused the proffered menu and gestured toward Becki. "She's the expert." So, turning to consult with the waiter, she proceeded to order, flattered that Arnie was deferring to her judgment.

Finally a girl arrived with a large tray covered by one huge piece of slightly grey, flat bread adorned with little mounds of various foods. "You just grab and then tear off some of the bread to go with the toppings; it gets the grease off your hands too," Becki instructed.

"Hmm," Arnie sounded a little doubtful. "I've never

eaten my plate before." Again Becki laughed, but she was watching him closely, concerned now over the dinner selection. She rarely chose when dining out, at least for others. After the first few bites, he looked at her, "You're right about the heat factor, but this stuff is good. Tell me what I'm eating, if you think I should know."

"The sour pancake bread, that's *injera*, and the puree is made of ground lentils. This I especially like," she said, indicating another of the mysterious mounds. "It's called *tibs*, which is chicken that's been cubed and sautéed. But watch out for this," she cautioned, pointing a well-manicured finger. "That's *berbere*, the pepper sauce."

"All good," Arnie pronounced solemnly. "I'm going to have to remember this when I get back to Boston.

"You don't sound like you're from Boston."

"What no nasal 'yeps' or broad 'park the car in Harvard Yard'?" he asked, drawing out the sounds and affecting a New England twang.

"I suppose so."

"That's because I only live there. I'm really from Oregon."

"Gosh, that's supposed to be beautiful. I've never been to the West Coast. Actually," Becki added a bit wistfully, "I've never been much of any place. I had a chance to go up to New York and work, but that didn't seem a good idea."

"Too big a city?"

"No, well, actually..." she hesitated, "I've got a little girl. I just didn't think it would be a good place to bring her up. Besides, I didn't know if I'd make it."

"Make it?"

"Modeling. I model some, and I was asked to send my portfolio to a couple of studios up there. But it's such a tough business, and I'm getting so old."

"Old? How old are you?" he inquired puzzled. She couldn't possibly be out of her twenties.

"Twenty-four."

"Twenty-four is old?" Arnie was incredulous.

"In that line, yes. And I'm not sure I'm really tall or thin enough."

He surveyed her long, lithe body. "You're taller than me, say five nine, five ten?"

"Five nine," she answered.

"How big are these models?"

"A lot are about six feet and they usually weigh no more than I do."

"You're skinny," he observed. "What, about a hundred and twenty pounds?"

Becki was surprised that he was so accurate. "More or less. I like to eat."

"God, what do they look like in real life? Escapees from Dachau? Sorry, not good taste. I sometimes make wisecracks I shouldn't," he mumbled, abashed.

"They're fairly thin. The camera does strange things."

"You're better off here in D.C."

"Actually I am," she answered seriously. "It doesn't pay as much, but I get a couple jobs every month...mostly photo sessions. Usually they only want someone to hang clothes on."

"Nice coat rack," he observed, and she laughed appreciatively. "What else do you do?" he asked.

"Oh, I work part time at a place that does interior decorating and handles fabrics and accessories. They do consulting and even arrange for special jobs like *trompe l'oeil*, gold leafing, faux finish—high-class work for the rich and famous. They also mount some displays for the fancier conventions here in D.C. I'm actually pretty lucky. They're fairly flexible about my hours so that I can do the modeling and get to my classes. Sometimes they even use me at conventions, which means a special hourly rate. That's why I really can't complain if they dump something on me at the last moment like they did tonight."

"And your little girl?"

"Andrea?"

"Pretty name. Tell me about her."

"Oh, she's eight, third grade, takes after me in looks. She's a nice little girl, smart, funny."

"Lucky child," he murmured, envisioning a tiny version of his attractive companion. Then he looked at her inquiring. "Eight?"

Becki was embarrassed. "I dropped out of high school. I was pretty stupid."

He regarded her reflectively for a moment and then said quietly, "We're all stupid at times. What happened to her father?"

"Billy? We got married. I think I was so dumb that it was a few months before I realized I was pregnant. I was still fourteen and he was the first boy I'd ever dated. And I didn't know who to talk to."

"You couldn't tell your folks?" Arnie asked calmly.

"I don't usually talk about this," Becki replied, amazed that she was, especially on a first date, but the little man seemed to project sympathy, and his candor was refreshing. Talking to him was proving easy, which didn't happen often.

"Sorry. I'm just being nosey. You don't have to tell me anything."

"No," she agreed, "but I started. My parents drowned in a squall out on the Chesapeake the year before. I was living with my father's aunt, Aunt Mary in fact. That's why I was so surprised when you said you had a message from her the other night."

"If I'd known you were Becki Thatcher, I probably would have said Aunt Polly."

She smiled shyly. "You're nice, funny too."

"And well read," he teased. "Not Mark Twain alone. Ask me about Herman Melville or Joseph Conrad." It was a test, unfair he realized, but somehow he wanted to know if reading *Tom Sawyer* had been a fluke or whether she really did have literary interests. She seemed bright but a high school dropout and teenage mother! Who knew, maybe it had been her looks that had attracted him. Still, as spectacular as she was, it was substance that counted when it came to dating, even if he'd probably never see her again

Carefully considering his question, Becki answered seriously, "I don't care much for whales or taking boats up sinister rivers. The rivers I like are here in Virginia or Twain's books, even if his *Life on the Mississippi* made me cry. His poor brother, dying in that steamboat explosion, but I'd still like to go on a paddle wheeler sometime."

"Me too," Arnie concurred pleased. "So?" Reading had always been important to him and it was nice to know they had something in common, but he felt a little guilty over his test and wondered if she realized what he'd done. Would he have if he weren't surprised by her background? Although it was unfair, he had been shocked when she mentioned her daughter. Eight-years old. Unbelievable. Most of the women he dated were older than this lovely girl and none of them had children

"So, what?" she asked uncertainly.

"You were telling me about yourself."

"I'm not very interesting," she replied.

He could tell it was a sincere remark, not just fishing for a compliment, and countered, "I think you are."

He said it as though he really meant it, and Becki again felt at ease, deciding she would answer him. "Well, I married Billy. Our mothers had been friends and I guess his believed it was the right thing to do. He was a couple of years ahead of me in high school. The big football hero who never used his brains. After he graduated, he went into the Army and got his training down south before ending up at Vint Hill in Virginia as a MP. I was staying with his parents when Drea was born."

"I did some basic. I was in ROTC during high school for a short time."

"Then you know the drill. When Billy got back here, we went to Manassas to live."

"The South's glory."

"What? Oh, the battlefield. No, I'm afraid we lived off the strip. That's most of Manassas: one fast-food place after another. I doubt if even half the people who live there have ever visited the park."

"I bet you did," commented Arnie, encouraging her. She was proving to be more interesting than he'd hoped.

"Yes," she admitted, remembering how good it had felt to get away from the crowded apartment complex. She'd walk the vast green spaces, carrying Drea in a sling, and thinking about all the poor, brave men who'd fought and died on what had become a peaceful, verdant land—other women's babes. It was a place where even the scattered cannons now served as jungle gyms for visiting children, oblivious of the bloody past.

"Anyhow, Billy was too young for marriage. I guess I was too, but someone had to stay home with Drea. All he really wanted to do was drink beer with his buddies. Finally he moved out and began chasing other girls. Diapers and a screaming baby weren't for him and poor Drea did scream. She had colic all the time. I sometimes thought I'd never sleep so I'd take her for long walks. That's probably why I got so thin although my father was. My sister, Marty, takes after my mother, small, beautiful coloring and face, but always worried about her weight."

"You have beautiful coloring and a beautiful face although I imagine you're used to people saying that." Arnie wondered what possible attraction other girls would have had for the immature Billy, aside from affording an opportunity to escape the wailing baby.

"Yes," Becki stated guilelessly. "That's why I get the modeling jobs, but who knows how much longer I'll have them. As I said, that's one reason I didn't try New York. Also, I would have been out of my element there. I'm really just a small-town hick."

"You seem to be getting along ok here."

"Luckily my sister and her husband took me under their wing once Billy left, and I make enough money to help pay our way. They've got a townhouse out at Falls Church. Drea and I have the bottom floor, which means a couple rooms and a bath like our own private apartment—a real shotgun affair for the two of us."

"I thought that was New Orleans or do they have irate husbands here, too?" joked Arnie, picking up on the shotgun reference.

"I wouldn't know," smiled Becki. "But when I take that paddle wheeler, that's where I want to go and see the ducks at the Peabody on the way. Imagine," she drawled in wonder, "a hotel that rolls out a red carpet for ducks!"

"Me too," agreed Arnie, "although I'd head for the oysters and jazz. I could probably skip the marching ducks unless they stuff one with sauerkraut."

"Sauerkraut!"

"My German half," explained Arnie.

"Sauerkraut, whoever would have thought that," puzzled Becki, whose introduction to other cultures was through books, film, and food; still it was safer to talk about things she knew. "Anyhow, I wish I could afford to get a place of my own, but Marty's pregnant and not teaching first term next year so I guess I'll really help financially. At least that's what she always tells me, plus Jerry's in school another year and only working part time."

"Doing?" Arnie inquired casually.

"Law at George Mason University and being a paralegal for a new firm in Falls Church. They like him and probably will take him in when he passes the bar. He and Marty met at Mason. She went up there immediately after William and Mary to get a master's in education, and he ended up picking her up in the cafeteria."

"Kind of like I did you in the bar."

At this remark, Becki protested, "No, you saved me, remember?"

"I forgot," he smiled slightly. "Ye gentle knight."

"Well, it's pretty rare. I really did appreciate it or..."

"Or you wouldn't be here."

"You're right," she agreed candidly, "but I'm not sorry I am. Actually, I shouldn't have been in that bar. I was at a shower for a girl from work when Larry the Lizard came to pick up Jenny and she asked me to come along for a drink. Oops," she stopped, obviously embarrassed about her own acid remark.

Arnie laughed appreciatively. "Lounge Lizard, of course. Most appropriate."

Becki smiled back, once more relaxed. Social occasions could be such a strain, but it was easy to talk to this man. "Loathsome too, as well as lecherous." Arnie guffawed boisterously this time, imagining how insulted someone like the dapper Larry would have been by that description. "Anyhow, I didn't know Jenny was going to leave. For some reason, she wanted me to meet him and I guess they had arranged it. Too bad they didn't tell me. But what about you? You haven't said anything except that you've been to places like Tokyo and are from the great Northwest and I gather you do things with computers. We have them at work now. I've even taken an introductory class at NOVA."

"NOVA?"

"Northern Virginia Community College. That's how I spend my Tuesday and Thursday nights. I'm trying to get an associate degree. I only have a GED, so I guess I'd better finish and have something to show."

"And you're going to be a computer nerd?"

"No, I'm not smart enough."

"I wouldn't say that," he responded. Maybe this Becki wasn't well educated, but she certainly was no fool. Brains and beauty, a nice combination.

"Thanks, I think. I'm interested in interior design. They've got a program and I'm taking some photography and art classes too."

"You'd be good at that." He looked at her carefully, assessing her tasteful appearance. Tonight she was in a simple midnight-blue suit—Chanel style he thought they called it, with a pale blue blouse that looked as if it might be silk. Her blonde hair was pulled back and her makeup was discrete but enough to highlight her vivid blue eyes, made even deeper blue by the clothes ensemble.

"How can you tell?"

"Oh, from the way you dress and handle yourself—nice color sense, classic style. You've looked terrific the two times I've seen you."

Now Becki really was embarrassed. Men were always ogling her but Arnie's comments had sincerity. "Thank you, but I have to dress for work you know."

"So do I, but no one would ever ask me to be on a magazine cover."

She laughed again and confessed, "They haven't asked me either."

"Well, they should. Would you like to walk around the area a little, have a coffee or something? I noticed they had some places with music when I got here." Arnie realized he had made a decision. This was a woman he wanted to see again, not just a diversion for a lonely evening out of town.

Becki looked at her watch, surprised a couple hours had passed so rapidly for it was now well past 8:00, about the time she'd originally allotted for this excursion. But she was enjoying herself and she too made a decision. Besides, it was the weekend and even Drea slept in provided overly indulgent Uncle Jerry let her stay up for late TV. "We could have it here. Ethiopian coffee is famous but it is a nice evening. I really can't stay much longer. I don't like to catch the Metro too late as I have to walk a few blocks to our place when I get off."

"Don't feel you have to stay," he said, but he was looking at her hopefully.

"No, that will be fine as long as I'm on the train before 11:00." And surely Drea would be in bed once she got home.

"Sounds good to me." Arnie helped her up and the two strolled out into the night. It was a mild spring evening and the street was fairly crowded. Restaurants had set out tables and people were sitting, talking and drinking. From some places, music could be heard. "This kind of reminds me of the Quincy Market area at home," he noted as they found a small coffee house and took one of the outside tables. Their conversation became chitchat, pleasant but impersonal.

When it was almost time for Becki to catch her train, they began to amble back to the station, catching the Red Line to Metro Center. "This certainly beats the T—that's the MBTA, Boston's system," Arnie observed. "In fact, this is the nicest subway I've been on."

"I really can't judge," Becki commented since it was the

only subway she'd ever ridden, "but we like it. It just doesn't go to enough places though.

"Planning and good transportation don't seem to be the American dream," Arnie observed a bit cynically. Their conversation had slacked off now, but the silence was comfortable as they transferred to the Orange Line. By the time they'd almost reached his stop, Rosslyn in Virginia, he said, "This has really been pleasant, Becki. Could I persuade you come into town tomorrow and go to some museums or tourist attractions with me? It's my only weekend in D.C. and I wasn't kidding about not having been here before." He had that hopeful look again.

"I'm sorry," she replied, deciding she meant it. The evening had turned out to be fun. There had been no pressure and this Arnie Miller was interesting. "I try to spend as much time on weekends as I can with Drea and helping Marty."

"Bring Drea," he suddenly broke in. "We'll see things kids like. The Air and Space Museum, the Washington Monument."

"Are you sure?"

"Of course. I wouldn't have said it if not. I'm an uncle. My sister has three kids. I like them and besides," he answered honestly, his eyes eager and optimistic, "you wouldn't come otherwise, and I'd really like to see you again."

She was surprised at how quickly she decided. "All right, 10:00 tomorrow morning at the Smithsonian stop and we can take it from there." Drea would have to be asleep by now and they could be underway by 9:00.

"That's fine with me." Arnie reached out and took her hand a moment as he rose for his stop. "It's been a nice evening."

"It has," she agreed.

CHAPTER 3

Shortly after 10:00, Becki and Drea exited the Metro but when Becki looked for Arnie, she couldn't see him. Fifteen minutes of pacing in front of the New Agriculture Building and he still wasn't there. Suddenly she remembered there were two Smithsonian exits—the one on Independence Avenue where they were and another in the Mall itself. Perhaps he had taken the other! Grabbing Drea's hand, she rushed across the avenue, avoiding the whizzing traffic and hurrying toward the Mall. There he was. "I'm so sorry," she apologized, flustered at her error. "I forgot to say which exit. I always think the other one's fastest to Air and Space and I guess I just thought you'd be there. I didn't think about you not knowing the stops."

"No problem," Arnie replied with a pleasant grin. "I was worried you might have changed your mind."

"Oh no, I wouldn't do that without letting you know," she said with obvious sincerity.

For a moment, he studied her face. "I guess you wouldn't." Then crouching down, he gazed solemnly at Andrea. Taking one of her tiny hands in his, he shook it gently. "You must be Miss Andrea. I've heard a lot about you. I'm Arnie."

Andrea, a pretty child looking much as he had expected with her mother's blue eyes and blonde hair, stared back equally solemnly. "Hi," she answered in a little voice.

"Is seeing the airplanes ok with you or would you rather go to the Museum of Technology? It's got an old fashioned town and trains or we could visit the Museum of Natural History and see the dinosaurs and bugs. They also have a coral reef and some pretty fabulous jewelry there."

"For being an out-of-towner, you're certainly knowledgeable about the Smithsonian," observed Becki.

Arnie glanced up, a cocky grin on his face. "I like to read, remember? So, what is it, Miss Andrea? You're the boss."

Drea looked at her mother, eyes wide and obviously surprised at being consulted on an adult matter.

"I think he means it, honey. What would you like to see?"

"All of it?" Drea implored hopefully in a tiny voice, and the two adults started laughing.

"Well, we're really going to have to walk fast then," said Arnie. "But if you're game, so am I."

"What does that mean, Mommy?" the child asked.

"It means we're doing it," smiled Becki as much at Arnie as the little girl, and the three rushed off across the Mall. By the time they'd gotten through the Museum of History and Technology and back on the Mall, Drea appeared to be still going strong but the grownups were hanging back.

"She's a powerhouse, isn't she?" asked Arnie.

"She doesn't have a lot of opportunities like this," responded Becki matter-of-factly. "It's mostly school or child care since I don't want to take too much advantage of my sister. Then when we're home, there's a lot to do around the house. I try to do my share of the chores as well as take care of us. But I take her places on the weekend, if just to the library, and we go on long walks."

"Well," said Arnie to Drea, "to have pity on us old folks, why don't we stop at the merry-go-round? You go around a few times and then maybe I can pick up some hot dogs and popcorn, stuff like that. How does that sound?"

"Oh Mommy," pleaded Drea. "I can?"

"*May*, dear, and Arnie asked, didn't he?"

"Oh thank you!" shouted Drea and she threw her arms around him. "You're a nice man. I'm going to ride the Black Stallion. Mommy used to read to me about him but I'm big enough to read it now myself," she added proudly.

"I used to read the *Black Stallion* series too when I was little," said Arnie. "I think I wanted to be Alec, but we lived in a city and I never had a chance to go riding."

"Neither have I, except once on a pony at a fair."

"Well maybe we can fix that sometime," he remarked and Becki looked at him strangely.

Once Drea was in the carousel enclosure and had picked a resplendent black horse bedecked with eye-catching plaster jewels, Arnie and Becki sat down on one of the benches. "You're very kind," observed Becki. "Most men I've dated haven't paid any attention to her but you've answered questions and were telling her things about some of the technical items in the museum."

"I told you I like kids and she's a nice one. She's bright too."

"I wish you hadn't mentioned riding though."

"How so?"

"You're only here another week. I don't want her to think you've promised something she won't get."

Arnie looked at her thoughtfully and added quietly, "I'll probably be down to D.C. again. Maybe we'll get together then, if you'd like. In fact, I'm hoping you'll come out with me next week...any, every night you can."

Becki stared back equally thoughtfully. "Remember, I have classes Tuesday and Thursday. When are you going back?"

"Saturday morning."

"Well, maybe one night. Can we continue to play it by ear? I hate to have Marty baby sit too much but I'll see."

"Fine by me," Arnie responded, trying to be casual. He definitely did want to see this gorgeous lady again. "Do you want to go on the carousel while I go get us some nice junk food?"

"I go in circles enough," Becki joked. "I'll wait here until you come back. But make that a diet drink for me, please, so I don't feel too guilty and some juice or milk for Drea. It's hard working and trying to have kids eat right. I don't want her to grow up thinking that ketchup counts as the vegetable group."

Arnie smirked sheepishly, confessing, "I'm afraid I'm on the run so much that I eat a lot of junk food too with ketchup probably serving as my salad course and Tang, instead of real juice. Now you, you look as though you're an ad for one of those health-food magazines."

"You do have a way with compliments," Becki said. She was so used to getting all the bull from men on the make when she was modeling. Yet Arnie kept saying things like this but then just went on being nice, not pushy, with that cherubic smile of his. Definitely very different from the kind of man she ordinarily met, and he was being genuinely considerate to Drea, who seemingly had learned to identify phonies at an early age. That was something she wasn't always able to do herself, Becki reflected ruefully.

When he returned, Drea was back with her mother, looking excitedly at the array. "Pizza, hot dogs, coke, popcorn, wow! Can I have the coke?" The little girl's hand had already dipped into the popcorn and was shoving kernels into her mouth.

"*May*, and don't talk with food in your mouth," cautioned Becki, "but no, diet drinks aren't good for small fry. Juice is."

"Ah Mommy," but this was more the expected protest from a child than an actual complaint. In no time, Drea had her mouth refilled and was pointing at the dinosaur statue in front of the Natural History building. "Can I climb on it?"

"Why not, as long as you remember to stay in sight. We'll be over in a little while to go into the museum. There's an elephant in there you can't believe."

"And a whole exhibit of cockroaches," added Arnie helpfully.

"Ugg," said Drea, nose wrinkling up in obvious disgust.

"Ok, how would you like to hold a tarantula instead?" he asked.

"Really?"

"If your mommy will let you. They're usually nice and soft and fuzzy, although I wouldn't advise squeezing. They live in an insect zoo over there," he said pointing at the Natural History Building.

"Wow!" exclaimed the little girl, clearly intrigued by the interesting prospect.

"Not afraid of spiders, I see," Arnie remarked.

"Even if she's being brought up in the suburbs, her aunt and I were country gals. I even had a pet snake when I was little," Becki added.

"Somehow I would never have believed that," he said, looking at her. Today she was dressed in tailored beige slacks and a simple white shirt but she still looked stylish. It was the carriage, he thought. She held herself so tall and stately.

"Certainly, I told you I was brought up in the Northern Neck."

"You keep saying that, but I have to confess my ignorance."

"What? Something you haven't read about?" chided Becki with a slight grin. "It's a peninsula of Virginia that stretches down into the Chesapeake with the Potomac River on one side and the Rappahannock on the other. My father's family had a place on the Potomac down in King George County beyond Fredericksburg. That was one of the colonial areas. George Washington was brought up around there."

"You're one of those river plantation Virginians?"

"I wouldn't say that," she chuckled. "I wish I could. I suppose the family had some money once. My great aunt still has the family home. It's an old farmhouse on a hill overlooking the water and it's very scenic there. A lot of the land was sold, but there're still about thirty acres left and the river frontage. Sometimes you can even see eagles."

"Eagles around here?" Arnie's eyebrows rose in amazement.

"Yes, Virginia is fairly rural once you get away from D.C. and a lot of the wild life is coming back—geese, ducks, swans, herons. Lots of deer and small mammals too. It was a nice place to grow up when I was young." Arnie tried not to smile. Becki was still young by his definition, in spite of parenthood, though that had to color her perspective. "My parents had a little seafood place on the river and we'd spend a lot of time out on the water, crabbing, fishing."

"You miss it?"

"Oh yes!" The enthusiasm was manifest by the sudden

light in her eyes. Then more realistically, she said, "I'd love to bring Drea up there but I'd be working in some tourist shop in Fredericksburg or fixing hamburgers in a fast-food place. Maybe I'd be checking groceries if I were lucky."

"If you were lucky?" Arnie was genuinely surprised. He'd never really thought about that. Menial jobs were part of his adolescence, but he'd never gone the greasy fast-food route. Even by high school, he'd mostly worked in offices.

"It's one of the best-paying jobs around, but murder on the feet."

"I'd imagine so," he agreed.

"Besides, my aunt didn't want me after I got pregnant and once Billy deserted us, I didn't have a lot of options. I was so lucky that my big sister and her husband are so great. I hate to think what would have happened."

"You would have done ok," he stated seriously.

"How do you know that?"

"You're smart and obviously not afraid to work. I doubt if it would have been easy, but I bet it isn't the easiest now."

Becki looked at him startled. "Why do you say that?" Most men never even considered that being a single mother, working and going to school, might be tough. All they saw when they looked at her was her appearance. In fact, all most of them seemed to be interested in were her looks. She sometimes wondered if any realized she had brains or was a person with problems or goals and dreams. Dating, by and large, was not always pleasant, not that she did much. The world seemed to abound in Larrys although not all as crude or aggressive.

"My mom had to bring me and my sister up. You remind me some of her," Arnie said in part as explanation.

"You haven't really told me much about yourself."

"What's to tell? I'm a computer nerd. I work on software. That's what I've been hustling down here."

"And in Japan?"

"Well, it's software that deals with money and everyone is interested in money. But don't we have a date to pet a tarantula?"

"Better you than me."

"Hey, don't knock it until you try it."

"Only like James Bond if the thing is crawling up me. I don't mind spiders. I just have to know that they're there."

"Point taken, Miss Moneypenny," he conceded, although he really equated her with 007's bevy of beauties; but, he wasn't sure she'd like that analogy. Becki, if anything, seemed embarrassed by her good looks even though she capitalized on them professionally.

As it turned out, Natural History proved to be such a hit that they never got over to Air and Space. Drea enjoyed the insect zoo and did get to hold the tarantula. She was equally fascinated by the exhibit of a kitchen engulfed by 'yucky' cockroaches as well as the small, living coral reef, but it was the display of dinosaurs that had her enthralled. She and Arnie examined each in great detail, he helping her read some of the labels and telling her all sorts of extra miscellaneous facts until Becki asked, "Was it computers you said you worked with or paleontology?"

"I loved these things as a kid," he enthused, his face beaming. "I used to read about them all the time and I actually did think about being a paleontologist until I discovered numbers were more fun. I'm from Oregon, remember? It rains all the time. We stayed in the Ark all winter and read or played cards. My sister and I must have learned a hundred card games and we both built models. She liked planes and cars and I did the dinosaurs. *Godzilla* was my hero."

"I thought he was simply a loathsome lizard who made Geiger counters click," remarked Becki pertly, amused at his obvious excitement. Arnie grinned back appreciatively. She had obviously attended Saturday matinees too—another important part of his childhood. "Well if you all are going to spend a half hour on each one of these beasts, I think I'm going to head upstairs and catch a glimpse of the Hope Diamond."

Startled, Arnie now gazed at her in unfeigned surprise.

"Drea can stay down here with me?"

"I think she'll be fine with you," answered Becki, adding facetiously, "You're not a child molester are you?" Arnie looked so shocked at the suggestion that Becki almost had to laugh. Moving over to Drea, who was engrossed in examining some fossils, she leaned over and quietly said, "I'll be back in a little while, honey. You can keep looking at the dinosaurs with Arnie, but stay around here so I can find you, all right?" Drea nodded her head and turned back to her current interest. Then whispering in Arnie's ear, Becki added, "There, I've told her. Do you want me to tell her to scream her head off if you leave the exhibit? She probably would anyhow. Besides I have your business card and I know what hotel you're in."

"We'll be here," he asserted stoutly but still wondering if she was being serious.

In about fifteen minutes Becki was back. "My, you've moved all of ten feet," she drawled dryly. "Progress. Are you counting the bones in each one now?" It was another hour by the time they left the exhibit and Becki looked at her watch. "I don't think we're going to have time to go to another museum."

"Are we going to have to go home?" whined Drea, face now theatrically pitiful like some waif out of *Oliver Twist*.

"Don't be a whiner," whined back Becki, holding her nose to sound even more nasal. Then both laughed since this was obviously a family joke.

"I personally suggest dinner provided I have a vote," interjected Arnie hopefully.

"Oh yes," agreed Drea eagerly, jumping up and down and grabbing his hand. "That's a good idea, Arnie."

"Arnie's spent a lot of time with us today, honey. I'm not sure..."

"Please," whined Arnie and now all three were laughing.

"Well," said Becki, "there're not many places around."

"How about Chinatown?" he asked. "I saw it on the Metro map. Is it any good?"

"Yes," acknowledged Becki reflectively. "There're a few streets of restaurants and we like Chinese food, don't we, Drea?"

"Chicken with cashews and an egg roll," the little girl promptly replied.

"I see," said Arnie. "Do we all have to order before we go?"

"I'll think about it on the way," remarked Becki, and the three made their way back to the Metro. Drea was hopping along in between the two adults, her hands holding theirs tightly so at times she could swing back and forth.

"I'm not sure we can feed you," observed Arnie. "You're heavy."

"Silly man," replied Drea, giggling and looking at him coyly through her thick dark eyelashes. What a charmer she's going to be when she grows up, thought Arnie, just like her mother.

When they got to Chinatown, they slowly began to meander up and down the streets trying to make their selection. Arnie was looking at the old converted buildings and Becki told him that this had been D.C.'s main downtown area during the nineteenth century. "The Lincoln conspirators met here. That house across the street was Mary Surratt's boarding house. They actually ended up hanging her over at Fort McNair in S.W., down where the Potomac and Anacostia meet. John Wilkes Booth was supposed to have been buried there later under what's now the tennis court. Even Ford Theater is only a few blocks away from here."

Arnie looked suitably impressed but before he could say anything, Drea cried delighted, "Ford Theater! Can we go?"

"*May*," tried Becki again. "It's not a movie theater, sweetheart. That's where President Lincoln was shot during the Civil War. It's a museum now."

"Oh," said the little girl disappointed. But suddenly she brightened up and boasted, "I know about President Lincoln. He freed the slaves."

"Among other things," murmured her mother, "but I think food is next on the agenda, and after, you and I have to go home."

"Well," declared Arnie, stopping in front of a restaurant with a bright red marquee, "we'd best really enjoy the dinner then. Since you two can't make up your mind, I'm picking this place based on my keen powers of observation and subsequent analysis."

"What does that mean?" Becki inquired with curiosity, not seeing anything in particular to distinguish it from its neighbors save maybe a brighter entrance.

"I've noticed about six oriental couples go in which I think is an indication that it probably serves decent Chinese food."

"Kind of like the number of trucks in front of a highway diner?"

"That would probably be a good clue too, unless of course there was no other diner for a hundred miles."

"My," said Becki, "I hadn't thought about that."

"That's part of the scientific approach. You have to consider all the information."

"I'll keep that in mind. What's the rest of your analysis about this dinner?"

"A Shirley Temple for Miss Andrea, cold Taiwanese beer or one of those tropical things you like, egg rolls all around, other nibbles, and then the main courses, including chicken with cashews, of course."

Upon hearing this, Drea rewarded him with a big smile. Then jumping up and down, she pled, "And chopsticks, Mommy. Can I try chopsticks?"

"You don't know how to use them," her mother said, murmuring *may* under her breath one last time.

"I'll teach her," volunteered Arnie, turning to Becki. "Do you want to try?"

"If I ever go to the Orient...I like to get the food to my mouth."

"I'll remember that," he grinned and when the chopsticks came, he showed Drea how to curve her fingers. Of course by the time the adults had finished dinner, she was still working away at her meal. They sat, sipping tea for another hour and chatting quietly while the little girl laboriously picked up, lost, and recaptured her food. "Most persistent child I've ever seen," Arnie stated with absolute conviction.

"You encouraged her, but you're nice to let her try. I think though, we really are going to have to switch to a fork, or do you want to take the rest of the food home?" Becki asked her daughter.

It was obvious that Drea didn't want to admit defeat. "Can I take the chopsticks too?"

"I suppose so," said her mother. "They're disposable, aren't they? Besides, now we can open the fortune cookies." Drea's was 'Long Life' but Becki and Arnie got the same one: 'A stranger will be entering your life'.

"It should have mentioned two," he chuckled and Becki blushed. When they got to the subway station, he said to her hopefully. "You and Drea wouldn't care to come back in tomorrow, would you?"

Drea looked optimistic but Becki answered, "No, tomorrow isn't good, I'm sorry."

Drea started to protest, but Becki glanced at her sternly and put her finger to her mouth. The little girl became quiet and looked away, leaving Arnie feeling sorry for both himself and the child. At Metro Center, where they had to change trains and were waiting for the Orange line, he tried again. "Well you did say maybe another day and Monday's kind of an anniversary. We met last Monday, remember?" To emphasize the point, he was whining slightly.

Becki looked at him in amazement and began to laugh. "All right, Monday. You're definitely a salesman. I can only stay for a drink. I've got to study."

"Drink and dinner after," he bargained hopefully.

"Drink at dinner," she conceded.

"Deal," he readily agreed, not wanting to push his luck. "But where? You know, you haven't even told me where you work."

"Oh," she answered surprised, "off K Street, near that bar where the girls from work like to hang out." But you don't, thought Arnie, and probably don't at any bars, although he said nothing. Becki continued, "There's a little German place about a block down."

"Great, 6:00 again?"

"Fine with me. Give me a piece of paper and I'll write down the address but I really, really have to be on the train home no later than 8:00." This time she'd keep that deadline.

Clicking his heels, Arnie bent over. "*Sehr gut, meine dame.* It vill be done."

"Aren't you supposed to do a *sieg heil* or something?" she asked.

"Wrong period. Think Austrian Empire or something. Waltzes are much nicer to contemplate."

"I don't think I've ever danced a waltz."

"I don't suppose I have either," said Arnie.

Both considered what it would be like dancing together, but neither spoke, although he could see her regarding him speculatively. She'd be fantastic, he thought. How she would have looked in one of those turn-of-the century ball gowns. Tall, that golden hair piled high, attired in something shimmering so she'd really stand out in the crowd. There would have been flowers in her hair and diamonds or pearls around her long, slender neck. Dashing men in dress uniforms would have been bowing and clicking their heels all over the place, and he'd probably have been too small and dumpy for her to even notice.

When the train reached Rosslyn, Arnie hopped out again. Both Becki and Drea were waving to him, Drea in fact blowing kisses, and he pretended to catch one, smiled and blew it back. He could see she was laughing delightedly as the train pulled out. Cute kid, he thought, reflecting that it had been a pleasant day even if seeing the child's mother had been his major objective. Definitely two for the price of one.

By Monday, Arnie was waiting eagerly for Becki, hoping that perhaps he could get her to extend her stay but she was adamant. Beer, dumplings, green pepper salad and schnitzel, accompanied by a lively conversation about anything and everything. Then suddenly it was almost 8:00 and she exclaimed, "My train!"

"Not to worry, I'll get a cab if I have to."

"Don't be ridiculous! Whoever heard of a cab for three blocks? We'll just walk fast. They only come every fifteen or twenty minutes now so we have to go *schnell*, which is about the only German word, I know. All those prison guards in the World War II movies making everyone hurry when there was nowhere to go."

"It sounded good," observed Arnie, whose own German wasn't much better, although his grandmother had tried to teach both him and his sister. The two marched or at least walked as *schnell* as possible, scarcely arriving on the platform as the Orange train pulled in. "I told you we'd make it. Now, I know you can't come in on Tuesday or Thursday, but what about Wednesday or Friday? Remember, I have to leave on Saturday."

Becki thought a moment, "Friday?"

He broke into his nice smile. "Good. Would you like to eat at the hotel?" Then realizing what she might be thinking, he added, "I'm not sure how great the food is but the roof bar has a fabulous view. Why don't you come for a drink and we can watch the sunset. Then if the menu doesn't please you, we'll go over to Georgetown."

"That would be nice, Arnie." Becki squeezed his hand and he again got out of the train a second before the doors started to close. She was half surprised that he hadn't tried to kiss her, but he had simply grinned per usual. When the train pulled out, he was on the platform, as he'd been the time before, lifting his hand to wave goodbye.

CHAPTER 4

THis Friday for a change, no one had any last minute work and Becki was able to leave at a decent hour. There should be no problem getting to the hotel on time and she thought about the evening. Arnie was undoubtedly one of the sweetest men she'd ever met, and he'd certainly impressed Drea, but he was going back to Boston. Even if he were to come back or stay in D.C., what would be the future going out with him? He'd never even tried to kiss her, and if he did, would she be interested? Nice wasn't the same as being sexually attracted, unfortunately. Well, it had been nice—two weeks of nice and she hadn't had anyone who'd been genuinely interested in her for a long time. She'd thought Mike was, and then it turned out that the bastard was married. Six months since she'd slammed the door in his lying, two-timing face and there had been no one since, or for that matter really before.

When she got to the hotel, she called up to Arnie's room. "Hi, I'm here. I'm a little early; is that all right?"

"Great," he said in that nice radio voice, "more time before I have to put you on the mysterious Metro to somewhere. You know, I still don't know where you work or live or even your telephone number."

"Oh, I guess you don't." Becki was startled. How strange, she had never thought of that and he had never asked. She could have stood him up any time if she'd wanted and he wouldn't have been able to find her. Had she wanted it that way on purpose? Yet here she was.

"Well never mind, do you want to come up?"

"Come up?"

"Sure, to the roof bar. I'll meet you there and then we can decide what to do."

"Fine," she agreed. For a moment she had thought he meant to his room. Again she wondered how she would have reacted. She was so tired of men who tried to maul her, but Arnie had never made a single move.

When she stepped out of the elevator, he was waiting for her. "Beautiful as always. Is there any color you can't wear?" he asked, gazing at her simple black dress and admiring her golden hair, pinned into a sophisticated hairdo. It was just as he had imagined it might look if she were wearing that ball gown. All that was missing was the string of pearls.

"Black's not a color," she rejoined.

"I suppose it isn't, but you look fantastic. Every guy is going to wonder what you're doing here with me."

Becki laughed. "You're my knight in shining armor, remember?"

"Darn tootin'—show me a dragon, fair damsel." Becki blushed again, but Arnie pretended not to notice and merely enthused, "Now what magical potion can I have them mix for you?"

"I don't know. I don't drink much...beer sometimes."

"So I noticed, but since this is kind of a special evening...I mean, well hell, what do I mean? Since it's the last night I'll be in town this time, how about something exotic?"

"What would you suggest?"

"Maybe some nice tropical drink—a frozen daiquiri or a piña colada or something of that ilk."

"Piña colada, that sounds good, like that song."

"Except there's no rain. I especially requested no rain so we could watch the sunset."

"That was thoughtful," she replied, but then Arnie was thoughtful in reality as well as jest. They were now seated by a table overlooking the river with all of Georgetown spread out before them. Beyond, they could see the monuments.

"I like Boston," he observed, "but D.C. really is beautiful. We always hear about the politics and inside the Beltway crap, but aside from Cherry Blossom time, they never seem to talk about all the parks and flowers and the walks along the river. That's what I did last Sunday when you and Drea couldn't come in."

"It is beautiful," she agreed, "but sad, too—the crime,

people sleeping on the streets, which seems to be getting worse. We can't use those parks all the time."

"Yeah, that's cities. I don't know why it should be that way, but it's happening. How did we get on this topic?"

"I don't know. I'm sorry, maybe un *peu triste*."

"Madame *parle français*?"

"Madame hopes she passed her French exam last night."

"Ah, now I understand why you had to study and couldn't come out with me on Wednesday. Too bad you didn't tell me. We could have gone to Georgetown to one of the French restaurants and let you practice on the menus."

"Hey, none of them have the view."

"No," he concurred. "Would you like another piña colada?"

She looked down at her empty glass. "We're still eating here?"

"If it's ok."

"All right. I guess it is. I don't usually have a second drink but these are a weakness. We'll be having dinner soon, right?" she asked a bit anxiously. Billy had introduced her to alcohol, proving liquor was quicker, and she'd learned that lesson the hard way even if she still did enjoy indulging.

"Soon," he promised and another frosty cherry-topped drink swiftly arrived. "I'm not trying to get you drunk. It's just so pleasant up here. These two weeks have been nice, and a lot of it has had to do with you."

"For me too." She smiled, knowing she meant it, and was glad he felt the same.

"When I come back again, will you see me?"

Becki regarded him soberly a moment and then answered, "Yes."

"Good. Now how about dinner?" Signaling for the waitress, Arnie told the woman they'd be dining and the two were led to the restaurant section on another side with a different view. The sun was almost down now. In the buildings below, lights were beginning to twinkle. A different waiter appeared, lit a candle, and handed them the menus.

"Anything special?" Arnie asked Becki.

"The seafood, I think. I love seafood. My parents were the best cooks. You should have tasted their crab cakes and the spiced crabs and shrimp. Everything they prepared was good."

"And you cook too? Not that you look like you eat anything, as thin as you are."

"I like to but mostly it's food Drea likes or a fast pick-up dinner for all of us. Children seem to be born without taste, although that Chinese dinner was a hit."

"Yes," he acknowledged. "One of my nephews would like to live on peanut butter and jelly and the other thinks hot dogs are haute cuisine. At least my niece likes spaghetti, but I believe that's because she can throw it all over. She's the baby."

"You never did tell me about your family."

"Not much to tell. My dad died when I was little. My mom worked in a bank. She never remarried. I have one sister who's a CPA, married to a lawyer. She's older than I am—mid-thirties and she's got three kids. Timmy age ten going on about a hundred. Josh is nine and Molly is three and an unholy terror but the cutest little thing so that everyone forgets and lets her get away with it. My sister got all the looks, unfortunately."

Becki smiled slightly. It was true after all, but she placed her hand on his, saying, "And you got the charm." That was also true.

"Good comeback," Arnie answered with what definitely was a charming smile. "How about some wine with the dinner?"

"I had two drinks," she replied cautiously.

"Well, I'll have some wine then and maybe you'll help me a little."

It was dark outside now and Becki appraised the new view of the city. The monuments were lit and streams of traffic ran up and down the parkway, shifting chains of sparkling rubies to the right and diamonds to the left. "What's Boston like?" she suddenly asked.

"Oh, historic like here, but different, an old city for the States—bigger modern buildings but none of the classic styles really like your monuments or older government buildings, except for a few private homes. You'd like it. You'll have to visit some time."

"I'd enjoy that," she said seriously. "There's so much I haven't seen but want to."

Arnie was obviously about to say something when a young, eager-looking man appeared at his side. "Dr. Miller?" Arnie glanced up in surprise. "Dr. Miller, I heard you speak over at Treasury. I merely wanted to tell you that that software program of yours sounds very interesting. Did you develop it at MIT or what?"

"Or what," smiled Arnie. "Thanks. We're kind of excited about it too. Hopefully you all are thinking the same."

"Well we certainly want to hear more about it. Anyhow, I just wanted to tell you how interesting your lecture and demonstration were. I'm going to be in Boston next month. Is there any chance I can come by and talk to you?"

"Sure," said Arnie amiably, reaching in his pocket. "Here's my card; call me when you get there. Do you have one?"

"Oh certainly, I'm John Peeling. Excuse me and I'm sorry to have interrupted your dinner, but I didn't get to talk to you the other day. There was such a crowd around you."

"Nice to meet you, Mr. Peeling. I'll look forward to your call." Arnie stood to shake his hand. When the man left, he looked back at Becki. "Sorry."

"Dr. Miller? MIT? A lecture? I thought you were supposed to be a salesman."

"Did I say that?" Arnie asked, well aware he'd been steering their conversations away from what he actually did and speaking only in generalizations when the subject came up.

"Not exactly, but..."

"Ok, I have a Ph.D. and I teach a class at MIT. That's where I got my doctorate and some of my buddies from there and I have been working on a software package, which is what I've been hustling down here. We're hoping to get it on the GSA schedule and then all the government agencies can automatically buy it."

"About money."

"That's right. It tracks money, inventories, payrolls, etc. Now that people are going into computers, they need an integrated package. We just hope it will be ours. We also are working on something that can be used for the stock market."

"And you're how old?"

"I'll be thirty in about six weeks."

"You must be a genius."

"I wouldn't say that."

"But you wouldn't deny it either," she asserted, nonplused that Arnie wasn't the simple sales rep she had thought.

He shrugged and laughed dismissively. "Hey, I'm merely going into the wave of the future. There're not too many others out there yet so I get more credit than I'm due."

"I bet," she said, upset that she'd underestimated the man and had been babbling about so many unimportant things. He probably thought she was a fool. "MIT and?"

"A small school in California," he replied casually. "I was lucky enough to get a scholarship. Actually, I've been lucky to get them all along...kind of like your sister did."

"Where?" she persisted.

"Caltech."

"Oh! The two scientific biggies and here you've been taking out someone going to NOVA part time."

"And enjoying every minute," he responded. "I told you, you're about the nicest part of this trip."

"Thanks," she said a bit archly, surprised that she was annoyed to discover that she hadn't been prominent in his thoughts, but then she was still irritated that he hadn't told her who he really was, although he hadn't lied about anything. Creative geniuses who taught at prestigious schools were clearly out of her league, even if he'd never been in the least condescending.

"I didn't mean it that way. I've been here on business after all. The fact that everyone's interested in our software has been pretty nice too."

Becki smiled, determined to make the best of the situation. "I was just teasing. I'm happy your business worked out."

Suddenly Arnie placed his hand over hers. "Will you come to my room?"

She looked at him startled, almost hurt at the suggestion, particularly now. Maybe she'd been wrong and this had been his purpose all along. Big-time academics just didn't date girls like her. "I..."

"No pressure," Arnie said quietly, but with obvious sincerity. "I'll take you to the Metro now, if you'd prefer. I just..." Unable to say more, he picked up her hand and kissed it gently.

She gazed at him gravely, contemplating, still wondering if she were wrong to have doubted his intentions in spite of this advance. "Are you married or involved with anyone?"

Surprised, Arnie answered, "Of course not, are you?" She shook her head. He continued in a low, serious tone, "I can't really promise that this would go anywhere. That's about the best I can do...be honest." Then he added, "If you don't come, I'd still want to see you again when I come back, but I've got to warn you, I'd keep trying to get you into bed." He'd wanted to from the moment he'd met her, he realized. He'd never dated such a beautiful woman and thoughts of holding, caressing, loving her had been dominant throughout the last few days.

She nodded, accepting his explanation, which sounded true. Then he leaned across the table and placed a light kiss on her lips. "Listen, I'm going to pay the bill. You think about it. My room is 429. If you'd like to come, that would be wonderful. If you don't, I understand. If you want me to walk you to the Metro, call and I'll come down. If you want to leave and never let me know how to find you again, that's your decision too. You've never given me your number, remember? Anyhow, whatever you want." He stood, bent over, and kissed her again—a soft, sweet kiss—and left, forcing himself not to turn and gaze at her for what might be the last time.

Becki sat looking out over the city thinking and staring down at the river, her Potomac, but small, contained and civilized here—not the wide lovely river of home but still a connection. His room, she pondered. Somehow she hadn't really expected a request like this. Such a gentle kiss and yet surprisingly so pleasant. For about five minutes she just sat, playing with a spoon, staring ahead, seeing the darkened river flowing towards home.

Then slowly she got up and made her way to the elevator. Pushing the number four, she waited as it descended, puzzled as to whether she was doing the right thing. When the doors opened, she stayed a moment, her finger on the 'open' button. There suddenly was an angry buzzing and she knew she had to make up her mind. Quickly she stepped out and made her way down the hall. At 429, she stopped indecisively, started to turn to leave and then stopped again. She waited another minute, her mind racing. Then she knocked, a quiet, hesitant little knock, analogous to her feelings.

Arnie had the door open almost instantly and extending his hands, he took hers. "I wasn't certain you'd come. I hoped you would, but I was afraid you wouldn't. Are you sure?"

She looked at him, a quiet and now somber, but plain, man. Not handsome, but when he smiled and talked, he was so alive, so natural yet confident. She'd never met anyone like him. She nodded her head and his face broke into a beautiful, tender smile and he pulled her inside. Shutting the door, he placed his arms around her and began to kiss her— a kiss that turned from gentle to passionate and she found herself responding. Finally, pulling away, she said embarrassed, "I didn't bring anything. I mean I'm not prepared."

"No pills, no coil?" he asked somewhat surprised.

"I can't take pills, I get sick. I use a diaphragm but I haven't had to use one for months. I just never thought..."

"That's ok," he assured her, "don't worry. I have something. Now come here," and he led her over to the bed. Sitting, he pulled her down beside him. "You're beautiful, so beautiful. I couldn't believe it when I saw you in that bar and then when you didn't call that night, I felt like such a fool that I hadn't taken your number but somehow I knew you were going to have to be the one to contact me."

Becki said nothing. She had made her decision. Slowly he began to take off her clothes until at last, she was there only in a bra, half-slip and panties, black to match the dress but simple, utilitarian. She reached up to unpin her hair, but he stopped her. "No, wait, please. Let me do that last," he implored as, tenderly, he pushed her back down on the bed and then removed her undergarments. Finally, he took the pins from her hair and began to spread the soft, thick tresses over the pillow. "God," he sighed, "you're even more beautiful with everything off. All that golden hair and lovely tan skin. I just knew your hair was natural. You look like some magnificent tawny cat, long and lithe. You should have gone to New York, honey. You would have taken it by storm but if you had, I never would have had a chance to meet you."

Then he began to undress and to her surprise, his stockiness turned out to be a compact and muscular body. Lying down beside her, he began to run his hands lovingly down her torso. At first he kissed her languidly as if savoring her very taste, his tongue gentle, and again she was surprised at how good it felt. In response, she kissed him back, a long, long time. "Hmm," he murmured as he started to play with her nipples, fondling them lightly with his fingertips until she found herself aching. Then his hands moved further down her body and he stroked her between her thighs and she felt herself straining, pressing against him and hugging him tighter.

"You feel so good," he sighed. "Let me put on something so you'll be ok." At last he penetrated and began to move back and forth and she was clasping him to her and holding on tighter and tighter. It was as though she never wanted to let go and yet at the same time she was longing for release. Exquisite torture, she thought, just like they write about in all those silly romances. She didn't know it could be so good. And then suddenly, she was there and he joined her and it was incredibly satisfying. She couldn't believe it.

"Fantastic," he uttered, "just fantastic." Raising himself up, he looked down at her. She said nothing, but reached up and softly stroked his hair. There was a bemused smile on her face and then she pulled his head down and kissed him lightly, gratefully. He lay there, his head on her breast and she kept stroking his hair. This beautiful little man, she thought. He was beautiful. He was beautiful inside and he was beautiful as a lover and she held him quietly.

After a while, Arnie rolled over. "Can you stay the night?" She nodded, smiling, unable to say anything and he pulled her to him. "Beautiful, you're so damn beautiful and it was beautiful too." She nodded again and just held on to him.

Later that night and then later still, they repeated the exercise until at last, totally exhausted, both fell asleep. When Arnie woke in the morning, he stared at her in the clear daylight. She had to be the most beautiful woman in the world, and she'd ended up coming to him. Delicately, he began to run his hands up and down her body and when she opened her eyes, Becki smiled at him and then parted her legs so again he could enter her. God, he thought, I just don't believe this. But both were silent and it was a leisurely, kind, and considerate lovemaking. After, they remained there for a long time, saying nothing.

Finally, he got up and looked at her. "You have to be the most quiet woman in the world and one of the most passionate too." Leaning over, he kissed her. "Jesus, I wish I didn't have to go back to Boston. I'd like to stay locked up in this room with you for a whole week though I probably wouldn't survive."

Now she did speak, laughing. "Me either. But I think

we probably did what most people wish they could do in a week."

This time he laughed. "You do talk. Maybe what they do in a month. It was truly fantastic. I'm a very lucky man." Becki smiled shyly, unable to say anything but her eyes were bright and that, he believed, was a good sign. "You're one beautiful lady, inside and out," he said, and she thought, how odd. It was what she'd thought about him but she remained silent and just kept smiling.

"Tell me," he asked hesitantly, "why did you decide to come?"

"Chopsticks," she murmured, blushing at her unexpected but genuine response.

"Chopsticks?" Arnie was flabbergasted by her answer.

"I figured any man who'd be willing to sit in a restaurant for an extra hour so my daughter could try chopsticks had to think I was really special." Arnie laughed uproariously. She was indeed special, and he gave her a gentle kiss and hug.

After, he called room service and once they'd showered and dressed, they sat there over breakfast and just gazed at each other, wondering what the other was thinking, but content. Then knowing he'd soon be departing for the airport, she got up to leave. His hand reached out, grabbing hers. "Haven't you forgotten something?" She looked at him puzzled. "I don't really want to have to hire detectives and tell them to find the most beautiful blonde in D.C. unless you don't want to see me again." He regarded her expectantly.

"Oh." She reached for her purse, but he'd already picked up a hotel note pad and pencil. Carefully, she printed out the Falls Church address and telephone number and then as an afterthought added Jerry's and Marty's name, happy that he'd finally asked, knowing this time, he'd have to be the one who determined the next step.

"And you've got my card, right?" he asked concerned. She nodded, reassured that he was being genuine. "I don't know when I'll be down here next but it should be this summer. You'll let me know if you want to see me, right? No games, we're honest about this. If you meet someone else, tell me right up front, ok?" But God, I hope you don't, he prayed, wondering how soon he could get away from Boston again.

Becki nodded and he stood with her, taking her into his arms and kissing her. "Oh Beauty, I'm sorry I have to go, but thank you." He walked her to the door where she took his hand, holding it a moment, and then turned and left, still unable to say anything. What a surprise it had been, she thought. All the way home on the Metro, she considered what had happened and thought about all the handsome men she'd dated in the past, only to discover it was a little plain-looking guy like this that really had it. Good things in small packages. Why did he have to live in Boston?

CHAPTER 5

Marty looked at Becki speculatively when she got home, but said nothing. The late night call saying she'd be home in the morning had come as a surprise but Marty wasn't her sister's keeper or at least tried not to be. Still, it was so unusual that Marty had to wonder about the little man from Boston.

It had turned into such an ordinary day, Becki realized, as she organized a wash and cleaned their downstairs rooms before heading off with Drea to visit the pet shop. Goldfish were this week's promised treat, and Becki remembered all the animals she had had and loved when she was a child. But, Jerry was allergic to fur so even a cat was impossible. Maybe someday, she mused, maybe someday she'd have a house and pets and Drea and a husband...a thoughtful man like... No, she mustn't think that way. She was just being foolish.

That afternoon when she got back, Marty pulled her into the living room. "Look," she cried excitedly, "they came just after you left." There were two dozen long-stemmed red roses. "Do you have any idea what those must have cost!" exclaimed Marty. "My heavens, I've never gotten anything like that."

Becki reached for the little envelope and pulled out the note: 'Thank you, Arnie.' No 'love', she noted sadly, but still something and she smiled at her sister. "I told you he was a nice man, a really nice man."

The week passed and each evening when she got home, Becki looked eagerly in the mail or nonchalantly asked if there were any telephone messages. By the beginning of the second week, she stopped asking. She had looked at Arnie's business card two to three times a day, but no, she couldn't call. At the end of the second week, she put it with the rose she had pressed and the note that had accompanied the flowers in her bedside table drawer. It had been a nice little adventure with no one hurt. Maybe next time she met someone, she'd be a little more careful.

Drea asked her often about Arnie and when they'd go to the museums again or riding a horse. Becki would just smile and say, "He lives in Boston, honey. That's pretty far away. He just wanted to share a day with us, and it was special, wasn't it? This summer when you're out of school, we'll get down to the Mall and maybe we can also find a place for you to go on a horse sometime, all right?"

The little girl nodded, but seemed disappointed. "Arnie's not coming back?" she asked in a small, sad voice. No theatrics this time, just truly dejected.

"Maybe sometime if his work is here again. If it is, I'm sure we'll see him," her mother answered, trying to hide her own sadness. Of course, Becki doubted that they would. Perhaps she had been a fool, but Arnie had seemed so genuinely nice and truly interested. Still, he'd never promised anything. The decision to sleep with him had been hers. She would have to live with that and the sense of loss she now felt.

Then one day, amazingly, there was a postcard in the mailbox when she got home. It showed an Oriental woman in a kimono standing in front of an exotic temple shrine and the word *Nippon*. The message was brief: 'Sorry. Had to go to Tokyo as soon as I got back from D.C. Will phone when I return. Say hi to Drea. Arnie.' No 'love' again, but he hadn't forgotten. That night Becki took the postcard to bed and placed it carefully under her pillow.

The following day when she got home late, Marty was waiting anxiously. "Your friend called."

"My friend?" Becki practically held her breath.

"Yes, the little man from Boston. I told him you had a class but should be back by 10:00 and he said he'd call tomorrow."

"Oh," Becki sighed, disappointed, but just then the phone rang and she reached to pick it up.

"May I speak to Becki, please."

"This is Becki."

"Hi, it's Arnie. I just got back today. I'm sorry it's so late, but I decided I couldn't wait until tomorrow after all. Can you talk?"

"Of course." Marty looked at her questioning and Becki mouthed 'Arnie'.

'Oh' her sister mouthed back and discretely left the room, an act of willpower at this point. It had been months since Becki had had a boyfriend, and for once, baby sister wasn't talking. Marty found herself consumed by curiosity. The man from Boston must be really special.

"How are you?" he asked.

"Fine," Becki replied, feeling utterly stupid at her conversational ineptitude. "How was Tokyo?"

"You got the postcard."

"Yes, yesterday."

"It took that long? Damn, I thought you'd get it a week earlier. You must have thought I dropped off the face of the earth."

I did, she thought, but instead she politely answered, "No. I got your flowers. Thank you, they were lovely."

"American Beauties for an American Beauty. When am I going to see you?"

"You're coming down here?" She tried to keep the eagerness from her voice.

"Actually I was hoping you might be able to come up here. I'll send you a ticket. My birthday is the Fourth of July weekend—July 2. I thought we could go to the Boston Pops and watch the fireworks by the Charles since you're such an aficionada of rivers."

"I couldn't do that."

"What? Come up or take the ticket?"

"Both," she replied tersely, "but I'd like to see you. When do you come down next on business?"

"Not until next month, but that's too long. If I were to fly down this weekend, could you come away with me?"

"I don't think so," Becki responded sadly. "I mean I just don't go off for weekends." I did once, she thought, and that was such a mistake. When Mike told her he was married, she was so mortified, so angry.

"Would you at least see me if I came?"

"Certainly," she answered quickly, probably too quickly, "but you shouldn't come down if it's not for business. That's so expensive."

"I think I can afford it," he replied. Then bluntly, he asked, "If I do come down, will you at least spend a night with me?"

"Yes," she said softly, wondering again if she was doing the right thing, but it had felt so good to be loved again. No, she corrected herself, to have someone make love to her. But at least it felt like love with him, not just sex.

"Good, I'll fly in on Friday. Can you meet me at National? I'll pick up a car and then we can have dinner and..." he hesitated, "and I'll bring you home."

"Yes," she said once more.

"And Saturday, maybe we can drive out to Northern Neck. I looked it up on a map."

"Oh," she smiled to herself, "but Saturday..."

"Hey, I know, Saturdays belong to Drea. We'll bring her along of course. Surely one of those seafood places down there has hot dogs."

"She's a proper Tidewater child, even if she hasn't been brought up there," declared Becki firmly. "She'll eat more crabs than you do."

"Want to make a bet?" Arnie was laughing happily now and she joined in. "It's so nice to hear your voice," he confessed. "I thought about calling from Tokyo but the time difference is fourteen hours. Anyhow, I'll check out the flights tomorrow and then give you a call. See, I am smart. That way I'll get to talk to you then as well. And maybe you can think of some motel near your place. In fact, make a reservation for Friday through Sunday nights. I'll catch the earliest shuttle back on Monday. Use my whole name, the way it is on the card, ok? You've still got my card, right?"

"Oh yes." Not that she needed it. She'd long since memorized everything on that small, well-fingered bit of cardboard.

"Good. I'll talk to you tomorrow night...no classes, right?"

"No."

"Fine, I'll call about 7:00 then. Good night, Beauty."

"Good night, Arnie," she replied in her soft, sweet voice and as she hung up, she started humming to herself about 'piña coladas and getting caught in the rain'.

CHAPTER 6

Becki was pacing eagerly at the plane's gate late that Friday afternoon. As soon as she saw Arnie exiting, she rushed up and threw her arms around him, forgetting all her resolutions to be calm and collected, just a friend meeting another friend. "That's a nice greeting," he said, a huge grin on his face. "Did you miss me?" She smiled shyly and nodded. "Cat got your tongue?" he asked. In answer, she merely stuck hers out and he laughed. "Ok, oh silent one, what's the agenda?"

"To get your car, I guess."

"You do talk. Amazing."

"Don't be mean," she protested, but she was still smiling bashfully. "Who did you rent from?"

"One of the places out on Route 1 so I guess there's a shuttle."

"Route 1. That's good. We can come back and stop around Crystal City. There're all sorts of ethnic restaurants there and then we won't get caught in the traffic. D.C. is supposed to be getting like L.A."

"Heaven forbid," uttered Arnie with feeling, "I thought Boston was bad."

"I only know by hearsay," said Becki.

"You don't drive?" He looked surprised.

"Not much. I use Marty's or Jerry's cars sometimes; otherwise I couldn't go to school. I can get to work by Metro. Besides," she added, "I couldn't afford a car."

"Oh." He really couldn't think of anything else to say. "Well, lead me to the rental shuttle and we'll calculate how to get there. Any specific restaurant?"

"No, there's a block of little ones. We could just walk around until you see one you like—more of your empirical reasoning. Most of them have tables outside and I thought that would be nice in this weather."

"Very nice," he agreed. "Just being here is nice."

She smiled again, taking his free hand, and they made their way out of the crowded terminal. Without too much trouble, they eventually got to the restaurant area and after parking a couple of blocks away, strolled down the sidewalk. Above, the trees were full of foliage with birds nesting and small grey squirrels running up and down the trunks.

"Trees and houses," Arnie noted, "even your immediate suburbs still look like small towns."

"With all those high risers up ahead?" She pointed to Crystal City.

"It depends which direction you're looking," he said, turning around.

"A matter of perspective again," she laughed.

"Most definitely."

"No wonder you're into design, Dr. Miller."

"Isn't that what you want to do?"

"I'm not sure trying to be an interior decorator qualifies, compared to what you mean by designing," she replied cautiously. Arnie's designing apparently was with a capital *D*.

"You're thinking of changing things, making adjustments, making things better or more pleasant aren't you?"

"Well, yes," she acquiesced uncertainly.

"Ok, I want to do the same, although in my case I'm looking to streamline things, to make business processes easier and more efficient. To find solutions."

"I think we're pushing this analogy. I also think I'm hungry," she stated firmly, deciding it was time to change the subject. Her work would never approach his level.

"So, which one?" he asked, glancing up and down the row of restaurants.

"You choose."

"Great, shall we just flip a coin?"

"No, surprise me."

"What if I pick one you don't like?"

"I like them all."

"Ok, how about this Italian place?"

"Well..."

"I knew it, you don't like Italian!"

She giggled, "Just teasing. That's fine." The two turned in and were seated at a sidewalk table with an umbrella where they could watch other people wandering by. There was amazingly little traffic and it was quiet, except for the neighboring diners who were talking and laughing at nearby tables.

After they ordered, he asked, "What's the itinerary?"

"Whatever you want," she replied.

"Well, we know what part of it is, don't we?" he asked, looking at her soberly.

She blushed, looking down before murmuring, "And what else?"

Arnie took her hand, his fingers stroking it gently. "You really don't say anything about..."

"About what?" She knew what he meant and added, "What's there to say?"

"Whether you like it, whether you like me?"

She looked at him surprised. "You couldn't tell?"

"Well I thought you did."

"It's so personal."

"I think that too, but I mean it's kind of personal between the two of us."

"Yes."

"And what's that supposed to mean?"

"I'll show you later," she replied, blushing again.

A little grin appeared on his face. "That sounds interesting." Then their dinner arrived. Becki said nothing for most of the meal, just smiling, happy that Arnie had really returned. Nibbling at the antipasto—an olive here, a bite of pickled artichoke there—and her veal parmesan, she listened closely as he told her about Tokyo and his trip.

Finally she sighed, "You make it sound so real. I try to imagine what it would be like to take a trip like that, but somehow I can't. I see movies and TV and read. Yet to really go on a trip like that seems so...so unreal. And then, someone like you does it, just like you come down here, and suddenly it seems very possible."

"You have an interesting way of talking about things. Most people would ask how long it took to fly out, or did I eat raw fish, or are the Japanese really inscrutable, or something like that."

"So, how long did it take, and did you eat raw fish, and..." Both started to laugh.

"Almost a day with stops in San Francisco and Honolulu. Yes. No. Just different."

"Now see how much more knowledgeable I am?" she giggled.

"Just take me to our next stop. You meant it about staying with me?" his voice hushed and he licked his lips nervously, surprised at his agitation.

"I'll have to go home after," she said.

"The least of our problems. We're still going to the Northern Neck tomorrow?"

"If you want."

"Oh, most definitely, and with Miss Andrea too."

"She'd throw herself in front of the car if we didn't let her come."

"You're too good a mother to let that happen."

Becki accepted the compliment. "Thank you. That's nice to hear."

"It's true. I saw the way you were with her when we went to the Smithsonian. Do you like all kids or just your daughter?"

"I like house broken ones," she answered truthfully.

"Me too," he agreed, "but if they're not, it's the parents' fault."

"Not always, but mostly," she concurred. "Yes, I do like children. So do you. You were so patient with her. You'd be a good father." Then she stopped, clearly embarrassed again, not believing she could have made a comment like that. What would the man think? That she was setting a trap for him?

Arnie appeared not to notice her discomfort. "I hope so. I'd like to try some day. Anyhow, where to?"

"We get back on Route 1 and then loop around the Pentagon until we hit Route 50. The motel is on that, almost at Falls Church."

"Why don't we plan for you to take the car home tonight and then you and Drea can pick me up after."

"You'd trust me?" she asked, surprised that he would offer her the car.

"What's to trust? You left your daughter with me when you went to look at the jewel collection. That was real trust. Besides, it's insured. If you don't show up in the morning, I'll just say you rolled me and stole it." In response, she slapped him lightly on the wrist. "Hey, that hurts," he complained.

"You insulted me," she intoned haughtily, but she was smiling again.

When they got to the motel, she waited in the car as he registered and then they drove around, parking by the room. Arnie got out and opened the door, taking the luggage inside, but she sat quietly for a moment. He came back out and looked at her, "You changed your mind—you're not coming in?" He sounded worried.

"I was just thinking," she murmured quietly.

"Penny for them?" but she said nothing although in her mind the thought was buzzing: cheap. She'd felt cheap when she'd gone to a motel with Mike only to discover he was married, but she hadn't felt cheap the night she had spent with Arnie in the hotel. Then it had seemed right. Was there any difference?

"That darn cat again," he said gently and gave her a hand out of the car. "Come on inside. I missed you and I want to show you. I'm not going to hurt you."

"I know that," she said. "This time I even brought the diaphragm."

He chuckled, pleased. "Prepared. Me too. We both must have been scouts."

"No," she said, "I was 4-H. I used to raise pigs."

"Pigs! I can't believe it."

"Pigs are beautiful," she protested indignantly. "They're

smart and if they had fingers and a thumb, they'd rule the world."

"You must have loved *Animal Farm*," he commented, genuinely amused at the image of the beautiful Becki shoveling manure or slopping a hog.

"No, they were mean. I don't like anyone that's mean and my pigs weren't. I still feel guilty every time I eat pork though Bar-B-Q is so good."

He was really laughing now. "You, a pig farmer!"

Becki looked actually hurt. "I had one you could even ride," she continued stubbornly. "At least when she'd let you."

"And what did she do, when she wouldn't—buck you off?" Arnie was practically convulsed at this point, trying to visualize a lanky, teenaged Becki being thrown from a bucking porcine caricature—wild eyed, snorting with a quivering snout and bristles, something out of a crazed *Loony Tunes* cartoon.

"Yes," Becki answered with dignity. "That's exactly what Snow White would do."

Arnie stopped laughing and looked at her. "You're serious and Snow White, no less! Why Snow White?"

"Because I wanted her to find her prince and I never joke about pigs," she answered, but then she grinned, "at least not often. She was my favorite and she was a good mother too. We had a special pen fenced around our barn and my father helped me bury an old bathtub in it. The first time we filled it with water, she couldn't figure what it was. She kept creeping closer and closer. Then all of a sudden, she fell in. Water splashed all over and she was so surprised, she was frantic. She was on her back with all four legs kicking up in the air and squealing like mad. We howled and I don't know who was louder, Snow White or us. When she finally got out, she shook off, went back and then got in again. We ended up calling her place 'two rooms with river view' because you could see the Potomac down the hill. She had one corner where she ate and another where she liked to sleep and another for...well you know. Pigs are really clean,"

Becki avowed. "It's only when they're confined and people don't take proper care of them that they're dirty. The mud is to keep them cool since they don't sweat."

"Kind of like hippos," Arnie commented, surprised he'd never considered the similarity although pigs had never been of much interest save for their products like a nice crispy slice of bacon. At heart he was a true city boy.

"That's right, water horses. Did you know that the Potomac comes from the same Greek root for water?"

"God, you come up with the weirdest things, interesting," he added, "informative, of course."

"Of course, although some think it's really from an Indian word, but I like the Greek better. Anyhow I liked *Jeopardy* a lot—I sure hope they bring it back."

"And I bet you always won."

"Maybe," she smiled smugly. "But in answer to your original question, yes, she'd buck you off if she was tired of the game and usually in her bathroom corner to get even."

"Bathroom corner...to get even." Arnie started laughing again. "You've almost convinced me of her intelligence. Maybe we can develop a Stanford-Binet test for swine. On big cards and they'll mark the right answer with their hoofs or something."

Becki scowled. "Trotters and listen, she was plenty intelligent. We couldn't drive by her pen without her getting up to lean those front trotters on the fence and cry. She'd practically go crazy when we came near unless we stopped and scratched her ears."

"Just like a cat. I had one of those. How did your snake like her? I can't believe this. I meet a girl with pet snakes and pigs."

"They never met. Snow White would have eaten her."

"Seriously?" Arnie's mouth dropped open and he reconsidered the allure of the crispy slice of bacon.

"Of course, why do you think they used to let pigs loose on some of the farms in olden times."

"To eat snakes?"

"Their skin is too thick for them to be hurt by a snake

bite. They'd just clean out the rattlers and other poisonous ones. Don't you remember your Mark Twain about the pigs that were on some of the Mississippi islands?"

"Gee," he said, wondering how he could have forgotten an interesting item like that. "I'll have more respect next time I order a pork chop."

"You're not nice," Becki complained flirtatiously, deciding that pigs was another subject, which had been exhausted, for Arnie had his arms around her now and was kissing her throat, his lips working their way down the dress opening at her neck.

"I'd like to be," he breathed heavily. "I'd definitely like to be." Slowly they began to undress each other and again, she was surprised by his looks. With clothes, he was just the stocky, maybe slightly overweight little man. Out of them, he was so fit and strong. She ran her hand lightly up his arm, feeling the flow of muscles. As if in answer to her unasked question, he remarked, "Nautilus and skiing in the winter. I also did some wrestling in college. Then I thought about triathlon training, because a couple of my buddies were, but I'm definitely not a swimmer and I got tired of running. My legs are too short and I also got tired of being knocked off bikes by road hogs."

In response, she looked closely at his face, noticing a scar close to his temple. She touched it quizzically. "Right," he said, "the damn car tipped me completely over and I slammed into the curb. If I hadn't had a helmet, I would have been brain dead or at least Humpty Dumpty scrambled. As it was, I ended up with a few broken bones and a smashed bike and the bastard just drove on. Fortunately there were some friends behind me even though they didn't get his license."

Becki looked slightly sick but held him a little closer, kissing the scar lightly. Then she said, "You didn't have to jolly Larry after all, did you? You really could have hurt him."

"Yes, even though I'm short, I'm fairly sure I could, but it was more fun the other way. I prefer to use brains than brawn in confrontation."

"Me too. I would have just broken his finger."

"What!"

"I told you Billy was a MP. He knew all sorts of little tricks that he showed me. I would have just snapped Larry's little finger back."

"Ouch." He looked at her, grimacing, deciding he hadn't been wrong in comparing her to a 007 girl. "You're a lethal weapon and now you tell me."

"Well, it's not exactly every day conversation," Becki remarked wryly.

"Gee, you could have taken him out yourself. You didn't need my knightly rescue service."

"It was nicer having it," she said smiling. "I told you. That was one of the nicest things anyone has ever done for me."

"Is that why I got the reward, Lady Rebecca?" Arnie asked seriously.

"No, my Lord Arnie. You made me want to go to bed with you, that and of course the chopsticks," and she started to kiss him again. By now they were on the bed and had become silent. Soothingly he stroked her and then more firmly, urgently, almost struggling in his passion. In minutes came their release.

"Need and greed," he sighed. "You're really something, Beauty. I wanted to tear your clothes off the second I saw you at the airport. Actually, I was fantasizing about this all the way down." She smiled and held him. "You're not talking again, you're so demure," he whispered.

"What's there to say," she answered, pleased by his comment. "It's so nice. You make me feel so good. I've never felt as good as when we do this."

"I wondered, I really wondered. It's the same for me too." He held her gently. "Can you stay long enough for us just to make sure once again?"

"I think so," she smiled and started giving him little kisses.

CHAPTER 7

Early the next morning, she and Drea were back and Arnie was waiting eagerly. "Hi, Beauty, and hi, little Beauty," he greeted them boisterously, as he slid into the front seat and reached to squeeze Becki's hand.

"Arnie," whooped Drea from in back. "I've waited all week for you." She leaned over the seat and flung her little arms around him, giving him a kiss.

"Gee, that's nice. I've been thinking about you too and I brought you something from Japan." He handed her a small paper bag covered with pictures of minuscule cartoon figures.

Drea looked at Becki. "May I, Mommy?" she asked, for once remembering her mother's grammar lesson.

"Of course. Arnie's our friend," Becki replied and Arnie smiled at her, a sexy little smile. She looked away, blushing, and he thought how pretty, almost innocent she looked when she did that. It had been a long time since he'd been around someone who blushed.

Oblivious of the undertones, the child carefully opened the bag and peeked inside. First she pulled out some pencils with tiny painted wooden heads, which were wrapped in textured, colored papers to look like they were wearing kimonos. Next she extracted a pair of bright red lacquered chopsticks and a little lacquer bowl to match. Then at the bottom, she found a small wooden box. When she opened it, her eyes widened as she saw a tiny china doll wearing a wig and dressed in a traditional kimono with an *obi*. Surrounding the doll were half a dozen other little wigs.

"Those are some of the different ways Japanese ladies used to wear their hair for special occasions," Arnie explained. "I'm not sure I remember which was for what, but I'm sure you'll decide. And the pencils are for school. Then when you finally figure out how to use the chopsticks, I'll take you to a Japanese restaurant some time."

As though insulted, Drea stated firmly, "I've been practicing with the ones we got in Chinatown, haven't I, Mommy?" At the sight of the chopsticks, Becki blushed again. Arnie glanced over, tipping her a wink as if daring her to say that he shouldn't make promises that he wouldn't keep.

"I'm glad to hear that, Drea. Now you'll have to teach Mommy." His grin broadened as Becki turned even redder.

Drea, suddenly timid, said in a barely audible voice, "I will and thank you."

Becki looked at him seriously. "That was really sweet, Arnie. She doesn't get too many presents," or treats she added mentally, knowing he meant what he'd said. Then turning to her daughter, she said, "Now you really have something special for show and tell at school."

"Do I have to use the pencils, Mommy?"

"Why no, does she Arnie?" Becki turned back to him.

"Not if you don't want to," he replied, surprised by the question.

"No, they're too pretty. They're really dolls too."

That was an interesting observation, he thought, but merely said, "Well, ladies, it's time to get this show on the road. Let's trade places and you read the map," he told Becki, "I'll pilot."

"Since you've never been in Virginia, we could do a circle," she suggested.

"Sounds fine to me. How's that?"

"We cut over to Route 66, get off at Gainesville, make our way down through Warrenton and then Fredericksburg. That way you get some glimpses of the Blue Ridge. Then coming back, we take I-95 and swing around the Beltway."

"Ah, the infamous Beltway."

"What's 'in famous', Mommy? Is there an 'out famous' too?" piped the small voice from the back of the car."

Becki and Arnie burst out laughing. "You figure this out," she said, "you brought it up."

"Well, 'infamous' means famous too, but not in a nice way. It's all one word," and Arnie carefully spelled it out.

"There's no real 'outfamous'." Indubitably a different approach to thinking, he decided. That's what made both of them interesting. He spent so much time around brilliant people but they weren't always interesting.

"Why is the Beltway famous in not a nice way?" Drea persevered.

"It's just an expression," Arnie explained patiently. "The beltway is a road that goes around D.C. like a belt around your tummy and because D.C.'s the capital, some people talk about the government as being inside while the rest of America is outside. Does that make sense?"

"But why is it famous in a bad way?"

"Wow, she's persistent," he said to Becki in a low voice and then spoke louder. "Some people don't like government. They're afraid of it so they like to think it's bad and therefore they say infamous."

"Oh," Drea was taking this in. A couple minutes later, she finally asked "Is it?"

Arnie glanced at Becki. "I don't think so, do you?"

Becki turned around to face her daughter. "As Arnie said, some people are just afraid. Sometimes the government does things that are mistakes just like people do, but no, I don't think it's bad and I think we need it. We're a big country, honey. That's what your grandpa always told me. It holds us together."

"Oh," said Drea again, apparently satisfied for she was once more silent and watching the traffic.

"About our round trip tour, does it matter when we get back?" Arnie asked.

"No, not really," Becki answered. "Drea can asleep in the car. It's whatever you'd like to do."

"Well, the Blue Ridge even from afar sounds enticing. Will we have a chance to see Fredericksburg too?"

"Maybe a little. We're talking about four or more hours actual driving and I don't know how much time you'd like to spend on the river. We really could have gone down by way of the Potomac too but that's very congested and I just thought this would be different."

"Maybe another time."

"That would be nice," realizing she meant it and thinking again sadly of how far Boston really was. She definitely liked this man. "Then you could see Mount Vernon and Old Town Alexandria."

"I'd like that. I will have to be here in late July or early August for a week. Will I get to see you?"

She flashed a brilliant smile, delighted at the news. "If you still want to."

"Oh, I'm sure I will," he answered enthusiastically, a huge grin on his face. "I'll try to work it so I can be here on both weekends too."

"Good," she said quietly, very quietly, not sure if he heard but he did.

Once past Warrenton, he began to see the Blue Ridge, slightly hazy, but decidedly blue. "I'd wondered why they called it that. Those mountains really are blue, aren't they?"

"After a rain when the air is clean again, they're practically indigo. When Billy was at Vint Hill, I used to drive out here after I dropped him at work. I never drove all the way up, but I liked being in the country and seeing the farms and mountains. I'm not sure I'd ever like to live in them, but they're so pretty from a distance." Then suddenly she changed the conversation and asked, "What's it like to ski? Where have you been?"

"To the Rockies a few times, but from Boston, I usually go up to New Hampshire. Once I went to the Alps."

"The Alps? Is there any place you haven't been?"

"Lots. I used to want to ski in South America too, but I'm not really all that great."

"I've only been on water skis," confessed Becki, wondering at a man who'd casually mention skiing on three continents. "I can't imagine what it would be like in snow."

"Cold, Beauty, cold but exhilarating. You'll have to try some day."

"They have day outings to Pennsylvania from D.C. I've read about them in the Post. Maybe some time, but I can't afford any broken legs."

"And bucking pigs don't break legs?"

"What are bucking pigs, Mommy?" asked Drea, once again interested in their conversation.

"Arnie's just teasing. I told him about my pigs."

"I wish I had a pig," sighed Drea, "and a cat too."

"The cat would try to eat your goldfish," observed her mother neutrally, sorry once more responsive pets couldn't be part of her daughter's life. Fish were pretty, even interesting in spite of the fact that a goldfish supposedly only had a memory span lasting seconds, but children—adults too—needed animals they could hold and love. Definitely a kitten or puppy for Drea would be high priority if she could ever afford a place of their own.

"Oh." There was silence again.

When they got to Fredericksburg, Becki showed Arnie how to cut down the river road and go below Chatham, the historic manor now being maintained by the Park Service. When she mentioned the name, he looked at her with interest. "That's odd, that's the name of the town where I go on Cape Cod."

"Do you want to stop?" she asked as they drove through the flood plain from where they could see the old town across the water. "If you'd really rather see it and Fredericksburg, we can skip going to the river. This is the Rappahannock, you know, not the Potomac. You're now officially entering the Northern Neck."

"No, you've said too much about it. I half expected flashing lights or trumpets or something to announce our arrival," he quipped and Becki looked at him in mock exasperation, her lips pursed. Knowing when to stop, he added, "We'll catch what we can of Fredericksburg on the way back."

"Fine," she concurred with an arched eyebrow and they made their way to Earl's Market where they turned down a winding rural road. Shortly after they had passed the sign for Fairview Beach, Becki pointed to a cut to the left. "Take that," she directed, and they were on a bumpy one-lane dirt road.

"What do you do if someone comes out?" asked Arnie, obviously concerned by the narrow pathway.

"Get off to the side, of course—especially if they're bigger. You are a city boy."

"Are you sure this is safe?"

"Arnie, I lived around here for over half my life. Once upon a time, all this land belonged to my great, great grandparents."

"You weren't kidding about being an old Virginia family."

"No, we've been here for centuries—both sides. My dad's family probably swapped beads with the Indians. And my mother's folks ran a small shop in Fredericksburg in the eighteenth century; they were the latecomers to the area and just shopkeepers, according to Aunt Mary, who knows everyone's pedigree. Mother used to tell me about how when she was a little girl, she and her brother would take tourists around Ferry Farm back on Route 3. That was where George Washington lived as a small child. They'd find some dead tree and chip off pieces telling the tourists that these came from one of those he'd chopped down and that they weren't supposed to be doing that—kind of like the Mediaeval trade in splinters of the true cross, Sir Knight. Then they'd cadge tips." Arnie looked actually shocked. "It's not just you city slickers that know how to con people," Becki said, smirking at his reaction.

Suddenly they rounded a bend and there on the right was an old stone fence. Beyond it Arnie could see a large white house and some small stone outbuildings. "That's the original farmhouse," Becki said casually, seemingly without emotion. "That's where Aunt Mary lives."

He stopped the car abruptly. "Do you want to go in?"

"I can't. She wouldn't see me."

"What do you mean?" he asked bewildered.

Becki looked back over her shoulder and saw that Drea had drowsed off. Quietly, she answered, "She called me a whore when I got pregnant and threw me out."

Arnie looked at her stunned. "You can't mean that."

"Listen, she hardly spoke to my father after he married my mother. It was a mixed marriage."

"So," said Arnie, slightly defensive, "was my parents'. My mom was Catholic and my dad Jewish." Suddenly, he turned to look at her. "Does that matter to you?"

"Of course not," said Becki. "My mother was Baptist and my father Episcopalian."

"That's a mixed marriage? You're joking."

"Not to my aunt. My parents just took turns going to one church one week and the other the next but my aunt hardly ever spoke to my mother. She wasn't even sad when my father drowned and she never once said anything nice about my mother. She only took me in because aside from Marty, there was no other close relative and people would have talked. That year I had to live with her was the bleakest I've ever had. I think that's why I got involved with Billy. Marty was away at school and I just wanted someone to love me," she added poignantly.

Arnie looked at her, thinking this was one of the saddest things he'd ever heard. "Why didn't you live with another relative?"

"Mother's brother died and my father was an only child. There was only her."

Slowly Arnie said, "I thought my parents had some problems. My mother's family—Irish Catholics—never really forgave her for marrying a Jew but my dad's mom, Leah, is really nice. I think my grandfather was upset that my mom wouldn't convert, but Grandma Leah said the mother determines the religion and she just accepted it."

"How did your parents handle it?"

"Oh, pretty informally, I guess. We lit a lot of candles around Christmas time," he smiled, remembering. "But we really weren't brought up either way. I was the only kid in kindergarten who brought matzos and a saltshaker to school to eat with my Easter eggs. My dad died when I was little. I was about seven, but I remember him as quiet and funny and really kind."

"Sort of like you," she responded, looking steadily at

this kind, funny man.

"That's nice, although I'm not too quiet." Becki smiled slightly, nodding her head in agreement. No, quiet hadn't entered her mind. Meanwhile Arnie continued, "Dad had been working in my grandfather's clothing store. Kind of tradition since his family came out west as peddlers from Germany. Too bad we weren't one of the big Jewish banking families, but hey, it was their store. My mom's family had worked on the docks but she was considered more upscale when she went to work in the bank and that's how they met. A love story...kind of *Abie's Irish Rose* updated. They apparently were very happy according to my sister. She's five years older and has some real memories, but my dad got pneumonia and that was that. My mom had to go back to work, but they'd partially bought a house and my Grandma Leah would slip us a little cash. We lived ok, nothing special, but ok. Fortunately both Eileen and I were good students, and we got scholarships and it worked out."

"Eileen, that's a pretty name."

"Yes, for one of my Irish great aunts—the only one who kept up with my mother. I was named James for my Irish grandfather and Arnold for my Jewish great grandfather, but aside from Aunt Eileen, the Irish side just didn't give a damn so I decided I preferred Arnie instead of Jim after my dad died. I was already James in school, though, so I have used that name legally."

Wasn't *Abie's Irish Rose* a play or something?" asked Becki.

"Not many people have heard of it nowadays," answered Arnie. "It was just a family in-joke for us like your *Tom Sawyer*."

"Oh my mother read more than Twain. She had all sorts of books of plays and poems. She loved to read. There was a series that came out every year and gave synopses of the ten best plays that season. I guess she always wanted to visit Broadway and that was as close as she got. When I was little, I started reading them too."

"It's nice to have collections like that. My folks didn't

have a lot of books. My sister and I hit the libraries."

"I don't have them anymore," Becki said looking down. "I do the libraries now too."

"That's too bad. No room?"

"No," she hesitated. "My aunt got rid of all my parents' possessions. She said it was her Christian duty to take me in but not their junk. I just came home from school one day and she'd sent off everything to a church bazaar. I tried to buy a few things back, but I didn't have any real money." Arnie looked at her, unable to say anything. "Families," said Becki finally, with a slight shrug. "Well, we'd better drive on before Aunt Mary comes out with a shotgun."

"I have a terrible feeling you may not be joking," he responded disconcerted.

"This road is public, more or less. I told you a lot of the land was sold off—all to the left and along the river on that side so it's used by everyone. No one's going to care if we go down there. Most of the places are summer or weekend cottages, and some even belong to distant cousins. We're all kin out here, Arnie. Even Billy and I were cousins removed half a dozen times on our mothers' side."

"My God, the Kallikaks and the Jukes."

"Upstate New York or New England, I think. Besides, they disproved that study." she declared.

"A class in biology too?"

"Naturally, but that was high school and a bit too late to be of practical help as far as I was concerned," she remarked wryly. "Anyhow, I prefer to think of the Incas and the Pharaohs when it comes to incest but no, I didn't marry my own grandpa. I was probably something like his sixth or seventh cousin. Even the Lees and the Washingtons were our kin way back. I read somewhere we're all sixth or seventh cousins although I don't believe it."

"Lees and Washingtons, I am impressed. Well, if we are all cousins, I'd just as soon remain a kissing one."

"Oh you," drawled Becki, tapping him on the wrist and once more flashing her brilliant smile, which seemed to capture his heart. They drove slowly down the hill and about a half mile on, she told him to stop. "They haven't built this lot up yet. This will be a good place." Turning, she lightly shook Drea. "We're here, honey. Wake up. We're at the river. This is where Aunt Marty and I used to come to family picnics and swim as little girls. Your grandpa and I would go out on a boat near here and fish. Then your grandma would grill what we caught over an open fire."

"Is this where you did the crabs, Mommy?"

"No, they came mostly from the Bay and we cooked them at the restaurant but we'd bring out a bushel at times and spend hours picking them apart and dipping them in vinegar."

"Yummy," said Drea. "Are we going to today?"

"If Arnie thinks he'd like to try. I thought we'd go to the restaurant that Grandma and Grandpa used to have and sit out on the wharf to watch the boats. But we couldn't watch eagles and egrets there. If we're lucky, we might be able to see them here and you can run up and down the beach awhile and wade a bit. How does that sound?"

"Wow!" Drea was now wide awake and climbing over the seat to get out of the car.

"Sounds pretty good to me too," said Arnie. "I like to go to the beach though I usually go out to the Cape and yes, Virginia seafood sounds like a great idea. Let's see who can get to the river first, Drea. I'll give you a head start," he challenged, and the little girl dashed ahead.

"Don't fall in," cautioned her mother. "I didn't bring a bathing suit."

"Did you need one?" he asked.

Becki blushed a deep red. "Sometimes we didn't. At night, we'd have bonfires down here. That's how I got into trouble," she stated matter-of-factly. "I'm older and wiser now."

"Yeah," he concurred and looking at her, added, "you don't seem like someone in her early twenties at all. I mean you look it—even younger sometimes, but inside you're not."

She regarded him thoughtfully for a moment, her eyes

steady and cool. "I can't be. I have Drea. I had to grow up after I had her. I probably had started to when my folks died. No, that's not really so, I still was pretty naive and young then. I just missed them so much and Marty was out of the house and of course we lost everything."

"How so?"

"Oh, my folks wanted to expand the restaurant and they'd mortgaged our place. The restaurant had a big mortgage too. My father didn't really have much insurance and my mother had none so the bank took both properties after they died. Maybe if Marty had been older, she could have thought of something but she was only a junior. She was lucky she could stay in college but she was such a great student that they upped her scholarship."

"Why didn't your aunt help?" Arnie asked intrigued.

"I told you. She didn't like my mother. She probably thought my parents deserved it and the little money left she took for my keep."

"And you had to go in a house like that? No wonder you were looking for someone."

"Yes, well the house is supposed to be partially ours too, but we'll never get it." Becki sighed, obviously resigned.

"What do you mean?"

"My aunt was one of three children. The place was supposed to go to all three but my great grandfather never wrote a will. When he died, one of the children was already dead and my grandfather let his sister stay there. Since there was never anything written down, after Grandpa died, Aunt Mary just had it sort of by default. She kind of told my father it would be his one day. She had never married so he never said anything to her. Then she was so upset about his marrying my mother that she said she was going to leave it to a distant cousin's family, not that I'm sure Dad really believed her. I do, though, and I guess that's what she's still planning to do. She's in her eighties now."

"You mean that place should be yours and your sister's?" Arnie was horrified.

"I suppose so," Becki said sadly, her face dejected, "but

nothing was ever recorded. We'll never get it and the distant cousins don't even live around here. They'll just cut it up if they can't find someone rich who wants the whole piece."

"Jesus!" exclaimed Arnie, noticeably perturbed. "Have you gone to a lawyer?"

"Who has the money?" she commented wearily since this had plagued her for years. "I kid Marty that's why she married Jerry and I know he's looked into some records but since nothing was ever written down or filed, he thinks there isn't a chance."

"How unfair!" Arnie was highly indignant. He was a man, who was used to getting what he wanted. In circumstances like this, he would still be fighting.

"Life's not too fair. My folks wouldn't have drowned if their friends had kept their boat up and had had a radio that worked. We wouldn't have lost the house and restaurant. I probably would have gone to college. It didn't happen, Arnie. That's just that." Shrugging her shoulders, she turned and walked away from him, catching up with Drea and pointing out things on the beach.

Arnie stared at her. No wonder she's so mature, he thought, remembering how mature and levelheaded he'd believed himself at that age. Hell, he'd started SofTek then, but he'd never realized how lucky he was—how lucky he'd always been. She was so damn beautiful and everyone probably thought that that's all she was concerned about yet here was all this history. What a shame, he decided ruefully as he admired the panoramic view of the wide, placid river. This place evidently meant the world to her and she was lucky if she could just drive out to catch a glimpse.

Thoughtfully, Arnie slowly wandered down and joined Drea and Becki. "It's lovely here," he finally commented, "and peaceful. Much more isolated than the Cape."

"Well, if it's not developed, maybe it will stay that way. I used to sit down here for hours." Becki's eyes narrowed slightly as she remembered. Right, and eventually Billy had come to sit by her and her life had taken another turn.

"When you weren't riding your pig?"

"I'm sorry I told you about her. No, I gave up pigs when I was fourteen. I was working some in the restaurant then and it was probably a good thing. Aunt Mary no doubt would have wanted to eat Snow White. She wasn't having many litters anymore."

"What did you do with her?"

"Oh, we put her out to pasture, so to speak. Unfortunately the people who took her didn't keep up her shots and one day she died, but at least it wasn't at a slaughterhouse. Pigs get things like pneumonia too, Arnie."

"Yes, they do." He put one arm around her and with the other reached down for a stone. "Do you know how to skip stones, Drea?" The little girl shook her head. "Find any that look flat and I'll show you how. I used to be pretty good at this and I bet your mom was too."

Nodding her head in agreement, Becki smiled but then suddenly she gestured toward the sky. "Shh," she whispered and got up, running as quickly as she could to catch Drea. Putting her fingers gently over the child's mouth, she pointed up and all three of them saw an eagle making slow circles and then landing on the top of an evergreen. They stayed there, quiet, until leisurely the bird took off and began to soar down the river.

"I've never seen one outside of a zoo," remarked Arnie in wonder.

"I told you it was special here," said Becki, "but let's have that rock-skipping contest now so we can go for a walk up the river. Then maybe we can see if we can find some crabs."

Later when they finally got to the little riverside restaurant, Arnie surveyed it and its surroundings with interest. The building itself was an unadorned wooden structure extending out onto a wharf with windows all around so everyone would have a view. There were no real decorations, just plain wooden chairs and long, marred plank tables. Yet in spite of the almost Spartan simplicity, the place looked comfortable. "This belonged to your parents?"

"They thought so," Becki smiled ironically. "We lived

about halfway between here and Aunt Mary's but I didn't want to stop there. After the bank sold the property, the people tore our house down so they could have something out of *House Beautiful.* There wasn't anything really special about our home but the view. It was just a small clapboard building but we had the little barn and pens and Marty and I each had our own room. You could see the river in the distance from our windows. Now the house there is redwood and glass and looks like it should be in California. They added decks and a big patio and they even have a swimming pool—I wouldn't be surprised if they never use the river," she shook her head in dismay. "The new owners fenced the grounds in and use the barn as a stable for their horses. It's as if we never lived there," she finally half-whispered sadly.

"Hmm," murmured Arnie, realizing anything he'd say would be inadequate.

"Progress," remarked Becki with the resignation of years. "But, more important now, food. Do you want me to order this time?"

"Sure, crabs, right?"

"I've got to warn you. They've become rather expensive. We could get a few and then something else."

"I think I can swing it. What do we get? A couple apiece?"

Becki burst into laughter. "You obviously have never visited the Chesapeake. If we're not getting anything else, at least a couple dozen."

"A couple dozen! How big are these things?"

"Oh, I imagine you'd get enough meat out of a dozen to about make up one of your West Coast ones."

"You're not serious."

"Try me. And if we weren't driving, I'd say a pitcher of beer, but maybe we should stick with soft drinks."

"Why don't we compromise," he countered. "A nice icy beer for each of us and then we can switch."

The waitress arrived, putting down brown butcher's paper on the table and returning with wooden mallets and a couple of saucers of vinegar. In a few moments, she was back with a huge tray, piled high with small, rusty-colored crabs.

"These are the famed Chesapeake crabs?" Arnie asked, clearly surprised and not sure if he was disappointed. Taste obviously would tell, but being from the Pacific where a crab was a crab, he couldn't refrain from making a dig. "They practice infanticide here!"

Not rising to his wisecrack, Becki merely called Drea back from the window where she'd been standing, staring out at the wharf. "Unfortunately, you're partially right, but these are adults. We'll just have to let Drea demonstrate."

"Crabs, Mommy, crabs! Can I start in?" the little girl squealed, sighting the heaped platter.

"Go for it," urged Arnie. "You're supposed to teach me how to eat them. After all, I showed you how to use the chopsticks."

Drea looked at him seriously. "That's so silly. Everyone knows how to eat crabs." Carefully, she pulled the largest one off the tray. Placing it on the paper covering, she lifted the mallet and smashed down. Then meticulously she began to extract the meat, daintily dipping it into the vinegar. Next she took the little feelers and started to suck out what remained. "See, Arnie, it's easy."

He reached over and extracted one from the heap, copying the process. At first bite, his eyes opened wide and he turned half reproachfully to Becki. "These are hot...pepper hot. I see why you need the beer. No wonder that Ethiopian food didn't bother you. But my God, the work to get a few bites. Is this really a meal or a hobby?"

Becki chuckled softly. "Both. If it's too hard for you, city boy, get some crab cakes or spiced shrimp."

"I think I'm up to the challenge," he retorted, "but you're going to have to try a New England clambake some time. There they know how to eat."

"So do we," she asserted sweetly. "We've just made it into an art so we can converse while we dine."

"I'm not sure picking crabs is quite the way I envision

gracious dining, but I grant you that they're tasty even if I do feel as though we're robbing someone's nursery."

CHAPTER 8

They stopped in Fredericksburg on the way back, and Becki took them to the Civil War battlefield. After seeing the Park Service's slide show, Arnie, shook his head. "The poor town. Attacked, captured back and forth all those times. I had no idea. How could they live?"

"It was hard. My great great grandfather was wounded and then paroled to go home. By the time of the war, it was just a farm—the horses and most of the animals were gone. Yet we, as a family, were actually lucky. We kept the place though it wasn't worth much after. Still everyone knew how to hunt and fish and they survived. I remember when I was about Drea's age, my grandmother would bring me to the cemetery here and point out names of kin. Some older people around here still fight the war a little, but it's silly. That's what my father always said, that we were all one country now. I mean who would ever have thought I'd meet someone from Oregon who lives in Boston and flies off to places like Tokyo on business or to Switzerland to ski."

"Switzerland," cried Drea excitedly. "Did you see Heidi's hut?"

Arnie looked at Becki quizzically. "We're working our way through the series," she explained.

"Series? I thought there was only one book."

"Oh no," answered Becki. "The translator wrote a couple more so we could see how Heidi and Peter grew up and lived happily after."

"Just like a fairy tale," interjected Drea enthusiastically.

"Well, I'm glad to hear that," responded Arnie seriously. "I always wondered what happened to them and I positively do believe in happily ever after. But no, I didn't see the hut though I did get goat cheese and some of those nice soft rolls the blind grandmother wanted with melted cheese. Have you ever had fondue, Drea?"

"What's that?"

"Oh, something like Heidi's grandfather used to make—melted cheese. I can make it too. Maybe sometime we'll try but I bet you'll like the chocolate one better."

"Chocolate?" Drea was decidedly interested.

"Yep," said Arnie. "They melt chocolate and dip all sorts of things into it—apples, strawberries, bananas, cake."

"Oh, yummy!" The little girl's eyes widened. "Can you make that too?"

"Most definitely," boasted Arnie.

"Doesn't sound so bad to me either, though I've got to watch that poundage," Becki commented. "I've got a photography session coming up."

"Really," remarked Arnie, interested. "You hadn't mentioned anything about that."

"Well, you haven't been around...I mean in the country. Things were pretty slow while you were away, but they want some autumn clothes featured for one of the department stores. It looks like I may be doing it in a week or two."

"That's great. Do I ever get to see these pictures?"

"If you'd like," she answered almost indifferently.

Drea broke in. "People pay my Mommy to take pictures of her! She's beautiful in them. I've got some in my room. I'll show you, Arnie. You're so nice; I might even give you one."

"I'd like that. It's a date right?"

"A date? How silly. I'm too little for dates. You really are a silly man."

"Thanks," he responded, "out of the mouths of babes."

"Only little ones," replied Becki, taking his arm. "Let's do something more cheerful now. Let's go back into town. We can get the car tour map from the visitor's center and follow their driving circuit. Then if you like, we'll wonder through the shops."

"And restaurants after?" asked Arnie. "Those crabs at lunch only counted as appetizers."

"You don't have to take us out to dinner again," Becki protested futilely, realizing Arnie was a determined man and Drea would agree. Still, this weekend was costing him money even if he obviously did have a good job.

"I know I don't, but I want to. Besides, I'm hoping we can have a little time together again this evening...just us. Ok?"

She smiled and he waited patiently until she answered, eyes cast down as if afraid to show her true feelings. "I suppose so, but you'll come in and meet Marty and Jerry and stay while I get Drea to bed?"

Drea turned. "I don't want to go to bed."

"Not now, sweetheart," her mother assured her. "We've still got more to see and do and Arnie's going to treat us to dinner."

"Fondue?" the child inquired hopefully.

"Somehow I think you're going to have to wait for that, but maybe the next time. The next time when we find that horse to ride too," he stated firmly, looking pointedly at Becki.

"You didn't forget!" Drea turned accusingly to her mother, "See, I told you he wouldn't." Becki just reached out and squeezed Arnie's hand, her eyes as bright as Drea's.

"That's your assignment," Arnie told Becki. "When I come back next month on business, you find a place to ride a horse and a place to eat fondue that'll let in an eight-year old. Otherwise your sister's going to have to let me take over her kitchen."

"Actually," remarked Becki speculatively, "that might be fun. You tell me what to get and we'll do that one evening."

"And you're going to make me lug down a fondue pot?"

"Yes, but I might even fix you crab cakes in return. My father's special recipe."

"Well that seems fair." Arnie gave her hand a squeeze back. "So you can cook real meals too. Do wonders ever cease?"

"You haven't tried my cooking yet."

"True, but I have faith."

The rest of the afternoon went as planned. Becki and

the Fredericksburg Visitor's Center supplied an abbreviated history of the little riverside town, which Arnie pronounced charming. The three of them drove and walked the old streets with Becki pointing out places like Revolutionary hero Hugh Mercer's Apothecary Shop or James Monroe's Law Office. At one corner, she showed him a small sandstone block with a step hewn in the side. "That's the auction block for slaves. Not everything was charming here," she commented dryly. He merely nodded his head in agreement.

When they got to Kenmore, the Lewis mansion belonging to George Washington's sister, they parked across the street and let Drea run back and forth on the green meridian to Hugh Mercer's statue and Mary Washington's obelisk. "That was a real Virginia mansion," stated Becki, indicating the handsome Georgian house. "Lewis lost almost everything when he supported the Revolutionary War but his family was still important—Merriweather was a cousin so I guess they were all adventurous. I like to think of Fredericksburg fighting for freedom rather than against it later. It's such a nice place although it's mostly tourism now but at least the town has the lovely old buildings or rehabs— not a pseudo recreation like much of Williamsburg. And all the modern stuff is out in the shopping centers. I expect that this is the way my parents and grandparents saw it even if these places are hustling postcards and overpriced antiques. At least conning you tourists keeps us in business, city boy," she poked him playfully to physically reemphasize her verbal jab.

Arnie grabbed her hand, laughing, and suggested hopefully, "And selling food too? What authentic Virginia dinner would you then advise, milady?"

"Frankly, I think we're not exactly dressed for one of those places. Why don't we go back to Caroline Street and stop in one of the little delis or we could hit some fast food on the way back. You've already been too generous with us today."

"I did not come to Virginia to patronize McDonald's or

even the Colonel, so called southern style chicken or not!" At this Becki let out a slight snort and Arnie wondered about real southern cooking. "And don't worry about the expense, I think I can afford to feed us."

"McDonald's," shrieked Drea excitedly, practically jumping up and down.

"My ears!" complained Arnie loudly, clapping his hands to his head and startling the little girl until she realized he was joking. Looking at Becki, he sighed, "You should tear my tongue out but I did promise she could choose, didn't I? Can we compromise? Is there some restaurant type place we can go to?"

"Well," considered Becki, "recalling my lectures on the delights of owning a pig, there is a good Bar-B-Q place out on Route 1 that's been here for ages. Then we could cut over and catch I-95 back. Will you consider that, Drea?"

"And French fries and cold slaw and chocolate ice cream?"

"I see she still orders before we get there, but whatever you want, kid," promised Arnie.

"Ok."

"Obviously food is the way to her heart," he told Becki.

"It is with most children. It's been known to work with me too. I can recall a candle-lit dinner this spring that..."

Shaking his head, Arnie protested, "The piña coladas contributed to our mood maybe, but not the food. Please tell me it wasn't just the food."

"What do you think," she said coyly, taking his arm. "Let's see how Bar-B-Q works."

Later that night, when she was nestled in his arms, he whispered, "Bar-B-Q works fantastically. I'm going to have to remember that."

She looked at him, uncomprehendingly at first, and then burst into laughter. "Not just Bar-B-Q," she conceded. "I think you had something to do with it as well."

"I paid for it?" he asked innocently.

"Stop it," she said, smacking him lightly on his arm.

"Ouch, that hurt," he complained. "You've got to stop

beating on me."

"Baby," she chided softly, but she kissed him gently on the arm and rubbed her cheek against its soft hair. "Men are such babies."

"And that's why women mother them."

"I'm not interested in mothering you, Arnie. No way am I interested in mothering you." This time she kissed him in a most non-maternal manner.

"Right," he agreed breathily, "no mothering. This is much, much better."

Sunday they drove back into the city. At the National Zoo, Arnie loaded Drea with peanuts, cotton candy and balloons—a child's notion of a perfect day.

"You're really spoiling her, Arnie," Becki complained when the two sat on a bench and Drea raced ahead to watch the keepers feeding the bears.

"What's wrong with a little spoiling? I like to be spoiled. Besides, you said she never sees her father. What happened to him?"

"Oh, he's still in the army. He met a German woman while he was in Europe. She had a couple of children and he married her. They're out west now at Fort Huachuca. They have a little boy of their own too."

"And he does nothing for Drea?"

"No, not really. Billy did send a few toys at first, but after he remarried, nothing. We never hear from his parents either now that there's the new grandchild. I don't know if they're embarrassed or possibly boys just count for more. They were decent to me when I first married him—at least his mother was."

"Well that's pretty shitty," declared Arnie clearly disturbed. "Drea's a doll. I couldn't imagine forgetting about her. All the more reason to spoil her."

"But not too much, please?" Becki looked at him, almost pleading.

"What do you mean?"

"She really likes you, Arnie. Let's just leave it at that, all right?"

"Ok," he agreed, "in moderation." He did not expound upon what Becki probably was trying to tell him, not to make the little girl care too much so she wouldn't be hurt when he was gone. "Ok," he said again, patting her hand. "Can you have a late dinner with me tonight after we get her home and spend the whole night with me this time? The last two nights were very nice, but I missed you after you were gone. I'll bring you back really early in the morning, before Drea gets up. I have to catch that first shuttle to Boston."

Becki considered a moment. "All right. Why don't you just let us off and then you can come back for me, say around 7:30. I'll be ready and I'll just wear what I need for tomorrow."

"Nice," he agreed, "and somewhere candle-lit and romantic where we can have a bottle of wine and grown-up food and be big people?"

"There're not too many fancy restaurants around the motel but there's a good place in Vienna—the Marco Polo. It should be late enough that there'll only be grown-ups though I don't know about the candles."

"Sounds good. You look good in candle light, but then you look good all the time, Beauty, so if I have to wait for that, it won't be a hardship."

The next morning when he left her at the Falls Church townhouse, she looked so sad that he wasn't quite sure what to say. Just before she got out of the car, he turned to her, taking her hand. "I am coming back, you know. In less than a month." Then he added, "God, I wish you could just stay in town with me the whole time."

"Hey," she replied, in her sweet southern drawl, "remember, I'm a student too. When I finish this summer, I've almost done it. Only two more classes."

"That's great."

"Thanks, Dr. Miller, although an AA probably sounds like small pickings to you. It's so hard to think of you as a professor, Arnie."

"Nothing academic is small pickings, Beauty— especially to someone working for a degree and trying to earn her living too. It's a good thing that my students don't look like you. They'd have me out of there for sexual harassment in no time."

"I doubt that."

"Why?"

"You'd never do something like that. You might look at the merchandise, but you'd never handle it."

Arnie grinned. "You're right, but I must confess I do believe in window shopping. Unfortunately or fortunately, I don't have too many women students and none of them look like you. You, Beauty, might have been worth the risk."

"It wouldn't have been sexual harassment in my case," she asserted, as she leaned over to kiss him. "You won't forget the fondue pot, will you?"

He burst into laughter. "Nor the skewers and when I'm here, we'll shop together and get all the ingredients."

"No," she said earnestly, shaking her head. "I'll do that. That and the crab cakes will be my treat. I can't afford to take you any place nice, but I can do that."

"Ok," he responded gravely, understanding. "That's the way it will be. I'll call you later this week. Now give me another kiss." He held her a few minutes and then she broke away, looking at him silently for a moment, before getting out of the car. As he drove off, he saw her in the rearview mirror. Standing tall, looking serious and dignified. Twenty-four, he thought. Some of his students were twenty-four. He was that just a few years ago but internally she was so old. She lost all those teen years. He shook his head thinking about the mature woman in the beautiful young body.

CHAPTER 9

The business trip back to D.C. in late July did not work out as Arnie and Becki had planned. When Arnie was finally able to give her the exact dates, it turned out that she had committed one of the weekends to a photography session. "You can't get out of it?" he begged over the telephone.

"Arnie, I'd like to, but I can't afford it. I make as much in one day doing this as I do in a week at work. I barely get by on what I'm earning with my job. There's never really anything left after I pay my share of the rent and utilities, buy some of the groceries, and pay for our insurance and my Metro tickets. Taking these jobs means I can go to school, get some things for Drea and me, even try to put a little money away."

When he heard that, he knew there was nothing more he could say. "How much time can you spend with me?"

"Where are you staying?" she asked.

"Wherever I can be closest to you. I'll rent a car if that would help you getting home."

"Two or three nights during the week, a day if you stay over the next weekend," she said, trying not to show she too was hurt by the unfortunate timing. But she did need the job. As much as she cared for Arnie and wanted to be with him, he was her out-of-town, occasional beau. No, be honest, Becki thought, he's more than that; he's the only one, but Drea is my priority.

"Better than nothing," Arnie said resigned. "What about Drea on the weekend and the fabulous fondue feast?"

"You still want to do that?"

"I promised, didn't I? We'll take her riding Saturday."

"All right. One week night for Heidi's feast. Then if we spend Saturday with her, maybe after we get her to bed, I can come and stay with you until you leave Sunday afternoon."

"I think that sounds like a winning compromise," Arnie declared, somewhat heartened. As it turned out that was much the way the week went. Although his meetings were going well and it was apparent that his company would be getting some government contracts, it was really the time he spent with Becki that was the highlight for him. He discovered that he was thinking about her, more and more, in the moments when they were apart. As he'd told her, he'd make no promises, but now he was beginning to wonder if perhaps his bachelor days were ending. He'd never been against marriage. In fact, he'd often joked that some of his best friends practiced it; But, he'd also enjoyed an easy going social scene with various women and had been so involved with his work that he'd never before seriously considered getting married. Maybe, he now realized, it was because he'd never before found the right woman.

Since he'd met Becki, he'd dropped other relationships. Neither had spoken of any commitment, but it was beginning to be a matter of serious consideration as far as he was concerned. He was also worried because he knew that he would not be having any further trips down to D.C. until late in the autumn and she, he was sure, would continue to refuse any invitations to Boston unless she could afford to pay for them.

With some trepidation before he left, he asked, "Can you come up to Boston for Labor Day? I'm giving a big party out on the Cape that weekend—a real New England clambake. No hours of picking little pieces of crab, just digging into all the goodies: corn on the cob, potatoes, clams, lobsters, and all cooked in an open fire with seaweed."

"It sounds fantastic," she enthused, intrigued by the prospect. "I've read about that."

"You're the one who's fantastic, the meal's just good."

"I'll settle for the 'good' then," but she beamed at him, pleased at his compliment.

"I do my best," he nodded and then pushed on, encouraged by her reaction and intent on getting her acceptance, but acting as though he already had. "If you get up there on Thursday, we'll drive around Boston at night and go someplace fun for dinner. Then we can head out early Friday, hopefully beating some of the traffic. I can show you some of the Cape that evening and then work your tail off helping me get ready for the party." Becki started laughing while Arnie had the grace to look embarrassed.

"Well, that too," he mumbled, adding, "people are coming on Saturday and we'll just hit one of the seafood places in Chatham then. The bake is actually Sunday so most will leave that night or first thing Monday morning to avoid traffic. I thought maybe you and I could go back to Boston early Tuesday and have the day in town to see the sights. We'll dine some place nice that night and I'll put you on the plane Wednesday. How does it sound?"

Becki did some rapid calculations, considering. It was over a month away and maybe she could get a cheap ticket, plus Marty's baby wasn't due until the first week of October. "Let me talk to Marty," she finally answered. "If she thinks it's no problem, I'll be there. You're going to have to tell me what to wear and all that."

"Just be your beautiful self," he replied with the utmost sincerity. The more time he spent with Becki, the lovelier she seemed.

"Men. I ask a sensible question and you come out with a wisecrack."

"Ok, think New England at the end of summer."

"I've never been in New England, remember?"

"Sorry. Something you can wear to a decent restaurant—the black dress. That's really special," he said recalling her in it and then his having helped her out of it that first night they had spent together. "Beach stuff: berms, bathing suit, T-shirts, sneakers, maybe a sweatshirt in case it gets cold. Also, you need comfortable shoes for walking in Boston."

"Fine," Becki replied, thankful she didn't have to buy anything. Drea was growing so fast that she'd practically have to get her a whole new wardrobe for school. Plus the little girl had her heart set on ballet and slippers and lessons cost so much, but it seemed such a small request.

The month before the trip, Becki was lucky to get two modeling jobs, which relieved her anxiety. When had she last had a holiday? She suddenly realized not since Drea was born except for that one horrible weekend with Mike at Virginia Beach. There she had learned of his wife down in Florida, who was caretaking elderly parents. She'd felt so cheap and dirty. Why had she never suspected, especially since Mike left town so many weekends, but he was Air Force and she had assumed the travel was business.

What was with her and men and the water, she wondered? It must be a sign. Even with Billy, their so called honeymoon had been a weekend up at Ocean City, Maryland—his choice. Roaming the honky-tonk boardwalk, tired from her pregnancy, and too sick to go on the rides, she had tried not to cry. Meanwhile Billy had jeered, calling her a spoilsport.

But to take a plane! She'd never been on one, something she didn't admit to others since it seemed everyone in the world had flown, including their dogs. Heavens, dogs and cats on airplanes! Now, it was her turn. Would she be scared? Would it be as wonderful as she hoped?

The Thursday of her flight, she looked over her clothes for what must have been the forty-second time and, at last, carefully packed them into one of Marty's suitcases. It was the first time she'd be away from Drea for more than a couple of nights but it didn't seem to faze the little girl at all. "You'll bring me something from Boston, Mommy?"

"Sure will, angel," Becki uttered as she leaned over to hug her daughter, who couldn't seem to keep still, excited over her mother's trip. God, she was lucky, Becki realized. Knowing what she had, how could she ever have considered not wanting this child, but then if she could, she'd have had a dozen more. Kissing the soft, smooth cheek, Becki promised, "Maybe two things if you're really good." A sweatshirt and something for school, Becki decided as she mentally calculated how much money she'd have to spend. Even purchased early, the plane ticket had been more costly than she'd expected. But she had promised Arnie and she so wanted to go. To see Boston, of course, but to see him even more she now realized. It had been only a little over a month's separation but it felt like years; she'd never felt this way before about a man. Yet when Marty and Drea dropped her at the Metro, Becki was the one who felt like crying. At the Kiss and Ride, she got out of the car and gave Drea a big hug. "Now you're going to do everything Auntie says, right?"

"I promise, Mommy. I promised yesterday, too, and this morning."

"Sorry," apologized Becki. "And Marty, you have all the numbers?"

"I promise, Mommy," mimicked her sister amused, eyes rolling in exasperation.

"Smartah..." retorted Becki.

"Uh uh, little pitchers," cautioned Marty with a large grin, shaking her finger. She couldn't remember when Becki had last been as excited. "You just have a fabulous time. You deserve it and be sure and say hi to your Arnie for us. Tell him if he doesn't treat you right, I'm coming up there to beat the sh..."

"Ooh, Aunt Marty, you're saying something bad," scolded Drea.

"What was that about little pitchers?" asked Becki sweetly.

"Just have fun, Becki." Marty again shook the admonishing finger. So far this Arnie seemed just what Becki needed.

Finally the small Ford tootled off and Becki carried her bag into the Metro. Once at National, the flight was delayed and Becki became anxious. What if it didn't leave or what if Arnie didn't wait, but that was stupid, of course he would. At last, with her luggage secured in the overhead compartment and herself safely strapped in, she looked out the window. Was it going to be wonderful? Was everything going to be wonderful? When the plane finally took off, she felt a slight jerk to her stomach and then she looked out. Below lay the Washington Monument and the Capitol and Watergate and the whole city. Everything was getting tinier and tinier, just like the little pegboard town she had when she was small.

Carefully she listened to the stewardess giving instructions and examined the safety card, as well as noting the paper bag. How mortifying it would be to have to use that! Looking around she saw that most people were reading, not even listening to the stewardess or looking out at the wonderful sights below. Blasé, she thought, that's really what the word means and wondered if she'd ever be blasé about flying.

The landing at Logan, when it came, was just the slightest bump and Becki felt quite proud of herself. She hadn't been the least flustered, Miss World Traveler! Then she grinned, noticing little children and older people and all the business travelers around her. Sure, Miss World Traveler. She was probably the only one who didn't do this regularly.

Arnie was right at the gate, even holding a red rose in his hand. "My," she said, "I am impressed."

"Hey, it's your first time to Boston, and you deserve a flower. A long-stemmed American Beauty for my long-stemmed American Beauty, remember? And also this." He gave her a big kiss. "How was the flight?"

"Oh fine," she responded airily, hoping she too was properly blasé.

"Well I know all they gave you was a soft drink and some peanuts, so why don't we head into town and decide where we want to go tonight. Or, I could take you to my place first, if you'd like, and we could go out later," he remarked casually, visualizing her next to him in his bed, a vision that was becoming more and more frequent—in fact practically nightly, often causing a physical reaction he hadn't experienced since his teens.

"Whatever you suggest," she replied smiling. "I'm the tourist this time, remember?"

"You're right," he answered seriously, putting his

amorous thoughts aside. "And you've never been here. We'll go first into Boston and look around a little, have dinner, and then home for the night." His countenance changed slightly as he said that, again picturing her entwined in his embrace. She smiled, saying nothing, just taking hold of his arm as he picked up her bag and they headed for the parking.

Boston, Becki thought, and realized she was too excited to verbalize much of anything. Except she was horrified by the driving; Arnie just laughed, "Welcome to the real Bean Town, Becki. For being self-impressed by their academic and technological prowess, when it comes to cars, people in the greater Boston area are as mad, if not madder than anywhere in the world."

In reply, Becki practically let out a scream as she saw a car cut across the lanes, missing them by inches. When she had her breath back, she asked, "And you do this every day?"

"Nope, thank God. I'd have grey hair if I did. I bike or walk to MIT from home and I take the T to our office. Driving is for getting out of town. The only reason I brought my car today was because I figured we'd have your luggage and might want to go around first. What would you like to see up here besides the Freedom Trail?" he suggested, remembering the pride and interest she'd shown being his guide around D.C.

"Walden Pond," she answered promptly.

"Why doesn't that surprise me at all? It's out of Boston but we'll try on Tuesday. I have to warn you that I think you're going to be disappointed. Thoreau probably wouldn't have recognized it."

"That's all right. That's still where he was."

"And you want to pay homage?" Arnie inquired gently.

"Sort of," she grinned. But then she added with a wicked little smirk, "and see if Zonker was really there and where Spenser and Hawk are."

Arnie laughed. "I'll try to point out those historic settings to you too." But that night he ended up taking her to the fish market and Legal's in Back Bay, insisting, "It's time you try real seafood. You've got to get scrod in Boston and sample their homemade ice cream."

"Scrod in Boston," Becki murmured. "That's a joke?"

"Right, that also; past pluperfect, but actually it's baby cod or haddock."

"So you practice maritime infanticide here too."

"Touché," he replied, recalling his retort to the Chesapeake crabs.

After dinner, Arnie drove her around the twisting streets, remarking, "Ralph Waldo Emerson said these were laid out by cows; you see I know some history too." Becki laughed, agreeing that Emerson obviously didn't understand surveying. They then crossed over the Longfellow Bridge to Cambridge, passing MIT. "That's the alma mater," Arnie gestured. "Three years of suffering. Now I just stick it to the undergrads."

"Mean! Did you do your master's there too?"

"Yeah, that was part of the three years."

"I'm impressed," she commented, meaning it, thinking how long it had taken most of her instructors to get both degrees. Even five years was considered fast.

"Sometimes I am too," he laughed, as he turned down a side street near Harvard and pulled up in front of an attractive two-story red brick house with a small front porch and a large oak tree in front. "We lucked out tonight parking," Arnie commented jauntily, as he helped her out of the car. "Even with a resident's sticker, it's sometimes a chore to find a place."

"This is old, isn't it Arnie?"

"Not as much so as the place your aunt's in." He couldn't bring himself to say hers. It would likely hurt too much. When they entered, Becki looked around, noting the living room off to the right of the entrance hall and a dining room to the left. The house looked like it was occupied by a bachelor, with simple, functional furniture, and some abstracts and framed posters on the walls. Piles of books were stacked here and there but overall it was neat and efficient. "Come on, slow poke," prodded Arnie. "I'll take your case up to the bedroom and then show you around. There's a library and study down the hall and the kitchen is behind the dining room. If you go through the pantry, there's even a small garden out back, not that I do anything with it. I'm afraid where some people have green thumbs, mine are gangrene."

Becki sputtered, but she was certain Arnie could have run a greenhouse if he were really interested. He was the most take-charge individual she'd ever met in spite of being kind, sympathetic and fun. "And upstairs?"

"Oh a couple of baths and three bedrooms besides the master one."

"And you live here all by yourself," she asked amazed by the size of the house. "No roommates?"

"I'm a big boy, Becki. I can live by myself."

She felt herself blushing. "That's not what I meant." I've stuck her foot into it now, she thought. Arnie was going to think she was wondering how much money he made to afford a place like this.

But Arnie said nothing, just carried her luggage upstairs and then hurriedly returned. "Come on. It's lovely tonight. Why don't you look around and we can have a nightcap outside, if you like. I may not be a gardener, but my neighbors are and it smells nice out there, roses and other fragrant flowers."

"All right." She followed him into the kitchen, which looked utilitarian but obviously was not overly used. A fondue pot stood on one of the counters. Touching it lightly, she observed, "That was really a hit. It was nice of you to give them one." Arnie nodded his head in agreement as they both remembered the dinner at her place. "Drea is pestering me about more Swiss feasts so I may make one for Marty and Jerry's anniversary. They really enjoyed that evening too."

"Me too," Arnie concurred as he opened the fridge and pulled out a bottle of champagne. "Would you rather have this?"

"Goodness," she exclaimed, looking at the French

label. "I'm used to Californian."

"Well, I don't think this is too bad. There are some glasses in the cabinet by the sink."

Becki opened its door and pulled out two flutes, tapping them delicately with her finger to hear the ringing sound. "Crystal. It sounds so pretty. My mother had some." And they probably ended up at that church bazaar, reflected Arnie, as carefully he began to twist the bottle.

"I thought you were just supposed to push the cork out," observed Becki, interested in what he was doing.

"Makes a nice sound," explained Arnie, "but then you lose half the champagne." There was a small pop, though, and the wine started cascading into the glasses. Putting down the bottle, he handed one to her and with his, clinked them lightly. "Welcome to Boston, Beauty. We don't have to sit outside if you don't want."

She smiled slightly. "I am a little tired. Maybe I should unpack and clean up."

"Maybe that's a good idea," he agreed, and picking up the bottle, he led her up the stairs. "Maybe you don't even have to unpack."

"Maybe..." she agreed.

Setting down the bottle and his glass, he took her in his arms. "Hmm, so nice to hold you. Why don't you go get ready in the bath? I'll use the one down the hall and then we can have some more champagne and..."

"You have an iron?" Becki suddenly asked.

"You're unbelievable," Arnie chuckled. "Yes, I have an iron and we can iron anything you want tomorrow. I'm good at ironing, ok?"

Surprised, she laughed in response. Then when she'd undressed and showered, she came back into the room, wearing a short white nightgown she'd purchased especially for the trip. The only other one she had, she'd taken to Virginia Beach that awful weekend and she knew she'd never wear it with this nice man; actually, she didn't wear it period. Still, it had served as a cautionary reminder, she reflected, although now, caution was gone.

The lights were low and Arnie was waiting for her in bed, his hair damp and smelling of clean spicy soap. She slipped under the covers and he pulled her to him, holding her tightly and then he kissed her and began to make love to her. After, he asked bemused, "Why does it always feel so good, Becki?" She just held on to him, stroking his back but her face had a sweet, contented look. Later they lay there propped up on the pillows, her in the crook of his arm, sipping their champagne, silent and content. He had turned on the radio and the soft sounds of Debussy filled the room. The bedroom window was open and she could smell the roses from outside and everything was so peaceful. So perfect, she thought.

CHAPTER 10

Early the next morning, Arnie watched her unpack. "You only need the casual stuff for the Cape. I'll iron your dress while you get ready, if you want."

"I believe you would," she declared, "but if I don't need it until Tuesday, I think it'll hang out. I'm impressed, a college professor and you can iron too."

"Think lonely bachelor on the road a lot, and I'm not wild about that TV Magnum beachcomber look that's catching on."

"That too. And I gather we're about to hit the road?"

"Right, I'll buy you breakfast on the way or if you can hold out with coffee and a donut from the bakery stop, we'll get a lobster roll once we hit the Cape."

"I prefer tea but that sounds interesting."

"Not just interesting," he asserted, "one of the great culinary delicacies of the Eastern Seaboard. Also it doesn't take two hours to pick the food out of tiny little legs."

She picked up a pillow and threw it at him. "I'm sorry I introduced you to Chesapeake crabs."

"And told me about raising pigs and..." He grabbed her, pushed her down on the bed and began to tickle her. "I don't like women who throw things at me. They need to be punished."

Becki was sputtering and giggling, squirming to get away. "I wish I'd thrown another," she retorted.

"You are dangerous." He stopped, looked at her and then lowered his head to kiss her.

"I thought we were trying to beat the traffic," she whispered finally.

"This doesn't have to take long." He began to unbutton her shirt. "Maybe we should take this off so we don't have to iron it."

"Maybe," she agreed and she let him undress her and then held up her arms to receive him.

"Why was I dumb enough to think a clambake was a good idea?" he asked as he started to kiss her delicately up and down her body. She had her eyes shut and was making little entreating sounds while moving her hands seductively over his trunk. Suddenly she opened her eyes, stared at him and then pulled him to her. He entered and she gripped her legs around him, squeezing as tightly as she could. Now murmuring, she had her arms around his neck, forcing his head down to her breasts. He pulled back, rolling both of them over and then he was on the bottom, looking up at her. Her long, golden hair was cascading down onto his face and he breathed in the perfumed scent. "Oh Becki," he sighed, "this is wonderful." Pressing her to him as firmly as he could, he felt himself deep inside her until she began to spasm and he joined her. "Definitely worth a late start," he said, stroking the soft, smooth hair while she lay cuddled against him, her fingers running gently up and down his chest. Yes, gentle, quiet Becki, he thought, more at peace than he'd ever been.

Later when they reached the Cape, Becki saw that the beach house was high on the dunes overlooking the Atlantic. It looked just like New England cottages were supposed to look, grey, weathered, shingled. "This is old too, isn't it?" she asked.

"Nineteenth century," he answered as they started bringing things in. They'd stopped along the way for the promised lobster roll but had loaded the car back in Cambridge with most of the groceries and supplies he'd purchased earlier. "We won't get the seafood until early Sunday morning. I've already arranged for that and we'll go back into Chatham tonight. There's supposed to be a band concert and I thought we could hit one of the raw bars. There're some fancy places out here too, but I kind of decided we'd save dressing up for Boston when we get back. Maybe I should have asked you," he added, slightly chagrined that he hadn't considered offering her the option.

"That sounds fine with me, but we don't even have to go back. I love the ocean. I could sit here for hours watching it."

"Well, if you want. Tomorrow night there'll be other people."

"Then let's do that, Arnie, please?" Becki looked up at him happily, her blue eyes shining. "Just us on the beach? The food doesn't matter."

"I think I can produce something. It's fine with me. Maybe we can have a little fire. Red wine and something?"

"Hot dogs, peanut butter and jelly like your nephews, who cares? Just us, ok?" Her eagerness was infectious and any guilt Arnie had had about not consulting her quickly dissipated.

"Whatever you want; but if you look in the kitchen cabinets, I think you'll find some tastier items."

So after putting everything away, Arnie got a blanket and went out to build a small fire. Becki puttered in the kitchen, pulling out various tins and putting them on a rattan tray. Getting into their bathing suits, they carried the tray and a bottle of wine down to the fire. Arnie went back for some warm clothes and towels and then they rushed into the water, splashing and playing but after a while she began to swim out. Concerned, he called to her, but she laughed and swam a bit further before coming back in. He was ready for her with a large fluffy towel, which he wrapped around her sleek, damp form, and they settled down in front of the fire. "You should be careful, Beauty. That's the ocean."

"We always swam," she protested. "My dad could swim for miles. He should never have drowned."

Arnie had his arm around her, holding her close as he gently toweled her long, damp strands of hair. "Fate likes to play tricks. Sometimes things happen to people that they'd never expect—that shouldn't. Why don't you get out of that wet suit, honey, and put these on." He'd brought out an old Caltech sweatshirt and some sweatpants. "These are clean and you've long enough legs to wear them even if there's probably room for two of you in there."

"You're nice, Sir Arnie, continuing to be gallant."

"I hope so, milady. You can go in to change but no

one's out here now so they shouldn't see and I'll hold the towel for you."

"And won't peek of course."

"Peeking was the idea behind the gallantry."

"And honest too," she said.

"I try to be," he answered simply.

She looked at him intently, trying to read his thoughts, and he stared back silently. "I'd assume so," she murmured finally. Then when she was dressed, she sank down beside him on the blanket and he opened the wine. The two were now quiet, nibbling together. Arnie would stuff a ripe olive into her mouth and she would spear a smoked oyster for him and it was a comfortable, lazy evening. The last rays of the sun had disappeared and the stars were coming out. The surf was gently pounding. When they'd finished, they carefully stacked the empty tins on the tray and he put his arms around her. She leaned back against him and his chin rested on her shoulder. They stared into the dying fire, listening to the ocean. Then he rolled back, pulling her down on the blanket next to him, his hands sliding under the sweatshirt.

"Outside?" she asked in a hushed voice.

"I told you, no one's around right now. The neighbors on either side were going into Chatham. The rest of the weekend there're going to be lots of people. We'll just roll the blanket around us."

Becki considered this and then she snuggled against him. "All right," she agreed, and quietly, tenderly, lingeringly he made love to her on the beach and she heard the surf go in and out. She fell asleep after and he lay there holding her, looking up at the stars, thinking. It was after midnight when Becki awoke, surprised at first and then realizing where she was. The fire was dead now except for a last ember or two and Arnie was lying next to her, breathing softly. She leaned over, kissed him gently, before saying, "I have a feeling we should go in." His eyes opened and he smiled. The two slowly got up, gathered their things and made their way back up the bluff.

"A perfect picnic," he murmured and she nodded her head in agreement, giving him another small kiss before following him into the house. They took a shower together and, after, sank into bed, holding each other and drifting off to sleep. The shutters were closed and they slept in. It was the sound of loud voices and knocking that woke them.

"Arnie, hey Arnie, let us in."

"Oh hell," he groaned, reaching for some shorts and a T-shirt. "I overslept. You stay in bed a little longer if you want. I'll go let them in."

"No, that's all right," Becki said, finding the slacks and shirt she'd worn the day before. "Is this outfit ok?"

"Fine." There was more pounding and yelling from outside. "I'm coming," Arnie yelled back and rushed out of the room.

Becki could hear a half dozen excited and laughing voices as she hurriedly dressed. By the time she stepped out of the bedroom, she saw there must be ten or more people in the living room, loaded with sleeping bags, knapsacks, bottles of wine, cartons of beer, and more bags of food. As she closed the bedroom door, she felt as though every eye had turned toward her and the conversation died. Arnie looked around, grinning broadly as he saw her. "Everybody," he announced proudly, "this is my friend Becki from Virginia."

Shyly, she said hello softly and crossed the room towards him. He put his arm possessively around her, the pleased grin lighting his face. "I could start around the room but you'd never remember all the names. They'll sort out pretty soon, right, guys?" There were muttered hellos as people began talking again and unpacking while Becki just kept smiling silently. It seemed that everyone knew what they were doing, so she stepped back at first, watching.

Finally, feeling anxious to be useful, she turned to Arnie, now busily directing his friends as to where items should go. Tugging at his arm to get his attention, she asked. "Isn't there something I can do?"

"Nah, just take it easy. I've got to go into town to get

some more things but everyone will be changing and going on the beach pretty soon. Why don't you join them?"

"No, let me come with you, please," she asked.

"Well, sure, if you'd rather, but it's just sort of drudge errands. You'd meet everyone if you stay."

"I came to see you," she begged. "Please?"

"All right," he agreed, somewhat surprised by the intensity of her request. "Gang, I've got to drive back into town. Per usual, I forgot stuff."

"Funny, you never forget anything," yelled one of the group. Several others moaned in agreement.

"I refuse to dignify that remark by answering. You know where everything is. There's plenty of beer and soft drinks already cooling and lots of junk food and sandwich material in the kitchen. Why don't you start making that up and we should be back in an hour.

"Ok, boss man," acquiesced the original speaker.

"No problem," someone else yelled, looking at Becki with obvious admiration. "Take all the time you want. I would!"

Arnie merely smiled smugly, and Becki followed him out to his car. "How come you're doing everything?" she asked.

"Oh, I usually do a couple big parties every year and I thought it would be nice out here."

"What, you have this place for the weekend?"

"Something like that," he answered vaguely. "Do you like it?"

"It's beautiful," she said with real feeling. "To be right on the ocean like this."

"Good, I was hoping you'd like it."

When they got back later, there were even more people milling around. Soon Arnie was laughing and talking animatedly with everyone. Becki would smile when introduced, but everyone seemed to know each other. So eventually she slipped into the kitchen to make more sandwiches. A while later, Arnie came in, acting surprised to see her there. "I was wondering where you were."

"Oh, just helping."

"You're supposed to be my guest."

"The others are too."

"Yeah, but they've been here before. Come on, stay with me. We'll get our suits on and go on the beach. I doubt that anyone is going to want to go to dinner until late tonight, but promise me one thing."

"What's that?" Becki asked with curiosity.

"Don't swim out too far."

"I don't take chances with the water, but I promise." But of course, from his perspective, she did swim out.

"She's really good, isn't she?" observed one of the guys.

"Oh yeah," Arnie agreed absentmindedly. "I couldn't swim like that."

"Me neither," said his companion. "She's the one you found down in D.C., the model?"

"Yeah," said Arnie, distracted and worried. She'd promised, damn it.

"Well, she sure is a looker. I can see why you wanted to bring her up here."

"Yes," agreed Arnie absently, walking down to the surf. Then to his relief, Becki turned and was swimming back, with clean, strong strokes. Suddenly she seemed to burst from the water in front of him like a water sprite, sleek and beautiful.

"That was wonderful!" she exclaimed, a huge smile radiating on her face, the most animated she'd been all day. "Come out with me."

"You had me scared, Becki. Besides I can't swim like that."

"I thought you were from Oregon and went to the ocean."

"The Pacific is cold. We don't swim out there."

"Excuses," she laughed happily, catching his hand and tugging him. "Please come in."

"No, Becki, and please, please, you stay near shore, ok?"

"You were really worried, weren't you?" She stared at

him, surprised by his obvious concern.

"I told you so last night."

"All right, I won't," she said, the animation leaving her face. Dropping his hand, she walked back to the house to change. Several people were there and they looked at her rather strangely when she went into Arnie's bedroom. Apparently all the rooms but that one were open for grabs. Well, I couldn't help it she thought, my things are here.

She took a quick shower, changed, and came out looking for Arnie. The rest of the afternoon, she tagged after him, nursing a beer, smiling shyly and listening to his friends talking. Every now and then he'd say something to her and she'd answer; but, by and large, she felt excluded from the general discussion, which seemed to be about work and people and places she'd never heard of.

That night when they went to the restaurant, everyone was laughing and talking loudly, but the conversations were much the same. Becki ate quietly, enjoying the food, and leaned up comfortably against Arnie, who had put his arm around her and was once more possessively holding her close. When they got back to the house, it was obvious that the party would continue with Arnie's enthusiastic support. Feeling out of place, Becki whispered that she was a little tired and went into the bedroom, where she lay quietly until finally she dozed off.

Sometime in the night, she heard him enter the room. He didn't bother to turn on the light and after he got into bed, he went right to sleep. She rolled up next to him and he instinctively embraced her, but he didn't wake. She continued to lie there for the next hour or so, feeling lonely for the first time she'd been with him.

The following day was Sunday and late that morning, Becki was helping Arnie with the fire and wetting down layers of seaweed so there'd be enough steam when they added the lobsters and clams. The potatoes and corn were already buried. Suddenly Becki was surprised when someone came up behind them on the beach, placing a hand on her shoulder. "Hey, guys, need a hand?"

"Dickie," exclaimed Arnie, whirling around. "You got here! I'd expected you last night. Where's Carla?"

"Well actually, Carla's history," said the tall, dark and exceedingly good-looking man.

"Gee, I'm sorry to hear that," commiserated Arnie.

"Good riddance, says I, and who is this lovely creature?" Dickie asked, turning to give Becki a long, appraising look.

"Becki, meet Dickie Ramsey, one of the company's partners and one of my oldest friends."

"I'm honored," the man said, reaching down for Becki's hand. "You must be the special lady that Arnie imported from Virginia. Right?"

Becki grinned shyly but was somewhat disconcerted by the man's physical contact. "I guess so."

"You've outdone yourself, Arnie. He's known for escorting beautiful women, my dear, but obviously we had no idea what a southern beauty was." Becki kept smiling but felt distinctly uncomfortable as the man continued to hold her hand, exerting a soft pressure. "Well what do you want this grieving, heart-broken male to do," Dickie inquired before finally releasing the hand. Then she began to relax realizing this was just the kind of show-off he was. Even Jerry's best friend was always touchy-feely and that was never threatening. After all, this Dickie and Arnie apparently went way back.

"Actually, I've got to watch this stuff so perhaps you can take Becki around and introduce her to everyone. She met some of the people last night, but the party got pretty wild and I'm not sure who all she's talked to, especially since someone new seems to be arriving every minute."

"My pleasure," said Dickie, turning back to Becki, the appraising look reappearing in his dark blue eyes. "You'll have to tell me if all the Virginia ladies are as lovely. Maybe next time I'll ask Arnie if I can make the trip down there."

"I guess we're like any other place," Becki responded politely. "Are you sure you don't want me to stay and help, Arnie? How else am I going to learn to do a New England clambake?"

"Hey, it takes hours," groaned Arnie. "That's another thing I forget each year. Just cruise a little and then maybe in a little while you can bring me a nice, cold beer, ok?"

"Of course." She didn't really want to leave although Dickie had grabbed her hand again.

"Come on," the big man coaxed, pulling her away. "Arnie gets really serious when he's on a project and this Labor Day Party is one of his big things. We'll just take a walk along the beach, say hi to folks, and you can tell me about D.C. I hear you model."

"Just a little. Mostly I work with a small decorating company."

"Ah design. Are you an interior designer?"

"I'd like to be. I've been taking classes."

"Oh really, where?"

"Just a community college at home. They've got a decent program."

"A community college," Dickie repeated; and, to her ears it sounded like a sneer. "So you're a junior college student." This time there was no doubt he was being condescending.

"Sort of, not everyone gets a graduate degree." She left it at that.

Dickie glanced at her neutrally. "Is this your first time up here?"

"Yes."

"Well it was nice of Arnie to bring you up."

"Actually," she remarked annoyed, "I brought myself up. Arnie just invited me." Was this man purposely trying to patronize her, she wondered?

"Let's get some beer," Dickie suddenly suggested, changing the conversation.

"Not for me."

"Oh come on, you don't really mean that. It's hot out here today."

"Maybe a diet drink," she decided. "You have the beer. Should we get one for Arnie?"

"No, he said later. Besides, I'm supposed to show you around. When did you get here?"

"To the Cape? Friday."

"Ah, Friday. I thought everyone was coming yesterday."

"I'd never been here. Arnie brought me out a day early so I could see the place and then he also wanted to make final arrangements for the party."

"Sure, he did," said Dickie satirically. Then more pleasantly, he called to several women sitting together on the beach. "Hey girls, how are you lovely things?"

"Fine, good looking," answered one of the women. "Where's Carla?"

"Carla's broken my heart."

"Dickie, too bad, but you seem to be consoling yourself," laughed the woman with a knowing sound.

As if suddenly remembering Becki, Dickie replied, "No, this is Arnie's little friend from Virginia."

"Hi," said Becki softly, hoping she had misinterpreted what the woman said.

A couple of the women smiled in response but the others just seemed to look her up and down. Then, a small but curvaceous brunette jumped up and said with what appeared to be a genuine invitation, "I'm Madge. Would you like to join us?"

"That would be nice," replied Becki gratefully, but Dickie again firmly seized her hand.

"Nope," he said forcefully. "Arnie told me to give her the grand tour." As they walked off, Becki heard a distinct snort from one of the women.

"Actually, I think I would have liked to stay and talk," Becki protested mildly.

"Dull, my dear," Dickie declared archly. "There are lots of others to meet. Come on."

But it soon seemed that Dickie was more interested in grabbing a beer here and there and stopping to flirt with the women or swap a joke with the men. Occasionally he'd remember to introduce Becki, and although she'd try to say something, he'd soon drag her off. Worse, his risqué humor with its innuendos embarrassed her. There had to be at least fifty people at the party by now, but she hadn't had a chance to talk to anyone. "Dickie," she finally insisted, "let's get Arnie's beer and go back, all right?"

"The beer, of course the beer, how could I forget? Come up to the house. He always hides a few of those Pacific Northwest ones he savors from us common folk. We'll get one of them."

When they got to the house, it was empty, everyone by now being down on the beach. Some were in the water, others standing around the fire or in small groups talking animatedly. "Now where could those beers be? They're from some micro-brewery out there," Dickie said, opening the fridge.

"I don't think there were any special ones," replied Becki, puzzled. "We put a lot of things in there Friday and yesterday, but I didn't see anything like that."

"Arnie always keeps some," Dickie stated authoritatively. "I bet he's left it in a freezer chest in his room. That's where you guys have been sleeping, isn't it?" he commented nonchalantly, but again with an insidious undertone as he steered her towards the bedroom.

"I don't think that's any of your business," she rejoined irritated, yet not wanting to insult a man, who clearly was Arnie's friend.

"Ah come on, you must be really something special for someone as busy as Arnie to make a trip to D.C. just to see you, especially after he'd picked you up in a bar." Becki felt herself turning deep crimson. Arnie had told people how they met. She turned to leave but Dickie suddenly reached out and grabbed her, pulling her toward him and kicking at the door, which partially closed. "Why don't you show me what's so special. Arnie believes in going first class."

"What the hell do you think you're doing?" Becki exclaimed indignantly, her usually tranquil eyes now flashing warningly.

"You know. Come on, be nice."

"I don't want to be nice. I just want you to let me go."

She tried to pull away but Dickie was holding onto her arm with one hand tightly and trying to kiss her, while his other hand began to grope one of her breasts. "Stop that," she hissed, tugging as hard as she could. "I told you I wasn't interested."

"Sure you are," the big man said, pressing heavily against her. "Anyone can see you like it—that you put out. Why else would Arnie have brought you up? He has plenty of classy girls here, not little bar tramps. You've been strutting your stuff all weekend according to the guys. The first thing I heard when I got here was the hot piece of ass Arnie had. Now come on and share. Arnie's not going to know or give a damn if he does."

"I'll know, and I care even if he doesn't. I said no!" Becki jerked again to get away, but Dickie was holding on too tightly and had succeeded in pushing and pinning her against the wall. "Please," she pleaded, "just let go and I won't say anything."

Dickie laughed nastily, the handsome face now reddened and coarsened. "Who'd believe a dumb blonde bimbo even if you did say something? Now come here." Furious, Becki swung back her free hand and smacked him across the face. "Damn," he snarled letting go of her breast to catch and grip the offending hand. "You little bitch. You're going to be sorry."

"She's not a bitch, she's not dumb, and she's not a bimbo or a piece of ass. Also, I believe her," said a quiet, deceptively calm voice. Both Dickie and Becki turned. Standing in the doorway was Arnie, coolly observing the whole scene.

"Ah shit, Arnie, I was just fooling around, you know that," said Dickie in his most ingratiating manner, stepping back although he still had a hand on one of Becki's arms.

"What do you think, Becki?" Arnie asked soberly.

She looked at him, then back to Dickie, who now looked worried, and finally down at her feet. Her face was hot and flushed. "It doesn't matter. He didn't hurt me."

"But he did insult you, and he's still holding on to one

of your arms, and I notice there are red marks on the other."

"Well, shit, Arnie, you saw her slap me," protested Dickie.

"Why would she do that if she was leading you on?" Arnie inquired reasonably. "Why don't you let go of her arm, Dickie, or maybe she'll break one of your fingers. She knows how. If she doesn't, maybe I'll take a shot at busting your nose."

"Come on, Arnie, you know I was only horsing around. She led me on. I'm your buddy, right? You don't believe I'd just hit on her if she hadn't asked for it."

"Did you?" Arnie turned to Becki and asked with seeming curiosity.

"No," she answered softly, her eyes still averted, trying not to cry. "He's just been drinking too much."

"Yeah, Dickie does like to drink and Dickie does like to hit on women, but I thought he only picked ones who liked it."

"I told you, Arnie, she's lying."

"I really don't think so and you know what else I think?" Dickie and Becki both looked at him expectantly. "I think it's time for you to pack up and go back to the city."

"You invited me," yelled Dickie, unnerved.

"So, I can un-invite you. I want you out of here in the next five minutes, or we'll see how tough you really are. And by the way, Dickie, I also think, come Tuesday, it's time for you to pack up your office and leave SofTek."

"You're crazy," argued Dickie, clearly totally shocked by the turn of events. "You can't do that!"

"Read our partnership agreement and your contract," replied Arnie coldly. "Two weeks with pay and I have two months to come up with the current stock value of your percentage of the company. You're through."

"I won't do it!"

"I repeat. Read the contract and the agreement. You signed them when we started the company. I wouldn't have written the papers that way myself but that's how my brother-in-law helped earn his percentage. It appears he was right. You're out."

"You can't do this to me. You need me and you don't have the money." Dickie's face was now stark white.

"I'll get the money," snapped Arnie tersely. "I don't care what I have to get rid of if it means I'm rid of you. I know now if you'd try to screw around on me with my girl, you'd do it in business too. I'd been wondering about some things lately, but I was giving you the benefit of doubt."

"Jesus, Arnie, we've been friends since freshman year, for God's sake! I came out from California because of you. I've given you some of your best ideas. You can't do this to me! And for what, this little trollop you picked up in D.C.— a piece of cheap tail that would put out for anyone." Dickie's fists were clenched and he was trembling in anger. Becki looked worriedly at Arnie, afraid that the big man might strike out at him or even her, but Arnie just stood there, outwardly placid and in control. Only his narrowed eyes and tightened lips showed his rage.

"I can and I am. Now get out of here before I really lose my temper. And Dickie," added Arnie icily. Dickie stopped and turned to look back. "She's not cheap and she wasn't willing to put out for you, you miserable piece of shit." Then Arnie walked over to Becki, who was leaning against the wall, her usually healthy color now pale and pasty. "Are you ok?"

"Yes. You didn't have to do that for me. He's right. You two have been friends for a long time. Maybe I should just leave. I don't want to be responsible for your breaking up a partnership because of me or having to sell things to get money." She looked distressed and still ready to cry.

Arnie put his arms around her, staring concerned into her worried eyes. "The only partnership I'm currently interested in is with you."

She stared back at him stunned. "What do you mean?"

"I've been thinking about it for some time and I guess I would have asked sooner or later, but sooner seems the better idea now. What do you say?"

"You're asking me to marry you?" She was truly

astonished. "You don't have to do that."

"I know I don't. I never made any promises when we started to get involved, but I like you, Becki, I really care for you."

"You care for me," she said slowly, blinking, trying to maintain some composure. "Thank you, Arnie, but I don't think so."

"Why? You don't like me?" He sounded very hurt.

"You know I do or I wouldn't be here. I care for you too or I wouldn't be sleeping with you, but I don't think we're marriage material."

"I'm not good enough looking? I'm not what?" he asked seriously, his face now puzzled.

"I don't give a damn about looks," Becki retorted angrily. "That's all I get from people. I'm sick of it! You're nice, you're funny and kind and you've been good to my little girl."

"But I don't turn you on."

"You've got to be kidding! Do you really think I hop into bed with just anyone or act the way I've been doing with you?"

"Well I did think it was pretty good. Actually, I thought it was pretty fantastic," Arnie said, trying to belay the pain that he was sure was showing in his eyes.

"It has been good. I told you that before. Stop fishing for compliments."

"So, if that's not the reason, what is?"

"You don't love me," she replied simply.

"What the hell do you mean by that?" Arnie asked irritated. "I just asked you to marry me, didn't I? I don't have a ring or anything because I didn't think I'd be doing it this weekend but I knew I was going to ask eventually."

"Eventually," Becki said a bit sadly. "And you like and care for me."

"Becki, you know I love you!"

"But you didn't say that, Arnie."

"Well I do. Do you want me to spout poetry or something, to start quoting the Brownings? Let me count the ways...""

"No, I just wanted to hear you tell me that you want me because you love me."

"Ah shit, I love you Rebecca Thatcher, Ms. Becki with an *i*. I love your lovely daughter, Andrea, minus an *i*. I like your sister Martha-Marty with a *y* and her husband Jerry also with a *y* and I'm sure I'll think their kid is cute even if there isn't a *y* or an *i*. Now, Miss Thatcher, will you please do me the honor of becoming my wife? I'll even get down on my knees if I have to, although I already have to look up to you, you big beautiful blonde. Please marry me, or don't you love me?"

"Oh, I do," she told him poignantly. "I guess I must have almost from the start or I never would have gone to bed with you. It wasn't just the chopsticks." He smiled. "But, I'm just not sure I'm the right woman for you."

"Why?"

"I don't have much education, you're so smart, and there's so much I really don't know about you, that you haven't told me."

"So I'll tell you now, but you tell me too. Yes or no."

"Tell me honestly, Arnie. Why are you asking me? Is it because people find me beautiful or is it because you just decided I was a good lay or..."

Looking embarrassed, he admitted, "Yes, that too, but also because I found out I like you so much. I enjoy being with you. I like to hear what you're saying. I want to be with you and I'd like to have a family with you, starting with Drea. She's a marvelous little girl. I'd want to adopt her, Becki, have her take my name."

"Arnie," she hesitated, "I do love you, but I just don't know."

Arnie caressed her face lightly with his fingertips, tracing the fine features, and then gently kissed her. "Good. You said at least part of what matters. We'll work on the other part. You'll say yes. I may not be able to give you a ring now since I'm going to have to buy that bastard out, but I promise one day you'll have a diamond that'll knock your eyes out."

"I don't need a diamond," Becki said softly. "You're one."

"In the rough, you mean?" he laughed.

"Well a bit more than I thought before I saw you in action just now. You get what you want, don't you?"

"Yes, usually," he agreed. "And I am going to get you. I told you before I don't give up. You're going to say yes before this weekend is over."

"You really believe that, don't you?" she replied, startled by his absolute confidence.

"Definitely. You already told me you love me. That was the big hurdle so why don't you give up now, Beauty, and just say yes."

"Arnie, you don't really know me either."

"I know enough. More than you do about me." He still had his arms around her. "Now just accept," he whispered in her ear. "Then I'll let you go."

She stood there, her head resting against his, and then very softly, she answered. "Yes."

He stepped back and looked her in the eyes and she stared back. "You won't be sorry," he promised and he kissed her, a tender, loving pledge for once devoid of passion. "We'll discuss all this when we can be alone. I'm stuck with this darn party now and have got to go back outside. Also, I have to make a call right away. Ok?"

Becki smiled faintly, not sure what she'd just done. "Of course, I'll be outside."

"You don't have to go," he said, pulling her down to sit with him, as he picked up the bedside phone and dialed. "You are going to be my new partner so you might as well hear. Hello, Tony? This is Arnie. Listen Tony, Dickie Ramsey may be coming around the office today or tomorrow. If he does, don't let him in. Tell the other security guy that he's no longer with the company and that his badge is invalid. Do you have that straight? Fine, if there're any problems, just call me out here at the Cape. I'll be here until tomorrow and then back at my house by tomorrow night.

Sure, right, no problem, thanks Tony."

"Isn't that a bit drastic?" remarked Becki after he hung up, astonished by the conversation.

"I have a feeling that Dickie isn't going to give up easily and that maybe I've trusted him more than I should. Now warned, I had better be a little careful."

"But security?" asked Becki, even more surprised. "How big is this company of yours and how come you can make all the decisions."

"I'm president and CEO," replied Arnie, "also major stock holder—fifty-one percent."

"And what does that mean?"

"It means when I started out, I couldn't swing the whole thing myself so I got some partners. Some like Dickie came in for their brains mostly. Dickie really is smart, maybe more than I am. He is a good idea man, just as he said, but he doesn't always follow through and he has a tendency to be a loose cannon. I'm a good idea man too—far better than he wants to believe, and I do follow through. Then a couple of partners came in because they had some money. We needed more than just brainpower. In fact, my sister and brother-in-law came in with some cash as joint partners; he's the lawyer and she's the CPA so they also had other useful skills we needed. They helped set up the company and gave me the legal advice as well as that additional funding. I'm hoping if I can't swing enough money to get all of Dickie's stock, that they might be able to buy a point or two. If I can't afford it, the other partners have second option to buy his shares, but I'd really like to get control of more points if I can."

"How many partners?" Becki asked.

"Seven at seven percent apiece."

"And you have security people?"

"And secretaries and sales people and programmers and..."

"Arnie, how big is your company?"

"About sixty now."

"Sixty? You have a company with sixty people?"

8

"Sure, a lot of them are out here today—at least the original crew. Sixty are probably more than we need, but we've been making lots of sales and I've been wanting to start some new design programs."

"Arnie, how much is this stock worth?"

"Why is it that the fact that you started asking me these things after you agreed to marry me, instead of before, makes me feel so much better?"

Becki's face turned red with fury. "You think I'm only interested in how much money you have? Well hell, if I had the damn ring, you could have it back." Abruptly, she started to rise, intent on walking out of the room.

"Hey, Beauty, I was just kidding. Honest." He caught at her, gently pulling her back down.

"Arnie, I thought you were just a salesman at first and then I found out you taught at MIT and did consulting. Now you're telling me you're some kind of company executive. Who are you?"

"Still the same guy you came up here to visit. The one who's been taking you out in D.C. this summer and calling you almost nightly. The one who hopes you'll move up here with Drea as soon as possible and be my family, although we may have to find an apartment instead of the house if I have to sell it."

"That house is yours?" Becki was once more shocked.

"So's this place, but I'll get rid of this first."

"You're rich!"

"As long as my company is worth something and in answer to your question, it's doing fairly well. The stock value is really on paper since we're not open to the public, but unfortunately when Dickie leaves, I have to give him seven percent of the company's current value and I'm afraid that means I'm going to have to scrape up at least a million."

"A million dollars! That means you have over seven million dollars in stock and all this property! They're going to kill you on capital gains if you have to sell those things."

"Brainless bimbo, hmm," said Arnie, digesting this comment with interest.

"I used to temp in a real estate office when Drea was a baby," she explained.

"And I bet you're good at math too."

"I was one of these eleven year olds they ask to take the SATS," she admitted.

"And how did you do on the math?"

"Top forty percent in math, top thirty percent in English."

"I see, at age eleven against the majority of college-bound juniors and seniors, when of course you hadn't had any algebra or any higher math yet."

"I was just starting. Marty always said I should go on in math, but I really wasn't interested."

"Obviously there're lots of things we both don't know about each other, but it should be fascinating finding out, don't you think?"

"I think so, but what I really think is that you should think about this marriage more."

"I'm the one who asked you, and you're asking me to reconsider. This is the oddest proposal I've ever heard of."

"I told you, particularly now that you've told me these things: I don't think I'd contribute to your life, your business, your brilliant friends."

"I don't think you're going to have to worry about my brilliant friends," he stated cynically. "Some really don't have enough common sense to come in out of the rain. But now, what are we going to do about us?"

"What would you like to do?" She hadn't thought that far ahead. She hadn't thought at all, Becki realized with increased trepidation.

"You know darn well what I'd like to do right now, but there're too many people around. Maybe I can convince a couple of the others to help close up tomorrow so we can get back to Boston early. At least we could have a nice evening in town then, just the two of us, and we'll talk about when you're going to marry me. I'd planned to take off all day Tuesday and show you around, but now I'm afraid I'll have to handle this Dickie situation at the office. Is there any way you can stay through Wednesday instead of leaving that morning?"

"I don't know. I could call and see. I had to get a regular ticket after all so I suppose I could change. Some depends on how Marty feels. Remember, the baby is due in less than a month, but they can't read calendars."

"No, I don't imagine they can," he chuckled. "I think we're going to have a good partnership, Miss Thatcher. What do you think?"

"I would like to think so, Arnie, I hope so," but she didn't sound convinced.

Arnie put his arms around her and once more kissed her gently. "But you do love me, and you think I would be a good husband. I know you'll be a good wife. We'll be a good team," he stated with confidence, "really good. Who would have thought it?" Who, Becki mentally concurred, now truly frightened at what she'd done.

Outwardly the clambake was a huge success. It was apparent that few if any knew about the Dickie incident. Becki was so bemused by what had happened and the fact that she'd agreed to marry Arnie, that she was in a daze the rest of the day and ended up drinking far more than she ordinarily did. By the time people were starting to leave or bed down for the night, Arnie had to carry her into the bedroom and she fell fast asleep.

CHAPTER 11

B Becki awoke to bright sunshine and to find Arnie sitting on the edge of the bed, just looking down at her. "How does the party animal feel?" he asked with an engaging grin. "I just came in to check if you were still alive."

"In pain. What time is it?" She glanced toward the window, squinting her eyes at the glare, before turning back to him and asking hesitantly, "Did…did I do anything really stupid?"

"Almost noon and aside from eloping with me last night, no."

"I did not...did I?" She looked at him utterly flustered. "Oh dear..."

"I should be insulted by that response," he started to tease but then seeing a horrified look appear on her face, he took pity and assured her, "No, honey, you didn't and no, you didn't do anything stupid. You just sat around quietly, smiling at people, and I think you ate three lobsters, about three dozen clams, six cobs of corn, a potato and, oh yes, probably a pound of slaw or so."

"You're lying."

"Exaggerating slightly, but I was impressed."

"Oh dear," she moaned again, rubbing her aching temples.

"I told you real food beats picking crabs. You've probably just been starving all these years."

Becki looked for something to toss at him but he shook his finger. "No, I wouldn't be able to punish you now—too many people still here," he admonished with a leer and then to his delight, she blushed. "Anyhow, I've conned a few good souls into agreeing to do the KP so we can get out of here as soon as you're ready."

"Oh Arnie, I'll help," she offered, starting to push herself up and knowing for sure now that her head was ready to explode.

Shaking his, he explained, "The con consisted of bribery. I told them they could have the place for the next few weekends. For one thing, I think I may have to come down to D.C. so we can discuss a few important items. We're still engaged, aren't we?"

"If you want."

"If I want? I thought this was a mutual agreement." This time Arnie was taken aback. He'd only been glib, not meaning to imply that the engagement might not have happened.

"Yes," Becki agreed softly, it had been.

"Good, now pack up," he said, visibly relieved. "We'll get out of here as soon as you're ready." She nodded, a big mistake, but within an hour they were driving back to Boston, not really saying anything, but both happy and Becki again feeling human. Yet although she had said yes, she was still worried.

Just before they got to the city, Arnie started heading west to catch I-95. Becki glanced at him puzzled, "I thought we were going right back to the house."

"Nope, I'm not really sure what's going to be happening tomorrow so I wanted to take you where you asked."

"Where was that?"

"Walden."

"You don't have to do that, Arnie."

"Sure, I do. We can't stay long but you wanted to see it. When you move up here, we'll bring Drea and see the whole area—the Minute Man Park, everyone's homes—Emerson, Alcott, Hawthorne. We'll even get her all the Alcott books if you don't already have them. But today, at least, you'll get to see the pond."

"Maybe," she said hesitantly, "maybe we should wait. You're worried about tomorrow. I bet you want to make some calls or something."

"Are you sure?"

"You said the area has changed. Later, when I come

back."

"That sounds nice, honey, the bit about coming back. You're going to like it up here. There's so much to see. I'll teach you and Drea to ski and we're going to do all sorts of things." Smiling contentedly, Arnie turned back towards the city and the Cambridge house, again being lucky with the parking—a good omen, he hoped.

Once they'd brought everything in from the car, he excused himself to make his calls, saying they'd probably only take a little while. But the one he made to Oregon to his sister and her husband lasted an hour and then he tried several other people unsuccessfully.

Becki was sitting in the little garden and browsing through some magazines when he joined her, looking less than his usual calm self. "Everything all right?" she asked with concern.

"Sure," he answered a bit curtly. "How about our sprucing up and tonight I'm going to take you some place really good. The black dress, right? And your hair all pinned up?"

"You have a fixation about that dress," she replied, realizing he didn't want to discuss his calls.

"Oh, Beauty, anyone would once they saw you in it."

When she was ready, he was downstairs, sitting in the living room. He was wearing a neat dark suit and looked the most dapper she'd seen. Dignified even. Somehow, she'd never equated Arnie with dignity before. Yet, of course, he had   shown   it   all   along.

He stood as soon as she entered the room. "Come here," he said with a slight smile and he handed her a black velvet case. "These are for the dress. They were your souvenir from Japan but when you wouldn't accept a ticket to come up here, I knew you wouldn't take them. I wish it were your ring, Becki, but maybe they'll do for now."

Cautiously, she opened the case and there lying on the satin interior was a string of glimmering pearls. "Oh," she said softly. "They're lovely."

"Just cultured," he admitted, "but good ones. Someday

you'll have the real thing." He reached over, pulled the string out and fastened the pearls carefully around her neck, stepping back to admire the effect. "Just what the dress needed," he declared, satisfied. "I love you, Becki, I do love you."

She turned, put her arms around him and looked into his shining eyes. "I hope I'll make you happy."

"Without doubt, Beauty, without doubt." Then taking her arm, he escorted her out. The restaurant he had selected was downtown at the historic Omni Parker House. "I may not have gotten you to Walden this time, but you might as well dine where Emerson, Grant and JFK did. Plus it's the home of Boston Cream pie," confided Arnie. "I also figured I had to give you a choice beyond seafood too," he laughed, and then laughed even harder when she started her meal not only with the famous Parker House rolls, but also clam chowder. Still, as promised it was elegant and the atmosphere romantic. The two didn't say much, just held hands and looked at each other; Becki realized she definitely was in love. By the time they'd returned to the house, she couldn't think of when she had been happier and as they lay in bed, she whispered, "Arnie, I love you too."

"You've never said that to me when we were making love."

"I didn't know if you loved me. It just feels right, Arnie, it always feels right. It did from the very start." Her fingertips traced his lips gently and then she kissed him, soft, tender little kisses. She placed her face against his, lying secure in the crook of his arm and he drew her closer. "But promise me one thing," she said.

"What's that?" he asked.

"If you ever want out, want someone else, just tell me. I couldn't stand it if you just walked out like Billy did. If you do change your mind some time, I'll leave, but just don't cheat on me. I couldn't take that again."

"Becki, what on earth are you talking about? We've just gotten engaged. Why on earth would you think I'd be planning to cheat or walk out on you? I love you. Why do you think I asked you to marry me?"

"Just promise," she demanded in a determined voice, one Arnie had never previously heard.

"I promise, ok? I promise, but can we talk about what you've promised to do, to marry me?"

"Yes," she said. "When?"

"As soon as you'll do it," he told her.

"Marty's baby is due. I've got to be there at first to help. They also need my rent until she can go back to work."

"So what are we talking here?"

"Christmas?"

"You want to wait until Christmas! Don't say that please. I'm not going to be able to get down to D.C. all that often. I know you won't come up here. Can't we compromise?"

"It's only four months—I'll have finished my AA too," Becki stated firmly.

"That seems long to me. Let's think about this. Now that we've said sooner, I really want sooner." He pulled her even closer to him, cuddling her, cajoling, "The sooner, the better. I need you, honey. You could always transfer your credits here and go on for a full degree," he added as temptation, but she didn't answer and finally they dropped off to sleep.

In the morning, Arnie left early, not awakening Becki but spending a moment before he departed, looking down at her: the long, lithe form; the golden tousled hair; the beautiful, fine-boned face. The thought that one day she'd always be there seemed unbelievable. It was a lovely way to start a day, even though this was going to be a difficult one.

In the evening when he came back from work, Arnie was quiet, preoccupied and clearly upset. Jacket slung over his shoulder, he had a solemn, tight-lipped countenance when he walked through the door. Yet he smiled as soon as he saw Becki.

To his surprise, the dining room table was set and Becki had purchased some flowers and a bottle of Chianti as well as finding some candles. There was a spicy, aromatic odor emanating from the kitchen. For after surveying Arnie's nearly empty fridge and limited pantry, Becki had spent the day walking around the neighborhood, picking up a few things for dinner. When she'd returned, she had prepared a spaghetti sauce—the source of the delectable smell, tossed a salad, and had a loaf of garlic bread ready for the oven once he arrived.

"I had a feeling you might not want to go out," she said, by explanation. "It'll only take a few minutes to boil the noodles and I can leave first thing tomorrow."

"No, please don't, not until Thursday morning. Let me have another day. I promised you I'd show you Boston, remember? Tomorrow will be better. This was really nice of you to do Becki," he said, regarding her efforts. She stared at him expectantly and Arnie knew she wasn't waiting for more compliments about the dinner so at last he said, "You were right about today. It was pretty awful, and I'm not sure everyone agrees with me. We had a board meeting of sorts and Dickie obviously has been talking to everyone. He wasn't telling the truth, of course, and about the only one strongly on my side was our one female partner."

"Had he been talking about me?" Becki asked.

"Not directly," Arnie countered.

"You'd better tell me."

"I'd rather not," he said bluntly.

"Arnie, you asked me to be your wife, your partner, what did he say?" Her voice was rising and it was clear she was agitated.

"He didn't say anything at the meeting but it was apparent that he's been telling the guys at work that I'd come in on the two of you hot at it in my bed and was jealous and canned him out of spite, that I've lost it for some two-timing bimbo." Arnie saw the hurt in her eyes and wished he could recall his words, yet he knew if they were to marry, he'd have to be honest with her.

Becki looked at him sadly, tears ready to flow. "I'm sorry. I knew I shouldn't have said yes, to have let this happen."

"You're sorry! I wanted to kill the SOB, but nothing was said directly so I couldn't refute anything and you did not let it happen."

"But they're all going to believe it, aren't they?"

"Not once they get to know you."

"Arnie, they're not going to try to know me. They're going to see me the way the Larrys and Dickie do. That's the way a lot of people were looking at me this weekend. They see I'm pretty and then I become one of those dumb blonde jokes: 'How could you tell the blonde made chocolate chip cookies? Because there were M&M shells on the floor.' I'll never have a graduate degree like you and Dickie and your friends."

"Ah shit, Becki," sighed Arnie. "Besides, Dickie doesn't have one—he blew his exams."

"Oh..."

"Why, did he say he did?"

"No, he was just patronizing me and I made a comment about not everyone having one."

Arnie laughed cynically, visualizing Dickie's hurt pride. "Oh, my. He probably thought you did it on purpose. It's a very sore point with him. Very good, Beauty, almost as good as breaking his finger, that bastard. And don't worry about the others, they'll know that's all nonsense once they meet you and talk to you."

"Arnie, no one talked to me this past weekend. Only one woman even tried, that Madge from your office, and Dickie pulled me away before I could say anything to her. I wanted to talk to your friends but they all knew each other and they just figured I was someone you'd imported for a weekend fuck, no more, no less, so why bother."

"Jesus, Becki!"

"You've had other girls out there just for a fun time," she stated, challenging.

"Well," he looked at her, "not this summer."

"But in the past. I overheard some jokes about being this summer's number."

"I'm sorry, Becki. Yes, I've dated a lot of women and

I've gone to bed with quite a few. I like sex," he stated simply.

"So, they thought I was just another one passing through. They didn't say it to my face, but you'd apparently mentioned that I modeled some. Dickie said you told him you'd picked me up in a hot singles bar. He said people were making comments about me when I got there. I guess they thought I was just the D.C. bang."

"I did not say I picked you up in a bar," Arnie protested, agitated. "And I didn't tell anyone we were having an affair although it was pretty obvious since you slept in my room. But, you've had boyfriends too. I can't help that I've had other women out there."

"Arnie, the night you met me was the first time I'd been out in months and that's because my friend Jenny wanted me along. Then she left me with that horrid Larry. It's because of the Larrys and the Dickies that I hardly ever go out. The last person I'd been dating...had sex with..." she looked down, clearly ashamed, "that was Mike. He was at the Pentagon and I met him through another girl from work. I dated him for months before I went to bed with him and then agreed probably because he told me he loved me. I seem to be a sucker for that line. I found out after that he was married and that was that. I never dated anyone before Billy. I went out a little with one of his friends after he left me and I'm not too proud of that but I was so lonely and if you haven't noticed, I like sex too." Trying to keep from crying, she added, "I met a couple of other guys but I'm shy and nothing happened. I have a really hard time getting to know people and I don't have sex with just anyone."

"I know you don't," he said, remembering her comments about the diaphragm the night she came to his room. "What do you mean you're shy? Quiet yes, but shy—you certainly weren't with me." He looked at her disbelieving.

"You've only seen me with my family and that one horrible evening at the bar. It's difficult meeting people. I'm always the one who doesn't speak in class. I never would have done any modeling if my boss's brother hadn't seen me. He's a photographer and he gave me some jobs and then helped me get a few others. They pay better than what I earn and I need the money, but that's another reason I didn't try New York. I never could have done it." She was looking at him, still trying not to cry, biting her lips nervously. "I really won't make a good company wife. I just don't know what to say to people. If I meet them one or two at a time, yes I can talk. I function fine in an office when I have things to do, but it's so hard for me. This just isn't going to work out." Now she was finally crying.

"Why did you go out with me?" he asked softly, disturbed by the sight. It was the first time he had seen her in tears. He knew she'd wanted to cry after Dickie hurt her but then she'd toughed it out.

"You were so nice to me that evening we met. You didn't try anything and you really seemed worried about me. Then when I did go out with you the next couple of times, it was so easy. You're fun to be with and you listened to me but you're different. To the others, Arnie, I'd just be a Virginia hick. I've only gone to junior college. I've never had any brilliant job. I have a little girl eight years old and I look my age so they're all going to know I was some little tramp who got knocked up in high school. They're not going to see me the way you do. They're just going to think you're one of those dumb ones who couldn't come in out of the rain and that I caught you strictly by spreading my legs."

"Well that certainly helped," he answered without thinking.

Becki gasped, horrified.

"Jesus, I was making a joke. Oh, Becki, I'm sorry!" he said, appalled at her response. "I just reacted to your comment the dumb way I sometimes do. I thought you'd laugh because you know how great I think you are. I told you I sometimes make wisecracks without thinking—it's defensive. But, I can't help if you're also as sexy as you look and if I moon over you in public because of that. Yes, I told people you were a model and I have that pinup picture Drea gave me at the office. You're the most beautiful woman I've ever dated. All that's just a fact of life too. You know I thought you were special the second I met you. I didn't keep asking you out just because I wanted to have sex with you. I hoped I would—I'm human, I'm just a man. I told you Sunday when I asked you to marry me how much I like you and Drea and your family. You say interesting things, you are interesting, and you're smart. You're just going to have to hang in there. They'll learn. Please?" He was holding her now, frantic to convince her. "Please. I do love you. Ok? We'll work on this shy thing."

"I'll try," but she whispered, still trembling.

Arnie continued holding her carefully, thinking about what she'd said and then how he had hurt her feelings. How could he have been so insensitive? Right, truly dumb as in too dumb to come in out of the rain, when all he wanted to be with her was gentle. He had always believed in being gentle with women but with Becki, he actually wanted to be protective as well. He didn't feel it was the time to say anything more so he changed the subject. "Tomorrow, we're going to have a day on the town. I'm going to show you my Boston so that you'll know that you'll like it when you come back to me and so you can tell Drea about it. We'll even get her some story books and things so she won't feel strange when she gets here." There, he thought, thinking about Drea should help. Let her consider what she's going to tell her.

"You're a nice man, Arnie," Becki said finally.

Arnie exhaled slowly, knowing he was forgiven. "I'd rather be told I'm the lover of the century."

"Which century?" she asked deadpan.

"Now who's being funny?"

"All right, you are—at least this century," and she looked at him for a moment, a small smile starting to capture her lips. "I really think you are. You're fantastic too."

"You took a while to tell me that," he remarked, relieved they were no longer experiencing an emotional crisis.

"Just like telling you I love you. There are some things I

couldn't say before, not until I knew we were going to be together...I hope," she added softly, the smile fading, and her eyes sober.

"Not hope, we are," he stated firmly, "and now you can tell me?"

"Yes, everything," she pledged, the seriousness obvious.

"Good. Can I try to be fantastic again tonight?" he teased, afraid to respond to her evident sincerity. He was in love, he was sure, but this all-encompassing emotional intimacy was something new, something to be explored and still learned.

As if understanding, Becki smiled back, the coy, seductive look reappearing. "I'd have no problem," and this time she began to rub his arm, stroking the soft down. "So many muscles. You really are deceptive, aren't you?"

"Comes in handy in the business world," he murmured, a world where he was more at home and innately understood how to act. "Does this mean we're going to skip dinner?"

"What do you want?" she asked.

"Why don't we just delay it for a while?" Taking her hand, he led her upstairs. There, pulling her onto the bed, he lay back relaxing and let her be the one to slowly woo him.

"So deceptive, but this isn't the business world," she said as she ran her hands over him, "this is better."

"Much," he agreed. Then he began to kiss her and feel her and love her.

"Definitely lover of this century," she said when they had finished. "If I recall any past lives, I'll let you know about those times too."

"You do that," he answered drowsily. "I'm just thankful for this one." Clasping her to him, he fell asleep. It was midnight by the time they finally got around to the dinner and Arnie was embarrassed, but Becki just laughed and asked if that wasn't the way the Europeans did it.

"Not quite this late, but we'll have to check that out. Would you like to go to Europe for our honeymoon?"

"I thought you were going to have to mortgage everything."

"We'll see, but I think it's time to go back to bed if we're going anywhere later today." He was right of course and the next morning, they had a slower start than expected but even though Becki didn't see as much of Boston as she might have, it didn't bother her at all.

When he took her to the airport early the following day, he was the one who felt sad this time. "Please marry me as soon as you can," he begged.

"One of us has to be practical. We'll talk. Four months—really three and a half—isn't that long, Arnie. School will be over. Marty will have her baby and can go back to work. Christmas. You'll be Drea's and my Christmas present."

CHAPTER 12

But once Becki got back to Virginia, she began to have her doubts again. When Marty and Jerry asked her about the weekend, she gave them a superficial rundown of the events but she didn't mention the ugly incident at Cape Cod, nor the fact that Arnie had proposed to her. In fact, upon being asked when she'd see him again, she hedged.

What had she done, she wondered? She loved him. She was sure of that and she thought he was sincere as well, but to actually marry him? It had been a big enough shock discovering that he wasn't just a salesman but instead a professor teaching at MIT. Now to learn that the computer company he owned was worth millions of dollars overwhelmed her. How could she possibly live with someone like that and be an executive's wife? She hadn't even been able to talk to his friends.

When Arnie called her the next night and asked how everyone had taken the news, she tried to equivocate. Then he said to her bluntly, "You haven't told them, have you, Becki? Why?"

"Arnie, I really can't talk about this now."

"People are listening?"

"Not exactly."

"What exactly, Becki? You've changed your mind?"

"Arnie, we should think about this more."

"Becki, you said that up here. I have thought of it. Do you love me?" She was quiet and he waited, worried until he demanded, "Becki, answer me."

"Arnie...I told you. I don't think this would work out."

"You still haven't answered my question," he said as calmly as possible. "Even if you hang up on me, I'm going to keep calling until you do."

"Yes..." she finally replied in a voice so low he could hardly hear her.

"Yes, as in you do love me?"

"Yes, but I'm sure this won't work, Arnie." Then she did hang up. He stared at the phone contemplatively. If he wanted to get out of this relationship, now was the time. But, if he didn't, how was he going to convince her?

The rest of the week and the next one passed but there were no more calls from Arnie. Marty and Jerry were still curious as to what had happened, but Becki revealed nothing and Jerry told his wife that it really wasn't their business.

Becki went to work, to classes, to Drea's open house at school, and seemed to be functioning, but it was obvious to those who knew and loved her that she was very upset. On school nights, she'd sit down to dinner with everyone and then as soon as the meal was over, help clean up and disappear downstairs with Drea. Once she had her daughter in bed, she'd go into her room and sit in the dark, thinking confused, sad thoughts before eventually going to sleep. Some nights she spent hours tossing and turning and other nights weeping quietly when no one would know.

The following weekend came. Becki took Drea to the library, a fast-food place for lunch as the weekly treat, and then to the supermarket to buy the week's groceries, which she and Marty alternately provided. It had been a lovely morning but while Drea was jabbering about school, Becki was inattentive. It was unusual for her to ignore Drea, but of late she seemed to be on autopilot.

As they drove back to the townhouse, she saw there was a strange car parked in front. Loaded down with grocery bags, she made her way up to the front door with Drea bounding ahead. The door opened just as she got there and Marty was waiting in the entranceway, her face beaming. "How could you keep it a secret? What wonderful news!"

Becki looked at her, puzzled, and then she heard Jerry laughing in the living room and a moment later, Arnie's voice. She felt her face go white and she was afraid she would drop the bags. Drea meanwhile had rushed into the living room. "Arnie," she was screaming happily.

A moment later, he was standing there, holding the

little girl in his arms, staring at Becki seriously with those alert brown eyes. "Hi, Beauty. Yes, how could you have kept it a secret? They didn't even know I was coming down. Here, little Beauty," he said gently to Drea, "get down so I can help Mommy." He reached over to get the bags.

"What did you tell them?" asked Becki faintly.

A wicked grin capturing his face, Arnie replied, "That I'd proposed and that you'd accepted of course, and that you had told me, which you did, that we'll be married by Christmas."

"Mommy," Drea shrilled happily, jumping up and down. "You're marrying Arnie! Does that mean you're my daddy, Arnie?"

"As soon as it takes place. Is that ok with you?" Drea's head bobbed up and down like a yo-yo and Arnie leaned over to pat it affectionately, saying, "I brought you some pictures of your new school and our house in Boston and when you fly up to see it next month, you can pick which bedroom you want and tell me how you want it fixed. Then we'll decide if a kitten or puppy would be better and I'll take you to the shore and..."

Drea broke free in excitement and rushed back into the living room where Marty had discretely retreated, squealing happily, "Aunt Marty, Uncle Jerry, Arnie says I'm going to have a kitten and can fix my new bedroom the way I want and he's going to take me to the ocean when I take an airplane to Boston next month. An airplane—why Mommy never took one before last week!"

"How could you?" uttered Becki in a low whisper as she sank down into the hall chair. The groceries were still clutched defensively in her arms.

Arnie knelt down beside her, removing the bags. Then taking her hands, he replied. "All's fair. You told me we were getting married. You said before Christmas."

"I changed my mind."

"Can't. You promised—that's an oral contract and besides, you told me you still love me." Becki looked down. "Look at me," he demanded, "and tell me you don't." She kept her eyes down and he scolded, "You can't say it so you do."

"I..."

"Tell me, Becki, and you didn't tell me you'd never been on a plane."

"But can't you see that's why I can't," she replied sadly, looking up into his now solemn, pleading face. "I told you. I've no real education, nothing. You're somebody, Arnie. I could never be the wife of a professor or a CEO."

"But that doesn't mean you don't love me," he persisted stubbornly.

"Yes, I mean no, but it's not going to work."

"Of course it is. I wouldn't have asked you if I hadn't thought it would. And that's why I had to come down here and settle this. Your daughter approves, your family approves, my family approves." Becki looked at him questioning. "You don't think I wouldn't tell my family? I told my sister and brother-in-law on Labor Day when I called them. They were delighted. I just was so worried about everything else, I forgot to tell you."

"What did you say about me?" she asked anxiously.

"That I'd met a very lovely, kind, sweet, intelligent woman in Virginia with an equally lovely, kind, sweet, intelligent daughter and that I was getting two for the price of one. Now come on, admit it, we're getting married." He put his arms around her, embracing her gently but firmly so she couldn't spring away. "You're not going to be sorry. I really love you and Drea, and we're going to have more kids, and I'm going to take care of you all. We'll live happily ever after like Peter and Heidi and eat fondue at least once a week."

Becki started laughing and Drea, who had returned, was screaming, "Fondue! Fondue again! The chocolate one too?"

"No problem," answered Arnie. "Maybe tonight if everyone wants and we can get back to the grocery store."

"Arnie, you really play dirty pool," chided Becki, but she was smiling now.

"That's what you expect from diamonds in the rough,

which reminds me." He reached into his pocket, producing two small, velvet boxes, navy blue this time. "You're still going to have to wait for the mega diamond I'm afraid." He opened the larger box and pulled out a pearl set in a gold ring with small diamond baguettes on either side. "This pearl is real so I hope it'll do until we get the diamond." Taking Becki's hand, he slipped it on her finger and she began to cry. "What, upset it wasn't the mega diamond?" he asked concerned.

"No, I never had a ring," she replied, staring at it.

"Well that's ok." Then he turned to Drea. "This one, sweetheart, is for you, to show you're engaged to become my daughter." Inside the box was a little gold ring with a minuscule pearl. Drea's eyes were large and she couldn't say anything as he placed it on her tiny finger. Wordlessly, the child threw her arms around Arnie's neck, squeezing tightly. "Not bad," he said, giving her a kiss, "but what about big Mama?"

Becki leaned forward and kissed him. Then she whispered in his ear, "You win...chopsticks again." A big smile broke out on his face.

Groceries deposited, there was a quick return to the store for the fondue ingredients and several bottles of champagne. The afternoon became more festive with even Marty having a glass to toast the betrothed, although she warned everyone that with all the excitement she might just have the baby then and there. The pictures Arnie had brought were admired, wedding dates discussed, and questions posed about the size of the guest list until Becki finally put her foot down. "All right, I'm doing it," she declared, "but just us and at Christmas like I said. Christmas Eve after I finish classes and at the Court House if we can."

"Fine with me," agreed Arnie. "Does that mean I'm invited for the holiday?" Everyone started laughing. "But that also means I get to take the bride away Christmas night for our honeymoon, ok everyone?" Drea looked a little taken aback at this prospect until Arnie assured her they'd bring back even more presents for her when they returned and that as soon as the three of them moved to Boston, she'd get her kitten.

"This is going a bit too fast for me," Becki said.

"Well, you were going a bit too slow for me," Arnie rejoined. "Even Christmas seems slow but that was what you said you wanted. And you will bring Drea up next month to see the house and school and everything so she won't be frightened."

"I'm not sure I can afford it," she replied, trying to calculate her current finances, which had been greatly depleted by the Labor Day weekend.

"My God, you're my fiancée!" he exclaimed. "Besides, I invited my daughter-to-be and she's too little to come by herself so I'll have to engage someone to chaperon her. If you don't want the job..."

Becki poked him, "You really do get what you want."

"Yes," he answered candidly. "I like to hustle if it's worthwhile." He looked at her seriously. "You're definitely worthwhile. After dinner, do you think you can escape with me for the night? I mean now that we're official..."

"Arnie, I escaped with you some other nights when we weren't. Let me talk to Marty while you finish your chef duties. Surely Drea has grated enough cheese by now."

When she went off to find Marty, Jerry stopped her and took her aside. "Jesus, Becki, you never told us who he is."

"What do you mean?" she asked baffled.

"The last time he was here, you kept calling him Arnie and he just said he was doing some computer work with MIT. I thought he was an instructor or something. I didn't realize he was the Miller who heads SofTek. That's one of the hottest software companies around, and he's supposed to have designed a lot of their stuff himself. He's brilliant! I read about him in the *Wall Street Journal*. You're going to end up millionaires, kid."

"Oh, well, it's on paper, and he just doesn't talk about it."

"It's nice to know there'll be someone rich in the family, and he seems nice besides. Drea is really crazy about him."

"He's been good to her," Becki said. "That was the deciding factor."

Jerry suddenly looked at her seriously. "You're not just marrying him because you wanted a father for Drea, are you?"

"No," she reassured him. "I do love him, Jerry. He's the kindest man I've ever been with. And, if we're half as lucky as you and Marty, it's going to be wonderful."

"I hope so, you're a good kid. But remember, we'll always be here for you." In reply, Becki reached up and gave her tall, lanky brother-in-law a kiss on the cheek.

CHAPTER 13

The autumn sped by, beginning with the arrival of Marty's little boy, Jeremy, Jr. Then there was school and the trip up to Boston, which thrilled Drea. Indeed, nothing about the impending move seemed to faze her. All Becki heard were questions from the little girl about when her new room would be painted—blue and white, Drea's selection. What kind of kitten would she have—one from the pound to save it although Arnie had originally suggested an Angora until Becki whispered something about shedding. Plus other questions like when would they go to the ocean again, was Arnie going to buy her skis for Christmas, how soon would she get the terrarium he was fixing for her and so on. Finally Becki sat Drea firmly down and explained that although Arnie was very generous, it didn't mean that he was going to give her the whole world. But then, each time he'd call, he'd talk to Drea too and it was apparent that all of these plans were well underway.

Christmas Eve was on Wednesday. The day before, Arnie arrived with gifts for all the family plus two bulging suitcases. The honeymoon, he'd warned Becki was a surprise. They would be away for two weeks and she had to pack for both warm and cold weather. Everyone seemed to know where they were going but her. Even Drea seemed to have a hint and was running round whispering and giggling although that might have just been pre-Santa excitement.

"Not to worry. I'll supervise," Marty assured Becki, making the friendly conspiracy all the more apparent. So Becki spent the night at the townhouse staying up late with her sister getting ready, and she was clearly a nervous wreck. "It's going to be fine," Marty kept reassuring her, although she too seemed to have a case of the jitters. "He's a lovely man, just what you deserve and remember, you're bigger!" At this, both broke into hysterical laughter.

Wednesday morning, Becki, Drea and Marty headed for

the law firm where Jerry worked. The marriage license had been obtained earlier and the senior law partner, a certified wedding officiant, was going to perform the ceremony. For propriety's sake as well as tradition, Jerry had left earlier with Arnie so he wouldn't see the bride.

Baby Jeremy was staying with a neighbor to Drea's distress since she thought he should witness the big event, but Marty whispered that Baby was too little for cake and he'd be sad seeing it at the wedding luncheon. Drea merely nodded, deciding that made sense; besides, Marty told her she could have his piece.

When they finally arrived at the law office, Arnie and Jerry were waiting, wearing dark suits and white roses in their lapels. Arnie for once appeared nervous, something Becki had never seen. Becki herself was dressed in dark-blue velvet and her golden hair was piled high. She was wearing the pearls from Japan and carrying a single red rose and Arnie knew for certain that she was the most beautiful woman he'd ever seen. With her was little Drea, dressed to match, and he felt as though he had been given the rare opportunity of seeing Becki both as a child and an adult—an eerie but fascinating vision.

When the lawyer read the vows, Arnie was the one who seemed to have lost his voice while Becki answered softly but firmly. But as soon as he'd placed the plain gold band on her finger, he drew her to him and kissed her tenderly. "I can't tell you how happy I am."

She had her arms tightly around him, not wanting to let go. "I love you, Arnie. I'm always going to love you."

"And I you," he pledged, more certain now about emotional intimacy. Then he whispered, "Does this mean I can stay in your room tonight? I checked out of the motel."

Becki gaily broke into peals of laughter and answered softly, "It's Christmas Eve. No one's going to be sleeping too much."

"Who said anything about sleeping?"

The wedding luncheon was followed by festivities at the house with neighbors and friends dropping by to bring gifts and wish the newlyweds well. By the time an excited Drea was in bed, Arnie had moved their luggage into the car and Becki was helping get the stockings filled. Then with the remains of a bottle of champagne—the last of several consumed over the afternoon and evening—they collapsed into Becki's bed and arms around each other, dozed off. Several hours later, there was loud pounding on the door and Drea was inquiring if Santa had come. Becki looked in horror at Arnie. "I fell asleep!"

He looked back, equally chagrined. "So did I." The two dissolved into laughter. "Some wedding night, sweetheart," Arnie said, giving her a kiss. "Definitely we'll never tell anyone about this, promise."

"I promise," she declared wholeheartedly before laughing again. Then they got out of bed to go upstairs and see what Santa had brought and share an early holiday brunch. Shortly before noon, they arrived at Dulles Airport and Becki learned that the first stop on their honeymoon would be Portland, Oregon, to spend Christmas evening with Arnie's family.

"What if they don't like me?" she asked worried.

"What's not to like?" he replied, surprised at her concern. "I've told them all about you."

"Everything...all about Drea?"

"Becki, you've nothing to fret about. Of course they know all about Drea and how I met you. You'll get along fine."

Becki of course was far from sure, but amazingly, what he'd said was true. When they arrived late Christmas afternoon, Arnie's brother-in-law, Mel, was waiting at the airport with his two little boys. "The rest of the gang are at our house," the thin, slightly balding man explained. "We figured we'd let Becki meet us gradually. Welcome to the City of Roses, Mrs. Miller." Then he turned to his sons. "Boys, this absolutely gorgeous lady is your new Aunt Becki, although how your uncle managed to accomplish that, I'll never know."

"Mrs. Miller..." Becki turned to Arnie, her eyes radiant.

"That's the first time I've been called that."

"Well, I expect you'll get used to it over the next fifty years or so."

"It finally seems real," she sighed, a happy little smile crossing her face.

"About time," he answered, smiling back, and then they all hurried off to meet the rest of Arnie's family, which consisted of Eileen, her small daughter, Arnie's mother, and even his grandmother Leah, a diminutive, distinguished woman in her late eighties.

"So beautiful, Arnie," said the white-haired lady, peering closely through her thick glasses at the new bride, before patting Arnie on the hand. "You didn't lie. She is too good for you."

"Hey, Grandma, you're not supposed to say things like that about your favorite grandson."

The tiny woman turned back to Becki. "Arnie is my only grandson, but he's a good boy. He'll take care of you. I'm happy I've seen his wife. He was taking a long time but now I know why. Welcome." Becki leaned over to kiss the little woman and had the sudden realization that not only was she now the next Mrs. Miller, but she really had a new family and that they were indeed truly welcoming her.

The Christmas party lasted so late that night that both the newlyweds once more fell sound asleep as soon as they'd collapsed in bed. Early the next morning, when they awoke, they started laughing again. "Why, Arnie?" Becki asked, honestly perplexed. "We could find time before we married. Does this mean that marriage is going to kill our sex life?"

"God, I hope not," he answered fervently but when he reached for her, they heard his niece Molly at the door.

"Uncle Arnie, Uncle Arnie, you promised you'd play 'Uncle Wiggly' with me. Uncle Arnie!" The small shrill voice started getting louder and louder as little Molly began beating on the door.

"It's a conspiracy," he announced, shaking his head woefully.

Becki was just chortling by now, "Go on, Uncle Arnie.

You said we were leaving tonight. Surely we'll find some place just for the two of us."

"I swear," he declared fervently. "You try to get more sleep." Then he found his clothes and went out into the hall to appease the precocious and stubborn child, thinking that perhaps Drea wasn't as persistent after all.

Late that evening, he and Becki were on another plane headed for Honolulu and Becki had solved the puzzle of one of her suitcases. When they arrived early in Oahu the next morning, they were met by a car and driven to Turtle Bay on the northern end of the island. Arnie had rented a condominium townhouse near the resort hotel. When Becki saw it, she could hardly believe the beauty. The condo was tastefully decorated but it was the patio with a small swimming pool and earthen pots filled with exotic tropical plants, including birds-of-paradise and orchids, that overwhelmed her. "Arnie, it's Eden! I never thought I'd see anything like this. How can any place be so gorgeous?"

"How does the quote go? 'And beauty shall surround her…' except you're beauty itself."

"You're beautiful too," she declared.

"You know that's not true, honey."

"You are in my eyes." Hers were shining with joy.

He leaned forward and placed delicate kisses on her lids unable to tell her how happy she had made him. "Well," he finally said, "we can have a swim and get an early breakfast at the hotel after we unpack or, God damn it, we can finally go to bed and let me make love to you!"

"At this point, I think we could take turns doing that," Becki concurred, "provided…"

"Provided what?"

"Provided we can stay awake," and she started laughing.

"Mrs. Miller, you have a wicked, sadistic sense of humor," accused a pleased Arnie as he grabbed her and carried her into the bedroom. "I intend to stay awake and I intend to keep you awake." Putting her on the bed, he proceeded to do just that before both again fell asleep.

The last thing he heard before he did was her

whispering, "You were fantastic, Mr. Miller."

"About time you said it," he grumbled, but he was very, very happy. It was late afternoon when they awoke. "Come on," Arnie said, "clean up and we'll go over to the hotel and have a drink while the sun sets. We'll eat there tonight, and I think they have some music if you'd like to dance. Tomorrow they're supposed to have a fabulous champagne brunch, and we can get in some beach time."

"Hmm," she murmured lazily. "Do I have to dress up?"

"Nope. This is Hawaii. Just a sundress. Then maybe Monday or the next day we'll go into Honolulu and I'll buy you a mou mou, although to cover you up like that would be a sin."

"I thought the missionaries made the women wear them so they wouldn't sin," Becki grinned.

They got to the hotel just in time to see the sun's final descent into the Pacific. There Becki stared in awe at the rushing breakers and spectacular colors streaking across the sky, feeling as though she were in some movie. "Arnie," I can't believe I'm here. It's so beautiful."

"Just what you deserve, sweetheart." When the pretty Hawaiian waitress came, he ordered piña coladas, promising, "They come in different flavors here, so we'll just start working our way through the selection." Eventually they got some dinner, but mostly they sat holding hands and looking out on the ocean, watching the emerging stars and moon, which was full and brilliant, lighting up the rolling waves of rippling silver—nature's decorative holiday tinsel.

"Remember the night at the Cape, our own private picnic?" asked Becki softly.

"How could I not remember?" he answered half-indignant that she'd even have to ask. "That's the night I was sure I had to marry you. I'd been thinking about it already but I knew for certain then, you big beautiful blonde."

She smiled sultrily and leaned forward, taking his hand, squeezing softly. "My sexy little man."

He grinned back. "How about another piña colada?"

"You're getting me drunk. That's also what you did at

Cape Cod."

"You got yourself drunk there, and who cares? We're on our honeymoon. We've only got to walk a few yards to the condo. Besides if we can't, I understand they send a golf cart." Becki laughed, not knowing whether to believe him or not. "Live dangerously, Beauty," he urged.

Becki nodded happily in agreement and by the time they got back to the condo, she was more than slightly tipsy and unable to stop giggling. Arnie had never seen her this way, even at the Cape where she'd been inebriated but quiet. Here she was such a happy drunk that he was amused and he helped her into the house.

"The pool," she demanded imperiously, her voice rising. "We've got to go in the pool."

"Are you sure you wouldn't rather lie down?"

"No! Definitely the pool, lover boy. I love water. I love you. Live dangerously. That's what you told me," she challenged and started to strip off her clothes in the living room, tossing garments here and there, more daring than she'd ever acted or even felt as Arnie watched in amazement. Laughing, she pushed open the patio doors and ran outside.

"Well, if you insist," Arnie said, shaking his head in wonder. Following her lead, he undressed hurriedly and was outside within a minute. The townhouse was an end one and no one was currently on the other side so being totally natural didn't seem such a bad idea. "Where are the lights for this thing?" he called.

"No lights," she called back. "Find me." Because it was dark, he lowered himself cautiously into the small pool instead of diving and began to swim slowly across. His eyes hadn't adjusted to the dark yet and he wasn't quite sure where she was until suddenly, he felt her swim up behind and grab hold of him. "Caught you," she giggled.

"I thought I was supposed to be finding you?"

"Same thing," she whispered. "Kiss me."

"Let's get to the side," he said. "I'd hate for there to be headlines tomorrow about a honeymoon couple drowning during a midnight tryst."

"It's not midnight," she asserted.

"It's past that at home," he bantered.

"Spoilsport," she countered, still giggling.

Then with one arm on the pool's side, he put his other around her, drawing her close. "Is this what you wanted?" he whispered into her ear as he began to kiss her.

"Hmm," she murmured, hungrily kissing him back, her arms around his neck.

"Nice," he said. "But I think maybe I'm getting some other ideas too." He kissed her again. "Definitely ideas. Why don't you hold onto the side here and let's see what else we can do in the pool." Becki put her arms over the edge and her chin was resting on the smooth tiles. From behind, he held on to her, his hands pressed against her breasts. "This was a very good idea, Beauty," he breathed as he started kissing her neck and the tops of her shoulders.

"Arnie," she suddenly said. "I'm not wearing anything now. I took my diaphragm out before dinner. Maybe I should go back inside."

"Hey," he coaxed persuasively, "we're married now. You said you wanted another kid. I want one. So if it happens, it happens but what are the laws of probability?"

"I do, Arnie, but..."

"But you were the one who wanted to go swimming. I like swimming with you, Beauty, at least in a pool. I don't have to be afraid you're going to be halfway across the ocean. Not to worry, just hold on tight," and he entered her from behind, pushing her down upon him, one strong hand tight upon her waist, the other holding onto the cool tiled ledge.

"Arnie," Becki moaned no longer resisting, "Arnie."

"That's right, sweetheart. Just feel the water buoying us up, just relax. You hold on and I'll do the work. Nice work. Definitely the right way to spend time in the pool."

When they were done, he turned her around and held her pressed closely to him, his arms passing under hers to grasp the edge of the pool and hers tightly twined around his neck. "You are fantastic in all elements," he whispered. She was quiet, her head resting against his shoulder, breathing softly, and her long blonde hair stirred gently in the water.

"Time to go in?" he finally asked, and Becki nodded her head. "Ok, you wait here and I'll get some towels." Arnie pulled himself out of the pool and went inside. Moments later, he came back and the brilliant silvery moon had come out from behind a cloud so he could see her. She was floating on her back, her hair now spread out trailing, and he thought she looked like Aphrodite. No question in his mind, she was the goddess of love for him.

"Swim over here, Beauty," he called softly. Becki looked up and smiled at him. When she got to the edge of the pool, he gave her a hand up and then wrapped her carefully in the large beach towel. "You have no idea how you looked in there. Now I know how some of those artists used to get their inspiration."

The rest of the time in Hawaii was a dream for Becki. She was properly solemn at the Arizona Memorial, curious as they explored Chinatown, amazed by the huge hotels of Waikiki, and fascinated by the Mission Houses. "So few people," she mused, "and they changed a whole culture."

"Sometimes it only takes one," answered Arnie pragmatically, momentarily back in Cambridge wondering how SofTek's newest program was progressing. He'd been working practically non-stop before leaving for Virginia and hoped he'd caught the last flaws. The other programmers had assured him that they'd work these out, in spite of the holiday, and have something to show him when he returned.

"Well, I guess it was lucky for us but maybe not for them and who would have thought that this is where prefab houses started" Becki commented, remembering one of her course lectures and totally unaware of Arnie's mental lapse. Bemused, she studied the little buildings that had been constructed in early nineteenth-century New England. Dismantled, the structures were shipped around the Cape in wooden sailing vessels so that the missionaries could live on a tropical paradise the way proper New Englanders did at home and in proper New England homes.

"Spoken like a true interior decorator," remarked Arnie, once more grounded in Hawaii.

"Oh no, I would have lived the way the islanders did," she protested strongly. Arnie had no doubt that she would for it was soon apparent that the natural sights pleased her most. Although they had spent some time on the beach, Arnie was so terrified of her lengthy swims out into the ocean that he decided that tourism and time by the pool was the solution, even if he had to continue plying her with piña coladas. Becki cheerfully succumbed to the ploy and they drove around the island stopping at the various tourist spots, sometimes a bit to Arnie's consternation such as the time she insisted on sitting at the Halona Blowhole for almost an hour.

"Becki, are we ever going to get out of here?" he asked plaintively, unaccustomed to waiting for anything at length.

"It'll blow. You've got to learn patience."

Arnie merely shook his head in disbelief and then to his amazement, as if by magic, the lofty plumes of spray spewed forth like spume from a whale. Becki grinned, and even though he knew it was merely the matter of the currents being exactly right, he felt as though she'd willed it. Some of the frothy foam reached twenty or thirty feet and reminded him of geysers at Yellow Stone. Moreover there was the added beauty of small rainbows forming as the sun's rays passed through this spouting mist.

Becki also made him hike the two miles up to the Sacred Falls, while Arnie complained that being on vacation didn't mean having to work. "Too much roast pig and overkill on piña coladas," she retorted, reaching out her fingers for a playful pinch, implying weight gain. He merely rolled his eyes as she said, "We need this. Besides, we can swim in the pool at the falls."

"You are such a water nymph," he half-complained, detaching her fingers which had nipped, reminding him that he'd not been exercising in the last frantic weeks. Becki didn't reply but instantly she realized his comment was true. So much of her life seemed to be influenced by water: her childhood home by the Potomac, her parents and the Bay, Aunt Mary's riverside house, losing her virginity and getting pregnant by the river, the times at the shore with Billy and Mike, staring at the river the night she decided to go to Arnie, realizing at the Cape she loved him, and now on this small island having her honeymoon with him, maybe even becoming pregnant again. Water, one way or another, was a key element in her nature. She had even been born under its zodiac sign in late January, something she had never considered before.

Yet of all their ventures, it was the day they went over to the Polynesian Cultural Center with its tiny, recreated South Pacific villages that intrigued Becki the most. Run by a branch of Brigham Young University, the center was staffed by the students from various islands, who were duplicating real portions of their cultural heritage. For the first time, Arnie found himself having to tear her away from the sundry exhibits. All Becki's usual timidity had disappeared and she ended up talking with people at each and every stop. Soon she had accumulated gifts of tiny figures made of palm fronds and other handmade souvenirs from the demonstrations since the exhibitors genuinely responded to Becki's enthusiasm, far beyond their usual polite exchange with tourists. "I've never seen you ask so many questions," observed Arnie, as they waited for the luau and dinner show that night in the center's outdoor theater.

"But it's been wonderful, Arnie!" Becki enthused. "Those people literally running up the coconut palms and the way they really make coconut milk and do that intricate feather work and all the other crafts. Especially the woodcarving—imagine, a real war canoe! I didn't have to learn this from *Jeopardy*. It was like going all over the Pacific."

"Well, maybe we can do that one day and take a cruise around the world. The next time we're here, we'll island hop and hope the volcano is active on the Big Island. I want to go to Kauai too—it's supposed to be the Garden Island and has a great canyon. We'll go horseback riding on the beach the way they show in the movies."

"You mean there're places you haven't been? And I've seen you try to ride with Drea," Becki teased, shaking her head in mock resignation.

"I didn't fall off and I didn't notice you being all that graceful," he replied, with wounded dignity.

"Drea didn't fall off either and I never said I could ride," she retorted.

"Yeah, just on pigs. I still think they're for eating—particularly roasted in a pit although the poi I could do without." Arnie grimaced at what he considered to be an unappetizing and even less appealing dish. "But we'll do the other islands next time." He leaned over, draping his arm around her, and gave her a discrete kiss suitable for the public. Quietly though, he whispered suggestively, "Are you sure you want to stay and see this, Mrs. Miller, and not just come to the condo with me?"

"You can swallow fire?"

"No, but I know some other tricks, like maybe knowing how to start one."

"No, and stop leering. Besides, you know you wanted to see this too. You said it was probably the most authentic show on the island. You'll just have to show me your tricks later," she whispered back.

"Promise."

"Oh, no doubt," she readily agreed, with a sexy little look.

The next morning they rose late after Becki had kept her promise to Arnie. It was New Year's Eve and their last day on Oahu so they went over to the hotel, spending the day alternating between the beach and the large pool. Becki still could not get Arnie to tell her where they were going next. She knew they were supposed to be gone two weeks but so far only one had passed.

That night they returned to the hotel for dinner. There were parties of boisterous holiday celebrants around them, many obviously local, displaying the whole array of Hawaiian ethnicity. Yet the two might as well have been alone and they danced late into the night to welcome in the New Year.

Although Becki wasn't festooned in the Viennese ball gown as he had once fantasized, Arnie decided reality was better. She wore the black and white mou mou he'd purchased for her, with the string of pearls and white orchids in her hair. She looked radiant and he felt he was the luckiest man while she was thinking she'd never been so happy.

"Tomorrow," Arnie had kept saying mysteriously through that last day when she tried to learn their next destination. "You'll know as soon as we get to the airport and I've got a present for you."

CHAPTER 14

E arly the next morning, when they were checking in at the airline counter, Arnie pulled out two passports and handed her one. "Here, you'll need this."

"A passport? How did this happen?" Becki was shocked as she received the small booklet, which seemed to promise the world. It was something she'd never expected to have.

"Don't you remember those nice Polaroids we took when you were in Boston and the fact that Jerry was having you sign some papers? You really should read what you sign, sweetheart."

"He told me he needed them for the lawyer so we could get married at the office," she replied archly. "I thought I could trust my own brother-in-law."

"Well, it was a surprise and if you look up at that board, you'll see where we're going." Raising his hand, Arnie pointed casually over the counter to the departures listing.

"Tokyo!" Becki gasped. "How can we afford this? Hawaii and now Japan?"

"Business for me, Beauty. Frequent flyer miles for you and not buying the diamond ring paid for Hawaii. My expenses in Japan will be picked up and you're along for the ride."

"Arnie!" Her eyes were almost luminous, "Japan. I'd never even been anywhere before I met you and now I'll have crossed the Pacific."

"The first few days are going to be meetings for me, honey, but we're staying at a nice hotel and I've arranged tours of Tokyo for you. I've got to warn you though, Japanese businessmen believe partying is part of the process and without wives, not even big beautiful blonde ones, so I may have to stay out late a couple nights but I'll be good. I promised, remember?"

Becki nodded her head solemnly and he continued,

"The first time I was there, I didn't realize I wasn't supposed to empty my glass and before I knew it, I was three sheets to the wind. I've been doing my homework since about Japanese customs. Then after I finish the work portion, I thought we could travel outside of Tokyo for a couple of days to one of the resort spots—even take the *Shinkansen*—that's the high speed bullet train. We can stay in a *ryokan*, one of the old inns, maybe at one of the hot springs, and by the way," he reached into his pocket, "here's your present."

Puzzled, Becki unwrapped the proffered package of beribboned tissue and then broke out into a huge grin. Inside the narrow, little box lay a pair of lacquered chopsticks encrusted with mother-of-pearl. "I said I'd learn to use them but these are too pretty."

"Right," he answered. "But you'd still better practice. Otherwise you're going to be very hungry."

"I'm not sure about the raw fish," she murmured doubtfully. "I never liked raw oysters, even at home."

"That's ok, I don't either. I told you I wanted mine fried, New Orleans style; but, you're going to love tempura and the pickled vegetables and their beer. We'll drink Saki too and good green tea and maybe try Kobe beef, provided our Japanese hosts invite both of us to dinner. That's probably the one item that would break my budget, but somehow your coming along is unlikely. Women just aren't part of the business scene here and the Japanese really separate the home from work. Madge Norris, the gal you liked from work, came out on one trip and they just didn't know how to deal with her. They were either uncomfortable and aloof, or downright patronizing, so we decided afterwards that I or a male partner would make the other trips. She likes Europe better anyhow."

"You haven't really told me what you'll be doing in Japan. I know you've gone over a couple of times, but why?" Becki asked as they sat at the departure gate, waiting to board.

"Well, remember how I said our software deals with money and also more efficient ways to manage businesses?

Numbers are numbers and money is money whether it's dollars or pounds or yen. The same thing with efficient business practices like tracking payrolls or expenditures or sales, whether you're running an insurance company or..."

"A chopstick factory," Becki teased playfully, fingering the little box he'd given her.

"Definitely. Got to make sure that runs efficiently," he grinned back. "Anyhow, we may have been early with this tracking, a kind of computerized spread sheet that can be updated automatically, but it's not going to be long before other people are selling them too. Now we could try to control access to our model through copyright laws, but it doesn't take much for someone to make a few changes and claim it as their own, particularly if you're dealing with people in other countries where it would be hard to prove. In fact, we actually lost out on one of our programs that way almost as soon as it debuted and I've never figured out why.

"I personally believe it's better to cut potential competitors in on the deal from the very start so that they'll not only have an interest in protecting the current product but any updates. Also, if they're sole distributors in their countries, they're going to make sure no one else subverts their market. This industry is changing so fast, Becki. What's state of the art now is going to be like an adding machine in a couple years. Of course in the short run, we'd make more money by just trying to be the sole proprietor and distributor."

She considered this for a moment and then remarked, "So you deal them into the process at ground level. They, in turn, cover your back so you never have to worry about them cheating, and ultimately you probably make more with them as foreign partners than you would if they hadn't been invited aboard."

"In a nutshell, my brainy Beauty. I wish a couple of my partners could have understood that principle. I may control the company but I like consensus and we went around and around on this. Fortunately one of them is gone. I never could understand why he was so against this."

Becki stared at Arnie, not saying anything at first, but knowing of course whom he meant. Finally she commented, "You said Dickie thought he was smarter than you and that maybe he was right about that. I don't think so, Arnie."

"Me neither now, Beauty. I told you I picked the right partner that day. I also think the Japanese are making a big mistake by not taking advantage of all that nice feminine brainpower. We're going to make a business woman out of you yet."

She shook her head. "I think I'd rather be a tourist."

So, the first morning in Tokyo, while Arnie was off to his appointments, Becki, carefully bundled up for the nippy Japanese winter, now understanding the need for the second suitcase. Her days of sightseeing were to begin with the Imperial Palace District. The little tour bus started from the hotel, a bit frighteningly on the left hand side of the road, but another indication that she truly was in a foreign land. It then passed the financial district where Becki knew Arnie was having a meeting. Next it went to the Otemon entrance to the palace and the passengers walked to the garden. On the way, she was surprised to hear bloodcurdling shrieks. The English-speaking guide, with his surprising British accent, explained they were passing the National Police Agency dojo where students were practicing martial arts. In all, it was a fascinating and exotic day for her, but when she returned to the hotel, there was a message from Arnie that indeed he would not return until late. She dined alone, reading her guidebook until he returned.

The next day was much the same except this time the tour covered several shrines and ended up with the afternoon at the Tokyo National Museum. There she saw everything from archeological objects to the officially designated National Treasures. Again Arnie returned late.

The third day he finished his business and that evening he took her to a little *robatayaki*, Japan's equivalent of the local pub. Very informal, it was a place where they could order a casual dinner a la carte and drink beer at the counter while picking different items to be grilled. Becki particularly liked the shitake mushrooms and the *ao-to* or green peppers. "I thought you'd like the *kare-shio-yaki* too," Arnie said as he had her try the grilled flounder.

"Too salty," she complained after a bite from his proffered chopsticks.

"Try some with wasabi. It should remind you of all that hot stuff you eat at home."

He handed her the tiny dish of Japanese horseradish, innocently pistachio green in color, and then had to laugh at the surprised expression on her face after she'd taken a mouthful. "Told you so," he said smugly as tears came to her eyes and she frantically reached for his beer.

"Beast!" she managed to gasp.

"Of course, my dear Beauty."

The following morning, before catching a late train, they went to one of the large Tokyo department stores to purchase lacquer ware, some small ceramics, printed fabrics, and bright woodblock prints as gifts and souvenirs. Becki, who still hadn't got a clear idea of the current money exchange, was positive these must be exorbitant and was then shocked when Arnie insisted on buying her a rich red silk kimono and even a small blue one for Drea. After he took her to a jewelry counter and they picked out a pair of real pearl earrings.

"Arnie, how can we afford all this?" asked a concerned Becki.

"I told you, sweetheart, the business expenses are legitimate and the other I explained. Besides, I, for one, only plan to get married once and this is our honeymoon, even if I haven't been able to spend that much time with you in Tokyo. I do not consider the classes you registered for at Boston U. to be your only Christmas gift. The business this trip should generate will undoubtedly allow me to pay back my grandmother for her loan, and you know I've rented out the Cape place for two years, which means no second mortgage on that. All I really need is to earn enough to make the double mortgage payments on the house and I can do that; we'll just have to live a bit frugally for a while. I'll have the loans I needed for Dickie's stock paid off in no time. Honest. That's our financial situation shrunk to fit one of your nutshells."

"Maybe I should forget school and get a job." Becki's face flushed in memory of the necessity for the loans.

Arnie looked at her, sorry he had brought up the matter. He knew that her salary would be small and too insignificant to be of any great contribution unless she aggressively pursued the modeling, which he didn't think she wanted to do. Modeling, he'd soon realized, had been undertaken for the money alone and although outwardly calm when she worked, Becki was actually highly nervous and unhappy during these sessions. He'd never press her to continue.

Gently he said, "Becki, I want you to go to school, to have time to be there for Drea, to get to know Boston. This is going to be a year of adjustment for us all. We're going to do just fine, trust me." God, he thought, I probably draw down as much from MIT for teaching that one seminar course as she'd make in two or three months in some office or shop, and he hoped he'd assured her, without insulting her offer.

That afternoon, they boarded the famed bullet train and by evening had arrived at a small one-story wooden inn in the country. When Becki saw the garden view, highlighted by snow-covered mountains in the distance, she sighed in appreciation of the beauty. "Those Japanese prints, Arnie, they're real. I never would have believed it." Then the two were escorted to their simple, *tatami* room by a kimono-garbed maid, who soon returned with cups of refreshing, hot green tea.

After a long, hot and sensually relaxing bath, they put on the *yukatas* or cotton kimonos and the silent little maid returned with their dinner, served privately on a low lacquer table in their room. When she left, Arnie turned to Becki, "Someone more quiet than you." Becki gave a soft laugh and poked him with the chopsticks.

"So that's the way you've been practicing with those,"

he chided, as he poured her the warm Saki. Then picking up his own sticks, he began to feed her soba noodles, sukiyaki and other tasty items. "You'd starve if I weren't here. Drea does better than you."

"Tomorrow," she promised. "Let's practice something else today." So once the dishes had been removed and the futons unrolled, they snuggled together. "Beats lying on the beach," she remarked.

"But still romantic," he murmured, wondering how someone so gentle, so innocent, could be so passionate.

"Oh, yes. I think most times with you will be romantic."

"That's nice. I'll try."

"I know you will," she answered happily. "Me too."

Two days later they were headed back on a direct flight to the states with a change in San Francisco. For this Arnie apologized, "Sorry we couldn't do California too, Beauty."

"Arnie, you've shown me more of the world in the last two weeks than I've seen in the rest of my life."

"Well, it's just the beginning, Becki. Once we get your things up to Boston and get settled in, there'll be all sorts of adventures for us to have."

She looked at him seriously. "Just marrying you is one."

CHAPTER 15

After arriving in Boston with the small U-haul carrying Becki's few possessions, everyone started at school and gradually settled comfortably into their new home life. Only the loss of Arnie's beloved grandmother marred the first year. But then, as if in some divine compensation, it soon became apparent that Becki, not Arnie, had been correct about the law of averages. Their first child was due in late September.

Arnie now began to worry how Drea would accept a new sibling. "Shouldn't this be a mother-daughter thing?" he asked nervously, when Becki insisted he be the one to tell the little girl.

"I'd prefer father-daughter bonding," she answered reasonably. "Drea loves you. Tell her she's the first one you've told."

"She will be," he replied, and finally, reluctantly, he agreed. That afternoon, he told Drea he had to go and pick up a few things at the grocery, asking if she would like to come along. Perhaps they could stop for an ice cream and spoil their appetites for dinner, he hinted. Drea was delighted at the prospect and the two walked towards the neighborhood market. Purchasing a couple of cones at one of the shops, they crossed the street to a small park and sat there on a bench even though it was a chill winter afternoon as March was determined to leave like a lion.

"Drea," Arnie began a bit hesitantly. She looked at him expectantly, her blue eyes wide. "I have something to tell you." Now she looked concerned. "Your mommy and I have decided to have a baby," he continued, apprehensive of her response. Suddenly there was a beautiful smile on her face so similar to Becki's that he felt unbelievingly tender towards the child. If he could care for Drea so much, he knew that the new baby would be one of the finest things that could happen to him and he hoped for them all.

"Oh," Drea squealed. "I've wanted one forever but Mommy said we couldn't until I had a new daddy. Does that mean you're really my daddy now, Arnie?"

"I think so, I hope so." He wasn't quite sure what to say.

"Do I call you Daddy?" she asked practically.

"If you'd like," he answered. "I think I'd like that very much."

"Can I call you Arnie too, if I want?" she continued, the pragmatic child.

"You can call me whatever you like."

"You're so silly, Arnie Daddy. You wouldn't like it if I called you Kermit the Frog or something like that."

"I didn't think I looked like a frog."

She looked at him for a moment earnestly and then said, "No, more like Fozzie Bear." Arnie smiled and Drea leaned over and gave him a sticky kiss. "Can we have one of each?" she then asked to make sure she'd covered all bases.

"They usually come one at a time," he replied.

"Well, I hope you'll try again after," she said seriously.

Arnie started laughing. "I think you're going to have to talk to your mother about that, but let's just try for this one now, ok? I also think we'd better get going before I turn as blue as Fozzie."

"That's Grover," Drea corrected, but then nodded her head and it turned out to be as simple as that.

Leah was an easy baby even though several weeks premature. In some ways, it was as though she had two mothers for Drea doted on her. But with the infant's arrival, Becki argued that she should stay at home. Arnie insisted that she continue at least one class a term and she moaned that she'd be old before she had her degree.

"Yeah, in your thirties, all washed up like me," he retorted.

Yet it was a good time for them all. He had to travel some and because of the children, Becki couldn't come, but she appeared content with her new family and school and a home of her own. Nor did she complain at the long hours he worked. Their social life was limited but again he was too busy to miss it, and she apparently wasn't interested.

Then a year after Leah's birth, he arrived home early one August afternoon. As he walked into the kitchen, he saw her standing at the counter. The radio was on and she was softly singing along to an old folk tune. She was wearing one of his worn-out work shirts and a pair of white shorts and her legs stretched down long and brown from the summer sun. Her figure was as beautiful as when he'd met her and he came up quietly behind her, putting his arms around her and placing a kiss on the nape of her neck.

"Arnie, you scared me." She turned her head, a big smile appearing on her face.

"How did you know it was me?" he asked. "It could have been the Boston strangler."

"I knew, but I didn't expect you for hours."

"That's why I came to check if the milkman's here."

"He came in the morning. It's the plumber's turn in the afternoon," Becki giggled.

"I didn't know we needed a plumber," he remarked casually.

"We," she emphasized the *we*, "don't."

"Ah, I see," he said, as he moved his hands up to touch her breasts and kissed her neck again. "Did I ever tell you that the Japanese think the nape of a woman's neck is really sexy?" He nuzzled her some more. "Easy to see why when you think about it." Becki made a little purring noise. "Where's Leah?" he abruptly asked.

"Taking a nap," she mumbled.

"And Drea shouldn't be home from day camp for a while, right?"

"No," she sighed.

"Hmm..." He unpinned her hair, letting it cascade down. Then he slipped one hand into the front of her shorts and began to stroke downward. "My beautiful blonde from top to bottom," he murmured.

"You're kinky," she accused mildly.

"Just horny." He unzipped the shorts and pulled them

and her underpants down. "Step out and bend over."

"You're crazy, Arnie," but she wasn't complaining.

"Nope," he said and bent to kiss her lovely derriere. "Most beautiful fanny in the world," he avowed.

"I'm not wearing anything," she cautioned suddenly.

"That's ok. You said you wanted another baby, right? Isn't this how we did it last time...spontaneity?"

"Yes," she agreed softly.

"Definitely the prettiest ass in the world." He separated her legs and then unzipped his slacks and entered her, whispering, "So nice, so very, very nice."

She pushed back against him, making little panting and moaning sounds as he pressed her against the counter, holding her by her breasts and squeezing gently. His face was buried in her sweet smelling hair and she felt soft and warm all over. "God, this is wonderful," he sighed, and then it really was. For a moment after, he just leaned over her, covering her, feeling the light perspiration on her skin. She was still quivering slightly. Then he straightened, pulling her up with him, and clutched her to him. "You are the sexiest woman in the world."

"Well you're not so bad yourself," she finally said, once more breathing normally, "but that certainly was a surprise."

"I was in the neighborhood and I thought this would beat lunch at the deli."

"Thanks. You are so romantic."

"I also thought I might like to take you to dinner some place special tonight if you can get a sitter."

"I was working on dinner when you so rudely interrupted me."

"I wasn't rude," he protested.

"Well, will you let me go so I can get dressed now?" she asked, staring down at the abandoned clothes, lying in a heap at her feet.

He smiled. "Probably not a bad idea. I'd hate to shock the plumber."

"Or the Boston Strangler," she added.

"Not funny, Beauty. You should keep the doors

locked."

"He was caught years ago and I was going in and out, Arnie." She had her clothes back on. "Now what's the occasion?"

"An order big enough that not only should this year's profits pay back the mortgage on this place but put all three kids through college."

"Arnie! The deal went through and we only have two."

"I'm optimistic, Beauty." He gave her another kiss. As it turned out, nine months later Bruce arrived, a healthy seven-pound eight-ounce baby, named for Becki's father.

"Are you sure we shouldn't name him after you?" Becki had asked.

"You know how I feel about the name James. You named Leah for someone I loved; this is only fair," Arnie had replied. Then when he saw the baby, he knew he'd been right for the little boy was long and lean like Becki and her father. "Our basketball player. He's beautiful, Becki, just like you, and if he's half the man your dad was, we have a winner."

"All our children are beautiful," she answered pleased, but Arnie felt a little sad knowing that Leah, although cuddly, cute and bright, definitely was not. Why, he wondered, did the little girl have to take after him and the boy after Becki?

At first the new baby was no difficulty for Leah. Drea had told her that she'd asked their mother for a sister and a brother and that's the way it was going to be. Leah accepted this logic as much as a child approaching two could; but in the next months, she noticed how people would 'ooh' and 'ah' over Bruce, saying how gorgeous he was while not seeming to notice her. Becki tried to tell her that new babies always got extra attention but as the little boy grew, he truly was a golden child, and people would stop them on the streets to comment on his looks.

One day when Leah was four, she climbed onto Arnie's knee. "Why is Bruce so pretty?" she asked poignantly.

"Your mommy's pretty," he answered, at a loss for

words.

"Then why don't I look like that?" Leah persisted, snuggling closer to her father, who was gently embracing her, one hand tenderly stroking the child's smooth, straight brown hair.

"You're my little girl and named for my grandmother whom I loved very much. You take after us."

"If I'd been named after Mommy's would I have looked like her?"

"It doesn't work that way, sweetheart. Sometimes babies look like one parent, sometimes the other, sometimes a mix and sometimes just themselves."

Leah was quiet, thinking. "I love you, Daddy, but I wish I looked like Mommy. Drea does."

And I wish you did too, thought Arnie, but he held his daughter more tightly. "You look perfect to me," he said. "Mommy and Drea and I couldn't love you more. You're a wonderful little girl and baby sister and big sister and just what we wanted."

Leah stayed curled up next to him and he wondered what they could do, if anything, to help her. Finally she gave him a kiss and hug, got down, and ran off. Yet Arnie knew she'd keep thinking about this. She was an exceptionally bright and perceptive child, and he wondered if she'd said anything to Becki. It was something they'd have to discuss; and he hoped it wouldn't damage the relationship between the children. Bruce obviously was becoming Leah's shadow and devoted follower while both children seemed to worship Drea, who in spite of entering those difficult teen years, still had patience with her little siblings.

What a gem Drea was, he reflected. He really did get two for the price of one when he married Becki. If Leah and Bruce grew up to be as nice as she, they'd truly be blessed, even if she was turning into a teenager.

These were the good years in Boston. The business was thriving. Becki was busy and content with the children and, at Arnie's prodding, did continue to take a class almost every term. They had gone to Oregon several times to visit his family, although both missed his lively grandmother, who'd died so unexpectedly. There were also short trips as a family to Virginia to visit Marty and Jerry, who now had another child, named Lily Marie for Marty's and Becki's mother.

"How did your mother get a name like that?" Arnie asked Becki. "You and Marty have such nice Biblical names, Rebecca and Martha."

"I guess my grandmother read too many novels and dreamed of running away to Paris," joked Becki. "Father, by contrast, was from an ultraconservative background so we got the Bible ones."

Right, like your great aunt, thought Arnie, but he didn't intend to bring that up. "Well, yours pleased Grandma. She was sure there was some nice Jewish blood in your family somewhere."

"Your grandmother was a wonderful lady. I'm so sorry she didn't live to see her namesake."

"We couldn't have named Leah after her if she'd been alive. It was against her tradition. Your suggesting it was one of the nicest things you could have done." He took her hand. "You do nice things, sweetheart."

"Well, I would rather have not called her that and still had your grandmother, Arnie. She welcomed me to your family, and I know how much you miss her."

"Yeah, I do, but I've got you and the rest of the gang now. That would have made her happy." And it made him so too, but as he was beginning to be able to slacken up somewhat on work, he started to notice that their social life was fairly sparse. Worse, when they did go to some of the parties with people from work, he saw that with the exception of Madge Norris and her new husband, Becki seemed to be excluded from the conversations. It was subtle, almost undetectable, and he wondered at first if he were imagining it. By nature, Becki was always quiet in crowds, although when they had small parties at home, she would talk vivaciously but those functions were mostly with people from the neighborhood. Moreover, they did not seem to receive many invitations from others at work except to all inclusive events with huge guest lists. This in part, no doubt, was due to the fact that the company had grown and Arnie was the kingpin. Still, even among the remaining partners, it was really only with Madge that they spent time.

All this seemed to come to a head when Becki came with him to an office Christmas party. She'd been standing next to him talking to several of the old timers and their wives and stayed with them when he excused himself to go over and speak to one of the new programmers. When he glanced back, he was shocked to see that the group had in effect shut her out. Later that evening, he thought that two women, who seemed to be looking at Becki, now taken in hand by Madge, had ceased talking when he approached. What was going on, he wondered?

CHAPTER 16

Shortly after the office Christmas party, Arnie was having coffee with Madge one afternoon and he felt he had to ask. "What the hell is the matter? Why are people giving Becki such a hard time? I know you like her. She told me you were about the only person, who tried to talk to her that first time at the Cape; and I've seen you with her when we are at parties. You and Bryan are also the only people from work we really do things with."

"Oh Arnie," sighed Madge sympathetically, "I wish I could tell you. Jealousy I guess. You've risen right to the top and some see her as a trophy wife since she's so gorgeous. I like your Becki. She is one of the sweetest persons I've ever met. She's bright and funny too, but she just doesn't come across that way unless people make an extra effort to get to know her. Most of our peers don't. But there's more, and I'll be blunt."

"You always are, Madge," he grinned.

Madge snorted and then said seriously, "Arnie, the others see her as some stupid chick that you knocked up and then felt you had to marry."

"We were married," he snapped angrily. "She got pregnant on the honeymoon. We wanted kids, although maybe not that early, and Leah was early. She weighed four and a half pounds. Can't people figure out that's a preemie?"

"Arnie, you didn't tell anyone you were getting married on that trip. How the hell were they to know you'd planned it? For that matter, you never really told anyone you were engaged."

"I didn't tell anyone because it wasn't their business," he continued irritated. "Becki hadn't completely made up her mind to marry me, Madge. When she did decide, it seemed logical to have her come along for a honeymoon. She'd been almost scared off the Labor Day weekend. That didn't exactly turn out to be the nicest experience for her."

"No," agreed Madge thoughtfully, "it didn't. I don't know how you could have handled that better, Arnie. You'd already told everyone about this fabulous blonde you'd met in a bar in D.C. and then suddenly she was there and obviously staying with you. They figured you'd just flown her up as your entertainment for the weekend. After all, you did have a bit of a reputation for squiring some good-looking women, actually rather more than squiring."

"She paid her own way, Madge. She wouldn't have it any other way. She saved all summer for that trip. I'd asked her up before and she couldn't afford it. She had Drea to support."

"Well, there's that too. A big kid like Drea and Becki so young so that's a stigma."

"That shouldn't be! Drea is a great kid."

"But obviously one that your wife had as a young teenager. Add the clotheshorse looks, the fact she rarely says anything, the pinup picture you had in your office, you figure it out."

"Ok, I screwed up. I'd just never dated anyone as beautiful as Becki. I couldn't help showing her off. I was...I am wild about her."

"Yes, and Dickie didn't help," commented Madge cynically.

"No, but is that still going around?"

"Still! Arnie, everyone thinks you were sharing her."

"What!" He was astounded.

"I mean not only was Dickie dragging her around the picnic that day, but you know he told everyone that the only reason you fired him was that you got pissed because you caught the two of them screwing in your bed. After you tossed him out of the company, he apparently elaborated on the story and said it still wasn't over."

"Yeah, I do know he told people something happened at the Cape but I didn't know about the other," reflected Arnie sadly. "I hoped no one believed the Cape story any longer. I wish I had killed that SOB."

"I imagine a lot of people do. He is slime. If he can't

charm their pants off, he patronizes them or worse. I never could understand what Carla saw in him. She was well rid of him but it's a real shame it had to happen Labor Day weekend or he might not have gone after Becki."

"She did have to fight him off," Arnie murmured, his looks darkening as he recalled Becki's anguish and undeserved sense of shame.

"I'm not surprised," Madge said grimly. "He doesn't like to be turned down, especially if he's been drinking and he was."

"What do you mean?" asked Arnie surprised.

"Let's say, he is very forceful with women he wants, even if they aren't mutually attracted."

"Hell," swore Arnie, visibly upset at this distasteful revelation. "How come no one ever told me?"

"It isn't exactly a thing most women want to share."

"You?" he asked, incredulous.

"No, fortunately, but a couple of gals I know found out the hard way. I'm just one of the ones he wanted to patronize but that's hard to do with an equal business partner. That must have really pissed the hell out of him when you asked me to be one of the originals."

"Well Jesus, Madge, you're good. That teamwork we did together at MIT was top notch. I never could understand why you didn't want to go on for the Ph.D. too."

"A master's was enough," she responded dryly. "Whenever I thought otherwise, I just sat down and waited for it to go away. You're so nice and sweet, Arnie, you let the shit roll off you that they pour on grad students. Besides, you're smarter than most of the bastards."

"Madge, you say the nicest things," he laughed half-heartedly.

"Well it's true, Arnie. That's why you always got the gals too. Our clandestine Romeo, we used to call you." He looked at her shocked. "Come on, Arnie, you're no movie star idol but you could always charm them. The guys never could quite understand it, but women did. You treated them like a real gentleman and you were honest about everything."

A slight grin appeared on Madge's face. "At least no one had any complaints and most amazing, no one seems to have had any hard feelings after."

"You're embarrassing me," Arnie laughed, but he was sure his ears had turned bright red.

"Well, I might have been willing to do more if you'd ever asked."

"God, Madge, I never knew." Arnie was practically speechless at this revelation.

"Of course not, why should you. You always saw me as one of the team, another of the guys. To be totally honest, I think that was much better, but...if you had ever been interested, I probably would have."

"Thank you," he said quietly. "You flatter me, but you're right, we're better as friends and business partners."

"Yes, and then I met my Bryan, and he was worth waiting for."

"I'm glad," said Arnie, utterly sincere. "You deserve someone special."

Madge just smiled and then said, "But when it comes to Becki. I really don't know what to advise you. I like her tremendously, but I'm out of the loop in some ways too. I'm not one of the wives and even if I am one of the guys, I'm not one of the boys so no one listens to me. People do treat her like shit at times and she just takes it. She tries to ignore them, but she won't fight back. Yet she's the only one who could stop this."

"She's so shy," he said sadly. "She tried to tell me. That's one of the reasons it took me weeks to persuade her to set the date. I wanted to marry her practically from the start. I asked her after the Dickie episode and got her to say yes, but she wouldn't say when. Then she backed out after she returned to D.C. I had to go down to re-persuade her. That's really why I never told anyone we were getting married or even engaged. Too much pride, I guess, in case she said no.

"The same sort of thing happened at Boston U. She'd write these outstanding papers. They were really graduate level, definitely *A* work. Then she'd end up with a *B* for the course. I made her ask the profs and she was told that she didn't speak up in class. One bastard accused her of having someone do the work for her." Actually Arnie, at that point, had been surprised that none of them had hit on her with the promise of grade inflation. Probably being married with kids had prevented that scenario. Academics were changing and not necessarily for the better.

"No question she's well read," agreed Madge. "I sometimes wonder if that's all she does."

"No, not all," declared Arnie stoutly. "She keeps our places spotless, she's a fantastic cook, the kids couldn't have a better mother, and she's my confidante. I can talk to her about anything. She doesn't understand all the technical stuff we're doing but not many people do, thank God. Otherwise we wouldn't be making our fortunes." He grinned, Madge nodding in agreement; and then he laughed boyishly, before adding, "But, Becki does understand the economics and the administrative aspects and often she helps me work out problems there. Becki's not just a sounding board. Yet I'm sure when company come to our house, they think we've had everything catered and have a regular housekeeper and that all she does is stand around trying on clothes. Hell, she even makes some of them—another of those 4-H projects she did as a kid. Then those, that might suspect she has a brain, see her placid countenance as being stuck-up or superior instead of a defensive mechanism because she's afraid to talk to them."

CHAPTER 17

The final blow was to come the next year when Arnie was at last able to persuade Becki to go on a business trip with him to New York. She had become friends with a neighbor who had children at the same preschool attended by Leah and Bruce. One week Becki kept the neighbor's children while the woman joined her husband for a few days in Chicago. It was such a success that Becki, with Arnie's encouragement, agreed to leave their kids with her friend and accompany him to the Big Apple, a city she'd never visited.

He and a team from his company were negotiating with the Volkenant Corporation, a multi-service store which would not only distribute their products nationally but also promote them internationally through their world-wide chain of outlets—this to the exclusion of rival software abroad. Not only that, but Volkenant would further use the software for their in-house enterprises and had offered to provide financial backing for SofTek's latest software package if needed.

As Arnie explained to Becki, "The deal automatically ensures instant success to the newest offering. Of course," he noted, "they would have also liked some of our stock, but I really don't want to go public even though half the partners do. Maybe I'll change my mind someday if we want to run away and go around the world."

"That'll be the day, Arnie. You could never leave the company. You love the action too much," Becki teased, patting him affectionately on the hand. Business and her husband were synonymous. He probably dreamed in mathematical terms.

"You're right, I do. It is my ultimate game. Anyhow, Volkenant was considering software from a couple of other companies too, but ours is the best so they are finally seeing the agreement my way."

So, with the meetings successfully completed, now was the last night. A cocktail party was being given by Gustav Volkenant at his spacious rooftop apartment to celebrate. When Arnie and Becki arrived, there already was a large crowd and people kept coming up to Arnie to congratulate him. "Pretty heady stuff," he whispered to Becki, who nodded as she looked in awe, thinking the main room probably had more space than their Cape Cod place.

Smiling, she said softly in his ear, "You deserve it. I think they thought you were going to fold or let them take your package under their terms. I knew you had it in you, champ."

"Well I'm glad you did. I had some worries for a while."

"Why? Your program was best. You told me so and you're honest, remember? They'd be fools not to back you on your terms. Otherwise you might have started playing ball with the West Coast gang."

"Aren't you getting too smart," he said grinning, but he felt on top of the world. His company was a big enough player, although nothing like the opposition. For SofTek to have been picked as a partner yet able to retain its complete independence in this Volkenant venture, rather than just being used, was an accolade. "That's our host over there." Arnie pointed to a distinguished looking silver-haired man probably in his early sixties. "Come on, this is your chance to meet a true multi-millionaire, not just someone on paper like us." Taking Becki's arm, he steered her across the room.

"Ah, Arnie," Gus Volkenant greeted them. "So glad you could make it and this, I gather, is the lovely Mrs. Miller?"

"How kind, I'm Becki," she responded, extending her hand.

"You must be very proud of your husband, my dear. He's a real genius."

"I've never doubted it," she laughed. "I'm just so happy that you and your colleagues realized that."

"A charming young lady," Volkenant said to Arnie. "You're a lucky man."

"Oh I know that," agreed Arnie amiably. "There's never been a question in my mind. Anyhow, I wanted to thank you personally for your part in these negotiations and to tell you how much we appreciate this evening's invitation."

"Hopefully it will be the first of many," said Volkenant, and the three stood chatting for a few moments until some other people gravitated over to their host.

"What a crock of bull," Arnie quietly murmured to Becki as they finally moved away.

"Arnie!"

"Ah sweetheart, you know he was just buttering us up. He's happy it worked out all right, but he would have been happier if it had been all on his terms, their having sole distribution rights and a piece of SofTek."

"Arnie, you're terrible," she chided, but she had a slight smile on her face. Arnie had no intention of releasing shares of his company. They'd have to be pried from his dying hands, regardless of what his partners, thought or hoped.

"Well at least he was right about you."

"My hero," she sighed theatrically, hand placed on breast and eyelashes fluttering. "Want to get me a drink? I see Madge over there."

"Be delighted, charming young lady."

Becki stuck her tongue out at him and turned to leave but Arnie grabbed her arm, saying in a low voice, "Don't do that, it's dangerous!" Becki just laughed delightedly.

He was being served at the bar when he noticed that Becki was now in a nearby group with Madge near her. The look on Becki's face scared the shit out of him. She appeared outwardly serene if one didn't know her, but her eyes were utterly terrified and her face very pale. It was like looking at a deer caught in headlights during hunting season. What was going on? Not even taking the drinks, he started working his way rapidly through the close-knit crowd.

He was a couple feet from her when he heard an overly loud and familiar voice. "So I was saying, who knew that Arnie would pick up this beautiful babe in a D.C. swingers bar and import her up to the Cape for a weekend, but you know Arnie, he always could find them. That was some weekend, wasn't it Becki? I'll always thank Arnie for the opportunity of really getting to know you." Then the man laughed suggestively. "I also should congratulate you on the wedding. That sure was a surprise for everyone, your finally snagging our man of the hour. What was it? The little girl arrived a few months later? Good thing she looks like Arnie."

Arnie seized the man's arm, spinning him around. "Hello, Dickie, it's been a while," he said quietly, and he felt his other hand starting to clinch into a fist. It was Madge who stopped him from punching Dickie in the mouth by grabbing the threatening hand. Becki was just standing there, stricken. Then suddenly she turned, hastily making her way to the open roof garden while the rest of the group dispersed, embarrassed.

"Well," said Dickie nastily, a grin to match. "Always in the nick of time. You've done it again, haven't you?"

"What, arrived in time to hear you be your usual shitty self?"

"Come off it, Arnie, that agreement should have been with us. My program. What did you do, bribe them?"

"What are you talking about?" Arnie asked perplexed.

"You know, *System Alpha* is my program."

"No, as a matter of fact I didn't. Ours was just better. There was no collusion. And because our *FindIt* won is no reason you can say garbage like this. Why don't you just come outside with me and let's resolve this little problem. I've wanted to smash your pretty face in for the last five years. Let's see if you have the balls to give me a chance."

"Don't do it, Arnie, don't make a scene," cautioned Madge in a low voice, still clutching his arm firmly. "You'll be sorry after."

"I really doubt that, Madge."

"Honest, Arnie, go after Becki. I thought she was going to keel over."

"That's right, Arnie. Make threats and run off," sneered

Dickie, aware that others were watching and enjoying his play to the crowd, whether they could hear or not. "How typical to have a woman stand up for you. What is it, is Madge part of the picture now too? A *ménage à trois*? I'd always wondered about you, Madge; how come Arnie let you into the company but somehow I thought you were a dyke though I gather you've got some prissy little Harvard prof now. Or are you bi? Hey, maybe you're always with Arnie's little piece because you're the butch and she's the femme. Is that it?"

Arnie was now straining to get at Dickie, and Madge was pulling him back with all her strength. "No," she hissed, "you can't get into a fight here and he knows that. And you, you bastard," she snarled at Dickie, "my husband's not prissy or little but even if he were, he'd beat you, hands down. If you were all the male world had to offer, I'd be proud to be a lesbian. Arnie's right, you are a piece of shit, but if anyone is going to punch you, it's going to be me because I think he'd pound your worthless brains in once he got going. Come on, Arnie, go after Becki. Dickie isn't worth it. He never was."

Arnie felt as though he would explode in rage but Madge was right. How many people had heard, he didn't know, but getting into a brawl here wasn't going to help even though it was obvious to those close by that he and Dickie were on the verge. He looked at Dickie ominously. "That's twice. Madge saved you this time. I'm not going to forget." Giving Madge a quick hug, he turned to go and find his wife, infuriated to hear Dickie's laughter in the background.

Becki had made her way out on the balcony and was holding the rails tightly, her knuckles white, oblivious to the beauty of the city down below. He could see that she was heaving, trying to hold in little sobs. He came up behind her and put his arms around her, his head resting against hers, feeling her agitated gasps. "Hang in there, honey. It's ok. I didn't make a scene. You'll be fine. Just hold on, sweetheart. Do you want to leave?"

She turned and put her head on his shoulder, crying quietly. It was several minutes before she could speak and then only in a trembling voice. "I'm sorry. I just can't help it."

"What do you have to be sorry about," Arnie soothed. "He's the kind of person one should horsewhip. If Madge hadn't been there, I would have torn him apart, no doubt making everything worse. God I wish they still allowed dueling. Now I know how people get killed in bar room brawls. I've never been so angry."

"I'm sorry," she plaintively uttered once again, with a pathetic sniffle.

"Don't say that. He's the one that should be sorry. As it was, he made some cracks about Madge too. What a shit. Now tell me, can you stay a little while? It probably would be best, but if you don't want to, I can certainly understand."

"I'll try," she murmured dejectedly, "but don't leave me. I just can't be in there alone."

"I won't leave you," he promised. "Let me look at you. Here, take this handkerchief. Good thing they have non-running makeup now. You're the only woman I know who can cry and still look ok." She wiped her eyes and blew her nose. Then he took hold of her hand and they walked back into the room, but he noticed that several people were watching them and realized Becki knew as well. Dickie apparently had left, which seemed typical—all mouth and no guts but such a trouble-making mouth.

True to his word, Arnie stayed by Becki holding her hand. Her fingers clasped his so tightly that at times he felt she was cutting off the circulation and was going to squeeze them off. Somehow, for the next fifteen minutes, he managed to be pleasant and talkative with those he had to be. Then finally, they were able to leave. Becki hadn't spoken a single word since she'd left the balcony—an occasional polite, almost distant smile or nod of the head, but totally voiceless and eyes still moist and overly bright.

When they got down to the street, she at last released the pressure on his hand and he had the feeling that the experience had been pure torture for her. It hadn't been the greatest for him either, but he knew that in degree, she had been the one in absolute agony. As they waited for the cab, he said calmly, "I wish there was something I could say. It's not right or fair. I can only tell you again how sorry I am."

"It wasn't your fault," she said softly, looking down, refusing to catch his eye.

"Well it certainly wasn't yours either. I wish I knew how we could handle this but it's kind of like having the *National Enquirer* go after you. Dickie's utter scum and if there's any way I can get him, I will."

"No, Arnie," Becki protested turning, and he could see her eyes were sad, the wounded doe. "You're not that kind of person. I just don't think I want to go to things like this anymore."

"Honey, this is the first time we've seen him in over five years. Now that his company missed the brass ring, I doubt that we'll be meeting him at these occasions."

"Please, Arnie. Don't make me come next time."

"We'll talk about it, ok? You're my wife. I'm proud of you. I want you to be with me."

"Please." Becki was begging and somehow he knew that probably he would have to attend these business parties alone from now on. Arnie patted her ineffectually on the arm and then as a cab pulled up, helped her in. On the way back to the hotel, she sat staring silently out of the window. Putting an arm around her, he tried to draw her closer, but she remained stiffly where she was, as though she were chained to the opposite door. When they got back to their room, he started to say something but she looked at him placidly, her face now devoid of emotion. "I don't want to talk about it, Arnie."

That night in bed, she withdrew, huddled to one side and for the first time, he saw her totally defenseless, lost somewhere in her silent world. In the middle of the night, he awoke for some reason. It took him a moment to realize that it had been the sound of her crying. Her sobs were soft, almost gentle, like her, but he was shocked. In all their marriage, he had seen Becki cry only three times, one being when his grandmother had died and her tears had joined his. He'd said something to her about that and she'd told him she'd been all cried out during her mid-teens. But now, because of that bastard Dickie, the tears had flowed the Cape Cod weekend and tonight again, and his heart ached for her. He reached over and, reluctantly, she moved into his arms. He wiped the tears from her face but her eyes were tightly closed and she wouldn't look at him. Tenderly he held her, feeling love as well as anger and frustration, knowing there wasn't much he could do.

It had been the first business trip she had accompanied him since the kids had arrived and they'd had such fun in the evenings. Going to plays and fancy dinners—things he rarely did when away on business. He hadn't realized how much he missed her on his trips and had thought that now at last she would continue to join him. Instead, as a result of this embarrassing episode, he feared she probably would never come again. On the train ride back to Boston, Becki was unapproachable—the antithesis of the excited, happy companion on the trip down. Once home, it was as though they'd not gone and she never mentioned what had happened.

Worse yet, it was as though something had died in her that night. At home Becki was as loving and thoughtful as ever. She still worked on her classes but devoted most of her time to the children. Although she fraternized with the neighbors, it was obvious that she was greatly stressed whenever anything social with work took place. She would attend with him but she was a silent shadow, seemingly composed, but to his discerning eyes, unquestionably in torment.

The only place she was willing to travel with him was an occasional company trip to the West Coast. They'd go to Oregon first where he'd leave her with his sister or mother if he had business in California or Seattle. Then returning after the work portion, he would spend some time there with his whole family before he, Becki and the kids returned to

Boston. Clearly everyone enjoyed these visits and during them, Becki was the fun companion he'd first met.

The same happened when he had meetings in Washington, D.C. Then she would go to Virginia to her sister's. She had started making longer visits to Marty, who now had a larger home in Falls Church where she was still teaching and where Jerry had become a junior partner with the law firm.

CHAPTER 18

One day, when they were in Virginia, Marty casually mentioned that Great Aunt Mary apparently was on her last legs. "The old hag's ninety now and I heard she's in a nursing home. She probably won't return to the riverside house." Soon everyone was speculating about what would happen to the family home when Arnie looked at Becki and saw her lost in thought.

That night he tried to draw her out about the house and property and she began to cry. He mentally added a five to his little list titled 'Becki's tears'. "I just can't stand it! Someone will buy the house and change it or tear it down the way they did my folks' place. It's just not fair. It'll be ruined and it's so beautiful. When I was little, I wanted to live there by the river forever."

Arnie said nothing but the next morning he went over to the library to find telephone directories for Fredericksburg and King George, thinking how useful it would be if ever the Internet system the government and universities were developing became truly public. Compiling a list of local realtors, he started to make calls, asking that he be notified when the property came on the market. Within six months, the house, its complete furnishings, and the adjacent acreage, stretching from the woods to the river, was his. That night he came home with a bottle of champagne. "Come out into the garden with me, Beauty," he invited casually. "I have a surprise."

"What's the occasion, Arnie? Champagne even. You've made another million?" Becki followed him into the balmy late spring night. The small garden enclosure, so barren before she had moved to Boston, was now a profusion of colors and scents, rich lilacs predominating, plus the equally colorful scattered toys of their little family.

Stepping over Bruce's small yellow scooter, Arnie sunk into one of the comfortable lawn chairs. "Actually, sweetheart, I spent some money and I'm going to give you three guesses."

"Hmm, this is intriguing. A new Mercedes and you're going to tell me I can't drive it."

"Nope, and I would too let you. Try harder."

Becki looked doubtful about the car. Arnie was very possessive about his new Toyota, but ventured again, "A houseboat."

"That doesn't sound bad but try again."

"You know I can't guess. Silver chopsticks," she joshed.

"No, but I like that one," he grinned.

"Tell me or I'll do something drastic." She had entered the game and was obviously eager to know. Her face was exuberant the way it had so often been when they were first married although increasingly less so of late.

"You give up too easily and I should really make you work, but..." he said as he finally removed the bottle's cork. Then pouring the foaming wine into their glasses, he announced with great fanfare, "Ta, ta, we now own your great grandparents' house and property."

"Arnie!" Becki's mouth was wide open and she nearly dropped the glasses. The champagne was spilling all over. Setting them on the ground, she settled down on his lap and threw her arms around him. "Oh Arnie, thank you," and she started to sob.

"God, Becki, this isn't supposed to make you cry." Six, he thought inconsequentially; she was developing a pattern

"I was so afraid it was going to be ruined. Oh Arnie..."

"Better than a diamond bracelet? A sapphire one? Ruby?"

"Don't be an idiot," Becki retorted. "Better than a million bracelets—diamond, sapphire and even ruby! When can we go see it? Can we spend holidays there, what?"

"It's really yours, sweetheart, so whatever you want. I can get away next month when school is out if you can wait that long."

Becki looked at him seriously, her blue eyes clear and intent. "I've been waiting all my life. Let me tell Drea."

"I thought it was quiet around here. Where are she and the small fry?"

"She took them over to the Weinsteins for a birthday party."

"Hmm," said Arnie, "and that's good for how much longer? An hour?"

"Maybe," speculated Becki.

"Maybe maybe or maybe for real?"

"An hour is a good guess."

"So, if we were to take this champagne upstairs, we could probably count on an hour."

"Maybe."

"And what would you say?"

"I should have known there were some strings to this gift."

"Sweetheart, I expect at least weekly mortgage payments from you—maybe more. Interest compounds rapidly."

"Usurer," she whispered. "What if I don't have cash?"

"I'll figure out some other tender."

"And be tender too?" she softly asked, as she started to nibble on his ear.

"Most definitely." He was beginning to breathe heavily.

"And this is another of those oral contracts I can't break?" By now she was running her hands through his hair and her fingertips felt like fire.

"Yep."

"Well, I guess maybe I'd better give you the first payment." Becki got up, sashayed saucily to the kitchen door, and turned to look at him, a sly smile playing over her lips.

"Maybe I'd like that," he said huskily as he got up to join her.

CHAPTER 19

The next month with the whole family packed into Becki's faithful old station wagon, they left early one morning, driving straight through to King George. It was a trip of eleven plus hours and one that Arnie did not relish. He'd tried to persuade Becki that they should stay in a motel once they got there; but, she had loaded sleeping bags, play clothes, flashlights and all sorts of things, saying the motels were too far away from the house.

"Surely we're not going to have to camp out?" he asked.

"Come on, city boy, you'll do fine." She had the children so enthused about the venture that there was hardly a complaint or argument the whole ride down. Drea played games with Bruce and Leah, while Arnie began to think if he heard another hearty rendition of *Row, Row, Row, Your Boat*, he'd throw up. Still it was a family outing, something they hadn't done in ages. Even going to Cape Cod had become rare.

Although they had not discussed it, he was aware of the fact that Becki never truly had been comfortable there after the Dickie episode in spite of their wonderful first night picnic and subsequent engagement. And, to be honest, he continued to remain apprehensive when she'd swim far out from shore, although he knew she had curtailed most such ventures in deference to him.

They got to King George late that afternoon, having come down Route 301 from Baltimore, thus avoiding the D.C. traffic. When they got to the house, Becki just stood there at first after Arnie unlocked the door. Drea and the kids rushed in immediately and were shouting about various things, but she couldn't seem to move. Arnie went over to her. "Am I supposed to do something special, something like this?" Grabbing her, he hoisted her up and carried her over the threshold. "I think I forgot to do that the time you moved to Boston but you'd already been to that house so maybe this is the one that counts."

Still in his arms, Becki kissed him, her eyes moist and bright. "Any place counts with you, Sir Knight."

"You haven't called me that for a long time," he commented as he lowered her.

"I think of you that way," she replied. Then softly, she added, "my sexy little man."

"That's better. When can we put the kids to bed?" he asked with a happy leer and she laughed.

The next days were hectic. He'd arranged to keep the electricity as soon as he'd purchased the house so at least they had lights, water, and working appliances, after a fashion. Yet there were items dating back decades that would have to be addressed, things to be sorted or disposed, and cleaning to be done. In no time Becki had organized everyone into doing something. Even little Bruce was given a broom and encouraged to swat the numerous cobwebs while Leah, self-importantly, trudged back and forth carrying light objects. By the time Arnie had to return to Boston after a week, the place was beginning to achieve some order.

Two weeks later when he flew back down for the long Fourth of July weekend, Arnie was amazed by the changes. Half the old furniture and all of Aunt Mary's possessions had been either donated to charity or hauled to the dump after Becki had borrowed a neighbor's farm truck and paid the owner's teenage son, who now had entered her employ on a part-time basis. From the way the boy was ogling Drea, Arnie wasn't sure if the youth was working for the cash or the opportunity to be near the blossoming girl. Fortunately so far, Drea, at fourteen, seemed to have her hormones in check; but Arnie knew he'd better discuss this with Becki, realizing that somehow he had evolved into an overly protective father and that the boy was too good-looking for Drea to ignore much longer.

Meanwhile he was dragooned into helping paint an upstairs bedroom. "After all," Becki told him sweetly, "that was one of the selling points you used on Drea when we were moving to Boston."

"Who says I'm the only one, who plays dirty pool?" complained Arnie. By the time he got back to Boston, he told Madge and his secretary, that he'd had to return to work to rest. But he also fondly remembered his surprise birthday party that weekend, which Becki had organized with some help from Marty. Still working upstairs, he hadn't even realized anything was happening until people began to arrive and Becki shoved him into the shower. It had indeed been a surprise that she would do something social like that and he was touched that she wanted to.

The afternoon had been perfect—sunny, not too hot, and the river calm and lovely. Distant cousins and friends of Becki's and Marty's parents plus some high school friends, mostly Marty's, had come. Even the few neighbors who weren't kin appeared. There had to have been over fifty people—a huge crowd by Becki's standards.

She had ordered bushels of the hot, spiced crabs, kegs of beer, and additional picnic items from the seafood place and grocery deli in Fredericksburg. The guests brought a variety of picnic dishes just like an old-fashioned potluck supper, the kind Arnie had seen in movies. That night, people shot off fireworks over the river. Then close to midnight, after everyone had left or was settled down, Becki and he went out to sit on the veranda swing and watch the moon reflected over the Potomac—large, full and silver, like the one when they were in Hawaii. They swung back and forth, holding hands, and he felt like he was in some time warp crooning 'In the Good Old Summer Time' from one of the grand old Hollywood musicals.

Becki leaned next to him, her head on his shoulder, humming softly. He hadn't seen her so happy or relaxed for ages and inside him, there began to grow a little worry. The contrast to the way she had been of late in Boston was disturbing. There, outside their home, she was morose, whereas here, she seemed the girl he'd met years before. He really didn't want to consider what this might mean. Instead, he just held her hand, enjoying the beautiful night.

Arnie managed to work his schedule so he could come to Virginia every other weekend, spending three to four days with his family. Although he was lonely when he'd return to the Cambridge house, he was working long hours and involved in monitoring new updates of *TrackIt*, *PriceIt*, and *FindIt*, which the Volkenant Corporation had been first to distribute.

Meanwhile the house in King George was becoming more and more livable and the kids seemed to be thriving. All three were swimming now—even little Bruce, and when Arnie went down to the shore, he was astonished by their progress. Becki, of course, continued to be a mermaid and would go far out into the river. One afternoon when Jerry, Marty and their kids were visiting, Arnie mentioned something about his fear for Becki and the water.

"Marty says she always was like that," replied Jerry sanguinely. "So was their father, which is one reason Becki couldn't believe he'd drowned. Marty was never much of a swimmer and their mother could barely float. When the boat disappeared, Becki would to sit for hours on that wharf, waiting, hoping they'd come sailing back up the river. She was fourteen then and she did that for months until she finally got involved with Billy. Marty learned about it later and I think she still feels guilty, but she was just a college kid herself and she couldn't have done much."

Arnie looked at Drea, the same age Becki must have been, and thought about what it would have been like to be a young teenager secure in a happy home one day and then the next all alone. The thought of Becki, the sensitive and imaginative child, having to depend on a bigoted and nasty old woman, who exalted in performing her so-called Christian duty but believed the child to be socially inferior due to her mother's family, sickened him. It was a fairly bleak picture, but then the more he learned about Becki's teens, the sadder they appeared. Yet in spite of that, she clearly seemed at ease back in that same environment.

By the end of the summer, the house was not only livable but was beginning to take on a flare that undeniably was Becki's. With Arnie's Cambridge house, the changes had been gradual. Mostly the use of color and addition of decorative elements turned a bachelor's abode, albeit roomy, into a comfortable, family home where his possessions were incorporated into a tasteful and cheerful interior.

With the King George house, Becki was eliminating decades of gloomy grime and clutter. The furniture she retained was old, dating from her great grandparents, and slated to be her next project after refurbishing the house. She had even rented a steamer and spent days removing dingy wallpaper and was currently working on brightening the interior. Woodwork already painted countless times, and ugly with age, was being stripped and lightened. The upstairs bedrooms were now pastel or bright colors similar to ones seen at Mount Vernon or the Lee Mansion of Arlington—famed homes of her distant kin. The idea that Becki and now his children were technically descendants of the First Families of Virginia still amazed Arnie, child of latecomer immigrants.

"Just because it may have seemed the dark ages," Becki told her husband, "doesn't mean that people back around the eighteenth century really lived in dark houses. Wait until we get the light in here!"

So cleaning windows was another priority. Arnie begged her to hire some help but she told him, "It's my project and besides, I already have Ken two days a week. Moreover, how is Drea going to earn enough money for things she wants if we don't pay her for the hours of work she's contributing? Besides, I already purchased squeegees!"

This appeared to be a key point in her argument but Arnie continued to protest, "I'll get Drea what she wants, damn it, and 'Ken doll' can work five days if he wants." Becki at this point had him scrubbing the upstairs glass doors in the master bedroom that opened onto a small balcony above the front porch and looked out onto the river. "I don't come down here to be a day laborer."

Becki came up from behind, putting her arms around him and gently patting him on the stomach. "I thought you were worried about Ken being here even twice a week," she scolded lightly, remembering Arnie's concern about Drea. "And, you need the work...you've been getting too sedentary while we've been away. I bet you're not hitting the gym even once a week any more. If you're not good, I'm not going to cook you any more Italian food or fried crab cakes. I'll feed you only lettuce leaves next time."

"Ok," he murmured, acquiescing, "but you can't do all this work, sweetheart. We'll get someone professional in for the floors and sanding the stair railings. It would take you weeks to get off all that old varnish and you wouldn't have either of those pretty hands left." He took hold of them, noting the short nails and the fact she was getting some light calluses. "No hand ads now, Beauty."

Becki laughed, "No ads period. I was glad I got pregnant right away so I never did have to model again."

"You didn't tell me that. I just figured you were too busy with the kids and school.

"I never liked it. You know that, Arnie. It was just a way to make halfway decent money but I was always uncomfortable."

"You'd still be able to do it," he observed lovingly, looking at her long, slender figure. Maybe she'd gained a pound or two more about the hips, but that was the most. Even her breasts were still firm and shapely in spite of nursing all the children. Now thirty, she scarcely looked a year older than when he had met her. People probably thought she was Drea's older sister and would have mistaken her for the baby sitter with the little ones, if not for the fact that Bruce so obviously was her little boy.

"I'll compromise with you, Becki. You promise to get someone in here to do the woodwork and, God knows, what other repairs needed. I'll help you with some of the other things. But...big 'but'...we're getting someone in to redo the kitchen and bathrooms and all the other heavy labor. I especially worry about the wiring. And, I will promise to get back to exercising. You're right."

"Come swim with me, Arnie. That's a start," she

begged.

"Naw, treadmills, exercise bikes and gym pools at best, honey. You're the water nymph. I'm just your friendly, little troll."

"Never," she stated firmly, "not a troll, too sexy. Still a knight. Want to take a sleeping bag down to the shore tonight? You could build a fire and we'll have some wine and a picnic."

"God, Becki! What a bad example for the children."

"Bruce and Leah are too little to understand," she refuted pragmatically. "We'll get some videos for them and promise Drea a PG-13 or maybe even an R for later after they go to sleep."

"What kind of mother are you?"

"You don't think she doesn't see them with her school friends in Boston? Lots of their homes have that cable and you know she babysits for others, who do. This way we can pick the movies we think she should watch. I'd rather have her see a little sex and hear some bad language than a lot of violence in something like *Mad Max* or that *Nightmare on Elm Street* series. I think I saw *Footloose* at the video store. That deals with teen issues."

"Hmm...I think I agree with you, but I also think you're making this offer for some devious reason."

"Why Arnie, trust me." The look on Becki's face was too innocent.

"With my life, Beauty, but I still think this is something else—another rural Virginia con for the city slicker, more chips from George's sacred apple tree."

"Just a promise that we can come back down here for Thanksgiving and Christmas and spring holidays as well as next summer."

"No wonder Drea used to order food before we got to the restaurants! You do believe in planning in advance, don't you? Well, I see no problem." But, that nagging worry resurfaced in his mind. Still, he'd told her it was her house to use as she wished.

"And you'll be with us?"

"As much as I can. I can't predict my schedule. You know that, honey, but I'll try."

By the following summer, it was a given: holidays and vacations were in King George. Drea and the little ones had begun to make friends and were enamored of the country life alongside the river. Arnie was being begged for a pony and a puppy as well as a small rowboat. And also, as he gradually realized, that home be in Virginia.

And Becki had done wonders with the house. It was airy, bright, and looking as it must have when it was built a couple of centuries before. Only the modern kitchen and bathrooms betrayed the passage of time, but even these had been done in excellent taste and did not distract from the historic aspects of the rest of the house. Moreover, Becki herself thrived there. The melancholy, that had become more apparent when she would return to Cambridge, totally disappeared. Each time Arnie arrived from his New England commute, it was as though he entered a different world. Here he had a lively, vibrant wife—the Becki he had wooed—and his children, who seemed to flourish. Even Drea, it appeared, was a Tidewater girl, just as Becki had told him years before. Moreover she was integrating into the local teen social scene although neighbor Ken still appeared to be relegated to buddy status, much to Arnie's satisfaction and the boy's obvious despair.

Arnie tried to talk to Becki about some of the problems of separation. He also tried at times to talk to her about seeing a physician regarding her obvious depression when in Boston or her increasing hesitance in social situations. Somehow, though, Becki would always shift the subject and he couldn't bring himself to pressure her.

Personally, Arnie longed to have her accompany him when he traveled, never having forgotten the few joyful days in New York before the ugly scene at Gus Volkenant's. Although he had received subsequent invitations to the man's luxurious sky-high apartment, he'd found excuses, not wanting to relive the unpleasant event. Volkenant, he knew, had heard details of the fiasco, but was too polite to inquire, although he always asked after 'the lovely Mrs. Miller'.

Still, without doubt, the time Arnie did spend with Becki was wonderful; and maybe, that was just the way it was going to be. He now was on the road more for SofTek and staying even longer at the office. In effect, he had become one of those executives who seemed to thrive on eighty-hour or longer work weeks. The company and its products had become major players in the rapidly expanding computer world. Promoting them and experimenting with new ideas was personally exhilarating. Consequently, when not with his family, Arnie had developed his own lifestyle. He was enjoying the challenge, indeed the game of advancing the company and his concepts, since he could devote total attention to the business. It was where the action was, just as Becki had said. Home in King George, by contrast, was the escape.

It was also apparent by the second summer that Becki did not want to return to Cambridge. Although Arnie was concerned about the decision, they agreed that she and the children would try a school year down in Virginia and reverse the order of visitation. Arnie would still try to get down at least twice a month. She and the children would come up to Cambridge for the holidays and a portion of the following summer.

By the end of this year of experiment, it was clear that she and the children saw King George as home; and, as the years passed, Becki spent even less time in Cambridge. In spite of this, there was no doubt that she and Arnie continued to have a strong and loving marriage and that any time they spent together was precious to them both. "Always a honeymoon," she'd whisper, whether in the Virginia house's antique walnut bed, lovingly carved by some early Thatcher ancestor, or entangled in a blanket by a riverside fire, blissfully alone during one of their intimate late-night picnics.

Still, as the children started growing, Arnie kept in the back of his mind the hope that eventually he and Becki would be living together year round again. The fact that Drea decided to go to William and Mary did not help his overall plan. Then when Leah was ready for college, she picked Oberlin in Ohio for its excellent music program. Bruce, who had interned for a summer at SofTek, was planning on Caltech the following year.

Arnie decided he would have to have a serious talk with Becki. For one thing, he worried about her living in the country by herself even though Drea was now working and living in Richmond, a little more than an hour away, and Marty was equally close in northern Virginia.

So that first year when all the children were out of the house, Arnie was able to persuade Becki to come to Boston for a few weeks in the autumn. But at Christmas—with all the family home for the holidays back in King George—she announced that she thought it was time to finally finish her long awaited undergraduate degree. She wanted to attend Mary Washington in Fredericksburg full time as a day student. Arnie hid his disappointment. At least she had a goal that would get her out of the house and involved with others. Within a year she should finish, he thought. Then, at last, he would be able to persuade her to live with him full time.

All that changed that spring when Becki disappeared…

☐

PART II: THE YEAR 2000
CHAPTER 20

Awkwardly balancing the heavy grocery bag against her hip with one hand, Becki reached into her pocket with the other and pulled out the key. She was just turning the lock when she heard his voice, the radio one—low and melodious. "Hi." She whirled around and there was Arnie, sitting on the steps going to the next floor. He looked calm and unruffled, his usual self.

"How did you find me?" she asked, afraid her anxiety was apparent. She was sure the blood was rushing to her face.

"Not one of the kids," he answered.

"Good."

"May I come in?"

"What would you do if I didn't let you?" She was curious.

"Wait out here for as long as it takes."

"You probably would so I guess I'd better let you in. How did you know I was here?"

"Private detectives. I've known for over a week. I just had to decide what to do when they found you." Arnie glanced around the apartment, which was sparsely but well-furnished, including shelves loaded with books. Most of the decorations and wall hangings seemed to have come from Africa, a few even from Ethiopia. For a moment he had a sense of déjà vu, remembering their first date at the Adams Morgan restaurant. "Hansen—the name on the door, who's that?" he inquired, seemingly indifferent.

"A friend of Marty's. He's TDY in the Middle East for six months and was willing to let me have his place for half price."

"Nice," Arnie remarked, inwardly relieved. "I've missed you."

"Tough. Over a week? Why did you wait so long?"

"I just wanted to see if there was someone else."

"Your detective couldn't find out," she commented acidly.

"It was none of his business once he found you. Anyhow, I've spent a lot of time the last few days at that little park across the street."

"Well I got careless," Becki retorted, annoyed. "I never noticed."

"No, you seemed too busy running to catch the Metro or taking long walks when you got home."

"Lily Marie's summer graduation, right?"

"Yes," he replied.

"I didn't see you there either."

"I wasn't, but the detective was. He followed you back from Marty's. I gather you were using her car."

"I don't have one."

"You do. You have lots of things."

"Let's get this straight, Arnie. Those are your things, not mine. I don't want anything. Ever!"

"And that's why when I got home you were just gone."

"Of course."

"You came back later though."

"Yes, but just for a few of my things—things that were mine before I met you. That's not much. I left everything else."

"I know. I found the rings, your pearls—that was a nice touch—cutting the string—and the safe deposit box key and the credit cards and everything else. Why did you leave?"

"Don't make me laugh," she sneered angrily. You know perfectly well why I left."

"Tell me."

"Stop playing games, Arnie. You cheated on me. One of the few things—the only thing really that I asked when we got married was for you to tell me if you ever wanted out, that I'd just leave, but that you had to tell me. Not lie, not cheat, not be a sneak like Billy, just tell me. That was good enough, but you didn't have the decency to do that."

"What if I tell you I'm sorry?"

"I accept your apology if that's what you came here to say. You said it, so now you can feel better, but we're through and you can just get out!"

"You've toughened up since you left. I don't want to be through and I don't feel better," he said, coming close to her.

"I had to toughen up. I was going to be on my own again. Damn it, Arnie, you betrayed me, and I'd done everything you asked!"

"Actually, I thought I'd done everything you wanted, too, and this separation wasn't my idea." He was now inches from her, staring directly into her face. Quietly he said, "And I did not betray you, Becki." He reached out to caress her cheek.

"Don't touch me," she protested, jerking back, the groceries now forming a barrier. "It's always trouble when you touch me."

"You don't mean that," he answered, putting his hands lightly on her shoulders, the bulky bag pressed awkwardly between them. "You don't mean that at all. I love you. You know that. I wouldn't have been looking for you for the last three months if I hadn't. I've practically gone crazy since you left. Here, let me take the groceries. You can't use them to hold me off. It didn't work before."

Becki's arms tightened around the defenseless bag and Arnie wondered why it didn't burst. At last, she dropped it on an adjacent table, boxes, cans, a lettuce and some apples tumbling out. They remained standing, a mere foot apart, but miles as far as Arnie was concerned. Becki's scowl and defiant stance were unnerving.

"Very funny, that was twenty years ago. You should have thought about all that before you put your pecker where it didn't belong."

"Nice talk," he replied, a wounded smile on his face. "You always did have a flare with words—all those English classes at BU and Mary Washington finally paying off. Besides, you haven't answered me. How did you know I cheated on you?"

"Because I got the pictures in the mail."

"Ah, I'm surprised you didn't leave them." At the same time he was shocked. Pictures? What pictures?

"Jerry has them. I gave them to him resealed in the envelope and told him he could use them if you contested the divorce."

"I see. And what about the kids? Why haven't you told them where you were?"

"Leah would have told you."

"You're probably right," he agreed. "But Bruce wouldn't nor Drea."

"No, but I didn't want them to be in the position of having to hide that from you."

"Well, I didn't ask Leah or Bruce, though I know you've called them. And Drea wouldn't tell me anything, but then she is your daughter. Neither would Marty or her family."

"But it was her daughter who sent you the graduation invitation."

"Sure, I'm her uncle. But actually what I got was an announcement after the fact. She didn't snitch either."

"Then how did you know about it?" Becki was clearly perplexed, wondering who else he might have contacted.

"Let's be analytic."

Becki snorted. As if Arnie wasn't always.

Seemingly unconcerned, he asked, "How long have we had the place down here in Virginia? At least thirteen years, right? So I'm well aware of school schedules. I just called her high school and asked when the summer graduation was going to be. The detectives were getting nowhere so I had to think of something myself."

"Very clever," she commented acidly. "You always were so smart and sure of yourself."

"Thank you," he replied. "I'll take that as a compliment."

"Yes, I guess you can," Becki's voice softened. It was true, after all, and she had loved these qualities. "Still, it was nice of you to send her the check. She told me. That was a lot of money for a girl her age. She's going to get a laptop for college, I think."

"I've got a lot of money and I love her. I love all our nieces and nephews, both sides. I'm just sorry I couldn't be there; but, I really wasn't invited or otherwise you wouldn't have come."

"No, probably not. At least not if I thought you were going to be there. Damn it, how could you do it to them too? Drea loves you like a real father, our kids adore you. Why couldn't you just have done this cleanly? Let me know you wanted out."

"I told you, I didn't want out. I've never wanted out! I didn't want this to happen. It was all a mistake. I came home early to tell you what had happened."

"I bet." Becki's eyes were dark with rage, something else new to Arnie, who was becoming more and more disturbed.

"Listen, Becki, I called you at the house that Tuesday after my final meeting to tell you I was coming the next day instead of the weekend, and you weren't there. I called every hour after, but there was no answer. I was worried as hell."

"Ha!"

"Believe me, I was. It was late that evening when I got hold of Drea, and all she would say was that you'd left but she wouldn't say where. Marty's, right?"

"Yes," she murmured.

"When I got there Wednesday, I called down to Drea's right after I saw the house and realized you really had gone. I thought you might have been there."

"But I wasn't so you figured that out right away, didn't you?"

"I know you, or at least I thought I did. I didn't have to be Sherlock Holmes or even your beloved Spenser to realize you'd left me when I saw the rings and things. You left everything. How have you been living? I've been worried sick about you."

"I'm getting along just fine, don't you worry the

slightest," she asserted nastily, arms rigidly bent to her sides and lips tightened.

Annoyed, he retorted, "Sure."

"Listen, I took care of myself and my daughter before I met you. I have a little money of my own, not something you gave me. I have some skills, more than when we met. I didn't need you before I met you and as the song goes, 'gonna get along without ya now'."

"What happens if you get sick or something?"

"I'll worry about that then. I'm getting by so do me the courtesy of letting me do just that and get out." Her voice was rising. If this were anyone else, Arnie was sure she'd explode with rage.

"Please," he pleaded, "please just listen to me. It was a mistake."

"A mistake! You call that a mistake!" She looked at him incredulously.

"I was set up."

"Swell, you want me to believe something like that?"

"Why else would you have gotten pictures?"

"That was our house at the Cape. No, that was your house at the Cape. That was you in that bed. I know that bed. I've spent plenty of time in it, and the woman with you wasn't me."

"Did you ever stop to ask why there were pictures? I'd really like to see them."

"Hell, how do I know if you're kinky with other women and want souvenir photos? How many, Arnie? How long have you been doing it?"

"I'm not kinky. I've never been kinky, and there haven't been other women."

"That was a woman."

"Yes, I admit that, but it was an accident."

"Define accident," Becki snapped coldly.

"Will you listen, really listen?" he begged, wondering how they ever could have gotten to this state. Becki was his emotional core, the human side of his being, and her antagonistic words numbed him.

"If you'll leave after you tell me."

"One, I was alone most of Sunday. All the business guests had left by early afternoon. Two, I planned to drive back into Boston early Monday. I'd been out on the beach and after I got in, I'd just called you to say I would be back in Virginia on Friday instead of Saturday, if you'll remember."

"So..."

"So, I went and worked out on the exercise bike because you'd given me another lecture, and after I was going to have a drink when someone was at the door. It was Pam Carter, who'd been at our meeting earlier with one of the consortium representatives. She was upset, crying, saying she was sorry to be there but she'd had a fight with her boyfriend, and could she come in for a minute because he was still at the motel and she was afraid to go back for her things."

"Sure...Sir Knight again, always there to help some damsel in distress," Becki sneered nastily.

Arnie was taken aback. He'd never seen her hostile before and even though she had reason to be, it was like being with a different person. "Stop. You said you'd listen, now listen."

She stared at him defiantly, saying nothing, but he could sense her anger radiating and even though he could understand her belligerence, he was becoming irritated. He had not instigated the incident, and Becki should have waited to talk to him before disappearing into the blue and scaring him half to death. After all, they'd been married almost twenty years. He deserved a hearing!

"I let her in and then she asked if she could have a drink. Well, I was standing there with a glass in my hand so what could I do? I poured her one and she sat down and started crying harder. Then she got herself another one and it was apparent she had been drinking before she got there. So I said I'd get cleaned up and take her back to the motel since she shouldn't be driving. I figured I'd get her another room or something and make sure she got her things.

Anyhow, I went into the bedroom and got into the shower, washing the salt out of my hair, blind as a bat with shampoo, and the next thing I knew, she was in there with me...naked and down on her knees."

"You honestly expect me to believe a story like that?" Becki was astounded.

"Do you honestly expect me to tell you something like that if it weren't true?" he asked.

"Frankly...frankly," she stopped.

"Yeah, well I was kind of at a loss for words too. I mean I was so surprised, I just, well you know..."

"I don't believe this," she said furiously, sinking into an armchair as he moved to the nearby sofa. Her knuckles were white as her fingers dug into the plush arms and he was glad for once that her hold was on the chair rather than him. Even Becki's playful pinches sometimes smarted— particularly now that he'd added a few pounds.

"I didn't either, but I pulled her up and somehow the two of us got out of the shower without falling and breaking our necks and then she was all over me telling me how sorry she was. It was obvious that she was drunk, and I didn't know what the shit to do. I mean for one thing, she was stark naked. Honest to God, Becki, nothing like that has ever happened to me—never! I finally got her out onto one of the living room couches and she just plain passed out, or so I thought. I tossed a quilt over her and then I went and washed the damn shampoo off and poured myself another drink and thought about calling you again..." He looked at her, sheepishly.

"I'm sure," Becki replied caustically.

"So help me, who else could I talk to but then how could I tell you something like this? You would have killed me."

"Yes."

"I'm glad you agree with my assessment of the situation," he responded sarcastically, wounded at her nasty tone of voice.

"Well what the hell do you expect me to say? Gee,

honey, I'm sorry you let someone suck you off," lashed back Becki.

"Cut it out. That's not the way it happened."

"And that's not what those pictures showed either."

"Why don't you tell me what the pictures showed?" This was perplexing him most, and he had to find out.

"Why don't you tell me what they could?" she jeered.

"The bed, right?"

"Yes...weasel out of that one."

"I went to bed, ok. I finished off the bottle and I guess I passed out. Then in the middle of the night, someone was coming on to me and to be quite honest, since you're the only one, and I repeat, the only one I've been sleeping with for all these years, I just reached over and went for it. Then to my horror, once I was fully awake, realized it wasn't you. It kind of put a damper on the whole exercise. I didn't know anything about pictures until you mentioned them, but if there were pictures, it was all done for a purpose and to be totally honest, I don't know why you, instead of me, got them. I mean the whole purpose of blackmail is supposed to be concealment, isn't it?" He looked piteously at Becki, who was glaring. By now the chair arms, if human, would probably be broken or the blood circulation stifled. "You have got to believe me, Becki," he implored. "I did not initiate this. I have not been sleeping around on you. I never did. Once we were married—hell, once I met you—I was a one-woman man and that's the way I wanted it. You've always been enough for me. There've been opportunities, sure, but I didn't want anyone else. I do not want anyone else."

"Touching, very touching. Now just get out," she rasped.

"You don't believe me," he sighed despondently.

"Why should I? I admit this is one of the wildest stories I've ever heard, and I really can't imagine why you'd tell me something this inane, but I still have the photos."

"And I'd like to see them. Let Jerry show them to me."

"And have you grab them?"

"You know I'd never do that."

"Well I also thought you'd never cheat on me, but obviously I was wrong. How often, Arnie?"

"Becki, it happened once, just that night, and I did not initiate it. Think of me as the rape victim."

"Some rape," she commented acidly.

"I told you I was drunk. I was asleep. I thought it was you."

"And she's about half my age and terrific looking. You really expect me to believe that, you miserable bastard? Your time's up. Just get out."

Her words were bitter but her eyes were full of anguish and Arnie felt like a real heel. Yet at the same time, he also was angry that she wouldn't listen to him or make an attempt to understand. The whole rotten episode hadn't been his fault; it was some terrible accident. "Would you have felt this way if it had been a car wreck and I had hurt someone?" he asked.

"If you had been drinking or doped up."

"You're hard, Becki."

"It seemed time to learn," she snapped. Being nice and trusting certainly didn't pay off, she reflected. How could she have been so naive all these years to believe he was faithful, particularly with all their separations? Arnie, the super salesman, he had sold her a bill of goods from the very start, and she'd believed him.

"I don't understand you and no, the woman's not half your age. She has to be at least thirty and she still doesn't look as good as you. You've always kept a portrait up in the attic, Dorian Grey's sister herself—but no wrinkles, no signs of aging on it." He got up off the sofa and approached her, leaning over and putting his hands on the tormented arms of her chair.

"I'll call for help," she said, feeling pinned in but trying not to panic. "We're separated. You have no rights over me."

"You could, but I don't think you will. You hate scenes. You always have. You get embarrassed. You might try to knee me in the balls, but you're not going to scream." She opened her mouth and he leaned forward, kissing her gently. "You won't scream," he said, quietly, seductively. "You won't knee me either. You love me. You're not going to hurt me—not even break a little finger."

She drew back as best as she could into the security of the chair. Her eyes were widening, sad and full of despair, and all the hostility was gone. Arnie could see her bravado was crumbling and she was beginning to sound like his sensitive, overly vulnerable wife once again. "Don't, don't do this to me, Arnie."

"What, try to make love to you? I love you. You're my wife. You love me. You like me to touch you." He sat on the arm of the chair and began to caress her, to woo her back.

"Don't," she repeated, "please don't. I don't want this. We're through."

"No, we're not, or you wouldn't be letting me do this to you." He drew her closer, kissing her more urgently, knowing he'd always been able to please her. Confident that intimacy, if nothing else, would win her back.

"Please, it's not fair," she protested weakly, but she wasn't struggling.

"Nothing is in love—I told you that when you tried to break the engagement." Standing, he pulled her up and held her tightly. "I felt as though I was going to die when I came home that night and you weren't there, Beauty. I called everyone I could think of. I was so worried. You know I came up to Marty's the next day but you were already gone."

"Yes," Becki murmured, "I was here."

"And you were so clever, sweetheart." Becki winced at the endearment, which Arnie tried to ignore. "All the mail was forwarded to Jerry's office and the stupid detectives never could figure where he was sending it."

"He wasn't. He took it home and then Marty gave it to one of their neighbors. I've been working for him and he'd give it to me."

"And you called the kids and told them to call Jerry or Marty in an emergency."

"Yes."

"But you didn't tell any of them why you left."

"No," she said quietly.

"Thank you," he said simply.

"They love you. I didn't want this to be me and them against you or vice versa." Becki's eyes were brimming and he knew if she finally started to cry, so would he.

"Why, honey, why would you ever think I'd want to leave you, to have an affair with anyone else?" Arnie was staring into the soulful eyes now, his own usually lively brown ones serious, intent, equally full of remorse.

"I'm getting older. I have no eternal youth. I am the aging portrait. You're a personable, filthy rich and still desirable man. Charming, brilliant—you're one of those people who improve with age. We both know you always knew how to attract women. The woman in the photos is young and needs no portrait. Time is catching up with me, Arnie."

"She may be younger. But, I swear, I've never ever cheated on you. I hadn't planned to when this happened. It was as much of a shock to me as you and I don't think it should count. As soon as I realized she was in my bed, I shoved her right out. I ended up tossing her and her clothes out of the house, which is what I should have done right away. Then I spent the rest of the night trying to figure what to tell you.

"I guess I should have flown right down but those meetings had been set up for months. Besides, I didn't want to tell you what had happened over the phone. I couldn't do that. I was ashamed and upset too. I didn't want to hurt you, Becki. You have to believe that! And then when I got back to Virginia and you were gone, I nearly went crazy. I realized somehow you had found out and I couldn't find you."

"Well, you must have spent a pretty penny doing so."

"Actually yes, but do you think it really mattered?"

"To your pocketbook, probably not."

"Take me back," he pleaded. "Don't leave me. Let's work this out, find out why this happened, please." He held her close, rubbing his hands up and down her arms gently.

"This is dirty pool," she said weakly, trying to pull away but at the same time knowing she wanted so much to stay in his embrace. It had been months since she'd seen him and his physical presence was making her body ache. Even with all their separations, they had never been apart for more than a few weeks at a time.

Tenderly he kissed her. She tried not to respond but then her body finally betrayed her and she began to kiss him back, hesitantly at first and then hungrily. Her little man, she thought for a moment, her sexy little man. He maneuvered her down on the couch and began to undress her. At first, she halfheartedly deflected his hands but then she just lay back and let him remove everything and touch her. Finally, unable to control herself, she reached down. Voraciously, greedily, she was grasping him, eager to feel and taste him. How long, so long, she thought, as she held him tightly. Their lovemaking was almost brutal, her nails raking up and down his back and he pressing hard, bruising kisses on her and holding her so securely that she was gasping for breath.

Once they had climaxed, he rested himself upon her and she began to stroke his hair gently. Then she began to sob to herself. Ten finally, thought Arnie, although he was sure the list had mounted during the months they were apart; certainly he'd shed more than a tear, if just in frustration, when he realized she was gone.

"I'm so sorry," he whispered into her ear, "I haven't lied to you. As crazy as it all sounded, that's the way it happened. You've got to come back to me, Beauty. From now on, you can't let me go off for these long periods of time by myself. You've got to be with me! The kids are grown now and you could. Nothing like this should happen again. I don't know why it did, but not again. Ok?" Gently he kissed her eyelids, tasting the salty tears, sorrowful that he was the cause.

Becki had the terrible realization that she had betrayed herself. It had felt right, the way it always did with Arnie, but she knew it was wrong. By not being able to deny him and herself, she was caught again. She'd never be able to escape now, to be her own person. Softly she began to cry more, disgusted by her weakness and dependency on a man who had deceived her. She couldn't say anything. She just lay there until he fell asleep. Then she extricated herself and went into the bathroom.

CHAPTER 21

When Arnie awoke, he was surprised to realize Becki was gone. From the bathroom he heard the water running. He lay back thinking about the whole mess, about what to do now. If he hadn't remembered Lily Marie's late summer graduation, he might not have found her. But now that he had, he still wasn't convinced that Becki would return to him. Why had that crazy Carter woman done what she did? He'd never given any indication he was interested in her. Sure, he could appreciate a pretty woman. He wasn't blind; but none had ever enticed him since he met Becki, his own true Beauty.

The fact that there were actually pictures made the whole setup even screwier. And why were they sent to Becki and not to him? He wouldn't have paid blackmail, of that he was sure; he would have told Becki. That part was true also, but Carter and her accomplice didn't know that. So, what else was involved?

Becki seemed to have been in the tub an inordinate amount of time and the water was still running. Arnie reached over to the coffee table and picked up his watch. It was now 7:00 P.M. He must have been dozing for almost fifteen minutes. Perhaps he should ask her if she'd like him to order some carry out. Jesus, he hoped she'd let him stay. She'd let him make love to her, but she was right, that was dirty pool. He'd always been able to turn her on by just touching her. Hell, she did the same to him, and he'd missed her so much all these months. From the almost savage intensity of her sexual response, she'd obviously missed him too. His back would probably be sore for days and he wouldn't be surprised if there was blood; good thing Becki kept her nails fairly short.

Getting up, he pulled on his trousers, zipping as he walked over to the bathroom door, and quietly asked, "Becki, are you hungry? Should I call out for something?"

There was no answer and the water was still running. So he knocked on the door and spoke a little louder. There was still no answer and now he was worried. Reaching down, he tried to turn the handle but the door was locked. "Becki, answer me! Are you ok, Becki?" His voice was rising but he heard nothing but the flowing water. He yanked ineffectually at the handle again. Then rushing into the kitchen, he began frantically pulling out drawers as he looked for something to force the door. Finally he found a large kitchen knife and returning to the bathroom, he called again, "Becki!" This time when there was no answer, he wedged the knife in the doorjamb and pried. At last it gave and he pushed in the door.

She was reclining in the tub, looking deathly white and the water was stained with blood. The ends of her long blond hair were wet and dyed by the rusty-tinted water. It was as though he was looking at some horror film. Arnie felt physically ill.

Leaning over the tub, he picked up one of her lacerated wrists. "Ah, Becki." He leaned over further to see if she was breathing. She was so still at first that he was afraid he was too late, but he felt a slight pulse on her throat and there was still some blood seeping torpidly. Reaching in, he pulled her out, limp as if her bones had melted. Clutching her tightly, he began to cry. Then looking around, he saw towels and tugged them down, wrapping them as firmly as he could around her wrists.

Picking her up, he carried her back to the couch. Laying her gently down, he took a pillow and propped her arms to elevate them above her heart, trying to remember a First Aid class taken in his youth. Then reaching for the phone, he dialed 911, wondering at the same time if it would be better to take her to the hospital himself. But of course, he suddenly realized, he didn't know where it was.

After making the call, he held her, his hands tightening around her wrists, hoping he'd stopped the bleeding. "Ah honey, why did you do it? Why?" It was the last thing he would have ever supposed but then he'd never believed she'd ever leave him either. All their years together and now something like this.

When he was sure the bleeding had stopped, he went into the bedroom to find a sheet to wrap around her and ended up stripping the top one off the bed. To his surprise as he did so, he noted his old Caltech sweatshirt lying crumpled next to the pillows. Odd, he'd thought it had been thrown out years before. He certainly hadn't seen it since...actually he couldn't remember for how long and then wondered why he cared at a time like this. Returning to Becki, he now saw her lovely skin was stretched taunt and appeared eerily pallid—none of her usual summer tan. Terrible, she looked terrible, not at all the beautiful, healthy woman he'd kissed goodbye just months before when leaving for the infamous Cape Cod meeting.

By the time the paramedics arrived, Arnie was fully dressed. Once they reached the hospital, he paced back and forth until a doctor was able to tell him, "Yes, Mr. Miller. We got your wife here in time, but we still don't know the extent of the injuries. She needs a transfusion and her right wrist has been badly gashed. There's certainly nerve damage and possibly worse, but we won't know for certain until after the reparative surgery. That should be immediate, but I have no idea how long it will take."

Feeling nauseated, Arnie gave his permission for the procedure. Then he asked the location of a telephone and went to call Jerry. Before his brother-in-law could interrupt or hang up, he said bluntly, "This is Arnie. I'm at Inova here in Fairfax with Becki. She tried to commit suicide."

"What!" Jerry was practically screaming.

"Can you get over here as our...her lawyer. The police are already here, but I don't want to talk to them without having you here. Also, I'm wondering if this is the right place for her, if maybe we should move her somewhere else."

"Ah hell," said Jerry. "I'll be there in less than a half hour. Don't let the police question you or her, if she can speak. This is my car phone number," and he rattled it off. "Call me in about five minutes and we'll talk as I drive over."

"Thanks, Jerry. I'll try to keep a low profile until I get hold of you." Hanging up, Arnie began once again to pace back and forth, looking at his watch. When the allotted time had passed, he dialed the new number.

"Hello."

"Jerry? It's Arnie again."

"Ok, tell me what happened," Jerry said, once more sounding his professional self.

"I found out where she was staying and I was waiting for her when she got home tonight. She let me come in and we started talking and I tried to tell her what happened."

"Which was?"

"She hasn't told you?"

"Not in detail."

"Well, when she wants to, she can. But for now, she listened to me and I asked her to come home and she wouldn't answer, but she..." Arnie hesitated. "She let me make love to her. Then when I was asleep, she went into the bathroom, locked herself in, got into the tub and slit her wrists."

"Christ! That's not Becki," Jerry blurted.

"I know it isn't. When I woke up, I didn't suspect anything at first but she wouldn't answer so I ended up breaking down the door and finding her. I have no idea how long she was in there. I just got her out, stopped the bleeding, and called 911. They haven't told me anything really except she needs surgery. She may have severed tendons and appears to have serious nerve damage."

"Ah shit. Ok, I should be there in ten minutes. Don't talk to anyone and get out of that emergency area immediately! In fact, just go to the front lobby. I'll come in that way and we can walk back together. And, Arnie, just for the record, I think you're a miserable turd and I'm doing this for my sister-in-law, not you."

"Fine," Arnie said, "fine." He hung up. Gazing around, he saw that no one was looking his way, so he slowly and nonchalantly walked out of the waiting area into the hospital corridor. Following the signs, he made his way to the main entrance. True to his word, Jerry came rushing in within minutes, all business and looking as though he were ready to argue in front of the Supreme Court.

"Ok, Arnie, show me the way. At this point I don't want to know anything about what happened between the two of you except for tonight. You've told me that, right? Everything you've said is true?"

"I swear it."

"Then when the police ask, you tell it exactly the same way. You can just say you've been separated for three months and that you came to see her to try to get back together, that you were intimate, and that this whole thing is a complete shock to you. I'll take it from there."

"Well it is!" Arnie's voice nearly cracked in emotion.

"I assume you want this as low key as possible. That you hope no one knows who you two are, nothing that might reflect on that precious company of yours and your reputation."

"We have fairly common names and hell, Becki and the kids have always stayed out of the limelight. Most people don't even realize we keep the two houses. All my main business is out of Boston and you know all my identification is listed as James Miller. Since I'm always called Arnie by the press now, I don't see why it should be obvious that a Jim Miller is me. I don't necessarily see why anyone should catch on, not right away."

"I hope so, for her sake more than yours, at least until we can get her to some private hospital. You know that this is serious and she may have to be committed."

"What?" Arnie's mouth dropped open. Becki was not insane!

"Oh, yeah," Jerry drawled out unhappily. "Also you'd better hope they believe she's the one that did this and not suspect you of being involved or we have big problems."

"Shit."

"That's an understatement. Now just be the worried husband and we'll do what we can do."

"I am the worried husband. I'm worried sick! I don't

know how badly hurt she is and until I got her out of the tub, I didn't know how she'd let herself go. She's lost weight and she looks terrible. You know she's never had a pound to spare."

"Well maybe you should have thought about that before you started tomcatting around," Jerry snidely remarked, glaring down at his brother-in-law, who was now glaring back. Another first in close relationships Arnie realized ruefully.

"Damn it, I didn't tomcat on her. She's my wife. I love her. I want her back. I want all this to go away. I don't know what's happening and I sure as hell never thought she'd ever do anything like this. This is insane." Oh God, he'd said the word. Maybe Becki was mentally ill. Sane people didn't attempt suicide, did they?

"Yes, it is and that's why I mentioned the possibly of having to put her into a mental hospital."

"A mental hospital," Arnie stopped abruptly, utterly shocked at the actual suggestion. Grabbing Jerry's arm and clearly distraught, he pled, "You don't mean that."

"Oh I do indeed," answered Jerry, shaking loose. "That's what they sometimes do with people who try to commit suicide, at least for observation."

"Jesus, that would destroy her!"

"From what you've told me, she's done a fairly good job by herself." Jerry's sarcasm was biting.

"Oh Jesus, I can't do that to her."

"You may have to."

The two arrived at the emergency ward. "Mr. Miller," said a harried-looking nurse, "we've been trying to find you. The police would like to interview you."

Arnie turned to Jerry. "Advise me."

"You talk to them. I'll be with you. How's Mrs. Miller?" he asked the nurse. "I'm the brother-in-law."

"Her vital signs have stabilized. She's having a transfusion now and we're prepping her for surgery. She's lost a couple pints of blood and one of her wrists was badly damaged. We've called in a specialist."

"Oh shit," moaned Arnie, putting his hands to his head and sinking into a nearby chair. "Poor Becki."

"Mr. Miller?" Arnie looked up and two uniformed policemen were standing in the room. "You were the one who called 911?" the taller one inquired, his face carefully neutral but no friendliness in his eyes.

"Yes, I found her in the bathroom...I had to break down the door to get her."

"Can you tell us what happened, sir?" The police remained standing, looking down, an intimidating tactic, thought Arnie, intentionally or not. But polite, so polite, yet still police. That they'd come to this. Becki and him and the police.

Carefully he answered, "We've been separated. I went to her apartment tonight to talk, to try and convince her to come home. We..." he faltered before adding, "...we made love. I fell asleep and when I woke up, I realized she had locked herself in the bathroom. I became alarmed and I went in to get her. I got her out of the tub, stopped the bleeding, and called for help."

"You say that she had sexual relations with you willingly?" The proper, courteous voice again, but seeming to have an underlying accusation.

"Yes, damn it. She did and why she did this, I don't know. She's my wife! I love her. Now what are you trying to say to me?" Arnie felt on the verge of losing his self-control and had jumped up.

Jerry caught his sleeve and stepped in front of him. "Officers, I'm Jerry Madison, an attorney." He pulled out a business card. "I'm also Mrs. Miller's brother-in-law and she had come to me for legal advice. She had not made up her mind yet if she wanted a divorce and if one was going to take place, it was to be no contest. There is no reason to think that anything occurred other than what Mr. Miller told you. If you think otherwise, I suggest you caution him at this point, in which case I'll be handling the situation on his behalf."

"No, sir, we're just trying to get all the facts," the

younger, previously silent, officer interjected. Just the facts, thought Arnie. It sounded like the original *Dragnet*, one of his favorite childhood TV shows.

"Fine, if you want anything else, my brother-in-law is more than willing to make a statement, but I'll be there with him. When Mrs. Miller can be interviewed, I'm sure the hospital will inform you and I'll also be present. She's been under a great deal of strain since the separation: lost weight, very nervous. Somehow she apparently also just lost perspective, but I'm sure she'll verify what Mr. Miller has said. Still, until her doctor says she is able to be interviewed, I think we'd just better leave it at that. Here's my card," Jerry said, thrusting one into the younger man's hand. You'll know how to reach me if there's anything else you need, and I'm sure the rescue squad will also corroborate Mr. Miller's story. Now if you don't mind, we'd like to talk to the doctor and find out her status and what should be done next."

CHAPTER 22

When Becki woke up the next morning, she found herself in a hospital bed. Arnie was sitting next to her. "Where am I?" she asked woozily.

"In the hospital. Why, honey, why did you do it?" he asked, his eyes sad. He had been there all night. In all their years, he realized he had never seen Becki ill. Certainly she had been in the hospital for the babies but she had always returned to her beautiful, healthy self within days, seemingly with boundless energy. The worse that had happened to her was a cold or two, but she was consistently the caregiver for the ills and accidents suffered by the rest of the family. Calm and collected, she would comfort them all. The sight of her like this, especially with the cumbersome bandaging on her right wrist and the knowledge that she had lost some of its mobility, distressed him immeasurably.

"It was a mistake," she whispered faintly and turned her head to look toward the window.

"You didn't mean to do it?"

"That's not what I said. Thinking I could go back to you, letting you make love to me. I shouldn't have done that. It was wrong, Arnie."

"Oh God, of course you should. You do love me. We do belong together. I couldn't believe you wanted to do this. You've got to come back to me." He'd never felt such anguish. No, that wasn't true—everything had been anguish since he'd found her in the tub. To a lesser degree, he'd been anguished since he'd arrived at King George and found her gone. But then...even though months passed, he'd never doubted that he'd find her eventually and bring her home.

"I'd do it again," she declared emotionlessly.

"How can you say something like that? How can you even consider something like that? You'd be killing both of us." His voice had risen, agonized, and he felt nauseated, knowing she was telling the truth.

She turned her head back towards him, staring at him with haunted eyes. "It's over. It's over or I am. I can't live with you again, but I didn't think I wanted to live without you. I thought I could. I thought I was doing fine but you found me and then I knew I couldn't keep you away but I have to. When I get out of here, you've got to promise you won't try to find me again. That you'll leave me alone. Keep this promise, Arnie, please!"

"How can I do that?" he asked poignantly, remembering the one other promise she'd ever exacted, not to cheat, which he'd broken even if unintentionally. "You're breaking my heart."

"Well, you broke mine." She began to cry.

"It was all a mistake. I told you. I didn't lie to you. I don't know how it happened or why it happened. I'm going to find out, but I need you. Please."

"Just go away," Becki pled. "Now."

"They're going to keep you in here for a while, not just for the hand," he finally said. "I've had no choice on that. The only way they'd release you now is to me."

"No!" Her voice was sharp.

"I can't help it. Jerry explained. Unless I can guarantee your safety and make sure you get to a doctor, they'll probably keep you confined."

"No!" Becki began to cry harder. "I don't want to go with you. Why can't I go home with Drea or have Jerry and Marty get me out?"

"I'm still your closest relative legally. I'm the one responsible for you."

"That's not fair, damn you!"

"What you've done wasn't fair. It wasn't fair to you or me or the kids. How could you do it?" Arnie's voice broke from emotion and he felt his eyes becoming moist.

"I'm so unhappy. I've been so unhappy. I'm just tired of it all. I didn't want to fight with you. I didn't want you to come after me again. I didn't want to keep loving you."

"I'm sorry. I'm so, so sorry. You've got to believe me," he was stroking her left hand until he realized that she was wincing from his touch. Not sure whether he was causing actual physical pain to that lacerated wrist or if it was just his proximity, he stopped. Then leaning over, he placed a kiss on her brow.

She jerked away. "Don't do that. Don't, please don't."

"Ah hell," he said in a deadened tone and got up slowly, feeling as though he had been struck. "I'll go now. At least I'll get out of the room. I want to talk to the doctor, but please think of coming home with me so I can take care of you. We'll get a nurse. I won't touch you. I won't come near you until you tell me it's all right. I just want to take care of you, to know you're ok. To see if maybe we can work something out when you feel better. I just don't understand this, I can't."

After he left, Becki lay looking up at the ceiling, not believing she was there, not believing that she had really tried to kill herself. When she'd done it, it seemed the only way to end the situation but she'd failed just the way she always did. What was going to happen now she didn't know and she started to cry again. She was so unhappy. She felt as though she'd been unhappy so much of her life except the time with Arnie and that had proved an illusion.

CHAPTER 23

When Arnie left Becki's room, he called Jerry at his office. "I've got to talk to you. Can you see me?"

"You know I don't want to talk to you, Arnie, but if you think it's anything that will help Becki, I will."

"I really don't know," confessed Arnie. "I hope so, but I'm at my wits' end. And, at least, I know you're almost as concerned about her. I would have liked to talk to Marty too, but she hung up on me when I called the house."

"I'm not surprised," remarked Jerry snidely, miffed at Arnie's protestation of concern. Becki wouldn't be lying in a hospital now if Arnie had truly been concerned. "If you can get over here in a half hour, I can fit you in."

"I'll be there."

When Arnie walked into the law office, Jerry was sitting there looking like a judge, not at all the friendly brother-in-law with whom he'd spent so much time. "This had better be good," said Jerry dryly, now strictly all business.

Arnie shrugged his shoulders, slumping uninvited into a chair. "I'll do my best. First I guess I'd better tell you that when I saw Becki this morning, she said she wanted to do it again."

"Ah shit, I don't believe this." Jerry's hand tightened on a pencil, snapping it in two.

"I wish I didn't either," replied Arnie, also wishing he could snap a few pencils, "but I was the one who found her. How well do you know Becki?'

"Now that's one of the most stupid questions I've ever heard," Jerry snarled, any vestige of a calm and collected attorney fast eroding. He loved Becki and this SOB had hurt her. "I've known her for twenty-five years. She's my wife's sister. She lived with us for almost six years."

"Given. But, I repeat, how well do you know her?" Arnie asked seriously.

"What...that she's gorgeous, smart, nice, obviously

loved you, you shit, is a great mother."

"Yeah, she's all that, but what about her socially, how she interacts with people—at work, outside the home."

"What are you trying to pull, Arnie? Trying to say there's something wrong with her, that you weren't the reason she went over the edge. She loved you, you bastard. She would never have believed you were unfaithful if she hadn't gotten those pictures. At least I assume that's what they show. She was frantic when she came up here that day. I've never seen her so distraught. I tried to tell her to go back to the house, to stake her claim, make you leave, but all she wanted to do was get out and she doesn't even want to use the pictures to put the screws on you. She doesn't want the house or alimony or part of your fucking company or any other damn thing. She just wants out and for you to leave her alone. But I tell you, buddy, I'm not going to let that happen. You're going to pay!" yelled Jerry, half rising, his professional composure now totally lost.

"Well, I don't want to leave her alone. I didn't plan to cheat on her, and I'd never refuse to support her!" Arnie retorted, irate at the very suggestion.

"Ha!" snorted Jerry, settling back into his chair and looking down at his watch. "You're wasting my time. I've got fifteen more minutes for you so if you really want to tell me something, you better do it now. If not, I'm going to find some way that Marty or even Drea can be her legal guardian until she's judged competent; and we're going to take you to the cleaners."

"I'm not sure I blame you," said Arnie, "but if I have fifteen minutes, you listen to me. First, I did not purposely cheat on Becki. I told her what happened and although it sounds totally improbable, it's true. I was set up. A young woman I hardly know showed up at our place at the Cape with some cock and bull story about her own problems. I had a drink and she'd been drinking when she arrived. Then she tossed down a few more and I was afraid to let her out on the road. I went to get cleaned up so I could drive her back to where she was staying and she got into the shower with me and...hell, she came down on me."

"You expect me to believe this? You're nuts!" Jerry's eyebrows had practically arched into his hairline. As a lawyer, he'd heard plenty, but this was ludicrous, especially from someone like Arnie, whose brains practically spilled out of his head. Right now he'd like to help them!

"It's my quarter hour so shut up. I got her out of there. She had passed out—I thought, and I took a bottle to bed with me and I ended up passing out too. In the middle of the night, someone was making love to me and I thought it was Becki, honest to God. Then when I realized who it was, I got her ass out of the house as fast as I could. I didn't even know there were photos until Becki told me she'd been sent some. I'd just assumed that the bitch had called her or told someone who knew Becki. The fact that there were photos means the whole thing was planned and what I can't understand is why I didn't get them instead of Becki. I'm the one that should have been blackmailed. Believe me, this has been driving me crazy since Becki told me; and, as soon as I get out of here, I'm going right back to Boston to see what I can find out. Hopefully a good detective agency up there will beat the crappy one down here. Hell, I was the one who figured out how to find her myself."

"How's that?" asked Jerry. The revelation of Arnie's use of detectives was a complete surprise.

"Your daughter's graduation."

"But she didn't send you an invitation."

"No, but I knew she was graduating and that Becki would go. I just had someone waiting there to follow her."

"So, what other cute little disclosures do you have for me?"

"You never answered my question about the public Becki," Arnie persisted doggedly.

"She's fine, Arnie. She was a normal person until this happened."

"You never noticed how shy she is?"

"Lots of people are shy, Arnie. That doesn't mean they're nuts. She was just fine. She was a lot of fun when she was living with us. She worked, she modeled, she had boyfriends—at least a few, she met you, she went off to Boston. What the hell am I supposed to say?"

"Well, for starters," asked Arnie, "what's she been like since she started working for your neighbors?"

"What do you mean? She's fine, I told you. She's competent, gets along with people, you know…"

"Does she have any social life? Does she have to interact with the public?"

"How do I know about her social life?" Jerry retorted. "She's been down in the dumps and trying to stay away from you. To be honest, I think she does mostly secretarial stuff now—typing, files, tasks like that."

"Did she ever tell you why we moved down here?"

"You were on the road a lot and she was tired of Boston. You guys had the chance to get the King George house and thought it would be a nice change for the kids to live in the country. She wanted to come back home. Shit, I don't know." Jerry shook his head, realizing he'd never really questioned Becki's motives for returning to Virginia.

"Becki's shy," reiterated Arnie.

"You said that."

"I mean really shy. Almost phobic. Think back to before I met her when she lived with you. She went to school, she had a job—again through some of your friends. She started modeling because her boss's brother was in the business. She met a couple guys because of people at work, but it was a fairly restricted life."

"Of course it was. She had Drea. She wanted to go to school."

"And she never went to New York."

"For the same reasons. She worried about Drea."

"No, only partially. She wouldn't have been able to cut it. She never really cut it in Boston either. She tried to tell me and at first I just wouldn't listen or accept what she said. I wanted to marry her right away. I was wild about her, Jerry—you know that! I still am, even if you don't want to believe it. And around me, just like you, she was functioning just fine. But when she came up there that first time, there was a nasty incident with a man from my company. It caused a whole shake-up at work and a lot of bad feelings. It wasn't her fault, but she got smeared because he started rumors. She almost didn't marry me because she was afraid, but I didn't understand. That time I came down here to tell you all, I was forcing the issue. She had reneged on our engagement and I wasn't going to let her. I bet you never knew that."

Jerry said nothing, but shook his head. Becki had never told him any of this, nor he doubted, had she spoken to Marty.

"Then when we did get married, more rumors started that I had to marry her, particularly because Leah was early. It was also obvious that she'd had Drea in high school. A lot of people at SofTek weren't very nice to her. But, I just didn't notice and she never complained. The kids came so fast and close together that all she seemed to have time to do or want to do was to stay home and be their mother. I spent a lot of time at work and we just didn't have much of a social life, not that it seemed to bother her.

"Then there was an incident in New York, when we managed to broker a deal with the Volkenant Corporation. It was the first time she went on a business trip with me after Leah and Bruce arrived. Someone humiliated her publicly to get back at me. She was so upset by what happened that she just wouldn't travel again with me on business."

Jerry looked interested. He'd often wondered why Becki hadn't traveled with Arnie more. Certainly when the kids were on vacation, they could have come to visit him and Marty.

"I wasn't going to force her at that point. I guess it was then I realized that we rarely socialized with anyone from the company...and I do mean rarely. I, of course, was spending plenty of time with them professionally. Becki and I'd give a big holiday party yearly but that was mostly an open house and she was always so busy being the hostess that even then she wasn't interacting. She'd go to a few work-related functions with me, but usually stay next to me like a leech unless Madge, one of my partners, lured her away. Even then, she'd mostly just stand there quietly, listening, smiling, not really entering conversations.

"It was a little better at home. She met some of the neighbors. We did a few things with them. She stopped her classes finally because of the kids. At least that was her excuse. She'd do things for their schools like baking cookies for class parties, helping at a fund-raising carnival or driving children places. But even there, she'd never do anything where she really had to talk to people.

"Arnie," interrupted Jerry, "where are you going with this?"

"I'm saying she functioned perfectly well in a small, safe world, which at least in Boston was getting smaller and smaller. I don't know what happened to her that year after her folks died and she had to live with that witch of an aunt, but somehow along the way, she was traumatized. She never really told me much except her aunt got rid of all their personal things and told her she was living there only as a Christian duty. When Becki became pregnant, dear old Aunt Mary called her a whore and threw her out."

Jerry looked shocked. "I never knew that. I'm not sure Marty did either. We knew she left but assumed it was to go to Billy's folks because he was marrying her."

Arnie continued bitterly, "Who knows what else the old harridan did to Becki. Imagine what it must have been like to lose your parents and home and have to live with someone like that. She once told me it was the bleakest year of her life. I think Becki probably always was a shy little kid, but with her parents she was fine. If they'd lived, I doubt very much she would have gotten pregnant in high school. She wouldn't have needed some creep to love her. I suppose you also didn't know the old bitch even used to tell her that her parents deserved to die, that it was some kind of heavenly retribution."

Jerry sat dumbfounded. At last he slowly said, "I can't believe it."

"Believe it," Arnie asserted forcefully. "Dear Aunt Mary actually told her that—especially about her mother. No, I think if her folks had lived, Becki would have gone to college, probably Mary Washington so she could commute. She'd have married someone nice locally...maybe a schoolteacher. She might have ended up teaching too. She'd have had her kids and no one would have noticed that she was a bit quiet. Maybe she wouldn't even have been that, since this was her home turf. After all, she somewhat blossomed when we moved back down here"

"I think this is BS," said Jerry finally, but he was looking doubtful. Arnie's comments were raising questions, things he himself may have noticed peripherally, but never pursued, satisfied that everything was going well for his sweet little sister-in-law.

"No, I've been thinking a lot about this since she attempted the suicide. I've been remembering all sorts of things."

"And trying to absolve yourself with pseudo psychoanalysis?" interjected Jerry, angry because Arnie might be right.

"Do me a favor," said Arnie. "You or Marty talk to your neighbor. I'm willing to bet that Becki does nothing in your neighbor's office that makes her deal with the general public. I'm also willing to bet that she barely utters a peep unless spoken to and just does a good job by herself. I'm not saying she is rude to the other people. They probably like her, but I'll wager actual money that she doesn't go out to lunch with them, or plop down in a chair with a cup of coffee to share some gossip, or anything else."

"She doesn't drink coffee," snapped Jerry.

"Stop being an ass," retorted Arnie irritated. "You know what I'm saying. You're going to find out she has become a total loner, a real introvert. And, she's been getting worse. I wanted her to have the damn family house because I knew how important it was for her, but do you really think I wanted her to be in permanent residence there, that I didn't want her and the kids living with me in Boston? I tried to figure out how I could move part of the business down here, but we're tied into MIT. That's our intellectual lifeline! Do you actually think I could operate something like SofTek out of rural Virginia? When I started realizing what Becki's problems were, I thought about playing ball with the big guys on the West Coast to get her out of Boston, but she wouldn't have been happier in Silicon Valley or Seattle. And although she likes my family in Oregon, Portland wasn't going to be the right city for my operation either. I started in Boston with people who were already there and we had all those connections. I've worked hard to accomplish what I have, Jerry, and I didn't want to lose it so I tried to do the best I could."

"Such as," Jerry asked, with a show-me attitude.

"I let her move down here, damn it! I waited for that house to come on the market because I knew she wanted it, and I alerted every realtor that I would pay top dollar. I arranged my schedule so I'd be able to come down to Virginia as often as possible—every weekend I could and the holidays. Sometimes she'd come up with the kids but rarely for long. You know we have a house up there! I kept it, hoping she'd be back. I tried to get her to go on trips with me, but that was almost impossible, and, of course, she had the excuse of the kids. Hell, I would have taken them too or gotten in a housekeeper or something. I called her almost nightly. Damn it, Jerry, this wasn't easy for me either. I really love Becki and if the only way I could have her was on some contrived part-time basis, that was the way it was going be. I did not cheat on her either, regardless of what has happened.

"Whether you want to believe me or not, I've been a God damn straight arrow because Becki was all I wanted. That's why this whole thing is so sick. Before this happened, I'd really hoped that I'd be able to convince her that now that the kids were gone, she could spend more time with me. I wanted her to move back when they left for school but she wanted to finish college here, not in Boston.

"You've got to believe me, Jerry. I've been trying to get her to talk to someone professionally for years. Becki knew she had a problem and told me from the very first, even though I wouldn't listen then. It just never came to a head, and I couldn't force her. I never could force her to do anything she didn't want. Hell, about the only thing I denied her was not making her pregnant again."

Jerry looked startled and Arnie explained. "If Becki had had her way, we probably would have had half a dozen kids, but I felt we'd contributed enough to overpopulation. She kept hinting though, and that was one thing I never gave in on. She's probably sent enough money to support half the orphans in Central America as a result, while I donate an equal amount to Planned Parenthood. Maybe I should have let her have another kid or considered adoption, though it wouldn't have solved her problems...our problems. But still, in lots of ways she would have been happier. Maybe a century ago it would have worked—a large family, living in one small community, not having to face much outside the home.

"Ah Christ, all I've wanted all along was her to be with me. I've really missed her while we were apart." Arnie bent over, his head in his hands. "Just believe me," he said quietly, staring down at the floor, unable to face Jerry for fear he'd break down. "I'd do anything. I'll even get out of the business now if that's what I have to do. God knows I've got the money. We could finally go public and I'd make a fortune, not just have a paper one. All I want is to have Becki back, even if it means I have to give up the company, work, everything else."

Dumfounded, Jerry sat there, saying nothing, just regarding Arnie as if he were an alien being. He wondered if he could discern what was true and what wasn't. Finally he asked, "What are you going to do now?"

Arnie looked up, eyes dull with a voice to match. "What I said. Go to Boston to figure out how all this happened. Keep in touch with the doctors to see what the prognosis is. There's no way Becki should get out at this point, even if it weren't for her hand. She's a danger to herself. We're just lucky she didn't try it down in King George. Knowing her, she might have swum out in the middle of the Potomac or taken the boat down to the Chesapeake to join her parents." Jerry looked disturbed, considering the possibilities.

"I'm also going to talk to the kids," stated Arnie flatly, inwardly nauseated once more at the unsavory prospect. "Try to tell them what's happened—Jesus, that's going to be tough. I hope that she'll want to see me again, that with counseling we can work out something. If Becki will take me back, even if it means I have to give up being active in the business, I'll do it. Hell, maybe we can buy her dad's old restaurant and run it. I don't know."

"You know, I almost believe you," said Jerry, in wonder that he did. Having Arnie to blame for Becki's problems certainly was the easier approach, but the man was right. Obviously they all had ignored some important issues, starting back when she was a kid.

"Why shouldn't you?" asked Arnie, wounded. "We always got along. I never lied to you. You know I never hurt Becki before this happened. I was part of your family, you were part of mine. We had some pretty good times if I recall."

"Yes," conceded Jerry, "that's why this got us so upset. Becki was happy with you. You've been great to Drea and all the kids—ours too. I mean you were big time, but you were just part of the family as far as we were concerned. We did like you, Arnie, but when you betrayed Becki, you did the same to the rest of us."

"Well, it certainly wasn't intentional," said his brother-in-law despondently.

"Nevertheless, it happened. What if she won't take you back?"

"Then we'll just have to make the best provisions for her that we can. That house is hers and so is all the stuff in it plus as much money as she needs or wants. You guys are just going to have to persuade Becki to be realistic about that. If she doesn't want to stay there, I'll buy her a place somewhere else...maybe near you or Drea, except I have a feeling Drea is eventually going places. She's one smart young woman and even if she isn't my biological kid, I sometimes think she's the most like me of the three."

"Oddly enough," remarked Jerry, "I do too."

"Yeah," said Arnie, "I really wanted her to go to MIT and come into the company, but I guess she got brainwashed down here by you Virginians. William and Mary is a great school, but she would have stretched more up in Boston. Odd, how of the three, she's the one that went into business and computers. She's going to do ok, but that job in Richmond just isn't up to her caliber. I still hope she'll consider something with my company. Yeah, if Becki takes me back and I stay here, maybe I'll do that or teach—Mary Washington or something. I think I still remember enough to do that."

"I'm sure you do," said Jerry in an ironic tone at such an inconsequential remark from one of the leaders in the computer field. "So what do you want us to do?"

"Short of fighting me? Talk to Marty. Tell her what I've said. Ask her to think about things Becki may have mentioned over the years. Find out from your neighbor if what I surmise about work is true. See Becki. Keep in touch with the doctors. I know you have her best interests at heart. I'm not asking you to plead my case. I'm just hoping you'll be fair and help me—help us. I'm even willing to sign something that you're representing me insofar as dealing with the hospital and doctors. I honestly don't think you'd screw me on this, Jerry. I want the best for her, same as you. But I also want her back and I'll do what I have to."

"I think you may have convinced me," admitted Jerry finally. "I'm not sure I can persuade Marty, but I will talk to her. And, I'll talk to you when…if…you find out anything. Ultimately though, it's going to have to be Becki's choice. When she can make that, I don't know. That's going to depend on what the doctors say." He got up, came around the desk, and thrust out his hand. "I really didn't believe I'd be saying this, but I am going to wish you luck, Arnie. If it doesn't work out, I'll be sorry. You made her happy for a lot of years. You know I don't have any sisters of my own.

Becki always filled that void and I love her. I'll try to help you guys work out something fair if you can't get back together, but I think I hope you do."

Arnie looked at him squarely. "I appreciate that. I can't say what's going to happen either. I'm going to head up to Boston tomorrow morning or tonight, if I can see the shrink earlier, and start finding out what I can. I'll try to get back down here by the weekend to see her again if she'll let me. I've been away from work for two weeks now so I've got to pick up some pieces and I want to cancel some trips and meetings so I can spend more time here. I also think I may have to fly out to see the kids and tell them in person. They don't know yet, unless you guys told them."

"Only Drea knows and she agreed to wait until we knew more about what was happening. Becki called them every week so I think you've got to let tell them something right away."

"Agreed, but how? That's the hard part. They knew we had separated but I told them their mother would talk to them and she never really did."

"That's something you're going to have to figure out," said Jerry sympathetically. "We'll keep in touch. You've got all the same telephone numbers?"

"Oh, sure," replied Arnie.

"Then if anything comes up that you should know right away from the hospital, I'll contact you."

"Jerry..."

"Yeah?"

"I already told the hospital that they should be letting you know anything about Becki, that I had to be out of town for a while."

"That was good, Arnie," Jerry said, a compassionate look now dominating his countenance.

"Also, they still only know her as Rebecca or Mrs. James Miller. I don't think there have been any connections with me so that the press would be interested in a cute little story on wife of multi-millionaire computer whiz in psychiatric ward angle."

"I hope not, I'll do what I can," said Jerry as he escorted him out.

As Arnie started out the door, he suddenly stopped and turned. "Thanks and I'll call you every day here at the office if it's all right."

Jerry nodded his head in agreement. "I'll take the calls," he added and Arnie looked at him gratefully. "I can't promise Marty will talk to you, but I'll try."

"That's all I can ask," said Arnie and he went back to his hotel to make arrangements for the return to Boston. His thoughts weren't overly clear, he realized. The shock of what Becki had said much less the whole episode had made him feel as disturbed as when he'd seen her in the bathtub.

What could he tell Leah and Bruce, he wondered? What could he say to anyone and where did he start with this mess? Should he just go and confront that bitch Carter? No, that would be a bad idea. Perhaps getting some confidential help would be best. What, worst of all, to do about Becki.

I really believe her, thought Arnie. She'd try it again at this point but, Jesus, he didn't want to lose her. Wouldn't it be nice if this were all a nightmare? He could just wake up and they'd be in bed together and he'd tell her his dream and she'd look at him astonished and maybe laugh. Then maybe they'd make love and it would all go away. Well, for Becki, it is a nightmare, Arnie perceived. How did she feel when she woke up in that psychiatric ward? And what will she do if it turns out her beautiful, agile hand is really crippled? He honestly didn't want to know.

CHAPTER 24

Mid-morning the next day, Arnie went straight to the office from the airport. There were a few strange looks from some of the staff when he ambled in since he wasn't expected. This was not a surprise since he'd left work with no apparent reason almost two weeks earlier, canceling meetings and telling no one his plans. But he'd been talking to his secretary fairly regularly so things per usual moved smoothly on. Also, aside from Madge, no one knew that he and Becki had separated. Maintaining two houses, especially when one was in rural Virginia, for once had its advantages.

"Harriett," he said to his secretary. "Give me a few minutes alone and then come in to brief me. I'll give you a buzz."

"Sure, boss man," the attractive brunette replied. "How was the vacation?"

"Vacation..." Arnie thought a moment, since of course that's what he'd called it—an impromptu getaway since he'd been feeling stress. Stress, what an understatement. "Dull, quiet, what I needed, even though I couldn't decide to go until the last minute. The niece graduated, in-law stuff like that."

"I wish we could all run away at times," Harriett said with feeling.

"What, I exploit you?" asked Arnie, curious.

"No, but when you're gone, everyone in the world suddenly wants to get hold of you, and I feel I am under constant siege. Then when you're here, they still do."

"And that's why I pay you so well," Arnie smiled.

"Hey, no argument," agreed Harriett, "but in my next life I'm going to go into a monastery and contemplate my navel.

"Nunnery, kid, nunnery. Plus, aren't you still taking off the month of December for a special event?"

"And I expect you to dance at the wedding," she replied pertly, her face brightening.

"I certainly plan to. December weddings are special. Becki and I got married in December."

"How is she?"

"Oh, a little under the weather," Arnie remarked as casually as possible while thinking that was probably as best to describe it. "Incidentally, if my brother-in-law, Jerry Madison, calls me anytime, track me down. Becki's probably going to be taking some tests." Yeah, thought Arnie, tests to see if she's still suicidal. Tests to see how much hand movement she'll recover.

"I'm sorry to hear that. I hope it isn't anything serious," said Harriett earnestly. Arnie felt a burst of affection for his lively young assistant, who he knew was one of the few at SofTek who genuinely liked Becki. Perhaps it was because Harriett too, although she hadn't told him outright, wanted to be a full-time wife and mother more than anything. He'd miss her when that happened, but then he realized, he might not be around either. He'd told Jerry that. Yet would he truly be able to make the sacrifice of leaving his company and Boston?

"I hope so, too," replied Arnie at last, wondering how could things, particularly for Becki, be much more serious. Life-threatening is life-threatening, especially when one wants to do it to oneself.

Once in his office, he glanced at his in-box, which was overflowing. The computer would be far worse, he was sure. Even though there was limited access to his e-mail, it probably was overloaded. The voice mail too.

He dropped his suitcase, but by contrast carefully placed the padded laptop and briefcase on his desk. Then he sat down in his comfortable chair, swiveling to stare vacantly out the window. His feet were propped on the climate control unit and he leaned back in the chair, his arms bent behind his neck. Where the hell to start? He'd thought of nothing else the whole flight up and most of the night before as he paced the hotel room.

Then he was equally annoyed that he hadn't been able to see Becki's shrink and angrier at himself because he knew he also couldn't face another visit with Becki until a little time passed—until she'd talked to someone. The one visit they had had was personally devastating, although he was sure it was worse for her. He wouldn't subject her to another now, but the thought that it hurt her to even see him was beyond his comprehension.

So...the solution. Arnie believed in solutions to problems and help when one needed it. Hadn't that been the basis of much of his work? Maybe the answer was a good detective agency. He mentally stressed the 'good' part, reflecting on the shortcomings of the Virginia firm. That would teach him to let his fingers do the walking through *Yellow Pages*. But how to locate one? This situation wasn't something he wanted to become public and then there was the question of whether anyone else should know. Who really did he trust? Aside from his sister and Jerry, whom he hoped he could trust; and Drea, whom he didn't want to involve; or the other kids, who shouldn't be, the list was fairly small. Of all his partners and friends, only Madge came to mind. She was also Becki's one true friend from the company and she was the only one who knew about the separation...not the reason...but at least the separation.

Arnie turned the chair around and looked at his phone, debating. And if I do call, he deliberated, how much do I reveal—the whole rotten mess? Also, where would they talk? Was the office a good place or had industrial espionage hit too? Was that what this is about? He'd never really thought much about that aside from isolating most of the computer system for security, compartmenting projects, limiting access to the public. Having one of SofTek's earliest projects undermined had been a costly lesson, dictating some security. Yet, the best way he'd hoped to counter such a problem was trying to instill enough team spirit and incentives for the people that worked for him so they'd be loyal to the company and also cognizant of the fact that protection of the products was to their wellbeing.

Yet this really didn't seem a company problem. Maybe he was getting paranoid. On the other hand, what had happened with the photos would give anyone reason for paranoia. Yet, if it had been a company problem, surely they would have come to him to pressure him in some way. Once they went directly to Becki, that hold was gone. All it had succeeded in doing was making them both miserable—tragically, in Becki's case. Telling her about the incident right away would have still made her miserable, but then, Arnie was sure, she would have believed him and the attempted suicide could have been avoided.

Somehow, the reason had to be personal, and maybe Madge could help him think. She'd been around the whole time. Certainly he couldn't talk now to Becki, who had always been his true confidante. His wife obviously wasn't in any condition to be thinking straight, and she hadn't ever met the woman who precipitated the whole mess. Also, Becki probably wouldn't talk to him. Hell, she wasn't now.

He pushed the direct dial. "Hi, Madge here," a voice answered after the first ring.

"What, no Ms.?"

"Welcome back, Arnie. The only calls that come in on this line are from jerks around here like you. What can I do for you?"

"You picked up, right? No speaker?"

"You know I hate to use that."

"Good. How would you and Bryan like to invite me for a drink after work?"

"No problem, but Bryan teaches a class tonight."

"Would Bryan be disturbed if you still invited me? We could collect him after class and I'll spring for dinner."

"I suppose he could be persuaded, but this sounds fairly mysterious."

"Let's keep it that way. I'll come by at 6:30 if that's convenient and then we'll have a couple of hours before we have to get him."

"Ah, a secret assignation with the boss."

"Don't say that," snapped Arnie sharply.

"Just kidding," Madge answered, surprised at his reaction to her usual joshing. "Half past six is fine. Besides the kids will be home."

"Just as long as we can talk privately."

"They'll probably be comatose in front of the television or playing video games. You know how that is."

"Yeah, I sure do, me the professional father."

"Ha! Professional maybe but when it comes to parenthood, Becki spoiled you. I've told Bryan more than once what I really needed was a good wife."

"No argument. I'll see you then and thanks." Arnie hung up and looked at his watch. It was 11:00 now. He'd try to get away from the office by 4:00, go home first, and then see what he could do. Meanwhile, he'd best find out what damage control was needed here, not that the whole damn place didn't seem to run perfectly well whether he was around or not. Maybe he could leave it and nobody would know. Yet he'd always been hands-on in his management. If he didn't know what was happening, how could he plan the next steps? He delegated plenty and at the same time believed in team efforts, but there was something to be said about being the captain of the ship. It was a fine line between being that and a micro manager but he concluded that he had succeeded. The good ship SofTek sailed on, returning with bounty, or at least profits, like successful whalers and merchant vessels of old. Definitely the preferred New England business tradition.

About a quarter to seven, he pulled up in front of Madge's place. "Howdy," she said as she opened the door, "where's your cloak?"

"At home with my dagger. I was afraid I might fall on that and you'd have to use the cloak for my shroud."

"Jeez, Arnie, what's the matter?" Madge looked at him with consternation. Even in jest, he sounded despondent, not the confident, collected Arnie who'd usually tackle most problems calmly and also usually with humor.

"Offer me a drink. No, better, have you got some coffee or something soft?"

"Sure, come in." Madge led him into the kitchen, surveying him anxiously. He looked awful.

"Where are the kids?"

"I forgot there was a game tonight. They've gone off with the neighbors."

"Good..." murmured Arnie, taking a chair and looking vacantly down at his hands.

"Well I know you're not here to seduce me so tell me, you want to buy me out, you're turning the company over to me, what?"

"Becki tried to commit suicide."

Madge looked at him, utterly shocked. Sitting down at the kitchen table, she reached over and briefly squeezed his hand. "Arnie...I'm so sorry. How is she? Is she going to be ok?"

"I really don't know," he responded sadly, looking at her dully. "Don't you want to ask me why?"

"Why?" Madge quietly inquired.

"Someone sent her pictures of me in bed with another woman. That was the reason she left me. I suspected something like that but I didn't know about the pictures. When I went to see her, she locked herself in the bathroom and slit her wrists. It was terrible, Madge." Arnie was having trouble breathing. "There was blood all over. She looked like a ghost. I thought she was dead when I got her out of the tub. When she was finally able to speak to me yesterday, she told me she'd do it again if I tried to get her back." Arnie stopped and began crying.

"Arnie, I'm so sorry. What can I and Bryan do?" Madge reached over, clasping his hand again, this time not releasing it.

"First you could ask me how the hell it happened?" he said, regaining control with obvious difficulty.

"Well, I did think of that, but I'm not the morality police. I really didn't think you played around, Arnie. I mean it's so obvious which of the guys do, but I thought once you two had met that you weren't interested in anyone else. I knew she wasn't, but this is one hell of a surprise."

"It's a long story," Arnie said and he proceeded to tell her.

Madge sat listening, saying nothing. When he'd finished, she looked at him, shaking her head. "You're a damned fool, Arnie, but I believe you. You'd never try to tell a tale like that if it weren't true. Now, what are you going to do?"

"If I knew, Madge, I wouldn't be here. I need advice. I'm worried sick about Becki. I don't know if she'll have me back or truly come out of this all right. Indeed, I don't know where to start. It was a set-up—it had to be," he said fiercely. "Someone was getting even with me through her."

"Maybe they were getting even with both of you."

"How do you mean?" Arnie asked interested, his brown eyes once more alert.

"Who hates you both?"

He looked at her strangely before answering, "You can't mean Dickie. My God, that was over twenty years ago. We haven't seen him for fifteen."

"And you fixed his little red wagon then too."

"Madge, that was business. I didn't even know he was part of the other group. They could have beaten us out too, remember?"

"I never said he was rational."

"Yeah, but look at all the trouble he's caused for Becki and me over the years. You know why she wanted to go home to Virginia. He more than got even when you consider how she's been afraid to live here, to go places with me. I know it's her phobia, but maybe without him, it wouldn't have happened."

"Did he know that? All he did was start some nasty little rumors. That doesn't mean he knew how they grew, how they poisoned her mind. Your marriage with Becki was private as far as most people are concerned. How many people besides me, and Bryan, really knew about her shyness and fear of gossip, why she lived in Virginia and rarely was up here?"

"None, I suppose," he replied reflectively. "It really

wasn't anyone's business especially since people weren't overly nice to her. She was upset and nervous enough when she would come here or go places with me so that I never wanted anyone to know."

"So, to the outsider, you had rather an odd set-up and Becki was either the superior snob or some gorgeous imbecile who was too stupid to say anything—the perfect trophy wife."

"Yeah, I guess so," agreed Arnie, "but that still doesn't mean that Dickie would be behind something like this. I mean how would he persuade some woman to hop into bed with me? She was at that meeting as a professional businesswoman not a hooker. And, I repeat, the last incident with Dickie was fifteen years ago."

"What have you done to him lately?" Madge asked calmly, not adding that sex for some women, as much as men, meant nothing emotionally, and that Arnie had always projected charisma and now power as well. She herself certainly had had to beat off first-time dates plenty in her younger days, but things had changed socially insofar as to which sex might be the predator. Christ, Arnie had been out of the loop for nearly twenty years, making his story all the more believable.

"What do you mean? I told you I haven't seen him since then," he persevered, still unable to comprehend such a scenario.

"You don't have to see someone like Dickie to aggravate him. He's my best guess. I'd suggest you find out if you, and by that I mean the company, beat him out again in some way."

"Well, I was thinking of trying to get some good investigators to track down information on this woman. I'd originally thought of seeing her myself, but then I realized that would be fairly dumb."

"I think dumb is an understatement," Marge commented wryly. Oh Arnie, she thought, you are a mess. The Arnie she knew never would have considered something so stupid before, even though he was a straight forward guy.

"Ok, what do I do? Who do I get to look into this and how can I have our records examined without getting everyone stirred up?"

"We could say there was some kind of audit or that we're trying to update our archives and bring in a 'consultant' to do the work for us," she suggested, stroking her chin thoughtfully.

"That might do it but who do I get? I don't ordinarily hire detectives, especially after the debacle in D.C."

"What debacle?" Madge's head jerked up as she stared at him in surprise.

"When Becki decided to leave me, she left me. I mean she really left me. I thought I was going to go crazy."

"Well, you weren't the easiest person to be around the last few months, but I'm not sure people noticed. I just sort of assumed we were the only ones you'd told about this separation and so I was being more observant."

"Yes," he answered slowly. "But I ended up having to get a detective agency to track her down. When I first went to King George, she had gone without a trace. She hadn't even let the kids know where she was. I had no idea until I returned to Virginia two weeks ago. Then it took me days to work up the courage to see her and then...well then this happened."

"Oh Arnie," Madge sighed with obvious sympathy, "I'm so sorry. I had no idea you didn't know where she was. You must have been worried sick."

"I assumed her sister would be looking out for her and if anything were to happen, the kids would find out and I'd hear. But I just love her so much, Madge. I had to find her and then after she'd seen me, that she'd do something like this..." He was unable to finish his statement, certainly not to add that it had probably been the seduction that tipped Becki over.

"Well..." said Madge, thinking rapidly, unsettled by Arnie's tortured, groping for words. An inarticulate Arnie was a heretofore unknown. "Between Bryan and me, we've got to be able to figure out who we can get to look into this for you. Anything I can do in the office—search files, ask a few questions, I'll do. I don't want to ask too many. You've done such a good job of keeping this under wraps. We'll want to keep it that way. Besides, most of the old timers know I hate Dickie's guts so they might wonder and the newcomers wouldn't know anything about this, except maybe those trashy old stories he started."

Arnie looked at her startled. "Still?"

Madge shook her head sadly. "Company lore. Besides, you're a legend in your own time at SofTek, boss man."

"Ah shit," groaned Arnie. "Becki was right, not to want to return."

"Probably so," agreed Madge, "if she wasn't going to fight back. But, if it's him, I'm beginning to wonder why he hasn't tried to hurt me."

"As you once said to me, Madge, he thought he was superior to women like you."

"That means I wasn't sexy enough for him to try to hit on, right?"

"Madge! No, it means when Becki refused to go to bed with him, I did the damage to the great career he thought he had. Then after he got canned, to add insult to that injury, she and I married so it makes us doubly the enemy. He probably thought we used to entertain ourselves in bed laughing at him, as if we didn't have better things to do!"

Madge let out a slight snort, sure from the times she'd seen Arnie and Becki together privately that there'd been some passionate nights between the two. Arnie was besotted with his wife and she had obviously worshiped him, which made this all the meaner. Just the sort of revenge a snake like Dickie would enjoy. It had to be him, she decided. "Sorry. This isn't funny."

Arnie nodded, for once not cracking a smile. "No. Maybe Dickie did decide to break up the marriage since he couldn't do the business in. I'm beginning to believe in your theory. Listen, I know I offered you and Bryan dinner, but may I take a rain check? All of this has caught up with me and I think I just want to go home and get some sleep if I can. I haven't been doing much of that lately."

"I imagine not. I'll talk to Bryan tonight when he gets home. We'll see what we can come up with. Why don't you give us dinner tomorrow night? Better yet, come back here after work and we'll talk. I agree with you about trying to keep this out of the office just in case we're wrong about who's done this or why."

"You are a woman beyond price."

"Right and I'm also your partner. Go home and sleep, Arnie, and Arnie..."

"Yes?" He was now standing by the door.

"Keep your pants zipped this time."

"Oh shit yes," he said fervently, and he turned and went out to his car.

The next morning when he called Jerry, there was nothing new. Throughout the day, he tried to concentrate on work and catch up with the piles of items that had accumulated during his weeks away. So much paper, he thought, and supposedly he was in a business trying to cut that down and streamline the work process.

When it was finally time to leave, he drove directly to Madge's. He knocked and it was Bryan who answered the door. "Madge had to stop by the bakery. She thought you deserved some home cooking at this point, even if she was going to have to buy it, so we'll eat here."

Arnie laughed, "Your wife is one in a million."

"Of course," remarked Bryan mildly. "Why do you think I married her?"

"Because you were smart," answered Arnie.

"Well we knew that before or at least I deceived Harvard, but with Madge, no question. I used to think you were smart too, Arnie, but it sounds like you've really screwed up."

"You could say that," Arnie acknowledged chagrined, particularly at the appropriate wording, whether Bryan meant it or not. "And, I deserve it but somehow I hope to recoup, to get a second chance. At worse, just to find out why this happened."

"Becki is a lovely lady," stated Bryan with conviction. "She didn't deserve this and if everything happened the way you told Madge, you don't either. And speaking of that other lovely lady, here she comes now."

Madge was walking up the pathway, a bag in one hand and a cake box in the other. "Good evening, gentlemen. How about helping a poor working woman?"

Bryan leaned over and placed a kiss on his wife's cheek and Arnie was amused for a moment at the contrast. Tall, pale, almost cadaverous Bryan, and tiny little Madge, whom motherhood had broadened: Jack Sprat and wife. "If that marvelous smell is hot French bread and that interesting box contains a Black Forest Torte, I'll be delighted to help you," said Bryan, dispelling the comparison to the man who could eat no fat.

"I've lived with him too long. He reads my mind, Arnie. How are you doing?"

"Surviving," he responded with a shrug, realizing that was true.

"Well, inside, fellows, I need a drink. That rotten company where I work had me hopping all day. It's run by some bastard who takes advantage of us peasants."

"Only fifty-eight percent," countered Arnie with a grin. "You exploit a full eight or nine, don't you now?"

"Ten, to be precise, and you know it," she answered. "I'm catching up with you. That way if we ever do go public, I can be filthy rich."

"You're beginning to think that's the way to go now, aren't you?" he asked seriously since through the years, Madge had usually supported him openly when the issue came up.

"No comment. We're not here to fight on business matters tonight. Where are the kids, honey?" she asked her husband.

"The neighbors were taking a whole gang to the movies."

"Thank God for neighbors," stated Madge with feeling. "We owe them big time tonight."

"I thought so too," agreed Bryan. "I defrosted that casserole and tossed a salad so we can eat anytime you want, but the drink sounds like a good idea. Arnie?"

"The biggest martini you can build."

"I didn't think anyone drank those anymore," remarked Madge.

"Actually, they're supposed to be in vogue again, and they do have their place," answered Arnie.

"Sure, putting someone under the table. Aren't you driving?"

"That's what cabs are for," he rejoined, wishing he'd called one months before out at the Cape. "This is the first time in days I haven't felt like I was under siege. That's right, isn't it?" he asked hopefully.

"You may have been a horse's ass," replied Madge, "but no. Actually Bryan and I talked a lot last night when he got home, and I think he has some ideas."

"What?" called the voice from the bar. "Wait until I get in there. I'm not sure I remember how to make one of these."

"Just bring the gin bottle and some olives," uttered Arnie, more than half despondently. Maybe tying one on wouldn't be a bad idea.

"And plenty of ice," added Madge firmly. "I refuse to take care of you if you get drunk."

"Here we are," said Bryan, bearing a tray with their drinks. "Scotch and water for you, my dear. This lethal one for you, Arnie, and...I guess a lethal one for me too. I'd almost forgotten how they tasted. Now before we get drunk and the children have to put us all to bed, let's reexamine the problem."

"No wonder he teaches philosophy," observed Arnie, dryly. "We'd just be throwing some figures up on the board at this point."

"Well actually," said Bryan, "about the only figures I have for you are these." He reached into his pocket and pulled out a folded piece of paper. "A certain member of my department was less than discrete in a relationship a couple of years ago. In order to extradite himself from the situation, he required some professional help, i.e. discovering that the lady, who was thinking of coercing him into marriage, had also been less than discrete and that her pregnancy could have been caused by one of several gentlemen. I think my friend seemed the best catch, and even though a blood test might have proved he wasn't the father, the publicity would not have helped his career. As it turned out, he wasn't the father and any possible blackmail was avoided. But, he had been fairly depressed when that was going on and had bent my ear one night, so I asked him today if he had any advice for someone caught in a similar embarrassing situation. This is the name and number of the firm he used. He says they equate discretion with their exorbitant fees; but, they have an excellent reputation and that much of their work comes from referrals so you may use his name, which is printed at the bottom of those figures. I doubted if money would be a problem so I'd advise starting with them."

Arnie reached over to accept the paper, unfolding it and glancing briefly at the information, before carefully placing it in his shirt pocket. "Fine, and then what?"

"Have them start with both the woman and Dickie," interjected Madge. "I'm still convinced he's behind this. Otherwise, I agree with you, there would have been no reason to send anything to Becki first. Who really cares at the company if you're playing around? If it got in the news, it would be embarrassing, but it's not going to hurt the sale of our software. I can't see Uncle Sam or anyone boycotting our products because you've supposedly started fooling around. Lots of snickering and bad jokes at your expense perhaps, but no monetary damage. After all, it's become the national pastime."

"Yes, it has," agreed Arnie. "But if it's Dickie, why did he wait this long?"

"I told you yesterday. I'm willing to bet anything that we've beaten him out again on some business deal. I mentioned his name casually at lunch today with a couple of our partners, saying I'd bumped into his old girlfriend, Carla, and she wondered what had happened to him. No one said a word so I really think people at work don't know or care where he is now or what he's doing, for that matter."

"Either that or he still is friends with some of those same partners, and they don't want to say anything."

"I really don't think Dickie keeps up with people if he can't use them any longer."

"He was with us for years, Madge," commented Arnie.

"True, but we were starting to go places and he was going with us."

Bryan broke in, "Whether it's Dickie or not is a moot point now. The damage has been done and what I think Arnie needs is some help in deciding what to do about Becki."

"God yes," Arnie declared impassioned. "According to my brother-in-law, she'll probably be in the hospital a few more days and then there's the question of whom she'll stay with. She can't be by herself—even if she could use her hand—and she was adamant about not coming with me or a nurse. She's already told me she'll try suicide again if I'm around and I doubt that Drea can take care of her—not that I wouldn't make up for her lost salary and any expenses. And Marty is teaching so I don't know what to do."

"What do you want to do?" asked Bryan seriously.

"Do you have the slightest doubt?" Arnie said unequivocally. "I just want her back, but I can't pressure her. One of the problems with our whole relationship was that I was always hesitant to pressure her about anything once I really got to know her. I was an enabler. I should have made her see a doctor when I realized she had problems. I shouldn't have taken the easy way out and let her move to Virginia when I knew the real reason she was going was that she was afraid to be up here, to face our peers. Yet when she tried to tell me her fears, I always pushed them aside. If I'd listened, maybe she would have told me more about her wacky aunt and childhood. I'm sure that's a major contributor to this whole mess. Then maybe I could have persuaded her to see someone, to put that aside at least.

"I spent too damn much time working and traveling even when I knew she wasn't going to go along with me. Letting her live there was a convenient way to salve my own conscience for all those hours and days I was away from her. Frankly, in retrospect, I feel pretty shitty about that—almost more so than this debacle, because if I hadn't done that, it might not have happened. I'd rationalize that I was spending quality time with my family, but it was also a way to avoid having her tell me she couldn't be part of my business life, which in lots of ways was my real life. Maybe I did make her this way. If she'd been vying for my attention all the time, I probably wouldn't have accomplished as much at work."

Arnie stopped a moment while Madge and Bryan waited patiently, knowing how hard it was for him to discuss this. Until he'd vocalized the thought, he'd never fully realized it. Had he really wanted Becki to be the way she was so she wouldn't interfere with his professional goals? It was a frightening awareness if so. But no, that wasn't right. She'd been the core of his personal existence, not just a pleasant diversion or temporary escape when work got too rough. He would give up his work if that was the choice now. He hadn't been bullshitting Jerry. If it was a case of his career or his wife, Becki won hands down and that was a realization too.

Slowly, he started talking again. "I had thought she was so mature at first. Certainly as far as Drea and family responsibilities, she was. She was accountable for our family but for herself, she was still a frightened little kid. All these years she's been a frightened kid and whenever she finally has had the guts to get out and face the world, someone like Dickie has hurt her. Actually, it's always been Dickie and me, hasn't it?" He looked directly at Madge.

"Arnie, forget Dickie for a moment, and let's concentrate on you," said Madge, staring back, appalled at the pain in her friend's eyes and wanting to assuage this hurt. "It's true you're the kind of guy that if he's not married to his work at least thinks of it as his mistress, but this isn't all your fault. I know you never wanted Becki to be a Stepford wife and that you wanted to include her as much as possible in whatever you were doing. Just seeing you with Drea and your kids..."

"Drea is my kid," avowed Arnie sharply.

"Ok, that's what I mean," continued Madge reasonably. "You love all those kids. You're a great father. Anyone who has seen you with them knows it. They dote on you too."

"Some days."

"Well some days is about the best we can get nowadays," remarked Madge pragmatically. "It's tough being a parent. It probably always was, but I think it's really tough nowadays. Kids can't turn their hostility towards thundering hoards. All they've got is us and the government!"

"I concur," added Bryan, more than slightly amused at his wife's tirade. He was well aware of a recent fight she'd had with their eldest and an ongoing battle with IRS. "I also support Madge's appraisal of your family. I don't know you as well but what I've known I've always liked and Becki, Becki is a bit fey. She's one of those people you can genuinely say is sweet and not mean it as an insult. Also, Arnie, you can't make adults seek help and it's logical to try to be protective of them when they won't, even if that's not for the best. We have some history with mental disorders in our family too…my brother, well that's another story. Anyhow, in some ways, Becki's actions may have a positive aspect insofar as she is going to have to get some help now. What you've got to make sure is that it's the best and that you stay involved. This time you're going to have to be there."

"Yes," Arnie sighed, "that's about what I've decided. If I want her, I may have to give up this life."

"And?" asked Madge, greatly interested.

"I already told my brother-in-law I would if that's what it took."

"I think you've answered your question," said Madge. "But don't flatter yourself. I think the company could cope with your taking a leave of absence. We might not be quite as brilliant as usual, but hell, if you'd been hit by a bus, we would have had to."

Arnie laughed, a genuine laugh—his first in ages. "That's what I've always loved about you, Madge. So incisive and compassionate besides. Are you telling me you'll run the place while I'm away?"

"I might. I could, I think," she asserted bluntly.

"I think you could too, but I might want it back."

"We'd plan for that contingency, but that wasn't really what I was saying."

"I know," Arnie nodded. "I appreciate the difference. You're right. I'll start what I can up here to see if we can locate the source of the problem. Then I'll make arrangements to divest myself of responsibilities. Do you really want to do this?" He turned to Bryan. "Do you know what it will be like if she does? It can overtake your life. Look what happened to mine. Your kids are still preteens."

"Oh I think we do," said Bryan. "This isn't collusion, Arnie. I didn't know Madge was going to say that, but I think it would be good for her. I'm the main parent in residence anyhow, which is fine with me. I knew when I married Madge that I wasn't going to have some little helpmate waiting with my pipe and paper at the door."

"You don't smoke, Bryan," Madge responded archly, and then her tone softened as she looked at the big, sweet man. "You really wouldn't object? It would mean those sixty-hour weeks regularly, more travel, and who knows what else."

"You promise to continue to respect me and keep me in the style to which I wish to grow accustomed?" her husband asked.

All three laughed. "I guess that means you expect more money too," said Arnie, regarding his friends wistfully. Their affection was so obvious—a comfortable couple just as he and Becki had been.

"Easily," Madge answered.

"Ok, it's a deal. Let's see what we can work out tomorrow. I suppose it will become public soon enough but I still don't want people to know about Becki."

"We'll just say you've been wanting time to write your memoirs—you know, the great American novel," ribbed Madge, "or go around the world or something. Most people will think you're just hiding somewhere so you can develop some fantastic new operating system that's going to take over the whole market and scare Microsoft."

"That'll be the day," Arnie smiled. "I wish, but I can't complain at what we have done."

"No, none of us can," she concurred. "Now, one other thing. We've got to see if there's anything in our own company that might have been the cause of this. If I'm in charge, I can start a search. I still think this is from outside, so we can't discount that either. And, further..." The men looked at her. "I also declare it's time to eat or you two are going to have another of those abominable drinks and I'll have to be responsible for you both. You, Bryan, set the table."

"Oh yes, mistress of my heart."

"Funny. Arnie, you can open some wine for me if you promise not to drink right out of the bottle, and I'll go nuke the casserole and put everything else out. We're all going to be happy if you get Becki back," she declared vigorously. "Then we'll have high class meals again."

Arnie looked at her, his eyes too bright. "Yeah...that would be nice."

The rest of the evening was low key, gossipy, a dinner among friends with no one referring again to the problem, although it was obvious that it dominated their thoughts. When Arnie left a couple of hours later, he shook Bryan's hand and hugged Madge tightly. "It's good to have real friends." It was, he realized. Becki had been his closest and after that her family, since his was a continent away, but now he'd lost that support. As unhappy as he'd been in the past months, he hadn't fully realized how much he'd needed someone like Madge and Bryan too. True friends to confide in, who wouldn't automatically condemn him and who would give him the advice and aid he'd always been able to get from Becki.

"Hey what are they for except to oust you as CEO," Madge laughed as he walked out the door, and he turned back, smiling kindly.

CHAPTER 25

The next morning, Arnie called the number Bryan had given him and discovered that he could be seen early that afternoon. Deciding to catch up on some work at home, he then called Harriett. "I've got to go to an appointment around noon so I may not get in until the end of the day. I was supposed to see Madge this morning so would you please let her know I won't be there until then?" He hung up before Harriett had a chance to ask how he could be reached and then put in a call to Becki's primary doctor, who was unavailable. Saying he'd phone later, he tried to reach Jerry but he was over at the Fairfax Court House.

Lose, lose, thought Arnie, but he was glad that some plan was getting underway. He just wasn't the sort of person who could sit and wait. He always had to be doing something. Maybe that's why Becki was so relaxing to be with. She could make him slow down and enjoy smelling those roses, looking at a sunset, listening to a songbird. How he missed her, he thought for what must have been the millionth time, how he had truly missed her. Even when she wasn't here, he always knew she'd be there when he needed her. Arnie didn't want to pursue that thought further so he opened his briefcase and began to look at some papers as he waited to go to the investigators' office.

It was shortly before 1:00 when he reached his appointment. Once there, he looked around with curiosity. He'd never had reason to visit a detective before and he discovered that he wasn't sure what to expect. Too many mystery novels on planes years ago and B-grade movies as a kid, he decided, but the offices he entered could easily have been those of a legal firm or insurance company. "Jim Miller," he announced, "I have an appointment."

The stylish young receptionist smiled, revealing a set of teeth almost as perfect as Becki's. "Oh yes, Mr. Miller, won't you please sit down while I buzz Mr. Jackson. He should be out in a minute." Discretely looking her over, Arnie saw another flaw in his perception of a detective agency. No gum chewing, hard-as-nails bleached blonde bimbo here. This was a chic, professional woman, who easily could have represented any top-notch firm.

"Thank you." and Arnie sank into a comfortable leather couch and picked up a copy of *BusinessWeek* while he waited. His mind wasn't on what he was glancing at and he thought he might as well have had *People* or some entertainment magazine such as he usually found at the dentist's.

"Mr. Miller?" Arnie looked up at a greying, nattily dressed man probably in his late fifties or early sixties, who could have been a banker or doctor or almost any profession but a detective. What was I expecting, Arnie wondered, Sam Spade? Becki's Spenser?

"I'm Bob Jackson, won't you come with me."

"Yes," Arnie said, getting up and shaking the man's proffered hand before following him down the hall. They entered a small office with handsome although not currently in vogue Danish-modern furniture.

"Take a seat, Mr. Miller, or is it Dr. Miller?"

Arnie was surprised, but remained composed, responding mildly, "You're the detective."

"Yes, but I also read an article about you in *Forbes* that included your photo not too long ago and recalled that your name is James although you usually go by Arnie."

"My middle name."

"I see, and naturally you want to keep whatever we're about to discuss confidential."

"I gather you have a reputation for doing that, which is why I'm here."

"Oh most definitely," affirmed Bob Jackson with a smile. "That's one of the things that keep us in business. Now what can we do for you?"

"Besides keeping this confidential, I want you to investigate two individuals for me—a man and a woman—and see if there is any relationship between them. If not, I want to know why the woman approached me and then sent some compromising pictures to my wife."

"How compromising, Dr. Miller? We are licensed, bonded, and have no intention of doing anything illegal."

"Sexually," pronounced Arnie firmly. This was no time for beating around the bush; Becki could have died. "Someone took photos of me with this woman and sent them to my wife, who lives in Virginia. I had never seen the woman before that weekend. I did not expect her to come to my house, much less end up in my bed uninvited; and quite candidly, I feel I was set up since unknown to me there was also someone present taking the photos. I am not happy over what happened but the bottom line is that when my wife saw these pictures, she disappeared. It took me months to find her and when I did, last week she attempted suicide."

Jackson looked at Arnie, coolly appraising him. Sexual peccadilloes, although personally distasteful, were part of the business. So was blackmail, which was probably going to be the next part of this disclosure.

"Frankly," said Arnie brusquely, "I don't care if you believe my story or not but I want to know how the incident happened and if the man was involved. He's a former partner, who once physically harassed and then later publicly embarrassed my wife. Because of the first incident I forced him out of my company—all legally, I might add. Then there was a second incident involving her. That apparently was the result of my company's outmaneuvering his on a business deal although it was strictly above board. I wasn't even aware he was involved with the rival firm at the time. In any case, that occurred approximately fifteen years ago.

"One of my partners believes that he's the most likely person to do something like this. There've been no attempts at blackmail so nothing really makes sense except revenge. I mean I'm groping here. I wouldn't like any of this to become known of course, but that's mostly because of my wife. She is reclusive—almost phobic—and if anything might tip her further over the edge, it would be public notice of this. As far as my business or own standing, this couldn't hurt me at all save for personal embarrassment, so she's been the genuinely innocent victim in this calamity."

"If we do find out that this really was a conspiracy or that there is collusion, what do you intend to do?" the detective asked calmly, but with real interest.

"That's actually my business, isn't it?" countered Arnie. "I supply the names, the date of the latest incident, the photos if I can obtain them..."

"Yes, where are the photos?" Jackson asked.

"My wife's brother-in-law has them." Now the detective looked nonplussed and Arnie continued, "He's a lawyer and she gave them to him in case I refused a divorce. He says he hasn't seen them and wasn't sure what they were. I believe him but I also believe that's what they show if my wife says so. She is one of the most truthful people I've ever met."

"I see," said Jackson slowly, wondering if he did entirely. "May I or my associates see them if necessary?"

"I'll have to ask the brother-in-law, Jerry Madison. He'll be the one representing my wife if the divorce takes place."

"And you don't want the divorce. A question of settlements, perhaps?"

"My wife is one of the most gentle, kind individuals I have ever met. No…she is the most gentle. We have three children—one from her previous marriage. I would never knowingly have done anything like this to hurt her. If the divorce does take place, and I fervently hope it won't, which is one reason I've come here, I will gladly give her anything she wants. I've already told Jerry that. I've also told him I'm ready to give up all active participation in my business and take her anywhere she wants to go if that would help. In fact, I'm planning to take a leave of absence now and let one of my partners take control of SofTec until this matter is resolved. What I want out of this, Mr. Jackson, is to be able to convince my wife that I did not initiate some affair, that it was all a horrible mistake, and that she should forgive me. I love my wife," Arnie expounded. "I'd never have planned to hurt her in any way. If I'd realized how she'd react when I did go to see her, I'd never have go..ne..." Arnie stopped, shocked at what he was starting to say, startled at another self-revelation.

Becki's leaving him had been traumatic, especially when he couldn't locate her, but work, the search for her, other things had kept him occupied. After all, deep in his subconscious he knew once he found her and explained what had happened, everything would be all right. But that wasn't what had happened. Becki's suicide attempt—that was something totally unexpected. In fact it was beyond his comprehension. That she'd rather kill herself than come back to him. Until now, that hadn't completely sunk in, although he'd skirted the issue. Becki, his Becki, the most important person in his life had chosen to... Arnie just stared ahead, the full implication of what she had done, and why, finally perceived and understood.

Arnie didn't know how long he was sitting there, unaware of what he'd been saying, of what he was doing, but suddenly he looked up and saw Bob Jackson gazing at him strangely and he realized that somehow he'd just drifted away. Nothing like this had ever happened to him before, either, and it was terrifying—a hint of the horror Alzheimer victims must face. "I'm sorry," he apologized, deeply embarrassed. "I just remembered something. Excuse me. What was I saying? Oh yes, I resent what's happened to me and I'm scared stiff that not only may I have lost my wife but that she may eventually succeed in taking her life. As it is, at best, I'm afraid she may have lost the use of one of her hands." And I may be losing my mind, Arnie suddenly thought. She really was trying to kill herself rather than come back to him! Oh God, what was he going to do?

It was apparent to Bob Jackson that the abrupt cessation in conversation indicated the strain Miller was under; but the look on the man's face just before he started talking again was unnerving. Something really terrible had just occurred to Miller and the detective was reminded of someone in his platoon in Vietnam who had snapped while they were out on patrol decades before. It wasn't just the poor wife who had gone over the edge because of this nasty mess. The creative computer whiz and confident, clever business executive in front of him was also apparently on the brink. It might not just be investigative services that the man needed. Jackson looked at Arnie quietly for a moment, making a decision, hoping it was the correct one. His company liked its low profile, but a scandal involving James Arnold Miller, Ph.D., SofTek CEO, had the potential of becoming very high profile.

Calmly, he said, "We don't take every case, Dr. Miller. Quite frankly, we don't have to. We're exceedingly expensive and greatly sought because we're among the best in the business. You got the appointment right away because one of our former clients referred you. I wasn't happy when you didn't identify yourself immediately, and yet I can well understand why you don't want this to become public. I think we can guarantee confidentiality at least on our side. Our employees are very professional and extremely well compensated for their work, which means you're going to have to pay us what may seem an exorbitant amount. I can see that this has to be a priority matter, which will drive the cost up higher. If you do want our services, I can guarantee that we will begin immediately and will keep you informed weekly. We expect at least a three-week contract. If after that time we have no information or leads for you, we will withdraw from the case if you wish. Otherwise, it will continue on a week-to-week basis at the set fee plus expenses. Is that agreeable with you?"

"Fine, do you want a check for the first three weeks now?" Arnie asked, feeling once more in command. But what a frightening moment or moments! For how long had he lost his sense of time? Apparently it was enough that Jackson had noticed. And would it happen again? But Becki had tried to kill herself rather than be with him. How could he face that? What could he do? Would she try again if he saw her? Certainly she'd made a threat in the hospital, but he'd still dismissed it as emotional aftermath. This time he knew for certain that his heart was breaking. Saying so hadn't just been rhetoric.

"You didn't ask how much our services cost," Jackson cautioned mildly.

"Who cares," responded Arnie with indifference. "It's the results I want." And, oh God, did he, but would he be able to face them?

"In that case," said the detective, "let's begin with the names of the individuals that you believe were involved. In the case of the woman, there's no question, but I'd like any information you might have about her as well as the man. And, I want you to call your brother-in-law and get his permission to see and copy the photos, which might give us some idea of who took them. You did have physical relations with the woman, right?"

"Hell, I don't know what happened at that point. There was a woman in my house who was passed out in the living room. I was understandably upset and I tossed down some drinks. In the middle of the night, I woke up with her all over me and to be totally honest, I was still out of it. I had not been playing around on my wife. Never! Something happened and some photos were taken and they were sent to Becki and I am fucking mad at this point," snarled Arnie. "The woman's name is Pam Carter, unless she came to the meetings under an alias. She was supposed to be a junior associate of Barnes, Inc. At least she attended a weekend meeting we were having out at the Cape with their representatives and some of our company members. We've been trying to keep these negotiations confidential.

"The man who may be responsible for this is Richard Ramsey, who was at Caltech as an undergraduate when I was. When I started the company after MIT, he and another classmate came out from there to join us. There were seven of us in all, three from MIT including me; Ramsey and the other guy from California; and one of the MIT faculty, who just wanted to put up money. Then my sister and her husband came in together as joint partners with the legal and financial advice as well as some cash. The others provided a little money as well as their programming expertise. After

Dickie was forced out—to the tune of $1,000,000 about twenty years ago—he apparently went with the Tech Group out in Silicon Valley. They were competing with us over new software that the Volkenant Corporation was going to use exclusively for their own business and then distribute publicly through all their retail outlets. We had the better package and we won. That was the SofTek *FindIt* in case you're up on that sort of thing. We've had four updates since, but it still is the best on the market for what it does." Jackson nodded; his firm used it for their finances. "That took place fifteen years ago and that was the last time I saw Dickie. I don't even know who he's working with now."

"And you say he also had problems with your wife," inquired Jackson.

"The first time he met her he tried to rape her and then lied about what happened. I stopped him and that's when I tossed him out of the company. To retaliate, he spread a lot of nasty and untrue rumors about her and after I married her, it caused her a lot of anguish. Then, a few years later, just after his company lost out with Volkenant, he insulted her publicly at a party and something in her just snapped. She was shy before, but she became more and more reclusive and eventually I ended up buying her family home back in rural Virginia so she could live there. Our marriage for over ten years has been one of my commuting down as often as I could. It's not been very satisfactory; but to be honest, I'd rather spend a weekend here or there with my wife than live or have relations with anyone else." And that's true, Arnie thought, as again he realized that he might have lost even that option. Oh Becki, what is going to happen to us, he despaired.

"And you're now planning to go down there, more or less permanently?"

"As long as she needs me, and yes, permanently if necessary." Oh yes…if she'll just have me, he prayed.

Jackson surveyed him. Miller, he knew from what he'd read in the financial magazines, was considered to be a brilliant, charismatic, and highly-competitive individual, who had been responsible for some of the more innovative software in the computer field. SofTek's financial systems dominated Wall Street and the stock markets internationally. Miller had made millions but still was considered very much a part of the creative process. His reputation professionally was outstanding. Until now, there had never been any indication of scandal. If anything, he was pretty much of a dark horse with little known about his private life and family. Yet, if the man were to be believed, rather than chance any widespread notice of this incident, he was willing to step aside and give up leadership of his company. All of this apparently to save his wife public humiliation and make sure no one knew that she had tried to kill herself.

"We'll do what we can," Jackson assured Arnie, surprised at the genuine interest and sympathy he felt. Hopefully it was justified. "I'll personally take charge of the investigation and get it underway immediately. Let me know where I can reach you once you leave Boston and I'll keep you informed on a daily basis if you wish."

"Thank you," Arnie responded gratefully. "I guess when you know something that should be often enough. I've got a few things I've got to complete up here in the next couple of days and then I'll be heading down to D.C. Quite frankly, I don't know where I'll be. I'm going to write down my contact information and I have one partner up here, Madge Norris, who'll be acting head of the company. You can ask her anything. She was going to see what she could find in our records but she also thought we might have to bring in an outsider to help with the investigation. I assume in this day and age that you have some staff capable of doing that?"

Jackson smiled broadly. "We no longer stand on street corners or sit in cars to do most of our work, not that that still isn't necessary at times. Computers are now the tools of the trade. In fact, one of the best people I have is a young woman who attended MIT. I think she might be quite suitable for that search."

"Fine. As I said, whoever, whatever. Just get me some

answers ASAP. I earned my money to use for some reason. I guess spending it this way is as good as any."

When Arnie got back to the office, he went looking for Madge, but she had called saying she wouldn't be in until the next day. He wondered whether he should phone her at home but there was so much that he still had to do before he felt he could leave town. So he worked on late into the evening. That night when he got home, he called Jerry. Marty answered and although she wouldn't speak to him, she did get Jerry.

"What's new?" Arnie asked, not sure if he really wanted to know. Since he'd left the detective agency, he felt as though he was in a living hell. Was this the way Becki felt, had felt all those years when he'd dismissed or ignored her personal problems in such a cavalier manner?

"About the same. Either Marty or I go to see her. It was my turn today. The doctors have her on new medication and are talking to her, but she apparently isn't talking to them so when she'll be released is still a question. The hand incidentally may be in better shape than we thought, but there is definitely severe nerve damage and loss of mobility. They want to wait awhile to see what time and therapy will do, but there may be more surgery later."

"Thank God about the hand. That sounds much better than what they said at first," Arnie enthused. It was time Becki had some luck. "Incidentally, I went to see a private investigator today."

"And?"

"You'll be contacted by a Bob Jackson. He may send someone down to D.C. and he wants to see those photos."

"I'm not sure I can do that, Arnie."

"Listen, they need to see the originals to track down the person who took them. You don't think I want anyone to see them otherwise, do you?" Jerry snorted. "I'll pay for your damn time if you have to go along to duplicate them. Or maybe they need the originals themselves and will give you the copies; I don't know. The fewer people who know, the better. Anyhow, you don't have to look at them, which was what you promised Becki. Ok?" There was silence on the other end of the line, but at least Jerry hadn't said no. Arnie continued. "I'm taking a leave of absence up here. One of the partners is going to take over and I'll be down there this weekend. As soon as I know where I'm staying, I'll contact you. I plan to stay until we decide what to do with Becki."

This time Jerry did answer. "Are you sure that's a good idea?"

"I told you when I saw you, Jerry. Becki's my wife. I love her, and I intend to do anything I can to get her back. I meant what I said about giving up the business if I have to. This is the first step." But will it be enough, will anything? The questions plagued Arnie.

"But you could get it back and then everything would be the same, wouldn't it Arnie?"

"Don't be such a cynic," Arnie replied, greatly irritated. "Whatever I do now is going to be guided by Becki. At the same time, I expect her to undergo the counseling. I realize now that I was an enabler. All of this problem isn't my fault." I have to believe that, he thought. If it were just him, he'd never get her back and maybe he really shouldn't, but if there was another reason, he still had a chance. "Something strange happened and I may have acted stupidly, but I am not the reason that Becki has been shutting down like this. Sure, our life style contributed to this, but she was already on her way. Did you talk to Marty about what I'd told you?"

"Yes..." Jerry hesitated.

"And?"

"And what?"

"Don't be a lawyer now, Jerry. Answer me like the friend and family you...were."

"She said you might be right about that part. That even Drea had mentioned to her that her mother was becoming more isolated. But she still thinks you're scum and that most of this is your fault."

"I'll accept it if we can work something out."

"I said I'd talk to you, Arnie. That's the best I can do now," replied Jerry.

"Fine, I'll call as soon as I get to D.C."

The next day, first thing, Arnie met with Madge to discuss how they would arrange the transfer of authority. "Are you sure we don't have to tell the other board members first?" she asked.

"Why?" he responded. "As far as they're concerned, it's just a leave of absence since Becki's ill or whatever we decide to tell them."

"Well, we'd better damn well get that story straight now."

"I agree, but as to the other—you, me, and my sister and her husband, since they'll always vote with me—we have control of the company. According to my calculations, that amounts to seventy-nine percent of the total stock."

"I am impressed," remarked Madge snidely. "Are you sure you don't have an abacus on your lap?"

"Sarcasm becomes you. You're going to do fine. Now what do I say about the other?"

"You've already told Harriett that Becki was having some tests. Just say she has some female problems. That's always a nice euphemism for a hysterectomy or something similar and that's not the sort of thing that starts a rumor mill or gets leaked to the press. It usually takes weeks and sometimes months for a woman to snap back so you wanting to be with her is perfectly logical."

"It takes a woman to think deviously."

"It was a woman that got you into trouble, Arnie," Madge remarked quietly.

"Ah yes. Well we're going to have to see what we can do about that."

"You saw the PI?"

"Yesterday. His name is Bob Jackson. He's getting started on this right away. I told him you'd be in charge while I was gone and your thoughts about looking around within the company. He says he has a bright young woman with all the computer know-how, one of our MIT grads, and that he's arrange with you for her to have access to our records. They apparently use her for industrial espionage investigations."

"Fine," said Madge. "When do you want to get away?"

"Today, now, this very minute, but hopefully by COB Friday. Let's work out what details we think we need and then call in legal and put the papers in place."

"Are you sure an announcement wouldn't be enough?"

"I'm not sure of anything, Madge, but just in case this wasn't all Dickie or there is some problem here at SofTek itself, I'd like to cover all bases to protect us both. Also, I have another favor to ask."

"Ask away. You're giving me power and money, it's the least I can do."

"I'd like to leave my house keys with you and hope you won't mind coming by once a week to check the place. I'm cutting off papers, mail, cleaning service, all that good stuff. Frankly I just don't want anyone in the place now; but there are Becki's plants and things like that. She didn't come to talk to them often in the last year, but I'd still like to take care of them."

"Sure, Arnie, no problem. I hope...I hope she'll be back to take care of them." Madge's face had a melancholy look.

"Not as much as I do," Arnie replied, sounding very dejected.

CHAPTER 26

When Arnie walked into Becki's hospital room, she was sitting by the window waiting. She looked better—alive at least. Her coloring was back and her hair glossy and gleaming again. Her beautiful golden hair, he thought. Would he ever really be able to look at it without seeing the blood?

"Hi," he said softly. "May I sit down?" She nodded. "Thank you for seeing me."

"I guess I owed you that." Then she added, "I'm not sure I could keep you out without a scene."

Surely she wasn't trying to be humorous, he wondered, but mildly remarked, "And we know you don't like scenes."

"No."

"How are you?"

"Physically? Alive," she answered dryly. "About the hand, I don't know."

Arnie inwardly cringed, but refused to ask the obvious about mentally. Instead, he plunged right in, "I shouldn't have seduced you when I came to see you. I should have been more sensitive to your feelings but I'd missed you so much. We'd never been apart that long and I guess I thought if we did make love, you'd forgive me and then I thought you wanted me too."

"I did. That was my problem."

Arnie didn't quite know what to say to this and was silent for a moment before commenting, "I went back to Boston to see if I could find out how all this happened. You know I didn't realize there were photographs until you mentioned them. I really didn't know what had happened with you, I could only assume."

"I know you went."

"Jerry talked to you?"

"Some, but mostly Madge."

"Madge!" Arnie looked at her surprised. "Madge called

you?"

"No, she flew down the other day to talk to me."

"Madge flew down here?" Arnie was still having a hard time taking this in but now he realized where Madge had been the afternoon he tried to get hold of her after seeing the detective.

"She told me you're turning the company over to her, at least on a temporary basis, but maybe forever. She told me a lot of things."

"Such as?"

"That you did work all the time when I was in Virginia so you could get down here as often as possible. That you were, as far as she and everyone else knew, totally faithful to me. That she believed you and that she thought Dickie was responsible for this whole mess and that..." Becki stopped, shutting her eyes momentarily, to take a deep breath. Arnie looked at her, afraid to say anything. "That...I was a damn fool to have done this when I had so much to offer and not only was I destroying you and hurting the kids, that if I didn't talk to someone and start straightening out my problems, I should have done a better job."

"Madge said that!" Arnie's face turned white in shock.

"She also said she was about my only friend in Boston anymore and that was my fault too. That I never should have been such a wimp and run away but should have stayed to fight."

"We never fought!"

"She didn't mean just with you, but yes, that probably was part of the problem too, Arnie. It wasn't natural, but I didn't want to fight with you ever." Becki looked at him with the saddest eyes he'd ever seen.

"I just thought we were living happily ever after," he sighed.

"I wanted to believe it was a fairy tale too, but Madge said now that something bad had happened, I was running away again and no one would want to help me if I didn't do something, but that she and everyone else would help if I did try."

Arnie looked at her, furious, frustrated, hardly knowing what to say. "Becki, I'm so sorry. I can't believe she'd do something like that. I thought she was our friend."

Bravely, Becki persevered, "She is our friend, Arnie. She's your very good friend and she was right, she was and is about my only friend outside of family nowadays."

"But how could she say things like that to you!" He was still clearly disconcerted.

"Because friends, real friends, do tell each other honest things. Because she was enough of a friend to come down here and tell me to my face. Because she does care for me." Becki looked at him, sorrowfully. "You and I used to tell each other everything when we were first married. You were my best friend and then...we just kind of stopped, didn't we?"

"I told you things, Beauty." Or at least I thought I did, he mused. So much of what he had thought was apparently wrong.

"Sure, you told me what you were working on, when you had to travel, what you thought about the children or the weather or the news of the day, but we just stopped talking about some things, didn't we?"

As she spoke, Arnie felt as though she were cutting into his soul. "What do you mean by that?"

"Oh, I guess what was happening when you were traveling, going away to meetings, things like that. Or, asking me what I was really doing, what I was feeling. Telling me what you felt."

"You wouldn't go with me any more so I didn't think that was important. You didn't want to see any of the people from work. You didn't want to be in Boston. You wanted another life and I thought I gave it to you." Feelings, how could he honestly address that, yet that was what this was all about, and hurt? He'd never hurt so much.

"You did, but what if I'd been wrong?"

"Were you wrong?" he asked quietly.

"I don't know...maybe. I don't know much of anything now, Arnie."

"What do you want?" He was afraid of her response.

"To get out of here. I'm still in the hospital because you told the doctors what I said, aren't I?"

"Yes, I guess so, and because you wouldn't talk to them at first."

"I want to leave here, Arnie." Becki was practically begging.

"Where do you want to go?" he asked.

"Maybe Marty's if she'll have me."

"Why wouldn't she?" Clearly there was something he was missing here.

"She's afraid. She's only been to see me once. Jerry came the other times. She stayed a few minutes and she really didn't say anything. My own sister is afraid of me." Becki started to cry. Arnie had given up trying to count the times he'd seen her do it. That little game was meaningless. He was sure they'd both cried more than they needed in several lifetimes by now.

"She's not afraid of you, Beauty. She's afraid for you, we all are," he corrected earnestly.

"And none of you have told the children except for Drea, have you?"

"I was going to see them after I came back down here. I didn't think it was something to tell them over the phone."

"Like you couldn't tell me what happened at the Cape over the phone."

"That's right," he admitted sadly. It clearly was the biggest error he'd ever made.

"What if I were to believe what you told me? Madge does, you know."

"I'm glad someone does," he replied.

"I think Jerry might too."

"Jerry's been talking about this?"

"Oh yes," Becki said. "Jerry told me everything you've said and what you told him you planned to do. Then Madge told me you were doing it."

"And?"

"And what? Does it make any difference? I don't know

yet, Arnie." He suddenly felt more hope than he had had all week, for months in fact, but then she continued and he was devastated. "Why should it really, Arnie? Madge was right, you know, we were having a pretend marriage. That wasn't fair to you."

"I didn't care about its being fair to me," he rejoined irately. "You on a part-time basis were better than you on no basis. I love you, Becki. I'll do anything for you I can, even if it means I can't have you anymore." Having said that, he averted his eyes, feeling very sad, but at least he'd told her the truth. If the only way she could be happy was through his losing her, that would have to be the way.

"Thank you," she said simply. "I know you tried to give me everything I wanted or thought I wanted. Maybe Madge was right, maybe we were both wrong. Being apart so much wasn't very healthy."

"I don't want to be apart anymore," Arnie stated sincerely. He never had.

"I know you don't but if we stayed here, you'd pretty much have to give up everything you've worked so hard to achieve."

"Becki, I'd still have the money, the stock, the power to dictate where the company is going."

"That's not the same, Arnie. You'd miss the action. You had all those things for most of our marriage, but it really was the action, wasn't it? You liked being a player, a mover and shaker, Mr. Innovator ahead of the masses."

He looked at her thoughtfully. "I liked the perks. I worked for them, but I guess you're right. I've realized that may have been one of the reasons I could live the way I did because I could then devote whole blocks of my life to concentrating on things like my work with no distractions."

"See, Madge was right. We both were wrong. I got to be an ostrich hiding my head in a sandy dream world and you could be the ruthless businessman," she commented.

"I'm not ruthless," he asserted tightly.

"I know and ostriches don't really bury their heads." She smiled slightly—the first smile he'd seen since he'd found her again. "It was just a figure of speech. You were always so confident but never ruthless, Arnie. Tough and determined to get what you wanted but that's not ruthless. You couldn't be and maybe that's why you let me do anything I wanted even if I shouldn't have."

"How could I pressure you to go to places when you were afraid? Or stay in Boston when you hated it?" And, I'm not getting what I want now, he thought despondently.

She looked at him, refusing to comment, and then changed the conversation. "What do we tell the children?"

"I can't speak for you," he answered truthfully. "I can tell them what happened and why I think it did, what I did, but that's all."

"And you'd do that? Tell them everything?"

"I'll probably have to. We've always tried to be honest with them."

"And with each other...at least as far as we went."

He wasn't sure if what she had said was a question but he replied, "Yes. I was, I did. I'm trying to be."

"Can you go now, Arnie?"

"If you want me to. May I see you again? Aside from seeing the kids soon, I intend to stay down here."

"Where?" she asked.

"Probably at a motel near here."

"You can have the apartment where I was. I'm not going to want to go back there."

"And you? May I see you, when you get out?" he persisted.

"When will that be, Arnie?" She avoided answering his question.

"I'll talk to Marty, if she'll let me, or Jerry. I don't think it's a good idea to go back to King George now, do you?"

"Because I might try again?"

"God, I hope not, Becki. But if you still want to commit suicide," he choked out the word, looking at her pathetically, "I doubt if we could stop you. I don't want you locked up. You're like some beautiful wild animal or bird. You don't belong in a cage."

"But I've kept myself in one, haven't I?" she gently asked.

"I can't answer that. I thought...I had hoped the river place wasn't a cage, that it was kind of your territory like for those eagles, that you were happy there."

"I think I was, as much as I could be. I wanted the house, but I hated it too."

"You hated it!"

"Oh yes," she said passionately. "Aunt Mary was still there."

"What do you mean?" Arnie looked at her carefully, clearly not understanding.

"Sure, whenever I had any doubts or something went wrong, she was there—even more so than when we were in Boston. She's always been there some with me, Arnie."

"What do you mean? You hardly ever talked about her after we married although I've always felt the way she treated you created or at least contributed to these problems. That year after your parents' death had to have been traumatic."

"It was. She was always preaching, hating. When I got the photos, she was there telling me that that was what I deserved because I'd sinned with you, been a whore, and that was the righteous payment."

"What do you mean?" He was horrified.

"I'd gone to bed with you before we got married just as I had with Billy."

"But we were adults. We fell in love!"

"She wouldn't have seen it that way."

"You mean you felt like we were sinning until we got married?" Arnie couldn't believe what he was hearing. This was mediaeval—sack cloth and ashes, self-flagellation. "You've been feeling guilty all our marriage because of that?"

"Not consciously. I told you, I liked sex. You know I did...you know I do, but that was supposed to be sinful too." Sex, Becki thought. She couldn't stop herself from wanting to have him, to let him have her even when she'd sworn to herself that they were through, and yes, she'd tried to pay, to atone.

"Becki, there's no commandment about not making love. Neither of us was attached to anyone else. We weren't committing adultery!"

"I did with Mike," she said ashamed, looking down at her wrists—atonement for that sin too.

"Damn it, you didn't know he was married! You never saw him after you found out." Arnie's voice rose, outraged at this unjustified self-guilt.

"I'm not saying this was rational. I'm just saying that's what she would have said to me, just the way she did when I got pregnant."

"Jesus," sighed Arnie, still flabbergasted. "What else did you hate?"

"The fact that everything was gone," Becki answered.

"Meaning?"

"When she threw me out, she did just that."

"I know she threw you out but I don't think I understand what you're saying."

"Arnie, she pushed me out the door when I told her I was afraid I was pregnant. She'd grabbed a broom and was beating me. I left wearing the clothes I was in and that was all."

Arnie looked at her, unbelieving. "Only your clothes...you didn't tell me that." A broom! Oh my God, the old hag really was a witch, he thought, and here we used to play make-believe about dragons and knights and damsels in distress and Becki had to face something like that as a little girl.

"Well, I'd grabbed my school books too when I ran outside. Then she locked the door so I sat on the steps and cried for an hour or more. When I finally realized she wasn't going to let me back in, I walked to Billy's house up by Fairview. It was after dark by the time I got there and I was so scared."

"That's miles," remarked Arnie, mentally trying to calculate the actual distance, seeing a frightened little girl trudging the dark, empty, back roads, holding a pile of precious but heavy school books. Fourteen-year old Becki would have been terrified.

"Yes and then I was afraid Billy's mother wouldn't let me in either but she did. I got to stay there but Aunt Mary wouldn't let me come back."

Stomach churning, Arnie waited for her to continue. Finally, he prodded her, "And then what happened?"

"Billy's mother told her that the whole damn county would hear what happened, not just about me being pregnant, but what Aunt Mary was doing. She said she'd start by calling everyone in Aunt Mary's church so Aunt Mary said I could take what was left of my things. My aunt always did worry about what people would say and I guess this would have been worse than my just being knocked up. Anyhow, when Billy's mother went with me, my clothes were dumped outside of the house, but..." Becki began to cry, unable to continue.

"Becki, Beauty, what happened?" Arnie approached her for the first time, kneeling by her chair. She had her face turned to the window and was making gasping sounds, her body shaking. He picked up the hand unencumbered by a cast. A light gauze bandage was still around the wrist and he kissed it gently. "Tell me, honey. Please say what happened."

"My other stuff..." She turned to look at him, but her eyes were actually staring far away, haunted. "My other stuff she'd taken outside and she'd set on fire. Mother's books I'd bought back at the church bazaar, my school papers, the 4-H ribbons, even my record books..." Here she let out a big sob. "In 4-H we kept record books and I was so proud of what I'd done with my pigs. I'd spent hours and hours and Daddy had helped me build the pen and everything. Those were just ashes or bits of charred green binders. They were the only things I had left of something we'd done together. And my awards from school and the jewelry box Mother gave me when I was twelve and everything in it—her baby ring, the cross I got when I was confirmed, Daddy's army medals, and the photos..." She broke down again. "All our family photos, all I had of my parents, it was all gone, Arnie. She destroyed everything—my whole family—my life."

"Becki, oh Becki," Arnie put his arms around her, feeling her heart beating wildly, wishing he could capture the hurt, destroy it, make time go back and stop Becki's parents from taking their fateful voyage. "Why didn't you tell me that before?"

"How could I, Arnie? How could anyone be so mean? Marty and Jerry weren't mean. Even Billy really wasn't mean—just young and irresponsible. I thought people wouldn't be mean to me again, even if there were Mikes and Larrys in the world, for they only wanted sex. Then I met you and you were so nice, so very nice. You were the nicest man I'd ever met and I thought, I hoped we'd be happy and then when I went to see you, something bad happened and I knew I shouldn't marry you. I even told you." She was looking at him and seeing him now. "It was a mistake, Arnie, I knew it but I really loved you and I wanted you."

"And I wanted you too, Becki, you know that."

"And after we married, no one liked me and I just didn't know what to do and then I couldn't even go places with you because bad things happened again. I was so afraid to meet people because I never knew what they were saying. It would be just like high school when I got pregnant and everyone talked about me. Some of the boys said I'd put out with anyone until Billy stopped them. At least then I was his girl—he hadn't accused me of trapping him yet."

Arnie winced. That little bastard! No wonder Becki, with all her pride, hadn't fought for Drea's support and signed the unfair divorce papers, which still upset Marty. Becki had always paid her own way, from the very start. And, no wonder she had been so upset about the Boston rumors regarding their marriage and speculation about the immediate pregnancy. If only he'd known this too, but he'd never asked, assuming it was just Billy's womanizing and immaturity that destroyed the childhood marriage.

"But it would have been worse with you. You might have gotten into a fight and hurt your reputation and business because you'd try to stop them."

Becki's concern was obvious even now and he asked

slowly, "You were afraid it might hurt me?"

"And the children. I didn't want them to hear that you'd married me because I was some slut you'd knocked up. That you'd made a damn fool of yourself because of me. That you were trapped too!"

"It was never true and do you think I would have really cared, that I did care?"

"Probably not, Arnie. You're tough, but I'm not and I did."

"But then why the hell did you let me buy the Virginia house? Why did you want to go there?" He was genuinely puzzled.

"You wanted…you wanted to give me what you thought I wanted most and part of me did want it. It had been a safe place when I was little before my parents died. It was my home even if I made a mistake." She stopped abruptly and then insisted, "No, Drea wasn't a mistake!"

"No one ever says she was, Becki," Arnie argued.

"Aunt Mary did."

"Oh Becki," he commiserated, nauseated at what he was hearing.

"Before living with her, I loved my childhood, my family, our history there, the river. I was happy there when I was little and I wanted my children to have some of that too. Also, I did want the damn house." Becki had stopped crying and was angry. "That was our house. That was supposed to be my father's house and then mine and Marty's. I wanted it back and…"

"Yes."

"I just hoped Aunt Mary hadn't destroyed everything. That something would be left of mine or my parents," she said sadly. "But she'd really done it. There were a few things from my great grandparents like our…the walnut bed, but everything else was hers and I wanted to burn it all. Papers and things like that, I did. The rest I gave to the damn church bazaar just the way she'd done with my family's things. Then I did my best to turn that house into a home the way my mother and father would have. But I didn't do too well, did I?" she asked poignantly.

"It was home! The children did have a happy childhood there. And, it's a beautiful place, Beauty. You should have become an interior decorator the way you wanted."

"I really didn't want that either, Arnie."

He looked at her surprised. "The classes you were taking when I married you?"

"It was a way I could get a better job; but, if I really could have done anything I wanted, I would have studied English and maybe tried to teach school." Arnie felt a little chill. It was exactly what he's said to Jerry and of course explained Becki's decision at Christmas to start at Mary Washington, her childhood dream before her parents died in the devastating storm.

"But...I didn't think I could afford to keep going to college after NOVA and taking care of Drea. Also, I'm not sure I could have gotten a teaching job and even that wasn't what I wanted to do most."

"What was that Beauty?" he inquired gently, wondering why he'd never asked—had accepted her at face value, not delving deeper. Was it because he was afraid of the hidden Becki, satisfied instead with the sweet, vulnerable, tenderhearted girl he'd met and loved?

"To write. I wrote a lot when I was little, especially after my parents died. I wrote about them and what it had been like when we were all together and what it would have been like if they'd lived. Aunt Mary burned all that up too. She burned my memories and dreams and I just didn't want to write again." Becki stopped, staring down.

Arnie sat there at her feet, holding her hand. They sat for a long time. It was getting dark outside now and he knew he would have to leave. Finally he said to her, "I'll talk to Jerry about you going to his place. You're not going to do anything to yourself now if you leave, are you?"

Becki wouldn't look at him but she said softly, "No, not now. I'll promise not now. And I'll talk to the doctors. I know I have to do that." Then she raised her head and gazed directly into his eyes. "I won't do anything now. I know I need help, Arnie. I've known for a long time. You apparently said something to Madge about my being a Stepford wife."

"I didn't say that," protested Arnie. "I never wanted a Stepford wife."

"But I was," she replied truthfully. "I let myself be. If I was a Stepford wife, nothing bad would happen. You'd be happy, I'd have the perfect home, I'd have the perfect children, everything would be perfect but that didn't really happen, did it?"

"There's nothing wrong with the kids."

"No," she agreed, "but they don't need me anymore and then when I thought you didn't either..."

"I do need you."

"Well, that's neither here nor there at this point. Drea is fine. She always was. Leah doesn't like me very much, but she's tough and smart like you and she's going to do all right. Bruce is more like me, but he's got part of you too. He's going to do something special even if he doesn't become a business whiz."

"Yes," Arnie concurred. "He'll be the one who designs the future."

"Maybe," said Becki thoughtfully. "I've sometimes worried he may turn out the ultimate weapon of destruction, not because he wants to destroy anything but because it would be the solution to the definitive puzzle. You and he— you've always searched for answers. He really is the genius in the family, isn't he?"

Arnie nodded his head, thinking he'd not searched enough, at least in his personal life, and hoping Bruce would never make that error. About his son, he too had sometimes had Becki's concern. "He'll just get us across the galaxy," he responded.

"I hope so," said Becki.

"But you're wrong about Leah," Arnie protested. "She loves you."

"I didn't say she didn't love me. I said she doesn't like me."

Arnie looked puzzled. "Why?"

"She didn't get the looks. She almost acts like that was something I did on purpose. I've never lived up to her expectations of a role model. She would have preferred to stay in Boston than in the country when she was older...lots of things. We should have sent her off to boarding school. She would have thrived."

"Perhaps," said Arnie doubtfully, not wanting to say that if Becki had returned to Boston, Leah might have been happier too. "Anyhow, I'm glad she picked Oberlin though I'm afraid you're right, she's not going to become the great dancer."

"No, and it's so unfair," stated Becki with a scowl. "She is good, but people want dancers to look like me, not like the stocky Galina Ulanovas regardless of how brilliant they are, and Leah looks like you." She looked at him sadly, her eyes begging his pardon for stating the obvious.

"We always knew you married me for the charm, right?"

She smiled, a sorrowful little smile. "But charm doesn't always do it for a girl. Looks don't either," she added, "if they're too much and there's no personality behind them."

"You have personality," he insisted ardently. "That's what I saw first."

"That's false, Arnie, you saw how I looked. It's like a candy bar—you went for the fancy wrapping but I was interested in the chocolate—the substance, something I thought I could depend upon, that would energize me. That's how I saw you—the man who could do everything. The wrapping didn't matter to me the way it did to you. If I'd been ugly, would you have gotten me out of that bar? Be honest and tell me that."

"If you'd been ugly, would someone superficial like Larry have been there with you, giving you a hard time?" Arnie retorted, wounded at her accusation. "But yes, I would have. How can you think I was that shallow? He was bullying you, and I hate bullies. That's one reason I snapped with Dickie too. I should have handled it better. Maybe we could have avoided some of his malice."

Becki looked at him and shook her head. "I doubt it."

"Anyhow, I gave you the choice about contacting me, going out with me, coming to bed with me. Sure I thought you were the most beautiful, sexiest gal I'd ever met. I still do. But do you think I would have kept after you or married you if that was all there was? Becki, you may give off something that turns me to water, but you, yourself, were outwardly one of the least seductive women I'd met. Ninety percent of the women I knew evoked more come-on than you, knowingly or not—pheromones, I guess. You had that chemistry but you were almost oblivious to it. It wasn't until after you went to bed with me that you just radiated sex appeal whenever I was around. I mean you didn't even carry any protection with you. You weren't on the great singles sex search.

"We both know it was just an accident, luckily for me, that you were there in that bar that night. I never would have met you in a singles joint or anywhere like that otherwise. It was obvious that it just was never the sort of thing you did. And then that's not how you were acting with other men either. That's why you so disturbed Dickie. He looked at you and thought you should be that way and was angry when you weren't and you rejected him. Even if I hadn't seen the whole incident, I would have known you weren't leading him on. You just didn't and don't do that sort of thing. You're too moral."

"Aunt Mary would have laughed."

"I hope your fucking Aunt Mary is burning down in hell where she belongs," snarled Arnie angrily. "I knew she'd messed up some of your thinking but nothing like you've told me. Have you said any of this to the doctor?"

"No."

"Well, you'd better, Becki. And I also think Dickie just became the next in line to replace her on my shit list. Maybe if you'd told me more about Aunt Mary and Billy too, I could have been smart enough to figure out some of this earlier."

"I'm not sure I knew," admitted Becki. "I told you. I

was the one who let myself become the Stepford wife, Arnie, but you let me too."

"Hell," he agreed gloomily. "Yes, I did, but I wasn't doing it to be mean. All I wanted was for you to be happy and that's what I thought you wanted. So, you'll talk to the doctors, right? But you don't know if you want to see me or for me to be part of your life."

"I'm sorry," she said with obvious sincerity, her eyes sorrowful. "I'm so sorry, Arnie."

"But you haven't said I might not be able to be part of your life later?" he asked hopefully.

"I don't know...I don't think so, but I don't know. That's as honest as I can be."

"That's better than nothing, Becki." Yeah, it's like how good it feels when you're not being kicked, he decided, aching. "Ok, I'll do what I can to get you out of here. I'm going to stay at the motel for now. I don't want to be in that apartment either. We both have memories." Then he said fervently, "You've asked me before, Beauty, if I'd have loved you or would keep loving you if you weren't beautiful and I usually took it as a joke. Then today you come out with this bizarre candy analogy. You were never just the fancy wrapping on some damn chocolate bar. It was the chocolate I wanted too. The pretty exterior just made it more enticing. I had never dreamed anyone as lovely as you would want someone like me. Hell, if you'd known I was a success, I probably would have worried that that was the reason you were interested in me, but you didn't know, and after that first dinner we had, it wasn't just your looks that counted. They were merely a bonus as much as my success has been to you—or at least it was," he added ruefully. "I know you've never given a damn about the money, just what the work meant to me. Think about that and the fact that there was nothing beautiful about you when I pulled you out of that tub and I couldn't have loved you more."

Becki looked at him, clearly surprised, but said nothing, not that he'd expected her to. Then he added, "I'll talk to the kids but until you let me know what you want me to say, I'll stall."

"Tell them the truth, Arnie."

"Everything?"

"Whatever you think they should hear."

"Fine, but you'll talk to them too?"

"Eventually. I really don't want to talk to them now."

"Ok. I'll go then, Beauty, but remember what I said the first time I asked you to be with me?"

"What's that, Arnie?" she asked softly but he was fairly certain she remembered.

"I told you that regardless of what you decided, I still wanted to see you and I'd keep trying to have you. I'll wait for now and I do believe you're not going to do anything foolish."

"Suicide isn't foolish," she asserted, staring at him challengingly. "It's a choice."

"Ok, but it's foolish when you're distraught and that's what happened that evening I found you. And Becki, I'm going to find out what precipitated this whole mess. I'm sure now that Madge is right about its being Dickie. If it was, he's not going to get away with it this time. I will find a way to stop him. I can't resolve your conflict with Aunt Mary. Even knights don't do well with dead witches though I would have tried if I'd known," he added wryly. "You're going to have to work that out yourself. If I'd really understood what happened with Aunt Mary, I would have done a lot of things differently, but if Dickie became the next step in turning you into what you are now, I will make sure he never bothers you again. I swear that, Beauty." He got up, leaned over, and kissed her gently on the brow, running his hands down her golden hair. "I love you so much. I hope we can work this out." Then, so she wouldn't have to say anything, he walked out of the room.

CHAPTER 27

As soon as Arnie got back to the motel, he began to make a series of calls. First he got hold of Jerry. "I've just seen Becki," he began.

"She was willing to talk to you?" broke in Jerry.

"Yes. I'd like to talk to you and Marty together."

"I don't think that's a good idea," Jerry replied.

"I don't think it's a good idea that Marty doesn't want to see Becki either."

"What do you mean?" Jerry sounded puzzled.

"You didn't realize that she's only been to the hospital once and that she only spent a few minutes with Becki?"

"You've got to be wrong!"

"I don't think Becki is lying, Jerry. She never has, and that's what she told me. She also wants to get out of the hospital. She's hoping she can stay with you so she can get the continued therapy for her hand and the psychiatric counseling here, but she says Marty's afraid. She also told me some very disturbing things about that year she lived with their crazy aunt which I bet Marty doesn't know. I even understand now why she never went after Billy for support. Anyhow, I believe her and I want to see her released. If she can't stay with you, I'll find a place for her and if need be, someone to be there with her. She'd hate that, but she's still shaky. At least she told me that she's not going to try to kill herself again now."

"And you believe her?" asked Jerry.

"I believe the 'now'" answered Arnie although he couldn't forget Becki's statement about suicide being a matter of choice. "And I believe it wouldn't happen while she was staying with you. She wouldn't want to hurt you that way, which is one reason I hope you'll let her. Where she's going, in her mind that is, I don't know. I also don't know what she might do later. The fact she talked today and says she'll keep up with the counseling, I think that's good. She doesn't want to see me now but she hasn't said forever. I can just hope. Anyhow, I'm going away for a while."

"So much for your great business sacrifices, huh, Arnie?"

"So much for your faith in me," Arnie retorted, annoyed. "I'm leaving to see Drea and then the other kids. I may have to go up to Boston if the detective I hired comes up with anything, but I've no intention of getting involved in the business now or who knows when. I did just what I told you I would do. Madge Norris is in charge of SofTek at present. What happens later still depends on what Becki wants, if she can ever decide. I intend to talk to her psychiatrist tomorrow, tell him what she's told me, and see what we can do for her. Does that meet with your approval, Jerry, or do you want me to slit my wrists too?"

Jerry was quiet and then had the decency to say, "I apologize. I'll talk to Marty. I hadn't realized she wasn't going over there. This is traumatic for us all. I'm sure we can work out something."

"Fine," responded Arnie, now cooled off. "If I can see all Becki's doctors tomorrow, I may start down to Richmond later and begin with Drea. Then I assume I'll just keep working my way west—Ohio, California. Becki told me to tell the kids the truth. I'm going to do my best."

"I don't envy you," commiserated Jerry.

"I don't envy me either but she's right." With that, Arnie hung up. Next he dialed Madge. When she came on line, he said without preliminary, "I don't know whether to punch you in the nose or buy you a diamond bracelet."

"Do I have a choice?" asked Madge, somewhat anxiously. Arnie rarely lost his temper but when he did, he was a terror.

"Why didn't you tell me you were coming down here to see Becki?"

"You probably would have wanted to know what I was going to say to her and have me pussyfoot around. Friends don't pussyfoot, Arnie. You both needed a kick in the ass and Becki knows I'm her friend. I wanted to tell her that I care about her and you and that she did and does need help and that suicide wasn't the answer. I also told her that if she really wanted to get even with you, to sue you for everything and then the two of us could control the company."

Arnie laughed. "I bet you did say something like that."

"Close. I remembered what you said about being enablers and I guess I was too. Maybe I should have just let Becki sink or swim when unpleasant social situations came up and I was there, instead of trying to help her avoid them. I just told her she had some damn good reasons for being depressed and that depressed people need help and that I really believed you, in spite of being a jerk, had been a victim too. I evoked the conspiracy theory."

"Dickie?" he murmured.

"Sure, it's still as good an explanation as any we've considered and I told her what you were doing, giving up to be with her, and about the PI. Speaking of which, their young woman reported in today and from first impressions, if that firm she's with doesn't treat her well, we should hire her."

"I see, you and Becki and some unknown female PI. What was this you just said about conspiracy theories?"

"You're beginning to sound like yourself, Arnie. There may be hope for you too," Madge laughed softly, relieved that Arnie could joke.

"Fine. Well, I've heard nothing from them yet and considering what I'm paying, I should probably call them right now, but hell, it's not been a week so I'll do it tomorrow. I've got to see Becki's doctor and learn what comes next when she gets out, what kind of treatment program they have for her. I've also got to hope that she can stay with Marty or otherwise make other arrangements."

"What?"

"Marty apparently is scared of what happened. Jerry didn't know that either. The marvels of close family relationships. Anyhow, I want to get out of here then."

"What do you mean?" Madge broke in, agitated.

"Becki still doesn't want me around although at least

she talked to me, possibly thanks to your kicking her pretty fanny. But she does agree that I should tell the kids what's happened."

"I don't envy you."

"Odd, you're the second person to tell me that today," he remarked cynically. "Anyhow, I'll see Drea first, then Leah, and finally Bruce. I'll keep you posted. I'd say get in touch with me on my voice mail but that's still jammed up with people who don't know I'm not running the store anymore. You are cleaning that out, aren't you?"

"Sure. I must say I almost feel guilty."

"How so?" he asked surprised.

"Some of your buddies are more than slightly candid. They'd probably be mortified if they knew I was hearing their messages."

Arnie snickered, "What was it you said about not being one of the boys? Now you can be. If any of the stuff is really personal, which I doubt..."

"Like requests for rendezvouses with attractive young women?"

"Low blow, Madge."

"Just want to keep you on your toes, Arnie. Don't trust anyone now."

"That's the problem, Madge. Say hi to Bryan and..."

"Wait, Arnie, just a sec. I tracked down Carla. I haven't called her but I thought you might want to talk to her or have the PI do it."

"Let me think about that," said Arnie. "It was so long ago that she was involved."

"But she was, Arnie. I never knew why since Dickie was such an SOB with women and she's so nice. I'm still willing to bet something really unpleasant happened with her. Considering how he went after Becki right after he broke up..."

"Becki cost him the partnership. Carla was a girlfriend."

"I think both upset him equally. He did...does...not take rejection or failure kindly and we're still looking on this end to see what may have happened lately."

"Lately could be years," Arnie protested.

"I really don't think so. I know the set-up took planning on someone's part. I mean if it had happened in Boston, you would have called a cab right away to get rid of her and not worried about her damn car. I think Dickie always liked immediate gratification and in this case that equates to instant revenge."

"Well, try it from that angle, but then try it from all of them. I'll call you from wherever I unpack next and Madge, thank you for kicking butt—mine too."

"Any time."

"Now for the big one," thought Arnie. Picking up the phone he dialed Drea's number, getting only an answering machine. Should he leave a message or should he just go down there? God, he was beginning to sound like Hamlet, that indecisive jerk. But if he did leave a message, would she call back? Finally, he compromised, "Drea, this is your dad." There, state it as it was. If she didn't like that she could tell him when she saw him.

"I saw your mother today and I'm driving down to see you. I'll either be in Richmond tomorrow or the next day, but I'll let you know as soon as I have some idea." He hung up, leaving no number. If she couldn't call him, she couldn't tell him not to come, he rationalized. At least this way he could try to see her. The worse she could do was slam the door in his face and she might just do that. She was the spitting image of Becki but in some ways they were mirror images. No one was ever going to stomp on that kid. She'd get her licks in first. Arnie felt strangely satisfied. Drea, little Drea, had been shy too, but once he'd married Becki, she'd become a dynamo. Some of that had to be due to him or at least he hoped so.

The next day he spoke to the psychiatrist as well as Bob Jackson. The latter had no news of significance yet, but had spoken to Jerry and gotten permission to take the original photographs once duplicates had been made. The former refused to give any concrete information, saying it was too early to make any prognosis although he was pleased with

Becki's reaction to the changed medication. He was also interested in what Arnie had told him, including the remarks about Aunt Mary and Billy.

CHAPTER 28

A s Arnie drove down I-95, he was caught in the D.C. traffic and had to concentrate more on not being killed than his personal problems. He did almost get off at the first Fredericksburg exit, and felt a wrench emotionally as he passed it. It was about 7:00 P.M. when he finally pulled into Richmond. He thought about going to a motel directly, but decided it would be better to go to Drea's first, hoping she'd be home. What the hell he'd do if she wasn't, he didn't know. Try her at work the next day, he guessed, and pray she'd talk to him.

Drea's apartment was in one of the elegant renovated nineteenth-century mansions near the Virginia Museum of Fine Arts with its fabulous collection of Fabergé. He remembered how enthralled Becki was by the Imperial Easter Eggs although he preferred the magnificent collection of Georgian silver. Wistfully he recalled what a pleasant visit they had had there just a month before she left him. That now seemed centuries ago and he wondered how life could turn in such a short time.

They'd gone down to see the Richmond ballet with Drea, adding the museum visit as an extra treat. He'd teased his wife that with all his technical know-how, he was going to mount an operation like the heist of the Topkapi Museum, featured in a favorite Peter Ustinov film years before. "You'll get the eggs and I'll take a tea set," he vowed.

"I'm the real tea drinker in the family. But if you're good, I'll let you use it too," she'd offered magnanimously with a dazzling smile as she squeezed his hand. Then fully entering the game, she added all sorts of improbable suggestions for their projected robbery and pointed out the items she especially wanted in addition to the eggs and tea set.

As a result, Arnie had planned to see if any Fabergé was currently on the market to surprise her for their next anniversary; but, of course, that had gone completely out of his head when she disappeared. Just like the pearls, he suddenly realized. He'd never gotten her a real string although he'd promised when they married. Certainly he had the money. And, somehow she'd never wanted to upgrade the pearl ring for a flashy diamond. It wasn't that he wasn't generous to her and all his extended family and friends, but it seemed there were so many little things, things that mattered he'd either forgotten or put off. The trip to the Pacific and the one to Europe. The trips he had instead offered had always been business related. Why was that, he wondered? Had he just been drifting along in their unconventional existence, accepting things as they were, not seeing the need for other diversions?

Parking on a side street, Arnie walked up to Drea's door. It was a minute or two after he knocked that the door opened and Drea, looking like a clone of her mother dating to the time when he'd met Becki, was standing there. "Arnie!" she exclaimed in surprise. A partially filled glass was in her hand and to his amazement, it appeared to contain wine. Moreover, her face had a slightly flushed look.

"May I come in?"

"Sure, why not." Drea moved back, opening the door wider.

"Good, I was afraid you might have a clove of garlic or a cross to ward me off." Worse yet, a silver bullet, he added mentally as he stepped inside.

"Still silly Arnie. Why are you here?"

"To talk to you about your mom...about what's happened."

"And you'll tell me yes and no or no and yes?"

"What's that cryptic comment supposed to mean?" he queried, "and may I sit down?"

"Of course. Yes, she did cut her wrists and no, you didn't cheat on her or no, she didn't and yes, you did or maybe yes, yes or better no, no."

"Yes, yes," he answered tersely.

"How could you be such a shit?" Drea inquired,

looking at him sadly, as she curled up in an arm chair. "You were her whole life."

"I'd like to still be her whole life. There were extenuating circumstances and how the hell did you know about the cheating? Did she tell you?"

"No, but Aunt Marty did."

"Thank you, Marty," he sighed, resigned. "Well it wasn't that simple."

"Life's not simple, Arnie. You tried to teach me that and now I'm learning."

"Meaning?" He looked around the room, which seemed less cluttered than usual. "Something's changed with this place."

"Sure, all of Chip's stuff is gone. He moved out last week, shortly after Mom tried to kill herself. Men are shits, Arnie. You too."

"I'm sorry, Drea. If he left you, he wasn't worth it."

"Well you left Mom."

"No, that I did not do. She left me. I don't want to leave her. All I want is to have her back. May I try to tell you what happened?"

"May, can...you sound like Mom and why not," shrugged Drea. "Want a drink?"

"Since when have you started drinking? It always interfered with your personal health program. Next you'll be telling me you've started eating meat again."

"Oh, I drank a little. Lately I've been drinking more. This summer has not exactly been the highlight of my life."

"Mine either," agreed Arnie, feeling that was the understatement of the century. "Pour me what you're having."

"A fine vintage screw-top California red by some company I've never heard of, but cheap." Drea unfolded her long, lean body and went over to her Pullman-kitchen. There she tilted a three-liter jug to refill her glass, discernibly jelly quality, and then went to get another for Arnie. The jug was nearly empty. "Sorry there're no real wine glasses. Those were Chip's."

"No problem but this is putrid," remarked Arnie after the first sip, yet he took another. "You were saying about this summer."

"Oh, right," said Drea. "My mother runs away from home, I lose my father..."

"You didn't lose me," protested Arnie.

"Oh, no? I haven't heard from you since the night you called me after Mom left King George. I wouldn't have known anything if Aunt Marty hadn't called. All I knew was that Mom was somewhere up around D.C., but she was Polyanna when she called, saying nothing, and you, you shit, you never called again."

"Drea, I didn't know if you'd talk to me."

"Why not, Arnie, aren't I your kid too? You told me I was, right from the start." Drea looked down at her hand and Arnie realized with a pang that the tiny pearl ring, he'd given her years before, was absent from her little finger where it had taken up permanent residence once her hand grew.

"You are, but...you're your mother's and I..."

"Haven't you gotten hold of Bruce and Leah?"

"Yes, but..."

"But that's different. They're your kids."

"Damn it, Drea. You're my kid too. I haven't told Bruce and Leah what happened, not even about your mother trying to kill herself. I'm here because I wanted to talk to you about everything, because I love you, and because she needs you."

"Ha!" snorted Drea furiously. "As soon as Uncle Jerry phoned to tell me what happened, I called up there. I tried to speak to Mom. I've called a half dozen times and she hasn't returned any of my calls. She had Aunt Marty tell me not to come up to see her, my own mother!"

"She's ashamed and, at first, she wanted to do it again." Drea looked at him, terror stricken. It was one of the first times he'd ever seen that haunted look of Becki's on her face.

"Jesus, I'm sorry I said that, Drea." Immediately he

jumped up and held out his arms to her, giving her a hug and patting her back. "Please, kid, I don't think she's going to do it again." He hoped he was right. "She promised she'd go into counseling. They've got her on anti-depressants and some other medication. I'm hoping she'll stay with your aunt."

"Why not you, Arnie?" Drea moved away, staring at him belligerently.

"Because she doesn't want to see me either."

"Well that's understandable, but why not me?" Drea's voice was filled with hurt and a tear had started down her cheek.

Arnie didn't know how to answer. He couldn't say that maybe Becki would try again and wouldn't want her daughter to find her. "I don't know. She doesn't want to see any of you kids."

"Swell, so why are you here?" Drea sniffed, reaching up to rub her eye. Arnie wanted to hold her again. But she wasn't a little girl now, not the child who'd sat on his lap begging stories or who came to him for intervention or sympathy the few times she'd angered her mother. This was a young adult hurting as much from his actions as Becki's.

"To talk about your mother, about what's happened, about what may have happened. To ask you to forget what she's said to you and have you see her—to beg you to if I have to. To hope you're still my daughter."

Drea sat back down looking at him, obviously still angry. Again he felt as though he were seeing a younger version of Becki and was disturbed by this hostile variation. Yet Becki had been practically volatile the night she tried to kill herself, displaying a hardness he'd never seen and he had been shocked. Then Drea relaxed slightly and said slowly, bluntly, "You're the only father I've got, Arnie. Billy never wanted me. I saw him once, actually twice, you know." Arnie looked at her, surprised. "He was in King George seeing his mother and he came up to me in the grocery store. I think he thought he was seeing Mom when he'd started screwing her." Arnie winced, but Drea didn't seem to notice. "I must have been the same age, fourteen. Anyhow Mom came up with the kids and he just looked at her embarrassed, turned away, and walked off."

"What did she do?" Arnie asked, staggered that Becki had never mentioned the incident to him. He knew she had remained ashamed of the circumstances of her first pregnancy in spite of never hiding this teenage indiscretion. In fact, he'd wondered, at first, how she could want to return to King George with her fear of gossip. Now he realized it was something she had had come to terms with on her own turf and obviously felt would never harm him there.

"Told me who he was. We never had any pictures of him around, you know, not as an adult at least. And, he'd changed a lot—the beer guzzling was catching up. Not like Mom. She always seemed the same, didn't she?" Arnie nodded in agreement. Becki and Dorian Grey, but she was good inside. Her portrait would have stayed beautiful.

"I saw him once more when my grandmother died," Drea continued. "He was back for the funeral and Mom and I went. He was out of the army, divorced, and had really put on weight by then—all those football muscles gone to fat. He sells used cars somewhere out west. He didn't talk to me that time either," Drea added bitterly.

"I didn't know you'd been seeing your grandmother."

"Mom took me there once after we moved down. She said Billy's mother had been kind to her and me when I was a baby, and I should meet her. She didn't seem too sorry that I didn't meet my grandfather—he apparently died when we were still up in Boston. I guess he wasn't much good either, like Billy. Anyhow, I really never wanted to go back and Mom didn't make me. I think she's sorry I never got to meet my half-brother, but he didn't even show up for the funeral. Leah and Bruce are my real sister and brother just like I thought you were my dad," Drea stated flatly, clearly still irritated.

Arnie nodded his head again and then slowly, he began to tell her what had happened and her angry countenance changed to one of incredulity. She asked nothing during his recitation, just sitting there as if in judgment, and he didn't know how she'd react when he finished.

"I suppose you've heard this, but you expect me to believe what you've told me?" she finally commented tartly.

"From everyone," answered Arnie with a despondent shrug.

"And you really believe that this may be some kind of plot to hurt you through hurting Mom?"

"To hurt us both."

"Mom would never hurt anyone...except Great Aunt Mary from what you told me and I think I wish I could do that. No wonder Mom has been so unstable at times. Now what are you going to do?"

"What I've started. Hope we find some proof, stop the bastard if he's really done this or stop whoever did, hope we can convince your mother to keep up the counseling, tell your siblings the whole story so that none of you would be shocked or embarrassed if this becomes public."

"Shocked, no more than now. Embarrassed, I can't say, but Leah would probably thrive on being part of the news and Bruce is in another universe. Leah doesn't like me, you know."

"What do you mean?" asked Arnie, disconcerted. There were all sorts of undertones to his family he'd obviously been too obtuse to notice, and it didn't make him feel very good about himself.

"The same reason that Mom said. She's jealous of the looks. If I had her talent, I wouldn't worry, but Leah feels it was some great conspiracy against her that Bruce and I took after Mom and she looks like you, Dad. Even Lily Marie looks like Mom, and I don't think Leah likes her either."

"I can't help it that I wasn't Paul Newman," he said sadly.

"Well, no one runs away when they see you either. You always reminded me of a nice big cuddly teddy bear when I was little."

"I know, Fozzie, but not so big."

Drea laughed, her anger now completely dispelled.

"You know what I mean, but still warm and loving, a great father. That's why that part of this summer hurt so much too."

"I'm sorry, Drea. I'm truly sorry. I just didn't know if you wanted to see me."

"Well, you should have tried."

"Yes," he admitted, dejected. "I should. Will you forgive me even if this doesn't work out between me and your mother? Still be my daughter? Everyone tells me you're the most like me...looks aside...of all three of you kids and I think so too."

"What no super genius like Bruce or angry creative soul like Leah?"

Drea's voice was defensive again and Arnie inwardly flinched, but he answered calmly, "You could say that. Really bright, innovative, good business sense. I'd still like you to leave here and come up to Boston to work for the company, maybe start grad school at MIT. You could stay at the house. It is your home too, after all."

"Is that bribery, Arnie? You'll paint my room again and build me another terrarium?"

"You know it isn't. I've wanted you to do that for a long time. Why should we let Madge have it all after I leave? We'll groom you as the heir to the throne and yes, I'll even throw in another terrarium if I have to."

"Why not Bruce?"

"Bruce is going to do ok. He's just never going to want to handle the business details. You do that. And, if you can get him on board as the new ground-breaking genius, you two could take on Apple, Microsoft, the world!"

Drea laughed and then added seriously, "I worry about Bruce."

"How so," asked Arnie, "besides the fact that he lives in some intellectual ivory tower."

"Oh, whether he'll ever have a normal life, girls..."

Arnie started laughing, delighted that he wasn't the only one missing out on family secrets after all. "Your baby brother knows all about girls." Drea looked at him surprised.

"Remember the summer before this when he was interning? Well, his supervisor informed me that Bruce had found a resourceful use for one of the computer labs when everyone was out to lunch. One of the student interns, grad school no less, was joining him for their own private picnic."

"Bruce, little Bruce?" Drea was astounded. "A girl intern?"

"Yes, Drea. Your baby brother is disgustingly heterosexual. He apparently had two or three of the gals at work interested in him. He even had them convinced he was already in college. He started on his feminine conquests years earlier than I did. I was so terrified of rejection that I was almost through university before I had a real girl. Of course he's far better looking. Anyhow, I had a long talk with Baby Brother about birds and bees and just turning sixteen and sex with women in their twenties."

"Did he listen?"

"If he didn't, he's being more discrete. Also, I think he's so caught up at Tech now that that's his main interest."

"God, he does take after Mom too." Then Drea had the grace to blush. "I mean she had me by fifteen...hell, Arnie, as soon as I figured out what sex was, I knew she was wild for you. Remember those old comic strips with the girls' eyes lighting up? There was a box with china wrapped up in them in the attic at King George and one was about a baby whose eyes sparkled and the other a reporter who had stars for eyes, *Brenda Starr* I think."

"It's still running," interjected Arnie mildly. "I saw it in a foreign paper my last trip abroad. She'd ended up divorcing Basil, the one-eyed sex god."

Drea seemed shocked. "Poor Basil...well Mom's eyes looked like that when you were coming down or actually were there, but when you'd leave Virginia, it was as though the lights went out. She'd hug that old Tech sweat of yours whenever you were away."

"Caltech?"

"Sure, I caught her with it once in bed and teased her. She finally told me it was her Fozzie Bear, something you'd given her when she first visited you up on the Cape. I guess she needed something of yours when you were gone." Oh, my God, thought Arnie, remembering the crumpled shirt on Becki's bed at the Hansen apartment, when he was frantically tearing off the sheet to cover her. "But, then when you were there, she'd just radiate. It was embarrassing at times to be around the two of you." Arnie looked at her surprised. "That's why I just couldn't believe this happened. She loves you so damn much and I thought you did the same."

"I do. I'll do anything."

"You really mean it about giving up work if you have to, don't you?"

"Oh yes."

"Well, before we get too drunk and maudlin, why don't you take me out to dinner? Do you want to spend the night here? I've got the spare couch. Then we can get plastered and talk some more about this and maybe you can persuade me to go up to Boston with SofTek after all. I think it was Chip that kept me down here."

"Are you sure?" asked Arnie. "That is about wanting me to stay here?"

Drea looked at him strangely. "Arnie, you'll never stop being silly. You're my father, for Christ's sake. Isn't that part of what we've been talking about? You took me to the zoo when I was little and to the emergency ward when I broke my wrist. Remember? I was screaming so much and wouldn't let Mom touch me? And then there was the time you grounded me in high school when I got in at 3:00 A.M. instead of midnight the way I was supposed to. Plus who was there to help me prep for all those math exams or make computers simple playthings? As long as I know you still want to be my parent, I want you to be, even if we can't figure out how to have Mom take you back."

"You'd want her to?"

"God, you really are a total jerk."

"And you have become a very sassy and impertinent child."

"Arnie, I'm twenty-eight years old. At least I didn't sass you when I was a teenager."

"Which is more than we can say about Leah," he replied.

"She sasses everyone. If you're finally going to take a hard line with Mom, you'd better take her on too."

"You think I should take a hard line?"

"You've got to stop seeing Mom as that princess in an ivory tower. She used to tease you about being her knight. I think it's time to kill the damn dragon, get her off the pedestal, and return to real life."

"You may be right," he mused, and he gave her a hug. "Clean up unless you want us to end up at McDonald's the way you used to."

"You're not getting off that cheaply, Daddy-O."

Arnie nodded, staring at her. "God, you've grown. You're bigger than your mother even. I feel like a midget around you two."

"We'll look smaller when you're back up on that great white horse Silver."

"That was the Lone Ranger, Drea, not a knight."

"Same difference, Dad."

The next morning when Arnie awoke, he felt slightly hung over, but not so much from the wine, although they'd had Chianti at the Italian restaurant and he'd purchased another bottle with an identifiable label on the way back to the apartment. Part of the feeling came from staying up until almost 4:00 A.M., discussing Becki, the siblings, their life together, everything. Part of it was just the pressure that was still there although he felt much, much better having had his talk with Drea. She'd been such a special little girl. Now she was a special big girl. Chip was a damn fool and she was well rid of him. He'd mention to Madge when he called next that Drea was thinking of coming to Boston.

Then Arnie thought about Drea in Boston. Definitely she should have the house until he decided what he was doing. He'd like that. To have family back there. Maybe after Bruce finished Caltech, he might come out too. The house had been so empty once Becki and the children moved to Virginia. It had gone from being a home to a place to stay—comfortable enough and convenient—but just a stop when he was in Boston. And yet, he'd been so pleased when he'd first purchased it, so relieved he was able to save it when he bought out Dickie, so happy when it became Becki and Drea's home and the babies arrived.

And it had been Becki's home, damn it! She had turned a bachelor's abode into a home. Bright, cheery colors in the kitchen and bathrooms; plants everywhere; art work to match—usually water scenes or some of the Japanese woodblock prints purchased on their honeymoon. And the books! He thought he'd had books, but Becki seemed to find every used bookstore or sale in Cambridge plus weekly trips to the library. Then there was Drea's kitten and the aquarium and terrarium and after the babies came, the myriad toys. And music, always music there and then at King George until Leah hit puberty when loud and raucous sounds had to be curtailed.

But once the family was in Virginia, the Cambridge house became just a place again where one slept and changed clothes. The signs of Becki were still present, but her radiant light was gone. Arnie had no problem working late or taking business trips then. The efficient but impersonal cleaning service arrived weekly to make sure he was comfortable but home, real home as much as he had one, had moved to the Northern Neck.

After reading Drea's note, which indicated that somehow she had managed to get off to work on time, he proceeded to straighten the living room before going to clean up. On the way to the bathroom, he glanced into Drea's bedroom. What a mess, he thought, another way she differs from Becki. He wondered if Becki would be capable of ever making a mess except, he considered sadly, of getting blood all over. But that was not positive thinking. He had to stop that.

After showering and shaving, he began to make his usual calls: Becki's doctors, Jerry, Madge—mentioning Drea, and finally the PI. Mr. Jackson was out he was told. Could Dr. Miller be reached later, although there still was nothing to report? Almost a week now, reflected Arnie. Well, this had been building up for years and he had signed a three-week contract. He thought about seeing if Becki would speak to him but decided that that probably wasn't a good idea at this point. Instead, he began to call the airlines and discovered if he could get to National within the next three hours, he could catch a direct flight to Cleveland and be there by 5:00 that afternoon. It would take him an hour or so to reach Oberlin and who knew what Leah was up to. At least he could get into a hotel or motel if he couldn't see her that evening. Actually, that would be probably just as well. The baring of souls with Drea had not only been exhausting physically but more so emotionally. For that matter, he wasn't sure he was ready to handle Leah yet. Making the reservation, he packed, left a note for Drea saying he'd call once he got to California or heard anything new, and departed.

CHAPTER 29

Arnie felt more optimistic on the drive back. Jerry had said Becki could come to their house. He had been able to talk frankly with Drea and their relationship seemed intact. In general, he felt some progress was being made. Moreover the ride back up I-95 was amazingly smooth, in contrast to his harried trip down. Sometimes when he'd returned before, he'd felt as though he was lost in the twilight zone as he was going through the Occaquon region and found himself sucked into D.C.'s quagmire of traffic. Now he was going against the flow and everything seemed to be working out. He managed to drop his car and was at his gate by 1:30.

Sitting there, he idly watched the other travelers. He'd traveled so much but usually he was working as he went, his laptop with him, or standing at public phones picking up his voice mail in the days predating mobile phones, calling people around the country, studying notes, whatever. He still preferred landlines and never kept his annoying bulky cell on, wondering what would happen when the newer streamlined ones, he'd been reading about, actually hit market. Now he resorted to it only in emergency. Becki and the kids alone had the number although it had been weeks since he'd found a call in the in-box. For a while, he'd not even bothered to check.

He couldn't recall when he'd last been free. Although he felt strange not doing something 'constructive', it was kind of nice to be like it was when he first started his business. Not encumbered by electronic gadgets, able to pick up a mystery at the bookstand, or just stare and daydream, not worrying about a deadline. How long had it been, he wondered, when he wasn't hustling? The exaltation from that had been great and he realized that even when he used to come to see Becki in King George, he never really escaped work. The modem for the laptop was plugged in each morning, the calls were made. Even if he hadn't brought his computer, each child had a PC, often contacting him when he was traveling by Internet since they knew his aversion to the mobile although Becki always used the phone. So that was a fallacy too. Arnie had still been partially in Boston or elsewhere even when he was sitting on the front veranda of the house, looking out at the sun setting across the river. Becki must have always known, he now realized. She was kidding him and he was kidding her; and because they loved each other, each probably thought the other didn't know.

The flight arrived on time and Arnie mentally thanked heaven that it was Cleveland, he was trying to get out of, rather than D.C. or Boston at this time of day. Prior reservations meant the rental car was ready and he was soon leaving the International Airport headed toward Oberlin. Again, luck appeared with him and within an hour and a half from landing, he was entering the small college town.

When Leah had first mentioned going to Oberlin, he was frankly astonished. Admittedly it was one of the leading colleges in the country but somehow the location had surprised him. Still, compared to King George, it and its proximity to Cleveland undoubtedly seemed cosmopolitan even though the campus was relatively isolated. By contrast, Boston and its conservatory were too close to home and a parent. Further, although Leah was talented musically, she wasn't going to be asked to join some major ballet company.

This, therefore, seemed the perfect compromise: Oberlin's renowned Conservatory of Music but also the opportunity to get a solid academic degree in case she gave up her hopes of having a musical career. Even though she hadn't said anything yet, Arnie suspected Leah was becoming realistic. Still, she no doubt wanted to be involved somehow with the theater. Knowing her persistence and supreme self-confidence—similar to his own or so he had been told, he felt that someday she might indeed be managing a small company or even running the business end of one of the larger ballets. It might not be her true dream, but there was something to being the power behind the throne and Leah clearly had a taste for power. If she'd been the one with the technical inclination, she probably would have taken over SofTek. Shit, no question. She'd probably even have ousted him if he'd delayed too long in leaving the company according to her schedule of personal advancement to CEO.

Checking into the Oberlin Inn, he gave her private number a call and again luck was with him. "Hello," he heard his daughter's low, melodious voice. Becki had once told him that if radio were still king when they met, he would have been a star. Leah had that same quality and not for once, he wondered why the girl hadn't considered that possibility. Public Radio had certainly revitalized the media. Maybe he should drop a hint; she'd be good.

"Hi, it's your Dad."

"Dad, where are you?"

"Here."

"Here as in Oberlin? You're kidding."

"No, sweetheart, I'm down at the Inn. I just got here. Are you busy or is it convenient for me to see you later tonight?"

Leah laughed, that rich vivacious laugh she had when she was happy. "Dad, this is college. No one goes to bed before midnight. Of course I can see you sometime tonight. Surely, even in your college days, people stayed up."

"To study, of course." Arnie heard her began to laugh again. "I haven't eaten yet. Do you want to join me for dinner or am I too late for that part."

"It is never too late for free food," Leah intoned dramatically. "Surely, even in your day, people craved real food."

This time he laughed. "You're right. Some things don't change. Do you want to come here or is there some special place you prefer? I'd like to talk to you, so some privacy would be nice."

"How deliciously Byzantine," she remarked. "It'll be ok there.

"Can you get over here all right or should I pick you

up?"

"No bother. I can be there in a half hour or less."

"Fine, I'll meet you in the restaurant then." Next he placed calls to Jerry and Madge, letting them know where he was and that he planned to be there at least for the next night. Looking at his watch, he decided he had time for a quick shower, but he was still down in the restaurant waiting for Leah when she arrived, some twenty minutes late.

"I was afraid they might close up before you got here," Arnie commented mildly.

"Ah, Father dearest, still a slave to time."

"The Protestant work ethic, what can I say?"

"You're not Protestant, Daddy."

"Nope, I guess not. How are you? You're looking good." She was, he saw. She was casually but neatly dressed—not the usual glaring and dramatic colors she ordinarily affected. She also looked relaxed and very different from the last time he'd seen her at home in Virginia, when she'd seemed mad at the world. The softening suited. Her big brown eyes, always alert and lively like his according to Becki, seemed warm and friendly. The eyes of someone people would enjoy getting to know, no longer strident or hostile as they'd been too often in her mid-teens.

"Well, Daddy, why the mysterious visit? Why the secrecy?"

"Oh, I just hadn't seen you for a few months nor gotten much chance to talk to you."

"What chance? It's been weeks since we spoke."

"Sorry," he apologized. "When did you last talk to your mother?"

Leah looked at him strangely. "Are you here to pump me about Mommy dearest? I don't know where she is, Dad. She hasn't told me and Bruce says the same and Drea never says anything, not that we've talked for ages. About two weeks, I guess."

"Leah, we have to talk." Arnie reached out and took her hand.

"What, you're going to finally tell me about the great split?" She was starting to look nervous.

"Your mother's been in the hospital," he said quietly.

"What!" Leah was now clearly upset and all affectation disappeared from her voice. "Something serious?"

"Yes."

"Oh God, cancer?"

Arnie cringed at that thought but knew that what he had to say would be equally shocking. There was no way to soften the news. "No, your mother tried to commit suicide." Leah's face turned stark white, her expressive eyes widening. For once she was speechless. "I was there," he continued. "She slit her wrists. It was touch and go for a while."

The sophisticated college student disappeared before his eyes. In front of him was a frightened little girl with tears starting down her cheeks. "Why, Daddy?"

"My fault," he stated bluntly. "This whole mess was my fault, honey. Your mom is going to stay with Aunt Marty and I saw her this week. She said I was to tell you everything about what's happened. I felt I had to do it in person. Drea knew about it, but not why. I visited her yesterday after I saw your mother. Bruce doesn't know yet so I'm going to have to go to California. This is something I felt I had to tell each of you personally, ok?"

Leah nodded her head and Arnie knew she'd wait until he'd seen her brother before talking to him. Bombastic and showoff, though she might be, his daughter always kept her word. Diligently, he continued, "If you've got some free time tomorrow, I'd like to spend it with you and really talk about this. But, I felt I had to tell you some of it tonight."

Leah was crying silently; and, for once, Arnie saw her mother in her. "I'm so sorry, sweetheart. We think she's going to be ok, but she's going to have to see a psychiatrist."

"She should have for years," murmured Leah almost tonelessly.

"Yeah, well I guess so. Everyone in the world seemed to have seen that but none of us tried to convince her to go."

"Why didn't you, Daddy? You were always the boss."

"When I was there, we pretended I was. I did try to talk to your mother a couple of times about doing something but she seemed to be happy with her world. I didn't want to upset it. I figured she'd had enough problems being married to me."

"How can you say that, Dad? You're a great father."

"It's nice to have a testimony from one of my kids, but I made mistakes. We all did. I'm just hoping we can recoup."

"I don't want to wait until tomorrow," said Leah truculently, sounding suddenly like the stubborn little four-year old he'd often faced, the only one of the three children, who even when small, got his dander up at that early age, according to Becki. "You brought this up so let's finish it now."

"Why don't we eat first?"

"I'm no longer hungry."

"Actually, I'm not either, but I think I'd better. I haven't been too consistent on food since this happened." I haven't been too consistent on much of anything, he thought. "A salad, dessert, something?"

"A small salad and coffee."

Arnie signaled the waiter. After the young man left, he began to speak in a low and serious voice. "Someone sent your mother some pictures of me with another woman. That's why she left."

"You, Dad?" Leah looked at him as though she couldn't believe it. "You worship Mom. You always have."

"Yes, damn it, but it was a mistake and I'm trying to find out what happened. Just listen, please." Here I go again, thought Arnie, and it doesn't get any easier. He should have made a tape recording and just distributed it. But Leah listened, looking pained, for once not uttering a sound. When Arnie finished, he said, "I know, you're going to say you can't believe it."

"I wish I didn't, speaking of Byzantine. Who was this man?"

"Someone I had the bad judgment to think was my

friend years ago. It still may not be him, Leah, but he appears to be most likely if the detectives finally get cracking. I hope they're better than the ones in D.C."

"D.C.?" She looked puzzled.

"That's how I found your mother."

"Oh!" The thought that her father actually had to hire detectives to locate her mother obviously shocked her.

"I don't know what's going to happen next," Arnie admitted ruefully. "I felt I had to be the one to tell you this. You have to decide what you feel yourself."

"Feel?"

"About me, about what's happened."

"How should I feel about you, Dad? You think I'd stop loving you if you really had been cheating on Mom? I love you." Embarrassed, she stopped. "Well I do."

"I love you too, but this story may come out. I hope not. I frankly no longer give a damn about me. The damage has been done but it's your mother and you kids I worry about."

"Screw it," declared Leah flatly. "But about Mom, you're right. Is she going to be ok?"

"I think so," but I hope so, was what he was thinking. "She's got more problems than just this."

"Yes," Leah agreed.

"One is you."

"What do you mean?" Leah asked belligerently. The brown eyes narrowed dangerously.

"She thinks you don't like her, so does Drea."

"Drea is too damn bossy," snapped Leah, "and yes, she pisses the hell out of me most of the time, but Mom...I love her, Dad, but we never have anything to say."

"She needs you now. Can you at least tell her that?"

"She didn't even let me know where she was," acknowledged Leah half sorrowful, half resentful.

"Honey, she didn't let any of us know. After she attempted suicide, she wouldn't see Drea much less talk to her. Your sister was utterly crushed."

"I imagine she would be," responded Leah, surprised

and now thoughtful. Drea and her mother were the storybook mother-daughter team. Mother loved her too, Leah knew, but somehow they could never communicate. But, hell, Bruce and Dad couldn't seem to talk either whereas she had never had any problem with her father, albeit some of their conversations had escalated into arguments, she conceded ruefully. "Sure I'll talk to her, if she'll talk to me. Send some flowers, something. I do love her, Dad. I just don't know what to say to her."

"Telling her you love her should be enough."

The waiter returned and the two sat silently, trying to eat. Leah played with her salad and slowly sipped the coffee, to which for once she hadn't added cream or the usual spoons of sugar. Finally, she asked, "What are you going to do if you can't find out who did it?"

"I really don't know," Arnie answered truthfully.

"Are you guys getting back together again?"

"I can't answer that either, but I think it's fairly obvious I want to."

"Yes. How are you going to tell Bruce?"

"That's a hard one, isn't it? I just don't know. Do you have any suggestions?"

Leah shook her head sympathetically. Bruce—he would be a problem. None of them really could talk to Bruce, except maybe Mom. "I'll think about it, Dad. I've got to get back to the dorm now. I don't have any classes in the afternoon tomorrow. You want to take the historic sites tour or go to the museum or something?"

"I want to do anything you'd be willing to do with me. Do you want me to drive you back?"

"No, that's ok. I need to think about this. I'll see you around lunchtime. That's included, right?" she added with a wan grin. Arnie stood and his daughter gave him a tight hug.

"Hang in there, Dad," she admonished gently as she turned and walked out. Two down, he thought, his darling girls. Leah's probably right—no, not just probably. Bruce will be the tough one.

Arnie slowly finished dinner, not really tasting it but

knowing he needed some sustenance. After, he went back to his room, kicking off his shoes and collapsing on the bed. Sometime in the middle of the night, he woke up. The TV was still on but the station was dark and buzzing. He got up, took off his clothes and lay back down, tossing and turning for another hour or two until he again fell asleep. It was almost 10:00 A.M. when he awoke and at first he couldn't believe he'd slept so late.

This time when he called the detective agency, Bob Jackson came on the phone immediately. "Good morning, Dr. Miller. I think we're beginning to have something for you."

About time, thought Arnie, but he waited politely, murmuring a non-committal, "Yes."

"The person who took the photographs wasn't all that clever after all. There were some identifying marks and I think we've tracked him down. Someone will be talking to him today and after that, we intend to have an interview with the young woman. She is an employee of Barnes, Inc. There was no fraud about that. Also, your partner steered us to a Carla Marino, who apparently was Mr. Ramsey's former girlfriend. After I talked to Ms. Marino on the phone, she agreed to see me today and give me names of some of Mr. Ramsey's other women friends. Our young woman at your company has also discovered that he had access to all company data before he left. According to the way you were beginning to compartment SofTek then, I believe you thought only you had total access."

"Christ," exclaimed Arnie, "no wonder he knew exactly where I was going! I didn't keep our goals secret but I sometimes wondered how outsiders knew the precise status of our products back then."

"I'm sure there might have been some other advantages for him in having that access, which we're following up. In any case, it appears your original supposition about his being the culprit may be correct. We should know within the next few days. If not, we'll have to try another line of reasoning if you want us to continue. There still is the possibility of industrial espionage."

"Fine," concurred Arnie. "How long until you can get me this information?"

"Hopefully we can send you a registered overnight package within three or four days. Do you know where'll you be?"

"Nothing faxed?" Arnie asked, not wanting to wait any longer than necessary.

"I wouldn't advise it."

"Yes, that was dumb of me." Was it ever, thought Arnie. He of all people to suggest something like that sent open—it just showed how upset he was. "Ok, I'm here through tonight and then I'm heading out to L.A. to see my son. I should be there by tomorrow night. I'll call as soon as I know where I'm staying."

"Good, we'll be in touch."

Arnie hung up. Industrial espionage? Was he going to have vibrators installed on the windows at SofTek or sweep offices electronically if this wasn't all Dickie? Then shaking his head, he realized that would be Madge's problem although he might make the suggestion.

Still, what was important now was Becki and maybe Jackson and crew finally had the real answer. But then what would he do? Get a gun and shoot Dickie if he were the culprit? It undoubtedly would give immediate satisfaction but the aftermath and possibly even self-guilt would be a problem. Arnie did not consider himself a violent man but right now he knew he was very close.

Leah arrived shortly after noon. When he opened the door, he saw she looked tired. "Not much sleep," he commented sympathetically.

"No, not really," she answered, looking around the room. "I wondered what this place looked like."

"Want to have lunch in the room or should we go out?"

"I think I'd like to go out, to walk, to think," she said. "Why did this have to happen, Daddy?" She was looking like the little Leah again as if he could fix some toy of hers or make a hurt knee go away—the other side of her sometimes volatile personality.

"I was stupid," he said simply.

"Yes, but you wouldn't have been, if someone hadn't wanted you to be."

"Thank you. You're about the only one who's said that. In fact, you are the only one."

"And it's not just you. It's Mommy too."

"She's delicate or maybe we let her be delicate. Anyhow, it was just too much for her. She's always had too much imagination, been too introspective. It was the final straw for her back."

"It's so unfair," Leah lamented, the four-year-old's plaintive cry.

"So's life, baby. But there may be some news. I talked to the detective and they may have a lead. They're hoping to follow it up today or tomorrow. With luck, they'll get something to me while I'm out in L.A."

"Then what are you going to do?"

"Oddly, that was just what I was considering while I was waiting for you. I don't know yet. But now I think I'm going to take you to lunch and then to see those historic houses. Maybe after, we'll hit that art museum. I'd like to see the Frank Lloyd Wright house too."

"You mean the Allen? I don't think we can get in that house during the week."

"Well then you'll just have to find another way to entertain me. I'm on a date with my beautiful daughter today."

Leah looked at him steadily. "Not beautiful, Dad. You said last night that we're all going to have to be completely honest about everything now—even the little white lies."

He stared back at her a moment, feeling great compassion. "Well, personable and creative and bright, how's that?"

"I'll accept that," Leah replied with dignity.

"That's been part of the problem for you, hasn't it?" observed Arnie gently.

"Sure. Mom and Drea and even Bruce all looking like

Greek Gods. And me..."

"And you, poor chickadee, looking like me."

"I didn't mean it that way, Dad."

"Of course you did, since we're skipping even the white lies, and of course that's just another thing we haven't talked about in this family. You're the one with the most imagination and probably creative talent. You're aggressive like me and as smart as any of us..."

"Except for Bruce."

"Ah yes, well that's part of Bruce's problem. Sometimes he's too smart and he hasn't quite learned to handle that either. I seem to be having heart-to-hearts with all you kids. I probably should have years ago. I'm sorry that you didn't get the looks, honey, but your mother has felt they were a curse. Drea has usually been indifferent and Bruce couldn't care less. In fact, he probably worries at times that he's too pretty, which is why I think he's been so girl crazy."

"Bruce!"

"Are his sisters the last to know? Your brother is a menace to young women."

Leah was laughing, almost hysterically. "Bruce, I thought he was..."

"Nope, heterosexual all the way," confirmed Arnie, "which is probably just as well with AIDS and all the other rotten stuff those poor bastards have to face nowadays. I've never understood all this homophobia."

"That's because you've never doubted being masculine, Dad. You may not be a Greek God, but you certainly have projected testosterone. I used to think you and Mother must have been rabbits in an earlier life."

This time it was Arnie, who burst in laugher. "Out of the mouths of babes. I thought we were very discrete but first Drea and now you tell me we might as well have been filming porn flicks on the veranda."

"I wouldn't quite say that," said Leah, "but it did give me hope for a sex life when I reached middle age."

"Which to you probably means thirty at this point. Let's hit the road, I'm hungry and today I hope you are."

"I'm trying to cut back, Dad."

"Any particular reason?" he quizzed, thinking of how nice she'd looked when she'd arrived last night—truly feminine.

"Oh...just a guy I met," she admitted bashfully.

Arnie couldn't believe her demeanor. He was so used to Leah charging along, slightly belligerent, that the way his daughter had been acting really startled him. A young man. She'd dated rarely in high school although she'd been involved in lots of activities, usually leading or perhaps, more likely, whipping the pack. About her social life in college, he had known nothing. Well, it was about time. He hoped the guy would prove to be nicer than Drea's Chip. Of course Leah was young, just nineteen.

Late that afternoon, they returned to the Inn and for once he felt relaxed. It had been a good day for them both. The immediate problem of what to do about Becki had been avoided, and for the first time in years, he had had a pleasant outing with his usually mercurial child. Better yet, it appeared that she felt the same. Maybe now was the time to discuss Becki again.

"Would you like to call your mother?" he asked.

"I've been thinking about that," answered Leah, "but I don't know what to say."

"What would you like to say?" asked Arnie quietly.

"Oh, to tell her I'm sorry and that I hope she'll be ok."

"That sounds good. Shall we make a call? I'll go out of the room if you'd like."

"No, that's ok."

"Fine, I'd like to talk to her too, if she'll let me."

"Speaking of Byzantine again, Dad. I talk to her and then she feels she has to talk to you." But, a look of shock had flitted across Leah's face. Somehow she hadn't realized that her parents still weren't really talking.

"She won't if she doesn't want to, honey, but it wouldn't hurt to try. There's one thing I'd like you to ask her, though, if she won't."

"Sure. What?"

"Why she still had that old Caltech sweatshirt of mine."

Leah looked at him oddly, and then dialed. Becki did answer and he listened to Leah's stilted conversation, speculating about what her mother was saying. Finally Leah said, "Daddy's here right now, would you like to talk to him?" Becki obviously was answering. Then he heard his daughter mention the sweatshirt and saw Leah regarding him sorrowfully. "Ok, Mom, I'll tell him, and Mommy, I'm so sorry and I love you." She hung up and was silent, obviously distressed.

"You don't have to say it, honey. She didn't want to talk to me."

Leah came over and put her arms around her father, her soft, perfumed cheek resting against his. "I'm sorry, Daddy. She did say that she is going to Aunt Marty's and to thank you and that she's supposed to go to the therapist every day for the next week or two—the shrink one, and that they're working on her hand now. I guess they're also hoping to cut down on the dosage of anti-depressants."

"Well, that's good, I guess. I'm glad you were willing to call her."

"Me too," agreed Leah. "God, I love you both, Dad. I really do even if Mommy doesn't believe it."

"I think she does," he assured her, "so what do we do tonight? What's the fanciest place around here if you promise to eat this time."

Leah smiled, "I think I could be persuaded. And oh yeah, she said she'd always had the sweatshirt and she was used to its being around. She guessed she just hadn't been able to toss it away." Arnie thought that was the saddest thing he'd heard, but also possibly the most hopeful.

CHAPTER 30

On the road again the next day, Arnie sank back into the morass of his problems. At least the news about Becki's impending release, and projected stay with Marty, was good. Further, Leah, like Drea, felt that anything that could resolve the puzzle of why things had happened was the right course. If any publicity were to result, that was just tough.

Bruce, though, worried Arnie. Bruce was introverted and Arnie had never been completely comfortable with his son. His discomfort with Leah had been the normal sparing between parent and a strong-willed child as the latter made attempts at breaking from the familial authority. The relationship with Bruce was not the same. Arnie may have been amused by the very human quality he discovered when Bruce got involved with the young woman up in Boston, but his son did live on a different plane. Arnie was smart, a genius Becki had called him, and if IQ were truly the whole answer, he was. So for that matter was Becki and the girls too, but Bruce...Bruce was something else.

Caltech was the right place for his son. At least there were people at the university who could understand what he was saying. Arnie could too, of course, but it took him a little longer. His own giftedness, he'd long realized, was a combination of creativity, the ability to see something through to the finish, self-confidence, and enough intelligence. Mensa material definitely but Bruce, Bruce was one in a thousand or maybe ten thousand. And when someone was that smart, it was hard to relate to others, much less as a son to his father.

Fortunately Arnie arrived in L.A. early enough, with the time difference, to be in his car heading toward Pasadena before rush hour. That of course was a joke, just as it was going around D.C. In L.A. all hours were rush hour, but he was registered and in his room by 5:00. Did he want to call

Bruce now, see him tonight, or maybe just have a drink by the pool, an evening to be by himself without anyone knowing where he was? He hadn't had that luxury since Becki tried to kill herself. The last weeks had been harrowing. Being up front with others about things so personal, so embarrassing, had been dreadful. No, he'd be a coward just this one night he decided.

Getting into his bathing suit, he went out to the pool, ordering a drink from the bar. There was some kind of convention going on at the hotel and there were groups of young people splashing and cavorting in the pool. Becki, if she were there, he knew would be doing laps. She was such a water creature. They were lucky she hadn't been by the river when she attempted suicide, Arnie thought. The tub was bad enough.

He wondered if she'd still love the water now. Certainly she had tried to share that love with all of them. She'd even tried to help him improve his strokes, but he'd always tell her that people from Oregon didn't swim. They rusted in the rain, not the ocean, because the ocean was too cold. She'd never really believed him until one summer. The kids were still small and they'd gone out to see his family.

One day they'd gone over to the state park near Tillamook for a day at the beach. Children were playing in the sand, racing back and forth with pails of water, building forts and castles. A few teenagers were in the water, splashing happily, but no one was really swimming. The waves, even though the tide was receding, were too unruly, and the water too cold, in spite of its being a hot August day. As if disbelieving what Arnie had told her, Becki started to take the little ones wading, when she'd looked at him in horror. "It must be fifty degrees."

"That warm," he'd replied sweetly from his vantage point, seated high above the chilly water line. With self-righteousness, he had wanted to be close to enjoy her inevitable discovery and subsequent discomfort.

"I never believed you, Arnie. I apologize."

"Grovel," he ordered with equally self-satisfied

arrogance. "You've given me a hard time for years about this damn swimming."

Becki merely walked over, shook some of the frigid water on him, making him lean back, protesting in laughter. Then she bent down and whispered in his ear, "Don't push your luck. If I grovel here, you don't get any apologies later."

"Madame! I owe you the apology." He lifted his face and kissed her. "We'll apologize to each other, ok? Just don't drip on me anymore!"

"Acceptable," she answered and went back to the little ones, who seemed impervious to the chill. Drea was running up and down the shore line with Molly while Tim and Josh, as mature older teens, were playing frisbee with some girls they'd met on the beach.

Arnie had sat there, a happy, smug smile on his face until his sister Eileen said to him, "Stop looking like you've eaten a canary, Arnie. You're setting a bad example."

"Just happy, sis, just happy."

"Anyone can see that, little brother. You did well. Lucky as always."

Luck, it had always been there for him; and yes, Arnie thought, he'd done well. Even though he was no slacker at work, he was aware that things usually fell in place for him with relative ease. But he'd gotten too damn complacent and unobservant. Maybe his luck in the really important matters, his marriage and personal life, had finally run out. Well, he'd do what he could. He also wasn't a quitter—just as he'd told Becki so long ago.

That night he ordered room service and drank more than he should until finally he fell asleep. When he did call Bruce the next morning, the boy was already at class. Arnie left a message and then went down for breakfast and the paper. Once back in his room, he made his obligatory calls to Madge, Bob Jackson, Jerry, and Becki's physiatrist, who related that yes, Becki was being released; and yes, she had become receptive to continued therapy; but no, there was nothing definitive that could be reported.

Nothing. Arnie was sick of that and the waiting. Action,

Becki had been so right about that too. He always craved action, even now in a situation like this. There was a problem here and he had to solve it. All his software had resulted from problems waiting to be solved—challenges intellectually, but he had avoided the biggest one of all, Becki. He had just accepted that beautiful, calm exterior and not probed her inner self. Maybe her candy comparison was valid after all. He had been satisfied with the wrapper.

No, that wasn't true. He'd wanted the chocolate too, but he still hadn't bitten far enough to know what was in the center—caramel, fruit, nuts? Who was Becki? It hadn't mattered. She was candy sweet and he loved her and that had seemed enough. That did make him no better than a Stepford husband.

Around noon, Bruce called, "Dad, you're out here?"

"For a few days," Arnie replied. "Are you free sometime today?"

"Sure, dinner I guess."

"Good, what time?"

"Oh, I guess 6:00."

"That's fine. Do we meet or do I pick you up?"

"I guess you can get me at the dorm."

"I'll be there," confirmed Arnie, and Bruce hung up on him. So much for close father-son relationships. Yet he'd never really had any actual problems with Bruce. Although his son had been standoffish from early childhood, he had played with his parents and sisters, even exchanging hugs and kisses when he was small. Still, it was obvious that he preferred to spend time by himself: reading, building things, daydreaming.

In public, Bruce was always polite. People usually liked him, at least on a superficial basis. Of course teachers at first would complain that he was inattentive. Then when he'd consistently ace tests, they'd just let him read or do what he wanted in class. If there were any accelerated programs, he automatically entered them. Like Leah and Arnie's mother, he did enjoy music and was an enthusiastic member of the school band so he had a common interest with his classmates there. Fortunately he was also fairly athletic so no one tried to bully him. Although he was never particularly popular, plenty of girls admired his tall, blond, good looks. On the other hand, no one seemed to dislike him either. Science projects, the computer club, and, for a short while, a stamp swap group were his outside interests. Then too, like Becki, he loved animals, perhaps because he was never disappointed in their lack of higher intelligence; a deficiency that had puzzled him about playmates when he was small.

Odd that, Arnie suddenly thought, Becki and her beloved pigs and the all-important 4-H. None of the kids had joined the organization nor had it seemed to matter to her. He'd never considered that before. Was that part of the trauma caused by Aunt Mary's actions too? What a loss, he thought sadly.

Bruce, though, had drifted through high school. Arnie had thought about letting him go to college at sixteen or even as early as fifteen; but, since the boy didn't really seem to care and obviously loved his mother and home, he said nothing. As it was, Bruce did enter Caltech only a year after Leah went off to Oberlin, but as a freshman, just turned seventeen and in effect a year ahead of his sister. Arnie himself had been barely seventeen when he had started college.

Promptly at 6:00, Arnie arrived at Bruce's dorm where his son was waiting for him. "How's it going?" he asked once the boy got into the car, irritated with himself that such inane comments were their usual conversation. This time, unfortunately, it was going to be different. Bruce looked well, none of that deadly undergrad pallor from too much pressure or late hours studying that so many of Arnie's own classmates had had when he was at Tech.

"Ok, I guess," the boy replied.

Fine, thought Arnie, that tells me a lot. "So who do you have this year?"

"Old man Irving and..."

"Albert Irving?" Arnie asked, astonished.

"Yes."

"What is he? Ninety now? I had him when I was here, and I thought he wasn't going to live through the term then."

Bruce looked at him with interest. "You did? Was he as boring then?"

"My God, yes," replied Arnie with feeling.

Bruce began to laugh, a pleasant sound not heard often enough as far as Arnie was concerned. Leah may have been slightly manic with her moods but there was never any question when she was happy. "Why do you think they keep him?"

"I always figured he knew where all the bodies were buried. They probably died of boredom in his class," Arnie added facetiously.

Bruce stared at him and started laughing again. "Somehow I thought it was different when you were here, Dad."

"You mean the dark ages? No, I think we probably went through the same sort of thing. I imagine Irving is still around because he was an expert on his subject even if he is one of the deadliest instructors I've ever had. The man actually became an inspiration for me."

"How so, Dad?" Bruce, for once, appeared truly interested.

"When I started teaching at MIT, I just knew I couldn't be as bad as he was. Any time I approached a lecture, I'd wonder how Irving would give it. Then I'd do just the opposite."

"You were pretty good, I heard," remarked Bruce casually and Arnie glanced at him surprised. Compliments from Bruce had never been the norm. "Some of the people I met in Boston had your class there and even one of my instructors here. He really liked you. He asked me if I was your son."

"That's nice to hear," replied Arnie. "Who is he?"

"Henry Guilliani."

"I remember him. I didn't know he ended up here."

"Yes, in fact, I think he's doing a seminar that touches

some of the stuff you developed. Your early software was really considered innovative."

"That's nice to hear. I just hope our present products continue to get good reviews."

"They do," said Bruce, and then abruptly asked, "Why are you out here? Is it about Mom?"

"Nothing like cutting to the chase. Let's get to the restaurant and yes, I am. Can we talk about it then?"

"Sure," his son agreed and the two were quiet for the rest of the ride. They'd picked a Thai place and after the dishes of chicken satay, shrimp rolls and salted eggs were placed in front of them, Bruce observed, "That's what Mom usually orders."

"We like a lot of the same food," remarked Arnie. "We've always liked a lot of the same things."

"And you usually were the one that saw to it that they were the ones you liked. That's why I can't understand this thing about her moving out. She always has done what you wanted."

Arnie was getting annoyed. "Yes, I called the shots on a lot of things but your mom also got her own way. Whether consciously or subconsciously, she moved our home to Virginia while my work remained in Boston. I thought of King George as a summer or vacation place when we got it. I never realized it would become home for my family—you kids and her. I hated the separation even if I could concentrate more on the business. That was your mom's decision, not mine, not ever, so don't tell me I always asserted my will over her."

Bruce ignored this, dipping the chicken into the spicy peanut sauce. "So why have you guys split then?"

"It's a little worse than that," Arnie said gently. "Your mother has been in the hospital." Bruce looked at him, staggered. "She tried to commit suicide." Bruce was hastily trying to swallow his food and coughing. "She's ok now, at least physically," Arnie swiftly said, ignoring the matter of Becki's hand for the moment. "She's going to be staying with Aunt Marty and remain in therapy."

Coldly, Bruce asked, "What did you do, Dad?"

"I admit it," said Arnie, throwing his hands up in exasperation. "It was my fault. Someone sent her some pictures that I was cheating."

"You bastard."

"Well there were some unusual circumstances. Are you going to listen or have you just judged."

"Talk."

"Thanks, son, for the vote of confidence." Arnie responded.

"Well what do you expect, Dad? You come and tell me Mom has tried to kill herself and that this separation and everything is because you were cheating on her."

Arnie looked at him, speculating on how to begin. Here I go again, he thought. Bruce listened, glaring, but at least staying quiet until Arnie finished. Finally the boy said, "So, what rabbit are you going to pull out of the hat now?"

"I wish I could tell you," Arnie answered truthfully. "If it's Dickie, maybe I'll just kill him."

"Bad joke, Dad."

"No joke. None of this is funny. I don't know. I won't know until the detectives find out something and maybe they'll never discover anything. Even if they do, maybe it wasn't him. I'll do what I can, ok? I've told all you kids; that's been bad enough. I've told you because your mom and I never believed in lying to you and this is serious. I'm hoping she'll take me back, but if she doesn't, you should know why. I'm mainly hoping she'll be ok. That's the big thing. And, this may even get messier. We've got money. Our company is a major player in its field. This would be nice material for the scandal sheets and if this becomes public, it just may. I felt I had to warn you."

"Warn me? Why? What did the sibs say?"

"They said do what I can. Stop the bastard if I can. Make it go away."

"How do you know you can make it go away?" asked Bruce puzzled, clearly an unusual experience.

"That's the whole point," replied Arnie. "I don't. I'm

doing my best. Maybe it will work, maybe it won't. I just wanted you to know, ok?"

"I don't like you, Dad," his son stated bluntly.

"Well, I haven't liked me very much lately either."

"Do what you want," muttered Bruce angrily, pushing his partially filled plate aside. "I think I want to go back to the dorm now."

Arnie called for the check. The drive back was ominously silent. Bruce was staring out the window. When they got to the dorm, he looked antagonistically at his father as he unsnapped the seat belt. Hesitating a moment, he opened the car door, as if he wanted to say something. Finally he just got out and slammed it. Well, thought Arnie, I was lucky with the other two. I guess I needed a reality check. He pulled away, driving slowly back to the hotel. But two out of the three kids, he kept thinking, only two, and he felt very depressed.

That night he stayed up for hours, surfing the channels, becoming increasingly more upset. Even a favorite old Tommy Mason flick with the cowboy hero predictably blowing away the villainous Kris Anders couldn't grab his attention. He wondered if tonight he'd be plagued with dreams of facing off Dickie and riding into the sunset with Becki—or worse, Becki slung limply, wrists bleeding, across Dickie's saddle, and him sprawled on a dusty wagon trail.

Then sleep finally came, for once without the nightmarish fantasies. So often he'd awaken the following morning, unsure of what exactly had happened even though he was certain Becki had appeared.

CHAPTER 31

The next day Arnie considered calling his son, but Bruce knew where he was. If Bruce wanted to speak to him, he'd call. And he remembered waiting in a hotel room years before, hoping Becki would phone that spring night they had met. Sometimes one just had to wait and hope. Maybe when this is all over, Arnie thought, maybe Bruce and he could work something out; but, for now, it was all about Becki and finding out what really had happened that mattered.

So instead, Arnie had a long conversation with Madge. Business was booming according to her. Obviously he wasn't needed, which strangely didn't seem to bother him.

"And, I spoke to your Bob Jackson himself," Madge then reported. "I did decide to give him Carla's name as well as those of a couple more women Dickie used to date. One, I know is still in the Boston area, but I've no idea where the other might be. Jackson didn't seem too worried about finding her though."

"That's why I'm paying the big bucks," interjected Arnie, glad she'd finally gotten to the subject which interested him most.

"Well if he's as good as the young woman he sent over, they're worth it. She's really plowing ahead."

"Great." There were no jokes this time about female collusion or conspiracies. A real one was bad enough.

Arnie's next call was to Jerry for an update of Becki's status, but Jerry was in court again, and so he waited, trying to decide what next. Should he return to the East Coast or stay out here a while longer? Dickie was supposed to be working in the L.A. area, and he wondered if he should try to catch up on gossip from some of their Tech classmates; but, that might be a bad idea. At last he decided. He'd stay at least a couple more days. Then he went down to the pool. On the way, he stopped by the desk, telling them he was expecting some business calls and would be outside; but none came. It was a thoroughly depressing day.

The next day was much the same. Arnie refrained from buying a bottle of liquor. Drinking helped get him into this trouble, and he'd been drinking a lot lately. Time to stop that habit. For a moment, he almost considered smoking—something he'd given up even before he met Becki. Instead, he went out and bought half a dozen mysteries and decided he'd try to escape that way. He stayed up half the night plowing through other people's difficulties, which magically resolved by the final page. If only he should be so lucky.

The rest of the time the reveries returned. Sometimes he was back in the past with Becki. She would be lying next to him and she would start to move her fingertips lightly around his breast and place little kisses and he would know that in her quiet way, she was asking him to make love to her. He would lean over and respond, losing himself in her. After, she would whisper how she loved him before snuggling within his arm, her hand resting back on his breast and falling asleep. It was as though they had completed some mystical, erotic cycle to somewhere special and enchanted, and then returned safely to their more mundane point of origin. Enchanted adventures within a tiny measurement of actual space.

Twenty years, he thought, and he had never wanted anyone else. His beautiful wife silent in bed, but passionate with her knowing hands and willing body. Had the silence been due to the fact that all these years she'd felt guilty about her obviously energetic and healthy sexual urges? Would he feel those wonderful, gentle hands again—especially the poor maimed one. Oh, Becki...

At last he succumbed to agitated dreams, but the next morning he was awakened by a call from Bob Jackson. "Dr. Miller?"

"Yeah," said Arnie, still half asleep, rubbing his eyes.

"I think you're going to be interested in a package we've compiled."

"Yeah," Arnie mumbled again.

"It appears you were right about everything. I also think we have the proof to contain your Mr. R. so he won't come back at you."

Arnie was wide awake now. "How so?"

"Depositions, some proof of actual monetary exchange, some shaky business practices including his time at your company, a thoroughly nasty reputation with women..."

"God," murmured Arnie. He wasn't sure if he meant it as a prayer or a curse. "Now what?"

"We're expressing copies of everything to you at your hotel. You should have it by tomorrow. Also, you'll be interested to know that the subject is still in L.A. and now working at Elling Technology."

It was as though the comic strip light bulb lit up in Arnie's head. "Jesus, they came up with *Total* just as we were hitting the market with our latest package."

"Yes, you seemed to have beaten him to the punch again."

"And the young woman?"

"She has been his East Coast girlfriend for the last year or so, although not exclusively. I gather she's been friendly with quite a few people."

"So it wasn't any big sacrifice of virtue for her to come after me."

"I wouldn't say so."

"What was she getting out of this?"

"She was going to be offered a better job out there and maybe the opportunity to become the fourth Mrs. R."

"Dickie's been married three times!" Arnie was surprised. Three times in fifteen years.

"And not very happily remembered by any of his previous wives, although only one was willing to talk to us. I think in a pinch another might reconsider, but the third was afraid."

"And why did his young woman talk to you?"

"We promised her immunity from the lawsuit you were going to slap on Mr. R., the photographer, and her."

"I see," said Arnie slowly. "And that's your advice?"

"Part of it. Read the files when they get there and think about it. I believe you have several options, including possibly the criminal one. He procured a woman who in turn allowed unauthorized access to private premises for the purpose of taking unsanctioned highly personal photographs. These were used to harass the lady we're interested in protecting."

"You should be a lawyer," Arnie said.

"I am. Several in the firm are."

Although surprised at this revelation, another stereotype of a PI shot to hell, Arnie merely asked, "What else?"

"Well, if you do decide to talk to him, don't let him keep the files and make sure you let him know that several people have copies. Make a recording of the conversation."

"Isn't that illegal?"

"Not if you're not going to use it in court or for blackmail or something like that," laughed the detective.

"Fine," said Arnie. "Who gets copies of the files?"

"You decide," said Jackson. "Your personal lawyer certainly. Maybe some of your family. Whatever you do, even if you don't decide to start a suit, be careful."

"And a suit isn't your first choice?"

"No," said the detective.

"Ok, I'll fax you a list of how many duplicates of the files I want and to whom they should be sent. I have to think about that a little."

"One final bit of advice, Dr. Miller. If you decide upon the direct approach, make sure that Mr. R. is well aware of the ramifications if he were to try to intimidate any of the individuals we interviewed. He should fully understand a civil suit can be slapped on him or even criminal charges sought. I also believe that some of his former employers, as well as his present one, might be interested in his, how shall I say, work record."

"Oh, I think so," readily agreed Arnie, wondering if telling the truth could be construed as blackmail. "As a matter of fact, I know his present boss. Thank you and I do mean that. I'll be waiting for the package. You said you'd be available tomorrow if I want to discuss it with you?"

"I'll make sure my secretary knows how to get hold of me if I'm out of the office."

"Thank you again." Arnie felt as though he might be human after all. Something was finally happening. First he contacted Madge. Then in rapid succession, he called Jerry, Drea and Leah, telling them that the puzzle had been solved. Each would see a copy of the report, but he refused to say what would happen next. He had been concerned about giving Leah one but then decided she was a victim too or at least had been affected by this whole mess. If something were to happen, she should know the whole story. He next called Bruce, who was out. On the boy's answering machine, he mentioned what had happened and left it at that.

He was surprised that night when Bruce called back. "Dad…"

"Yes," replied Arnie, not knowing what to say.

"You be careful when you go see that guy, ok?"

"Why thank you," Arnie answered and waited.

There was no sound for a while and then Bruce added, "I still think you were a bastard to let this happen, but I know you love Mom and you didn't do it on purpose." Then Arnie heard the phone click. Still not three out of three, he thought, but the odds are improving. In his mind though, he couldn't factor Becki in. She was the ultimate one to convert.

Arnie had a difficult time getting to sleep and was up at the crack of dawn. He knew the package would not be there until early afternoon but by 10:00, he had been pacing for the last hour. Before that he'd tried to watch a film on cable and then gone on to the news. The bottom line was that the only news he was interested in was what he would find in the package and what he would do when he read it.

At last the phone rang from the desk telling him that the item he had been waiting for had arrived. He hurried down to get it, wanting to rip it open on the spot; but, somehow, seemingly composed, he stopped to pick up a cup of hot coffee before making his way back to the room.

Once there, he flopped down on the bed and tore off the protecting tape. Inside was a neatly bound folder resembling a prospectus. Slowly he opened it and began to read the report, looking at the attachments, including depositions—for that was what they were. The investigating firm had had a licensed attorney take the various statements and have the signatures notarized.

It was, indeed, all messily there, starting with the photographer who had entered the Cape Cod house without Arnie's consent or knowledge and used infrared equipment to take the damaging photos. Then there was the testimony of Pam Carter, who admitted letting her accomplice in so the planned seduction could be recorded. Both had been paid by Dickie—the photographer monetarily and the young woman by promises of furthering her career. She, to date, had not received the expected job offer from Dickie's present company nor the equally desired proposal. Now she was not only miffed but apprehensive about her part in the whole affair. Both were willing to testify if necessary in return for a guarantee that neither would be sued by Arnie. If there were no court case, they also agreed to remain quiet about the whole episode, again under threat of a legal action.

From Carla, there had been a list of women with whom Dickie had been previously involved and the name of one of the women he married later. Carla had said if Arnie were to sue, she would happily testify; in fact she would get her medical records revealing how Dickie had beaten her the weekend of the Cape Cod picnic some twenty years before. Two of the earlier girl friends said that Dickie had been guilty of date rape. His former wife acknowledged violence in the marriage and said he had harassed her when she tried to get part of their mutual property. There was, in fact, still a civil suit against him for unpaid alimony.

From the company records, it appeared even in its beginning days that Dickie had leaked information on their early programs, which was the reason that SofTek had not then been first on the market with its earliest product. That, almost as much as the abuse of women, shocked Arnie.

Dickie had been a partner. It was his own throat he was cutting by doing something like that. On the other hand, no wonder Dickie didn't want agreements with foreign enterprises. He was probably trying to sell them the information himself. Maybe that was another reason straight-laced Madge hadn't been welcomed that time she'd gone to Japan. Conniving, opportunistic Dickie had made the previous trip.

Dickie's relationships with other employers had deteriorated the longer he stayed at each succeeding job and, gradually, he would move on. It seemed that the Peter Principle had been in play as none of these companies wanted to give him a bad reference for fear of some reprisal later. Essentially, Dickie had just been getting away with it. And now, for the last two years, he had been out here in L.A. working with Elling Technology, which interestingly enough had not gotten to market fast enough with their *Total*, a parallel of SofTek's newest, and already very successful *CombineIt*, the completely integrated office management system. If Dickie had only played it straight, Arnie thought, we all could have been winners.

Well, what to do? A gun or a knife still had an attraction. Of course, he knew he would never use one, even if that was the way to permanently stop Dickie. Beating him to a pulp also remained high on the list and that was something Arnie was afraid he still might do. No, he'd have to think about it a little. Should he call the kids again? If things went wrong, they'd be paying some of the price too—probably amounting to negative press coverage. Yet each one had told him that justice should be exacted, regardless of that unknown price. So, essentially he was the judge and it was up to him. Talk to Becki? She'd been the primary victim. No, he couldn't do that either and how he missed that. Not to be able to talk to Becki about a problem but for now, she was the focal point of that same problem. So the final decision: confrontation of Dickie, therefore, was also up to him.

He knew where Dickie lived and today, after work, he'd

be waiting to talk to him, at least at first. It was time to settle this face to face. With Dickie's file, he could then begin his own smear campaign if he didn't get satisfaction. Although Dickie probably didn't realize it, Arnie could easily offer some enticement to Dickie's present boss in return for the favor of removing him from that company. In all probability, just telling some of the story would probably be enough.

Once Dickie was officially blacklisted, he'd be through. Certainly there were enough stories of bad faith that when it appeared Dickie was down, more than one of his past acquaintances or cohorts would probably enjoy getting in a kick or two. Still, that would also put the man's back completely to the wall and with no escape, who knew how desperate his actions might become? It was going to be a thin line.

CHAPTER 32

Dickie drove up to his townhouse about 7:00 that evening. By then, Arnie was beginning to feel like he'd been on stake-out in one of those bad TV shows or a couple of the mysteries he'd been reading. The PI's *modus operandi* as he had always imagined, not as it apparently was in real life. Parking his car in front of his house, Dickie walked up to the front door and was unlocking it. Arnie was right behind him, but Dickie had obviously had a couple of drinks and didn't notice until he was actually opening the door. "Dickie, again long time no see," said Arnie, shoving him through the door and pulling it shut behind them.

"What the hell?" Dickie turned and Arnie would have sworn that he looked frightened. "Get out of here you SOB or I'm going to call the cops."

"I'd be careful whom you call an SOB, and I really think you want to talk to me. Or, if you have any balls at all and finally want to face me off, I'll be happy to do that too. God knows I've been wanting to beat your pretty face in for years."

"Big talk, little man. You and who else?"

"Wow," exclaimed Arnie, "tough school yard repartee here. If you want to try, go for it. I could have taken you twenty years ago and I think I still can." God, Arnie thought, eyeing Dickie, he's really let himself go. The slightly bleary-eyed man in front of him had a dissipated look and soon would lose even the remnants of the classic appearance he'd so prized. No need for a portrait in his attic!

"Maybe that broken nose I owed you for hurting Becki the first time. Maybe a few teeth knocked out for the New York party. Maybe breaking your jaw and any other damn bones I can for this latest stunt. I'd really like to kill you, Dickie. I've never felt that about another human being. I have even wondered sometimes about the death penalty. But for you, I'd take a chance with it myself. Now do you want to talk or shall we really have a fight?"

"You're crazy, Arnie. I'd end up hurting you."

"Nice comeback, Dickie, but it's only the two of us this time. No audience now. None. So sit!" Arnie had his hand on Dickie's arm and he shoved him over to a stool at the small living room bar. Dickie clearly wasn't the man he had been. Under those expensive clothes, Arnie could feel the slackness of the muscles. Good thing Becki had nagged him over the years about exercise and diet. He at least was still solid and in shape for his age.

"I've some things to show you," Arnie said, dropping the folder on the counter. "Are you sober enough to read or shall I read this for you?" Dickie looked down at the case file. "Open it, damn you, and read," ordered Arnie angrily, sounding very mean.

Working to focus his eyes, Dickie finally began to skim over the report, turning pages slowly. "You expect anyone to believe this crap," he said after a few minutes. "It's bullshit. Everyone knows you screwed me twenty years ago."

"Yeah, that was the story you told everyone, but it wasn't what really happened. Keep reading, you shit."

Dickie browsed through the attachments. Finally he said laughing, "So, you're going to try to do a hatchet job on me. Who's going to believe it? All this just to get even with you and that stupid cunt? And after twenty years? Bullshit!"

Arnie's eyes narrowed, words couldn't hurt. But hell, they had certainly hurt Becki. Somehow he had to stay calm even though he wanted to tear out Dickie's tongue after hearing the word 'cunt'. Taking a deep breath, he asked as unruffled as he could, "But we know you did. Why? Because of *Total*?"

Dickie laughed nastily. "Oh Arnie, you always thought you were so damn smart and a lady's man beside. You'd walk into a room with your bimbo, strutting like a bantam rooster because you knew every man there wanted to get his hands on her; but she'd look only at you. Stupid bitch. And you, you prick, you were ready to do anything for her like tossing me out of SofTek. Everyone knew that. But she was totally dependent on you. Of course the way to get even with you was through her. But I'll just deny it and say you've used people who don't like me. Besides, no one's going to give a shit. What do you plan to do with this stuff anyhow, take me to court or something? It's nothing."

"Not nothing," said Arnie tightly. "You didn't read the file closely enough. When you paid that photographer, you were dumb enough to do it on your fucking credit card and he gave you a receipt. He still has his copy of that receipt and the credit card company has the records with the file number of the work he did for you. The stupid jerk had copies of the negatives in his studio, also with that numbered file, and was afraid enough to hand them over to my PI. Plus, you never came through with the job and whatever else you promised that bitch, Pam, and she was in those photos and is now pissed as hell."

"What!" Finally Dickie did look worried.

"I think that constitutes a chain of evidence. Once we found out how you were screwing around at our company...and tell me, Dickie, that's one thing I still can't understand, why would you want to cheat us when you were still a partner?" Dickie said nothing; but, from the slightly pained expression on his face, it was obvious that he knew what Arnie was saying. "Anyhow," Arnie continued, "I'm sure you did the same with the others and I know some of your former employers. I know your present boss too— Dean Elling. We once worked on a national committee regarding the Internet. Did you know that, Dickie? I'm sure if I were to talk to Dean and the others about that breach, they'd do a little checking too and find a few things at their companies. How much did you get for leaking information or was it planned industrial espionage? Who bought the stuff—just the Japanese or the Europeans too? And the women, Dickie, you really are a shit. I wish I could throw you into a pit and invite them all to come and hurl things at you or set wild dogs on you. God, you are a bastard."

Dickie remained quiet. Then he said cunningly, an evil-looking smile appearing on his face, "You're not going to do any of this, you miserable little kike."

"Why not?" asked Arnie, somehow continuing to control his temper, before adding, "I assume you know that Dean's wife had a grandfather, who was a Reform rabbi."

It was obvious that Dickie didn't, from the sudden flush on his face, but he charged on, certain he still had a hidden card. "You'd never want this to get out, to hurt that precious little cunt of yours."

"You already hurt her," said Arnie tightly.

"But no one else knows. You let any of this out and everyone is going to know, starting with the tabloids. You're too successful and too proper, Arnie. This would be news. A nice smear and, best of all, true."

"Only partially," remarked Arnie, "but try. It can't hurt me. I've gotten out of the company." At this, Dickie looked dazed as if unable to assimilate the unexpected information.

"That's right; Madge is running it and no one would give a damn anyhow. Our software wouldn't be any less efficient if those pictures showed up. My family? My kids all know about this and suggested I just deep-six you some place. Becki? You've already done the damage. She not only left me but she tried to kill herself. She may have even lost the use of a hand. I bet you didn't know that, you miserable fuck! So think, Dickie, what do I have to lose by pulling out a gun right now?"

For the first time Dickie actually looked scared. "Don't shit your pants," Arnie said coldly. "I'm not going to kill you and maybe I'm not going to do anything, now. But you're never going to know when, Dickie. My lawyer, the PI, and each of my kids will have a copy of this file, plus Madge knows the whole story too. You couldn't get rid of this if you tried. Remember, I said I know your boss, Dickie. I've met your previous ones, too. If you ever try to fuck with me or any of my family or the company again, this stuff is going to get spread all over and we'll be the ones doing it. Same thing if you try to pull any crap on the people who supplied this information. You'd also better hope that no one else ever decides to do anything to upset us since you'll get the blame, whether you're party or not. Do you understand?"

Dickie was still quiet and Arnie reached over to seize him by the coat lapels, jerking him halfway up. "I said, do you understand?" Dickie nodded in surrender and Arnie slowly released him. "Then say it out loud, damn it."

"I understand."

"And just for my own enjoyment, why don't you again mention what nasty little things you've done over the last twenty years to me and Becki and say how sorry you are and why you won't ever do anything again. In fact tell me why you won't even mention our names from now on or why, if you ever see us, you'll turn around and quietly walk away, hoping we don't see you."

"You're kidding."

"No, I'm angry. I want a complete, detailed apology and I mean complete. Remember, I'd still enjoy smashing in your face."

"All right." Resigned, Dickie began to recite the whole sordid tale, speaking overly fast and looking ill and tired. At last, exhausted, he said, "Is that enough? Will you get out of here now?"

"Nice testimonial," replied Arnie, with a mean little smile. Digging into his pocket and pulling out a mini tape recorder, he pressed a couple of buttons and Dickie heard his last words.

"You could never use that," protested Dickie, making a halfhearted grab, nearly stumbling from the bar stool, but Arnie by now had stepped back.

"Probably not in a court of law, but why would I have to? Still, other people might enjoy hearing it. Now remember, you cross me again and you're dead. I owe you for a lot of your sins but mostly for the twenty years of shit you dumped on Becki and I'm never, ever, going to forgive you for that." Arnie reached over, picked up the file, and walked out. I should feel better, he thought as he approached his car, but he didn't really. Maybe just one punch, he thought. One punch would have been nice.

CHAPTER 33

A rnie was sitting on the porch swing at Marty's house patiently waiting when Becki got back from the physical therapist. Jerry had told him the schedule. No cast, he noted, but still an elastic brace on her right arm. He stood as she came up the stairs. "Hi, Beauty."

"Arnie."

"You're looking well." It was true. She was looking the best she had since he'd found her, almost like she had before she ran away months ago—nearly five, in fact, when they were both still pretending they had a normal marriage, a normal life. "May I come in?"

"I don't think so," she answered, half surprising herself, that she now had the will to refuse his request.

"Will you sit outside a little with me?" He tried not to show his disappointment.

She looked at him contemplating. "I could. I guess so." Then she sank down in one of the white wicker rockers next to the swing.

"You won't sit on the swing with me?" he asked hopefully.

"I don't think so," she said again, asserting her new feeling of independence.

"You're not afraid of me," he commented, rather than asked.

"I was never afraid of you, Arnie."

"Well someone is," he replied and she looked at him with interest. "It's about twenty years too late, and I apologize to you for that, Becki."

"Dickie," she whispered.

"Yes, the villain of the piece. Did Jerry tell you?"

"Yes," she said quietly.

"I should have done him in that summer at the Cape. I'd have pleaded insanity. They would have let me out a year or two later, and we could have lived happily ever after."

She had a slight smile on her face. "It never would have happened that way and you never would have done it."

"I really thought about it this time around."

"Me too," she concurred.

Surprised, he looked at her, the previously hidden Becki. The Becki of old—the one he thought he'd known—would never have said anything like that. Nodding his head, he said, "Well, it's done. I think he's scared shitless but even if he isn't, he knows he's ruined and that he's living on borrowed time professionally. He finally realizes that enough people know the story that if he even steps out of line the tiniest bit, he's through."

"You really believe that?" she asked pragmatically.

"He's a coward, Becki, and a sneak. He always came up against people weaker than him and I guess he thought I'd never have the guts to face him off."

"Because of me."

"Maybe...I was wrong, you know, but I was too obtuse to realize all the damage he'd done. All the damage I was doing." She looked at him, questioning. "Beauty, I should never have let you hide from your and our problems."

"You thought you were protecting me, Arnie, being my gentle knight again."

"I was also giving myself an excuse to be the busy executive and letting you hold down the home front with the kids, rather than face things like that myself."

"That didn't work out the way I thought it would either."

"No," he agreed. "Drea thrived back in King George, but she would have done equally well in Boston and had wider opportunity. Bruce would have been in his own little universe anywhere, although Boston would have given him more outlets intellectually. Still, he liked the wild life—animals, that is. Leah definitely should have had the big city life, although in her case, she might have gotten in trouble—a different kind of wild life."

"I got in trouble when I was a teenager in King George," remarked Becki wryly.

"Those were unforeseen circumstances—kind of the way I hope you'll view what happened with me. Are you taking care of the Aunt Mary problem?" he suddenly asked compassionately.

She looked down, answering slowly, "I'm talking about her now. I've talked to Marty about her, about lots of things—about Billy too. The kids have been calling me— even Leah. Thank you, Arnie. I'm sorry about Bruce though."

"We have nice kids. Bruce, well, I'll have to see about Bruce. I haven't given up hope."

"I wouldn't," she agreed and he looked at her intently, hoping she might add something else.

When she didn't, he continued, "They all know the whole mess. I didn't want any of them to be hurt if Dickie tried to fight this. They all said go for the kill." Becki sat there, lazily rocking back and forth. Finally Arnie stood up and walked over to her. Picking up her unencumbered arm, he looked at her wrist. The scar was still red and stark. It would always be there. One day he'd like to give her some beautiful wide gold bracelets or even diamond ones to cover it and the angry gash marks on her other arm, but she probably wouldn't wear them. Still, he'd like her to have the choice and this time he wouldn't forget. Gently, he pressed a kiss to the marred flesh.

"Will you forgive me, take me back?" he asked quietly. She just looked at him, but she didn't pull her arm away, and he continued, "Will you go down the Mississippi on a paddle wheeler with me? Like Mark Twain, the way we used to talk. We could get off in Memphis, stay at the Peabody, and watch the ducks march out at teatime like you always said you wanted to do. Then we'd go to New Orleans and eat oyster and shrimp po'boys and listen to jazz, the way I wanted."

Encouraged that she hadn't said no, he continued, "Maybe we could hop a freighter then and go through the Panama Canal or around the world once the therapists say it's ok. Or maybe we could even take the Cunard World

Tour and live it up to the hilt on the QE II. But still, it would be just us and we'd see those Pacific islands you wanted to visit. Three, six months, a year if you like. If we like a place, we'll just get off and stop awhile so I can climb a coconut palm and get you some coconuts to squeeze the milk. Maybe I'd even try my hand at carving a war canoe." It seemed another brief smile flashed across her face. At least he hoped so, unless it was just her visualizing the ludicrous scene of him trying to hoist himself up a palm tree.

"Anything you like," he continued persuasively. "Maybe we should go back to Japan and see if we can find that inn we visited on our honeymoon and I'll buy you the genuine pearl necklace finally. We'll have the other fixed for one of the girls. Maybe, you could even teach me to swim properly," he added shyly, "and you'll finally learn to use chopsticks. They should be good therapy."

"Maybe, maybe," she answered softly and this time he was sure there was a speculative glint in her eyes. "That takes me back. You're still the salesman, Arnie, but I'm not the same person now. I don't know who I'll be."

"Maybe, maybe I'm not either," he answered, staring intently into her bright blue eyes. "I'm certainly not the slick huckster you accused me of being when we met. All I know is that I want our persons to be together even if we do end up running a chopstick factory."

"Well you're obviously still the comedian, but what about your other business?" she asked, and he thought he detected the slight smile again.

"It's been getting along fine without me the last month or so. Quite a blow to my ego."

This time she really did smile, revealing those perfect white teeth. It was like looking at a double strand pearl necklace at Cartier's. Everything about Becki had turned out to be natural and genuine. Cautiously, he added, "I think I've finally persuaded Drea to go up to Cambridge. Do you have any problem with that?"

"Drea will do what she wants. If she wants that, fine."

"I won't even take a laptop on our trip unless you want

to use it for therapy. Jerry told me the doctors think you should get back at least ninety percent of the finger action. That was encouraging." Becki nodded. "I might call every week to make sure the company is still worth something so they won't kick us off the boat or whatever," he added hurriedly. Then taking a deep breath, Arnie slowly and clearly said, "Becki, I've decided SofTek should go public."

She looked at him surprised, eyes widening. It was, she knew, his greatest offer. The move would lead to relinquishing hold of his beloved company, but she couldn't say that yet. Instead she laughed softly, "I doubt you'd run out of money either way."

It was the first time he'd heard her laugh since he'd found her again. "We," he answered. She still hadn't said no to him, and he leaned over, pressing his face to her hair. "Still gold, that's the only gold that really matters. Please, Beauty. The wrapper, it's fine, but it's the center of the candy I want, that I always wanted. I'll even stop calling you Beauty if you want, Becki."

She put her left hand up, capturing his and looked at him. "I don't know if I could ever go back to Boston," she said. "I'm not sure I can even go back to King George."

"We'd find a place. Maybe we could find another river to live by, on a houseboat even. I can always teach. You can finish school and maybe write the way you should have or run a shop or whatever you want." Slowly, he pulled her up out of the chair and put his arms around her. "Please. You don't have to make any promises, just be willing to try. I've loved you for twenty years. Like those poets said, come grow old with me, Becki. I'm no kid. I'm fifty now and I just can't conceive of passing the rest of my years without you. Give me twenty more," he pled. "Wrinkles, grey hair, none of that would matter. Your secret portrait will always be beautiful, the chocolate tasty."

"I've got to go inside," she replied, but she didn't push him away. Arnie moved back, standing there waiting, and she stared at him for a long moment, trying to picture the young man she'd met two decades before. His brown eyes were solemn now, but still alert, and his matching hair was starting to be sprinkled with silver. There were lines beginning to cross that once cherubic face, but if anything, he looked dignified. Not handsome ever, but possessing the character she'd sought, which far outweighed a handsome countenance. Turning, she walked to the door, opened it, and then glanced back at him calmly, the hint of a sly smile playing over her lips. She stepped in, but the door remained open and he followed her, shutting it carefully behind them.

ACKNOWLEDGEMENTS

With thanks to Betty and Gene Smith and Barbara and Tommy Segar for introducing me to King George County; Ellen Alderton for memories of Boston and Gloria Remington for ones of Oregon; Constance Ramirez for the candy analogy; David Alderton and Joyce Sweatt for proofing and reproofing; and Margo Alderton, who, per usual, probably should be listed as co-author for her many efforts.

Made in the USA
Charleston, SC
12 April 2013